About the author

The author was born in Scotland and, after serving in the Army, embarked on a career in industry.

He has worked in several different sectors in senior roles and was latterly CEO of a large international data capture company.

He retired for the first time in 1995 to take on a consultancy designed to help new businesses become established.

In 2018, he finally retired from business life to become a full-time author.

John lives in Scotland and Portugal with his wife and they have two grown-up sons.

THE AUCTION

The second DCI Burt murder mystery

JOHN REID

THE AUCTION
The second DCI Burt murder mystery

Vanguard Press

A CIP catalogue record for this title is
available from the British Library.

ISBN 978 1 80016 132 0

*Vanguard Press is an imprint of
Pegasus Elliot MacKenzie Publishers Ltd*
www.pegasuspublishers.com

First Published in 2021

**Vanguard Press
Sheraton House, Castle Park
Cambridge England**

Printed & Bound in Great Britain

Dedication

To my wife, Liz, for her support and patience while I have been locked away writing this novel. Also, to my editing team of golf buddies and their wives for their support, good humour and advice (that was not always taken).

Acknowledgements

To my mate, Jimbo, for his help and assistance in ferreting out more detailed information than I ever could.

Chapter One

Doctor Hans Raga PhD, Director of Organic Engineering at the Massachusetts Institute of Technology, was at work in his laboratory. At fifty-three years of age, he was the Senior Research Fellow in the department, which meant he had his own laboratory facilities and an independent research programme.

It was nine p.m. on a wet and cold Wednesday evening that only this part of the north-eastern United States could produce. November in Cambridge, Massachusetts often produced some of the most severe winters in the entire country, and this year was shaping up to be no exception.

The temperature outside was only just above freezing. Winter was beginning to show its teeth and snow was now mixed in with the rain. Fortunately, within the laboratory it was comfortably warm. It wasn't only the central heating that accounted for the temperature but also the experiment Hans was conducting. He was working in secret and not even his closest colleagues had any idea of his work — except for one.

Dr David Graham had been aware of Hans' project for some time. Whilst he encouraged his friend, he thought Hans was a bit eccentric and was devoting a lot of time and effort into what the scientific community would regard as a crackpot idea. The thought that water could be used as the basic ingredient of a super fuel was barmy. Still, David supported his friend and they often discussed progress and potential solutions to problems.

Hans had at long last worked out why his theory didn't follow the logic that it should have. He'd had his eureka moment an hour earlier and this had led to a series of frantically mixed concoctions derived from amended and recalculated formulas. He was about to discover if his theory actually worked. He saw no reason why it shouldn't.

His adrenaline level was off the scale, as was his heart rate. The next few minutes would determine his place in scientific history. He wished

David could be here to share the moment, but he knew he was attending a scientific dinner in Washington, D.C.

For the experiment to work, Hans had to show that a small amount of liquid now contained in a glass beaker was so highly flammable that it would combust upon contact with heat. To show this, he heated an old hot plate and set its thermostat to maximum. Then, having filled a syringe from the beaker, he allowed a single drop of the liquid to fall onto the hot plate.

There was an instant flash. The liquid had ignited upon contact with heat. Hans was struck dumb. He couldn't believe what he had just witnessed, even though in theory it was exactly the result he had expected. He repeated the experiment several times and got the same result each time.

His hairbrained notion of water-based fuels had actually worked.

Despite the lateness of the hour, Hans set to writing up his notes. He worked quickly to include every small detail of his work. He included all the formulas, biochemical analysis and a paper on how it was possible to scale up his experiment to produce sufficient volumes for field testing.

It was at 02.35 on Thursday when Hans finally closed the lid of his laptop. He was excited but tired. Since his wife died three years ago, he had thrown himself into his work. It was as though his life had been on hold. His work consumed his every waking hour but now that would change. He closed his eyes and his imagination took over. He saw his picture on the front of Times Magazine as the saviour of the planet, as a scientific titan, perhaps even a Nobel Prize winner. He sat back and smiled to himself at the thought. Yes, his future looked bright, or so he thought.

By 02.39, Dr Hans Raga was lying dead on the floor of his laboratory.

By02.56, his laptop was inside a briefcase in a car en route to New York City.

***

On arrival in Manhattan, the murderer, plus the briefcase, went straight to the home of Gregory Anderson. Mr Anderson lived in the penthouse on the thirty-second floor of the McClean Building located on 56th Street.

The murderer had been here before but was again amazed at the opulence of this apartment. The ceiling heights were over fifteen feet high and seemed to be hung with more chandeliers than had ever been manufactured. He felt his feet sink into the pale white carpet covering every inch of the floor, except for the foyer which was tiled. Everywhere the murderer looked he saw no other colour except white. Even the elaborately crafted and expensive furniture was white.

Gregory Anderson was dressed casually and was seated in front of a roaring fire. The murderer noted that the fire was gas-powered. He didn't know why this detail had struck him.

"Did you get it?" There was no preamble and Anderson remained seated. Gregory Anderson had seen the murderer being shown into his sumptuous living room unannounced by his uniformed butler. The murderer was expected.

"Yes, I got it. This means I don't owe you any more, right? You said if I brought you the formula, you'd write off my debts." The murderer was anxious to get away. This was the only thought he'd had on the drive south. He had hoped to hand over the laptop and be told his debts were now clear and that he was off the hook. Instead, he was now fearful that he might never leave this apartment and that Gregory Anderson wouldn't keep his word. He might have known it wouldn't be that simple to get out of his predicament.

Gregory Anderson smiled. He was a big man weighing well over 220 pounds. People from Europe would say he was a typical fat, successful American. His hair was slicked back and even at seven a.m. he was clean-shaven and ready for the day's work. His large cigar completed the stereotype, as did the cup of steaming coffee now sitting beside him on a glass-topped side table. "You know, David, it's easy to enjoy yourself with other people's money, but the fun disappears when you have to pay it back."

"But you said we had a deal." He was pleading now, almost in tears. "You said if I brought you the formula, you'd forget about my gambling debts. We'd be square."

"Very true — I did, and I meant it." He gave what might have been mistaken for a fatherly smile. "But you're asking before I've seen the proof that you actually have it." Anderson moved his bulk and rang a bell push located beside the fireplace. He held out his hand. "Give me it." The murderer complied. "Take your coat off and come and have some coffee. We could be here for some time!"

A younger man entered from another room in answer to the summons of the bell. The new arrival was smartly dressed in casual clothing similar to that worn by Anderson. He was thinner than Anderson and sported a full beard that was neatly trimmed. He was probably late thirties and had an air of efficiency about him that contrasted with that of Anderson. This slim man was not a typical gangster if indeed he was one. Gregory removed the laptop from the briefcase with some reverence. "You know, David, when you told me you could get your hands on something like this in exchange for me writing off your debt, I thought you were only buying time. But now, if this is real and you are right about its value, I'll have enough money to let you gamble and lose for the rest of your life." He gave another smile that was more of a smirk. "But if you're playing with me…" The message was clear.

He turned to the younger man and handed him the laptop. "Here it is, Rory, see what's on it. You know what you're looking for. Take your time. I just need to know if it's real."

The murderer didn't know who Rory was but assumed he was a highly-rated technician. In fact, he was a graduate of MIT with a double PhD in Bioengineering. This was the university where the murderer had recently killed the inventor of water-based fuel and owner of the laptop.

Gregory Anderson and the murderer sat by the fire drinking coffee brought to them by the same uniformed butler who had opened the door and let David into the apartment. The butler was calm and efficient and extremely stealthy. David Graham hardly knew he was in the room.

Dr David Graham was a fifty-two-year-old single man who was shy when around women. A quiet academic, he took pride in his teaching abilities and his contribution to university life. He had always been a bit of a loner, had never been married and hadn't even had a steady girlfriend. He'd lived with his widowed father until he passed away several years ago. David had no vices except one — he enjoyed the thrill

14

of gambling. Over the years he had lost big but had equally won large sums on the spin of a wheel or the colour of a card. He had developed a mathematical formula to beat the bank, but it had now all come down to this. Gambling had turned him into a murderer and he still hadn't been told his debts were cleared.

"How much did you gamble away in my casino and on the horses, David?"

"You know how much. It's around $430,000."

"Yes. $437,790, to be exact. That's of course without today's interest being added." Gregory paused to let this sink in. "Money you don't have and no way of getting, except by betraying your friend. You're not a very nice man, are you?" David didn't answer. Gregory carried on. "You know that's what I love about my business. Guys like you lose and lose but always come back for more. When you get desperate, you'll do anything but admit you're an addict, but you need your next fix. The more you lose the more I make. Don't you just love the simplicity of it?" Gregory smiled at his own joke. "It's the American way. Everyone's looking for an easy buck. The best part is it's legal. I'm dealing with addicts but don't have to get involved with street gangs and drug pushers selling powder on street corners." Gregory Anderson sat back and puffed on his cigar. "That's another part of my empire but we won't go there. You know, David, you can't be left out of anything that makes money. Ah! Yes. I love the American way. If you're not in it, you're dead."

David Graham had hoped to be on his way back to Cambridge by now. He was a frightened man, so he listened more than he talked. Both men continued to make small talk. Gregory didn't dislike this gambler turned murderer, but business was business. When he had decided David's debts had risen too far, he'd sent his enforcer to collect. He'd allowed David's losses to increase because he knew who David was and it might be useful to have a hold over such an academic. You never know when such people might be useful. He knew David didn't have the money or the assets to cover the amount he owed. Gregory Anderson considered himself a man of compassion; he liked to meet people who owed him money and couldn't pay. Over the years he had learned that such people usually had something that could be of value. If not, he always found a use for them and collected one way or another.

This was the case with David Graham. When Gregory had explained to him his range of options, from settling his debt now to life in a wheelchair, David had panicked and told Gregory of a project one of his colleagues was working on. He said he was developing a fuel that was based on water. In an obvious and desperate move, he'd offered to get the formula for Anderson in exchange for his debts. He'd said the formula was worth millions. Anderson was sceptical but David Graham was desperate to avoid life in a wheelchair and pleaded with Gregory.

Rory would soon confirm if David Graham would live beyond the next few hours. He had gone way beyond wheelchair status. No one made a patsy of Gregory Anderson.

Rory returned carrying the laptop and a memory stick.

"Well?" demanded Anderson.

"Based on the last notes Dr Raga made, it seems his experiment worked."

David Graham was shocked and relieved. He could hardly believe what was being said. He had no idea his friend had actually figured it out. He'd taken a chance, but now could breathe easier. He knew Gregory Anderson's reputation for violence. He'd thought an uneducated man like Anderson would have no way of understanding what was on the laptop and would have to take his word that the formula worked. He had assumed that by handing over the information he could buy some time to work out how to escape the clutches of this gangster. But now this revelation — it actually worked! He could be in the clear. For the first time in a few hours, David felt he might yet get out of this nightmare he had created.

Rory continued. "The basic science is extraordinary. Some of the molecular engineering is simply brilliant. To reach the stage Dr Raga had reached with limited resources was amazing. I knew Dr Raga at MIT but had no idea how brilliant he was."

"Yes, that's all very well. It can work as an experiment, but will it work in the real world?"

"Oh! Yes, it's so simple. That's the clever thing about it. Dr Raga has even worked out how the formula can be scaled up to produce enough

16

material for commercial trials in a matter of months. You do realise what we have here?"

"As always, you're going to tell me."

"This could put the oil companies out of business. Imagine your petrol-powered car, or a Boeing 747 aircraft, running as they are now with no modifications but giving out zero emissions and using a fuel that costs pennies. It's what the world's been crying out for, truly green energy. This thing could be worth zillions of dollars."

Gregory Anderson rubbed his hands. "You're sure? You can tell just from what's on that laptop?"

"From the explanatory notes, the chemical formulations and the calculations, plus an understanding of the science, then yes. As near as I can tell without repeating the final experiment, I think this works. From an engineering standpoint it's beautiful."

"Right, lock the laptop away and give me the memory stick."

Gregory Anderson pushed the bell by the fireplace and again his uniformed butler appeared as if by magic. "Simons — when Kay gets here, tell her to book Dr Graham onto this evening's British Airways flight to London, England. She'll also have to book him a hotel room for two nights."

Simons, who could have been dumb, simply nodded and left. Rory had also left and both remaining men were standing by the fire.

"Just a minute, Gregory. I'm not going to London." David was putting on a show of indignation. "I've got responsibilities here. I can't just up sticks and disappear." He was frightened and had no idea what was happening, but he certainly wasn't about to do this overweight gangster's bidding without a protest.

"David," Gregory spoke with menace in his voice. "If Rory had said this thing didn't work then that's exactly what you'd have been doing." Gregory was now standing directly in front of him. "Disappearing." He let his words register. "But you're still breathing because you seem to have delivered. Let's not spoil things. Do as I ask and all will be well, OK?" As happens in the movies, Gregory Anderson gently slapped David Graham's cheek.

"You'll stay here until your flight tonight. My secretary Kay will give you everything you'll need for a nice trip to London. Enjoy it. I'll

17

even arrange for you to meet a nice young lady who'll take the memory stick from you and maybe show you the sights or even more." Gregory gave a telling wink. "All you have to do is wait for her." Gregory was looking pleased with himself. He could smell dollars and lots of them.

David was now more frightened than ever but was reconciled. He'd have to make the trip but made one last weak protest.

"I don't have any clothes, not even a toothbrush. It's impossible for me to go."

Gregory rang the bell once more and the obviously faithful Simons quietly appeared.

"Simons —show Dr Graham to the guest suite. He needs travelling clothes and the usual accessories."

Gregory resumed the position he was in when David first arrived; clearly the meeting was over. David followed the butler from the room. He had no idea what the future held for him, but he suspected it wouldn't be pleasant. Perhaps this was retribution for killing his friend, an act he now bitterly regretted but justified as his only way out. Perhaps the fat gangster was right — he wasn't a very nice man.

David Graham was driven to JFK Airport in New York by two very large bodyguards who clearly worked for Gregory. Neither of them spoke. His flight was at seven p.m. and they arrived at six p.m. He was ushered through the check-in procedures and escorted to the security check area. His bodyguards couldn't pass this point into the airside part of the airport but neither could David Graham return to the landside. His bodyguards had delivered him and made sure he was going to London and whatever fate awaited him.

Chapter Two

Detective Chief Inspector Steve Burt was in his office reviewing the recent cases his department had been consulted on. Since his Special Resolutions Unit had been officially incorporated into New Scotland Yard's corporate structure, Steve had assisted in several high-profile serious crimes, including a couple of murders, all of which had led to an arrest and conviction.

In the past eight months, he had gotten his life back on track. He was only drinking socially now and was well regarded within the Met. Unlike eight months ago he was now always smartly dressed and clean and tidy when arriving at work. Best of all, he was still having a strange and fascinating relationship with a doctor he had met during his last solo case. He felt life was good.

But... something was missing. He was getting bored helping others to solve their crimes. He wanted and needed a juicy crime of his own to solve. He could only hope.

Part of the problem was that he was missing his previous colleagues. He had no permanent staff, only officers on temporary secondment to his unit when he needed them and then usually only to do the legwork and write up reports. He was beginning to feel like a training officer. He'd had detective constables with no experience and a couple of Fast Track sergeants just out of uniform. He seemed to spend all his time during investigations explaining the basics of detecting.

As he sat in his eighth-floor office part of a two-room facility given over to his unit, he heard a gentle tap on his open office door. There, stood Inspector Abul Ishmal looking resplendent in his uniform. As Steve looked up, Abul, aka The Cap, smiled and said, "Hope I'm not disturbing you, sir?"

The pair had not met for eight months since they had both been involved in solving a couple of impossible murders that had re-energised their police careers. Inspector Ishmal had been the second member of Steve's first team.

"Cap! Jesus, look at you. All scrubbed up and looking like a tailor's dummy working Human Resources." This was a reference to their previous working relationship. They both laughed. "What brings you here?"

"I've been summoned to the eleventh floor. I've an interview with Chief Superintendent Charles. I don't suppose you know what it's about?"

"Not a clue but it's got to be good news. Maybe you've served your time in blue and they are allowing you back to CID."

"I hope you're right. I'm getting fed up of dealing with all the rubbish the great British public bring to my door. Plus, all I do is fill in forms and write reports no one ever reads."

"Welcome to the club, it's good to see you. Got time for a coffee?"

The inspector looked at his watch. "Yeah, I suppose so. I'm not due upstairs for another forty minutes."

Steve stood from behind his desk and gently brushed past Abul to enter the outer office. A solitary man sat at a desk engrossed in something on his computer screen. "Andy, are you busy?" Andy was a newly appointed detective constable and was still wet behind the ears. Steve didn't have much hope that he would blossom into a great detective.

"Yes, boss, I'm finishing off the weekly returns."

"Good, then pop up and get us two black coffees and get one for yourself, there's a good lad."

Steve went back into his office and both men now sat down at Steve's desk, side by side, after Steve pulled up another chair.

"I must say you're looking very smart: new suit, new office, new job, but no green Fiat!" Abul liked his own humour.

"Talking of green Fiats, have you heard from Twiggy?" Twiggy, or Detective Constable Florance Rough, had been the third member of Steve's previous team. She was rather overweight, to say the least, and chose to drive the smallest car on the roads — a twenty-five-year-old green Fiat 500. Steve had driven with her a few times and knew there wasn't a lot of space when Twiggy was driving.

"Only an e-mail about six months ago. Haven't you heard anything? I thought that at least she would keep in touch with you."

"No, only the same e-mail we both got. Now she's a civil servant she's probably too grand to talk to the likes of us," Steve said as a joke.

Abul spoke up for his ex-colleague: "She'll be busy learning how to spot swindlers and how they cook the books." Twiggy's career had taken a different direction after their case was solved. She had impressed the Financial Crimes Unit within Scotland Yard so much that she was transferred to the Treasury and was currently undergoing intensive training in forensic accounting.

Andy arrived with the coffee. He'd spilt one down his front but gallantly placed two full cups on Steve's desk.

"Sorry, boss, I got stuck in the door and spilt one."

"Thanks, Andy. Go and get another one if you want. It's on my tab."

Andy left. Steve shook his head at Abul. "You see what I'm working with? I sometimes wish we were back together. At least we were a team."

Both men realised how much they missed working together.

They drank their coffee and spoke of their lives during the past few months. When Steve mentioned Dr Alison Mills, The Cap's eyes lit up. "When did this happen?"

"You know when. She was the doctor at the old folks' care home in Rye. We kept in touch and now… well I think we could be more than good friends in the future."

"Good for you, Steve. I'm pleased. Remember if you need a best man, I could be available." The Cap looked at his watch. "Look, I'll have to go, or I'll be late." Inspector Ishmal finished his coffee, collected his cap from Steve's desk, and with a handshake and a promise to keep in touch, left for his interview.

After a few more minutes of quiet reflection, Steve was back to being all business.

"Andy, get me the file for this afternoon's Serious Crimes meeting, will you? I'll have to read up on the Harding case."

***

Armed with his case notes, Steve joined the regular meeting of senior officers who commanded the Serious Crimes units within the Met. The meeting was chaired by Commander Sheila Southgate. A veteran of the police service, Commander Southgate had seen it all. She was in her late 50s and was due to retire within weeks. She had let it be known that the prospect didn't fill her with enthusiasm.

"OK, all. Let's get on with it." This was her customary opening gambit.

"I don't think we've anything to add from our last meeting. No new cases. The weather must be keeping our customers indoors. Frank, what have you got on follow ups?"

Superintendent Frank Dobson was a legend within the Force. He'd solved more murders than any other officer currently serving in the Met. He stood well over six foot, was still slim, and at around mid-forties, he was tipped to go far.

"From last week's briefing I was looking at five murders, one of which was a multiple. That's the Pearson file. We're still a bit stumped on that one. Still no obvious motive or suspects. Maybe it's time Steve took a look?" The Superintendent looked at Steve but didn't wait for a response.

"We've made two arrests in connection with the murder rape that's the Jackson case and the McDonald Soho knifing. In both cases the suspects have been charged. The other two cases are ongoing, but I've just put extra manpower onto them so hopefully we'll get results within the week. The lads tell me they think they're close on both."

Commander Southgate looked up from her note-taking. "Thanks, Frank. Well, Steve, do Special Resolutions want to look at Frank's triple murder case?"

"If Frank doesn't mind, ma'am, I'd be glad to help out."

"Fine. Frank will you please pass on what you have to Steve. Steve you're now designated Senior Investigating Officer on the Pearson case. Try and get ahead of it. I know Frank's been hard at it, but the press, are getting restless. We'll have to give them something soon."

"Yes, ma'am." Steve felt that a set-up had just occurred but didn't know why.

"While we're on you, Steve, let's have your report."

"Truth to tell, there's not a lot to add from last time. We collared the guy responsible for the kidnappings and killings of females from large houses just after our last meeting. I believe DI Ellis has it pretty much wrapped up." Steve looked at Frank Dobson, who nodded yes. "That's the Hawes case off my hands. The culprit is pleading guilty to everything including the killings and we're waiting for a trial date. The other case — that's the Harding killing I took over last week — is still a work in progress but we have a few leads. Those were the two cases we had until now. So, one solved replaced by another." Steve looked at the Superintendent. "Thanks, Frank."

Frank Dobson just nodded, relieved to be shot of a particularly nasty case.

The meeting dragged on. Everyone present seemed to want to impress and usually talked at length on what was obviously a self-promotion trip. Steve was amazed that perfectly normal people appeared willing to sit in meetings like these and enjoy themselves!

***

Steve was back in his office reading up on the case he'd just agreed to take over from the Murder Squad. It was a particularly nasty series of murders by strangulation, and the Murder Squad led by Superintendent Dobson had made little or no progress during the four weeks they'd been investigating. Steve was aware of Dobson's reputation and was a little uneasy that such a high-profile murder case had so easily been passed to him.

He was just about to re-read the file when he was aware of someone standing in his doorway who had just given a light tap on the door surround.

"Do you have a minute, sir?"

"I could have, but first I'd need to know who you are."

"Detective Sergeant Barry Gibson, sir. Murder Squad."

"And what brings you to my door, DS Gibson?"

"Well, sir, if I could come in, I can explain."

"Then enter, but it had better be good."

"My governor DI Chandler sent me down to see if I could be of any help to you with the Pearson file, sir. A kind of secondment."

"Did he now?" Steve was surprised and a little suspicious. "Why would he do that?"

"Well, sir, I've been on the case from the start."

"Mm, yes. But why you? Doesn't he like you?"

The Detective Sergeant actually blushed. "Truthfully, sir, no he doesn't."

"So he thought he'd offload you onto me, eh? Is that it?" Before DS Gibson could reply, Steve carried on. "Why doesn't he like you?"

By now the newcomer was well inside Steve's office. He remained standing.

"It's a bit complicated, sir. Can I speak freely?" Steve said nothing but shrugged his shoulders in an acceptance motion. "Well, to be frank, I don't think DI Chandler is a very good cop. We've had a few run-ins about how best to move the case forward, but he ignores me. He's accused me of being too outspoken and insubordinate."

"And are you?"

The DS gave a wicked smile. "Yes, sir, I suppose it must look that way to my DI but he's not handling the investigation properly. Even Superintendent Dobson seems to be holding back. There are follow-ups that haven't been done. There's forensics that nobody's looked at. I think this killer will do it again. He's already done three."

"Hold on, Detective Sergeant, take a seat." Steve pointed to a chair on the other side of his desk. "You're accusing a senior officer of running an inefficient murder investigation. That's pretty serious stuff."

"Yes, sir, that's why this is off the record."

Steve liked the look of this young detective. He'd get his file from HR, but he looked to be around thirty years old, well-dressed, slim, and about five eleven. His brown hair was on the long side and he sported a small moustache that gave him a look favoured in the 1950s.

"Do you want to be seconded to this unit?"

"Yes, sir. To be honest, I don't think I could carry on working for DI Chandler much longer and I know as much about this case as anyone."

Steve absorbed the implications of what Barry Gibson had said. He made his mind up. "Andy, are you out there?" he shouted.

DC Andy, who appeared to be surname deficient, appeared.

"Yes, boss?"

"Go get two coffees and one for yourself but get a tray this time. I don't want any more accidents."

Andy with no surname hurried off.

Steve moved around his desk and sat beside the detective sergeant.

"Right, Detective Sergeant Barry Gibson, let's hear it, the Pearson case. All of it — especially what's not in the file."

Barry Gibson gave a relieved smile.

"Right. First, we have three victims, each dressed like a tart in the middle of the day. Why? None of the victims lived in Hackney so what were they doing all dressed up in an area they shouldn't have been?"

Barry looked at Steve and continued. "Three months ago, mother of two Marjory Pearson, aged thirty-three, was found strangled in an alleyway just off Claymore Street in Hackney. The discovery was made at 3.07 p.m. by a traffic warden on his way home after his shift. She hadn't been sexually attacked nor robbed, just strangled with what Pathology said was a slim leather belt. There were no forensics at the scene. The post-mortem gave the time of death no more than three hours before the body was discovered. The victim's husband didn't know why his wife would be in Hackney and was convinced she wasn't having an affair. The couple lived in Peckham in a council house. The husband drives a taxi. So the first victim was a dead end from the beginning. Her friends and neighbours said she loved her kids. The family were always short of money but seemed to get by."

Steve was making notes. Andy appeared with three coffees on a tray. He proudly announced that he hadn't spilt a drop. After handing over two cups, he went back to the outer office and his own desk to drink his coffee and carry on doing whatever he was doing before. Steve didn't have a clue how this DC filled in his day.

"OK, Barry, that's victim one. It sounds as though you've nothing. So why criticise your DI?"

"Well, sir, we didn't do any house-to-house. We didn't try and find out why this woman was in Hackney. We didn't even query why she was dressed to the nines in the middle of the day."

"Mm, did the PM say anything about recent sexual activity? If she was dressed up and the family were short of money then maybe she was on the game." Steve sat back thinking.

"There you go, sir, you can see that angle, but DI Chandler didn't even think of that. He just said there was nothing to go on, so it had a low priority. As it happens there was evidence of recent activity."

"They took swabs for DNA analysis?"

"Yes, but there was no match."

"What about victim two?"

"Right. She was called Stacey Mathews. Divorced, but with a kid. Twenty-nine years old and worked as a part-time hairdresser. She was found in Beecham Park, Hackney. That's just round the corner from where the first victim was found. A dog walker found her at 3.10 p.m. Again, strangled but this time Pathology thought it more likely to have been a scarf. There was no evidence of rape or robbery, but she was also dressed up just like the first victim in what looked like her best party outfit. You know, short skirt, tight-fitting top and four-inch heels. She lived with her parents in Mile End. They said she liked a good time but was always short of money. They were more or less bringing up her kid for her, a four-year-old little girl. They said Stacey didn't have a regular boyfriend but was always dreaming of meeting Mr Right — someone with loads of cash. Again, there were no forensics at the scene and before you ask there was evidence of sexual activity, but the pathologist said it was probably consensual. Death was again put at around three hours before the body was discovered. Both victims were killed around twelve noon. A bit weird, don't you think?" Barry looked at his new boss who just stared back. "Stacey was found ten days after Marjory Pearson."

Steve was sipping his coffee. "So it seems there are enough similarities to link the two murders. Both young, short of cash, both dressed up, both had recently had sex, and both were found dead in Hackney."

"Right. My DI didn't see the connection, or at least he said he didn't. He was writing them off as sex crimes and said they must have been working as prostitutes. Once again there were no follow-ups."

"OK, I'm interested. So tell me about the third victim."

"The peculiar thing is the third woman was murdered exactly ten days after Stacey Mathews. This time it was thirty-six-year-old Barbara James, married but separated, no kids. She lived alone and worked as a barmaid at an upmarket pub in the city. She was found by a cyclist on his daily ten-mile cycle ride." Barry looked at the DCI and smiled, arching his eyebrows and giving a knowing smile. "Ten miles a day — he must be daft!" He carried on.

"She was again in a side street but this time off Hackney High Road. The cyclist called it in at 2.55 p.m. Like the other two she was dressed up, and to be honest looked like she could have been selling her body, but Pathology confirmed that although there were signs of recent sexual activity it hadn't been within the last 24 hours. They put the time of death around twelve noon. She was strangled and the pathologist said it could have been done with a slim leather belt just like the first victim. There were no useful forensics at the scene. Another dead end."

"So what did DI Chandler say about this one?"

"He said he could see similarities given they were, in his words, 'dressed like good time girls', but said the only common thread was that they were found in Hackney."

"So, did he do anything? And what about Frank Dobson? He's supposed to be the go-to man on any murder enquiry."

"I don't know, sir. All I do know is that there hasn't been a real investigation into these deaths and if the killer sticks to a ten-day timetable, then he's due to kill again in six days' time."

"Mm. Good point. Right, DS Barry Gibson, I'll officially request your secondment to Special Resolutions with immediate effect. Grab yourself a desk out there, preferably one with a computer sitting on it. God knows what Andy does out there all day but if you need anything, ask him. Oh! By the way, ask Andy to show you the Harding file. It's a case we're working on with Murder Squad Two. You might as well get stuck into that as well." With a wicked grin, Steve added: "If you do find out what Andy does all day, let me know." The DCI preferred to lighten the mood with a bit of humour.

"Right, sir, and thank you."

"No problem. From what you've said there may be something fishy about these murders, but we can't jump to conclusions. We'll make a fresh start in the morning. Oh, and Barry, when it's just us, Steve will do. In public, either 'sir', 'boss' or 'guv'. Got it?"

"Yes, sir. As you say, sir, boss or guv." Barry Gibson gave a mock salute. He was a happier man than he had been an hour earlier.

Chapter Three

Steve and Barry were sitting in Steve's office at 8.35 a.m. the next day. Steve had intended to take the triple murder file home to read but had left it with Andy on his way out the previous evening. He'd wanted to be as up to speed as his newly acquired detective sergeant but thought that as he'd already read it twice then that was enough.

One of the things Steve didn't like about his role within the Met was a lack of permanent staff. He knew when he'd agreed to take on the Special Resolutions Unit that he would only have seconded officers with special skills to assist on each investigation, but it was like a revolving door. He didn't have time to get to know them, at least the ones who were any good. He'd felt in the past he'd been handed officers that weren't up to the job. At least Barry Gibson seemed a cut above.

Just as the two detectives were about to start, Andy put his head around the door. "Coffee?"

"Good idea, Andy," Steve said as Andy was reversing away from the door. "Andy? Get yourself one and come and sit in on our meeting."

Andy's head re-appeared in what could have been a split-second. "Really? Wow! I'll be right back."

Steve knew Andy read every file that passed over his desk so he would know about the triple homicide case. It would be interesting to see his work close-up, because despite making light of it, Steve really didn't know why Andy was his only permanent member of staff. He'd been told Detective Constable Andrew Miller was his admin assistant. Steve felt he didn't need an admin assistant and wasn't sure what such a person would do. He still didn't.

With their coffee in front of them, Steve was about to open the discussion when he noticed Andy had the Harding file on his lap.

"Andy, we're going over the triple murder case, not Harding."

"Yes, but you need to know about the Harding case, sir. There's been a development."

Steve wondered how Andy knew this. "Go on…"

"Well, last night after everyone had gone there was a call from Essex. They'd picked up someone trying to steal a car. It seems they found some jewellery on him that matched the description of stuff taken from Harding. Remember, we'd circulated descriptions to all forces. Anyway, it seems this guy confessed to the killing and the robbery. They wanted to check with us because their guy mentioned the banana. We'd not released that detail and they needed to check. If he knows that detail, then it's likely they've got our man. They've asked for the file, but I wanted to check with you first, sir."

Barry looked surprised. "Excuse me, I know I'm new and I've only scanned the file but what's with the banana?"

Steve took over. "Samuel Harding was a fine art expert at Sotheby's. He was taking some jewellery to be repaired but was knifed when he was crossing Regent's Park. He was found with an old-style dagger in his chest and a banana in his mouth. Goodness only knows why. We haven't figured it out, but we didn't release that detail. If Essex have a guy who knows about it then he's either our man or he knows who is. We picked up the case around four weeks ago but to be honest we were getting nowhere. I've got a couple of seconded plodders on it, but I didn't have much hope. Now this."

Steve turned to Andy. "Good work, Andy. Let's play a little politics. When we're finished here, go and see DI Chandler. Tell him his suspect for Harding is in Essex. I presume Chelmsford?" Steve looked at Andy, who nodded. "Give him back the file with my compliments, and tell him Essex want the file, so if he wants his man he'll have to go and fetch him."

The colour visibly drained from Andy's face, but he said nothing.

"Right. That means we now only have the triple. Andy, can you mark up the board please? There's a marker pen by the board." Steve was referring to a large white magnetic board attached to the far wall of his office.

Andy did as requested, but instead of getting ready to write, he produced photographs from his file of each of the dead girls. He used magnets to attach them to the board in a single line across the top of the board. He then wrote their names neatly below each photograph.

"Ready now, sir." Steve was impressed. He was seeing Constable Andy Miller in a new light. It was true he was no male model. He stood about five foot, nine inches tall; his hair was an old-fashioned short back and sides; he wore multicoloured sleeveless sweaters over white long-sleeved shirts; he favoured heavy brown corduroy trousers with turned-up bottoms; and his look was rounded off by his heavy brown shoes. At twenty-eight years old, he looked as though his mother still dressed him for school, but the school must have been in the fifties. No one dressed like this now, except Andy.

"Right, Andy. As we get something, write it under the appropriate victim. So, victim one — Marjory Pearson. Age — 33. Lived in Peckham.

Victim two — Stacey Mathews. Age — 29. Lived in Mile End. Victim three — Barbara James. Age — 36. Lived in Stepney."

Andy wrote it all neatly down under each victim.

"All three were dressed for a party. All three were said to be short of cash. All three were murdered around twelve noon. All three were discovered in Hackney. Two had had sex within hours of being killed. The third victim didn't but was sexually active no more than 24 hours before she was killed. We have no semen so no DNA. We assume if our killer was their last sexual partner, he must have worn a condom. Finally, there was no evidence that any of our victims were on drugs. Have I missed anything?"

Andy was finishing his writing and turned to face Steve. "Well, sir, you have." With no hesitation, Andy carried on. "The third victim, Barbara James, was on methadone. The PM report includes a toxicology report, and it says she'd been clean for a couple of months but was heavily into the substitute."

The room was quiet, and Andy shuffled on the spot like an errant schoolboy.

"How the hell do you know that?" Steve was impressed.

"I entered all three cases into the computer last night. You see, if you're doing it properly then you have to input each line from each report. The methadone reference was in the middle of the pathologist's technical explanations that frankly no one reads. It's easy to miss. I've set the file up so we can cross-reference even the smallest piece of information going forward. I hope that's all right, sir?"

"Andy, where have you been all my life? Well done again. I´m not sure it makes any difference but good to know. Right. Off you go and see DI Chalmers about the Harding case. Barry — call up a pool car. It's time we visited the crime scenes. The only problem might be if they were killed somewhere else and dumped in Hackney to throw us off."

"It's always possible, Steve, but I'm not sure. I'll bet our killer has a connection to Hackney."

"Excuse me, sir." It was Andy. "As I was putting things on the computer it struck me that as the victims were female and all dressed up, maybe they were sex workers, but their families didn't know. I mean who else would dress up like they were. I've studied the crime scene photos and I can't imagine women dressing that way, especially at twelve o'clock. I mean, it's lunchtime."

"So are you saying they might put you off your lunch?" Barry smiled at his own joke.

Steve sensed Andy was going somewhere with this.

"I don't eat lunch. I only have an apple, but no, listen." Andy was getting animated. Steve thought this was a positive sign coming from his admin assistant. "I'm suggesting they were either on their way to, or coming from, work. I've pulled all the sex outlets registered in and around Hackney. You know, massage parlours, gentlemen's clubs, strip clubs, although strip clubs tend to only open at night unless it's one of those lunchtime pubs."

Barry was about to pull Andy's leg at his knowledge of strip clubs, but Steve spoke first.

"Andy. We should have thought of that. Do you have a list?"

"Yes, sir, it's on the computer. It'll only take a minute to print off. There are nine massage parlours, two gentlemen's clubs and two strip pubs. I've included strip clubs even though the timings don't work but there are only three of them."

Barry was more interested now in this line of thought. "Suppose they were strippers and had been at rehearsals or something. That might explain the timings."

"All good theories. Let's get into everything after we've been to Hackney. And Andy, I've told you over and over. My name's Steve, boss or guv when it's just us."

"Yes, sir. It just doesn't seem right. You're a DCI."

Andy left to go and have his confrontation with DI Chandler, Barry left to pick up the pool car, and Steve began to wonder if he hadn't unearthed a dream team. Time would tell.

Chapter Four

The flight from New York landed at London Heathrow twenty-seven minutes early at 6.14 a.m. David Graham had no luggage in the hold and was only carrying the one bag given to him by Gregory Anderson's butler. The memory stick was safely stowed away in the inside pocket of his jacket. After clearing immigration and walking straight through customs control, he found himself on the landside of the vast Terminal 5 building at Heathrow. He followed the signs for 'taxis' and asked the driver to take him to the Mayflower Hotel in Central London.

He didn't see the two men who'd followed him since he arrived at Heathrow. They got into the back of the next taxi in line, just behind the one David was using. All London taxis were similar-looking shiny black boxes on wheels and one didn't stand out from another. The driver was told to follow the taxi in front. The taxi driver thought of making a smart comment, but at 7.30 in the morning after a long night shift, and with two hard-looking men as passengers, he just drove.

The first and second taxis arrived more or less at the Mayflower Hotel at the same time. Both left empty after their passengers paid their respective fares. David Graham walked to reception to check in whilst one of the men made a phone call.

Room 1202 was a standard hotel room; clean and efficient, with a great view looking out over London. There was nothing a guest could complain about. The en suite bathroom was complete with a large walk-in shower; the bed was a king size and looked comfortable; and there was a minibar and a kettle to make tea or coffee. There were even a few plain biscuits sealed in plastic bags. David was unpacking his few belongings when he heard a faint tap on the door. He opened it to see the most beautiful woman he had ever seen, just standing there. Not that he'd come across many beautiful women. Without any preamble she walked straight past David. "Good morning, Dr Graham. I trust you had a pleasant flight?"

David was dumbstruck. He'd no idea who this woman was, but clearly, she knew him. All he could do was blurt out a "yes."

"Gregory asked me to check that you had everything you needed and to collect a certain item from you."

She sat down in one of the large armchairs located by the window and smiled sweetly at him. She kept her heavy winter coat on but undid the buttons to reveal a pale blue dress cut high at the neck and what David thought could be described as an hourglass figure. Her long, dark hair was tied back, and her large, penetrating brown eyes gave her an alluring presence that David found disturbing.

"Did Gregory send you?" This was all the conversation David could muster in the presence of this beauty.

"That's correct, Dr Graham. Do you have the memory stick?"

"Well… Yes."

"Can I have it please?" She held out her delicate and well-manicured hand but remained seated.

David couldn't be sure but he felt her voice betrayed her as being originally from the USA but thought that perhaps she'd spent enough time in Europe to disguise the harder edges to her speech. He lifted his jacket from the bed and handed this seated vision the memory stick.

"Thank you." She stood up and fastened her coat. "Please be in the foyer at five p.m. this evening. I'll leave you to catch up on your jet lag. Please only order room service if you're hungry. We made sure your minibar is fully stocked and there is sufficient tea and coffee for your needs. One of Mr Anderson's operatives is located in the hotel and he will stop you if you try and leave — is that clear?" This beautiful woman had a hard edge to her and was all business.

"Yes, but why? I was told I could see the sights of London. No one said I would be a prisoner in this hotel."

"Dr Graham, these are my instructions. I'll see you in the foyer at five p.m." With a flourish of her hand, she walked to the door and was gone.

He was even more frightened after this visit and assumed this was the lady Gregory Anderson had told him to expect.

***

At five p.m. exactly, David was standing in the foyer of the Mayflower Hotel.

The mysterious beauty arrived at 5.01 p.m. She was wearing the same heavy coat she had worn at their first meeting. "Dr Graham," she smiled. "Shall we go? The car's just outside."

David Graham said nothing, still in awe of this woman's beauty. They climbed into the back of a black Audi and David noted that beside the driver was another figure occupying the front passenger seat. Both men were large and wore matching dark grey suits. As the car set off, David asked his companion where they were going. "Oh, don't worry. It's not far. All this will be over soon." His companion turned away to look out of the side window. The rest of the journey took place in silence. He had a lot of questions, primarily over his own future, but realised asking them would be a waste of time.

The car pulled up at the entrance to an underground garage. The driver leaned out and punched some keys on a keypad attached to the wall. The barrier swung up and the car drove on. Once parked, everyone exited the Audi and entered a lift. The woman inserted a key into a lock that was marked 'penthouse'.

There was no sensation of movement inside the lift and David was surprised when the doors opened and he was ushered out by one of the men dressed in dark grey.

The two men David now thought to be bodyguards stood back, allowing the woman and David access to a penthouse suite. The apartment was on top of a block of luxury apartments located in London's Knightsbridge area. All David could see was a vast, open-plan space with large picture windows running down the whole of one side of the penthouse. He could just make out that these windows opened out onto a terrace overlooking the London skyline.

The furnishings were strangely simple, with only several large Chesterfield-style sofas set out facing each other, a very large dining table that would double as a banqueting table, and several floor mounted cabinets that took up most of one wall. David noted that there were doors off to the rear and assumed these would lead to more private quarters.

Sitting at the dining table were two men David didn't know. "Good evening, my dear." This was directed at David's female companion. "Did the good doctor come quietly?"

"Yes, no trouble at all." The woman was removing her outside coat that not only showed her long, shapely legs but confirmed she did indeed have an hourglass figure.

"Good, good, very good." One of the men seated at the table scanned the doctor, taking in everything he saw in seconds. "Dr Graham, let me introduce myself. I'm Julian St John. This is my brother Sebastian." Both men stood to shake David's hand. David was surprised by the sight in front of him. Julian St John stood around five feet, six inches tall and from his shape appeared to be very overweight. By contrast, Sebastian St John was over six feet tall, very slender and seemed to have a problem with his right shoulder or arm. He shook hands with David using his left hand. These two certainly didn't look as though they came from the same womb.

Julian continued: "Doctor, please have a seat."

Both brothers left their table and walked to the area where the sofas were positioned. "I presume you're wondering what's going on? Well, I don't blame you."

Julian appeared to be trying to be over-friendly. He was smiling a lot. "You see my brother and I are in the business of finding things people want. The odd old master, the location of a known terrorist, that kind of thing. Things that most ordinary folk wouldn't know where to begin looking for, you see, but we do. We think of ourselves as facilitators. If you have a high-value item that you don't want the authorities to know you have then we help. We buy and sell and of course make a profit in the process." Julian seemed happy at his prospects of making money from David's recent deed. "So, it's only natural that Gregory Anderson would offer us first refusal of your formula. We have offered to pay Mr Anderson a whole load of American dollars for your formula." Julian was smiling like a Cheshire cat, but his eyes were drilling into David. This was another frightening individual. "But, you see, we're not in the business of paying for something we don't have, and that's our dilemma, Dr Graham."

Sebastian St John had been quietly listening to his brother. Now he took up the narrative. David felt this had been well-rehearsed. "We're not scientists like you, Dr Graham." Sebastian's voice was surprisingly high-pitched whereas his brother's had been deep and gravelly. "We can't look at a piece of paper and say we'll buy it just because someone says it works. Oh no, you see we're simple businessmen and good business practice says you should always try before you buy." Sebastian chuckled at his own choice of words.

For the first time since entering this place, David felt brave enough to speak. "But it has been authenticated by Mr Anderson in New York."

Julian took over once more. "Yes, yes, and we don't doubt him. It's just as Sebastian says. We need proof. We can't simply pay Gregory Anderson millions of dollars just on his say so that it works. Goodness me, no, that wouldn't be good business." Julian smiled but there was no warmth in it.

Sebastian was again front and centre. "We've set up a laboratory not far from here and we want you to recreate the experiment and prove that the formula works. We're sure it does, but as we say we need to be 100% sure before we pay Gregory. We've had it explained to us. We just need to see the evidence. Nothing much. Just a small bang when the liquid comes into contact with heat."

David was shell-shocked. This pair had obviously been briefed, but by whom?

David had never seen Hans' experiment in action and wasn't sure he was capable of repeating it. He was also beginning to think he would never get out of this mess with his life.

"I don't think I can do that. I've never worked with Dr Raga on this project. I don't know enough about it. I'm sorry but what you're asking is impossible." David adopted his most threatening academic pose. "It's quite out of the question."

Julian rose from his sofa and went to the table. He returned with a sheet of paper. "Dr Graham, you're familiar with the Herald Tribune newspaper in your country?"

"Yes, of course."

"Well before you tell us you can't do as we ask you'd better read this morning's headline. It was e-mailed to us by Gregory Anderson." He handed the copy to David. David's heart stopped for a beat and he felt the blood draining from his head. There in bold print was the headline: 'POLICE SEEK EMINENT SCIENTIST AS MURDER SUSPECT'.

"I think you'll have problems returning to the States, certainly as Dr David Graham. Every policeman will be looking for you." Julian put on what he hoped was his serious and compassionate face. "But if you do as we ask I'm sure we can help you evade the law and maybe even make you wealthier than you could ever imagine. I think you call this a 'catch 22'?"

David was reeling from the headline. If only Gregory Anderson hadn't kidnapped him he was sure he could have talked his way out of being a suspect, but the fact he'd apparently fled now made that impossible. His mind was in turmoil. "OK, I see I have no choice but once I'm finished I'll go my own way. I don't want your help." David began to plan how he could escape. There had to be opportunities to run, if only he looked for them.

"As you wish, it's your decision. We only want the proof. Frankie?" Julian called out. One of the pair from the car appeared. "Take Dr Graham to the facility in Redbridge. You know what to do."

"Right, boss." Frankie waited until David had risen from the sofa and walked dejectedly towards him. The other large man from the car appeared by magic at David's side. The lift doors closed as the three left the penthouse.

Julian turned to his brother. "Well, what do you think?"

"I think he'll do as we ask but I don't trust him. At the first opportunity I think he'll skip."

"Regrettably, brother, I tend to agree with you." Julian was thinking over the problem before shouting out: "Ruby — will you come through, my dear?"

She appeared through one of the doors at the end of the room. Julian gave her an appreciative smile that didn't reach his eyes. "Sorry to impose further on you but we require you to carry out a little errand."

"Yes?" Ruby replied.

"We're a bit fearful our Dr Graham may be playing a game with us and might try to escape our hospitality. We need you to ensure he does not. Can you do that for us, my dear?"

"But he is going to verify the formula?" Ruby was concerned.

"Of course, it's just a precaution. He's on his way to our Redbridge facility under guard but I think it's best if you were there and, shall we say, escorted him back to his hotel when he's finished." This was said with a lustful sneer. Ruby knew exactly what Julian wanted her to do. She was in London as Gregory's eyes and ears and more besides. She knew Gregory owned her but if things worked out, she would soon be free.

"Perhaps once you have taken care of Dr Graham you might oblige me with your company one evening?"

Ruby looked at this horrible, fat man who was leering at her. As Julian sat at the table, she leaned forward deliberately, revealing her not insignificant cleavage. "You're a dirty old man and you'll wait a long time before I come anywhere near you. But just to make sure." Ruby produced a two-shot .22 Derringer pistol and pointed it at Julian's head. "You've got the message now, I'm sure."

Julian was impressed by this, and even more impressed that she could hide the pistol without it showing through her almost skin-tight dress. Julian fantasised where she might keep it.

Chapter Five

On arrival in Hackney, Steve and Barry went straight to Hackney Police Station. Barry mentioned, for Steve's benefit, that this was one of the last community police stations left in London, thanks to budget cuts in the Met over the years. Steve knew all about budget cuts. It was only the need for budget cuts that had kept Steve in his present job.

The station was a bit soulless and obviously in need of some cosmetic attention. Both detectives pushed through the double swing doors that gave access to a large waiting area. The only furniture was an old wooden bench presumably for people to sit on whilst waiting to be attended to. A burly, uniformed sergeant was behind a Perspex screen writing in a journal of some sort.

"Yes, gents, can I help you?"

Steve produced his warrant card. "Yes, I hope so. We'd like to see your head of CID." The sergeant appeared to be impressed by Steve's credentials but looked sceptical.

"That'd be DCI Bottoms. Just hold on, sir, and I'll buzz him. Won't take a minute."

The sergeant lifted an old-style phone and dialled a three-digit number. He turned his back to the waiting area so that his conversation couldn't be overheard. Steve thought this conversation with the head of Hackney CID took longer than he would have expected but eventually the sergeant replaced the receiver and turned to look at his guests.

"DCI Bottoms is a bit tied up just now but says that if you're here about the murders then you'd be better speaking with DS Robertson. He knows all about the cases and he's in at the moment."

For some reason Steve couldn't fathom, he felt this arrangement didn't seem right. A DCI too busy to meet a colleague from Scotland Yard and a DS who knew all about the cases. He decided to let it pass but reminded himself to make a mental note for later. Something was worrying away at him.

The sergeant, now looking pleased with himself, buzzed open the door that gave access beyond his desk. "If you'd follow me, gentlemen. I'll take you to Sergeant Robertson."

Steve and Barry did as requested. Beyond the sergeant's front desk was a long corridor with doors leading off. The corridor had no outside windows, and the walls were painted with gloss paint in two contrasting colours. The colour of the top half had at one time been white. The bottom half was still painted grey. Where the colours met someone had painted in a thick red line. Steve thought the arrangement was functional but ugly. He felt he was in a time warp and was back in the 1950s. This place was depressing, especially with overhead neon lights permanently on. Barry's comments about budget cuts came back to him.

"Here we are, gents." The front desk sergeant stopped at a door, opened it without knocking and ushered the two officers from the Yard into a large room that had four desks arranged around the walls and other bits of furniture scattered in an obviously random style.

"Thank you, sergeant." Steve was being polite.

As they entered, Steve and Barry saw a man probably in his late forties sitting at one of the desks reading a newspaper. There was no one else in the room. Steve assumed the seated man was the one they'd come to see. He had thinning grey hair, cut very close to his scalp. He had a large, grey-coloured beard; his once-white shirt didn't look as though it had seen an iron in weeks; and his tie had been pulled down when he'd opened the top button of his shirt. Neither newcomer could see what he was wearing below the waist as he continued to sit in silence and read his newspaper.

"We're looking for Detective Sergeant Robertson?"

"Really?" The seated man put down his newspaper. "Well, that's me, Davie Robertson. Who might you two be?"

Steve and Barry produced their warrant cards and introduced themselves. From Davie Robertson's name and accent it was clear he was a Scot. Barry, who knew a few Celts, thought Davie might be originally from Glasgow.

Davie remained seated, even in the presence of a senior officer. "I suppose you're here about the murders?" To Barry's ear this Sergeant Robertson had lived in England a long time. His accent wasn't difficult to understand, unlike those of other colleagues he'd known from north of the border.

"That's right. I understand from your DCI that you're the man we should talk to. We'd like to pick your brains to see if there's anything we've missed in the files. We only got these cases yesterday and we're just getting started. We're with the Special Resolutions Unit at the Yard."

"Oh! Aye, I see." There was still a bit of the Scot about this man. The sergeant didn't move from his chair but stroked his beard in thought. "Well, I was aboot to go for an early lunch. That means the way I see it is this." Sergeant Robertson's accent was now more pronounced. "If you were to stand me my meal then I would be all yours and we could have a nice wee chat."

Steve was even more convinced he'd taken a step back in time. A junior officer bartering with a senior colleague. It was as though if Steve didn't agree to fund this sergeant's lunch, then he'd get little or no cooperation. Before Steve exploded, Barry said: "Sir, we've not eaten and it's eleven fifteen. Maybe a casual nibble with Davie here would help us all relax and discuss the cases?"

Steve was glad he had Barry with him. "Is that a deal then, gentlemen?" The cheeky Scottish sergeant rose from his desk and put on the jacket that had been hanging over the back of his chair. "My usual's a nice wee café just round the corner. Nothing grand but good, robust food. No need to worry, sir, it's very reasonably priced." With a wicked grin, the sergeant set off, expecting his colleagues from the Yard to follow him.

Barry grinned at his boss. "Takes all sorts."

"Yeah, I suppose it does." Both detectives from Scotland Yard followed on, not knowing what to expect.

Davie had been correct about the location of his favoured café. The term 'greasy spoon' was a better description. It was literally just around the corner. The detectives from the Yard stood looking at a building that shouted 1950s. To call this café a greasy spoon was insulting every legitimate greasy spoon in London. With a broad smile, Davie pushed the café door open. Steve noted that it stuck and needed a good push. There was a bell attached to the inside of the door that rang every time someone entered.

The act of opening the door brought a smell of overly hot and reused fat that wafted over Steve and Barry despite them still being outside. The establishment was called 'Mary's Restaurant'. It had one large plate glass window that no one could see out of for the condensation that ran down the inside of the glass. The proprietor had hung a net curtain over the lower part of the window, presumably for the privacy of the clients. No doubt it had once been white but it wasn't any more.

Steve and Barry went in. The smell was overpowering. It was bad outside but a lot worse inside. The tables were mainly set for two people, and each table had a plastic cover over it. Steve noted that no two covers were the same. There was a plastic tomato on each table which obviously contained tomato sauce together with a vinegar bottle. The chairs were an odd mixture and again no two seemed to match.

Davie had seated himself by the window. This was the only place it was possible to get three people sitting together and able to talk to each other with any privacy, even though the place was empty. They reluctantly joined him. As soon as Steve and Barry sat down, a stick-thin woman in her early twenties arrived holding a notepad and put a cup of tea in front of the sergeant. She was dressed in a dirty overall that looked as though it was home to a colony of salmonella bugs. She asked if they wanted tea or coffee and pointed to a hand-written blackboard on the wall. She said everything was available that was on the menu, but the pie, egg and chips was on special. Steve ordered coffee and Barry plumped for tea. Davie had already had his tea and said he was having the special. Steve and Barry gracefully declined the offer of the special, stating that they weren't hungry enough.

Davie's special arrived and no more than four minutes later his plate was clean. The tea and coffee ordered by Steve and Barry arrived at the same time as Davie's meal. After a tentative sip, they remained untouched — both tasted like Nile water.

There hadn't been a lot of conversation during Davie's lunch, but he had divulged that he was indeed from Glasgow. He'd joined the Glasgow force as a cadet from school and had moved south twenty years ago when he married his first wife.

Davie was wiping his mouth with the back of his hand; there were no paper napkins in evidence. He called for another tea before turning his attention to his colleagues from the Yard. "Delicious. You always get a good tuck in here. Now, gentlemen, what can I help you with?"

Steve felt it was Davie who was the senior officer. He had to get the relationships back on track.

"We've read the reports and we know Hackney handled the first killing. That's the Pearson woman. What we need is what's not in the file. Anything out of the ordinary. For example, was she killed where she was found, or was she dumped?"

Sergeant Robertson sat back and stroked his beard. He wasn't a tidy man and Steve wasn't surprised when he started to scratch his over-sized stomach and simultaneously burped. He didn't apologise.

"I was the first CID officer on scene. Pearson was lying on her back. You know, arms stretched out, one leg cocked at a funny angle with a red mark around her throat. It looked like a strangling. My initial thought was that she was on the game. All dressed up in the middle of the afternoon. I remember thinking it was funny that she was there at all. It's a fairly busy cut-through so whoever did for her must've known she'd be found and pretty quickly. There wasn't any attempt to hide the body. Either he killed her there or dumped her. Now you see I don't think she was killed there." Davie was enjoying himself. "It's a fairly busy alley and someone would have seen him. It's more likely she was dumped. He'd have to be quick mind but that's maybe why there was no attempt to hide her."

Steve thought this was useful but flawed. "If she was dumped and the alley has people coming and going, how do you think our killer got the body into the alley without being seen? Anyone carrying a body might attract some attention." Steve smiled at his little joke. No one else did.

"I'm only a lowly DS from a satellite police station so that's for you boys from the Yard to work out. But I might look at carrying the body in something with wheels that might be pretty common in that area." It was obvious that this DS Robertson was no fool, despite his laidback manner, and had more to offer.

"What sort of thing on wheels?" Barry pitched in as Steve seemed to be deep in thought.

"You obviously don't know this part of Hackney. There's a fair bit of underground rag trade that goes on, especially in the area the lassie was found. That alley's got large bins in it that are used for getting rid of fabric waste from the sweatshops. If it were me, I'd put the lassie's body in one of those bins and just wheel it into the alley. Nobody would look twice. There's a lot of them."

"Barry, look up the file. See if forensics found anything to do with cloth or thread on our first victim." Barry set to work.

"Davie? Apart from underground rag trade set-ups, are there any other illegal areas we should look at?" Steve carried on without waiting for an answer. "We think she might have been on the game, especially by the way she was dressed. Is there any gangland stuff here that's into prostitution or drugs? Anything that might explain the way the victim was dressed and the timing of her death?"

Before Davie could answer, Barry was reading aloud from the file. "Steve." Barry looked up from his file. "There were particles of fine silk thread caught in her hair and dust on her coat that forensics say could be from cutting cloth."

"Thanks, Barry. So, Davie, what do you think?"

"Apart from I'm a clever clogs, you mean?" Davie was pleased his suggestion had proven to be possible. "We don't have any gang problems here. Sure, we've got pimps and the like. A few clubs that maybe offer more than watered-down champagne. But nothing serious enough to suggest murder. There are the usual massage joints, but this lassie was dressed for more than a quick romp on a tabletop. I'm no saying it's not sex-related, but I don't think it's anything to do with organised crime, not in Hackney."

"Do you know anything about the second murder?"

"Not a lot. The body was found in Beecham Park close to the first victim. When it came in, my DCI hit the panic button and called you lot in. That's when we got the whole circus. Fancy pathologist, guys with machines, search teams, white paper suits, even tracker dogs. Of course, they found nothing. I was told to stay away from it. You lot from the Yard took over, including the first case. That's all I know."

"Well, Davie, you may have conned me out of a lunch, and introduced us to the worst dining experience we've ever had, but I think you've helped us, so thank you. If I need anything else, I'll call you directly."

"Yeah, do that. My DCI's a waste of space. He's only a couple of months from retirement and suffers from gout. Poor soul." Davie said this with no compassion at all. "Remember, sir, I'm always happy to help but I do like a lunch." All three detectives laughed as they stood up and left Mary's Restaurant.

Chapter Six

After walking with Davie back to Hackney Police Station, the two detectives drove into central Hackney and parked in a supermarket car park. They knew from their London A-Z that this was close to the sites of all three murders.

They followed their map and quickly found the alley off Claymore Street where Marjory Pearson's body had been found. Steve estimated that the alley was about ten feet wide, but the width was restricted by several large metal bins sitting on the left against the gable end of the adjoining building. To the right was a low, single-level, flat-roofed building that ran the full length of the alley. There were multiple doors leading from this building that Steve thought must be the rear doors of whatever businesses fronted the other side of the building. The road surface had broken up over the years and was now an uneven mixture of black tar and compacted earth.

Barry produced the file and both detectives estimated the spot where the body had been found by orientating the scene of crime photographs. "I reckon it's here, Steve. You can see where the Scene of Crime boys put their steel plates — the indentations are still there."

"Yeah. Good spot. Right, Barry, what do we think?"

"The body was more or less in the middle of the alley. Look at the photo. From the position I'd say she was literally dumped. Chummy must have panicked, especially if there were people coming and going. He must have waited until the coast was clear, dumped the body and walked away."

"Yes, but how did he get the body here and how could he stand around without attracting suspicion from passers-by? Nobody has come forward reporting a stranger hanging around."

"What if he's not a stranger? Maybe he's a regular fixture and blends into this place?"

"Mm could be, but Davie said this was a cut-through. I'm not sure it's that busy and it's not necessarily the same people who use this alley every day. Everyone would be a stranger. Remember we've no witness statements. We still need..." At that moment a sound came from the entrance to the alley at the Claymore Street end. Steve and Barry turned to see what was causing the noise.

A small man of Asian descent was pushing an enclosed four-wheel cart towards the detectives. He was dressed in a brown warehouse coat and stood about five feet, six inches. He was slim and appeared to be having difficulty keeping the cart moving forward on the uneven surface. He saw the two men from Scotland Yard and eyed them suspiciously but continued his efforts moving his cart forward. He was heading straight for Steve who moved to one side. The man stopped by one of the large bins set against the gable wall. He lifted the lid of the bin and turned to his own cart's lid to gain access to what was inside.

Both Steve and Barry just stood and looked on. The man bent over and put his head into his cart with his arms outstretched. He re-appeared with his arms full of brightly coloured fabrics and proceeded to throw his bundle into the large bin. He did this several times before closing the top of his cart and pushing the lid of the large bin closed.

"Excuse me. I'm Detective Chief Inspector Burt from Scotland Yard. This is Detective Sergeant Gibson." Both men produced their warrant cards as they walked towards the small man and his cart.

"Can I ask you what you just did?" The man looked blankly at the DCI and shook his head. It occurred to Steve that maybe this gentleman didn't speak much English.

"Do you understand? I need to know what you are doing."

Again, the man just stared, his brown eyes enlarged and wide. He looked very scared.

"Do you speak English? It's OK. You're not in any trouble."

In broken English, the man replied. "I speak a little."

"Good. Can you tell me what you're doing?"

The man didn't look comfortable but seemed to recognise the authority of Steve and the inevitability of him having to answer.

"Work for Mr Hodge. Him very good man. He give me job. I look after waste so there no fire in factory. I collect from floor and sweep. Put in cart and empty into bins. That what I do now." The man pointed to the large bins.

Steve and Barry looked at each other. The man's cart was big enough to hold a body. Maybe Davie Robertson had been right.

"Can you take us to Mr Hodge?"

The man shook his head. He looked even more nervous than he had thirty seconds ago. "Mr Hodge no like visitor."

"It's OK, we're the police. Mr Hodge will see us, and you'll not be in trouble."

Again, the man seemed to accept that he had no choice. He shrugged his shoulders and said in a weak voice: "OK, follow please."

The man pushed his cart back up the alley, turned left into Claymore Street and continued to avoid oncoming pedestrians until he again turned left into what appeared to be a parallel alley. This alley was of a similar size to the one Steve and Barry had just left. It was obviously the other side of the single-level building with the rear doors exiting onto the alley in which the victim had been found. The front of this building wasn't shops as Steve expected but had a series of warehouse roller-style doors. It was clearly an industrial building.

The man carried on walking at a faster pace as this alley had a better road surface. Steve expected him to enter the building on his left but instead he stopped facing a wooden door on the right that proudly announced 'EASTERN FASHIONS'. The man rang a bell and the door opened. Before pushing his cart through this door, he signalled his visitors to enter before him.

The detectives entered what seemed like another world. This place was bigger than they had imagined when looking from the outside. Eastern Fashions covered a vast space and probably all of the building. To the left were rows of sewing machines that, even to the uneducated eye, were performing different tasks. Steve quickly counted around a hundred women seated in front of these machines. There were carts similar to the man's except these had no lids. Instead, it appeared that each was filled with partly completed garments. Barry spotted several men in brown warehouse coats sweeping the floor and loading their efforts into carts with lids just like the one they had seen outside.

To the right of these sewing machines was a long table with a rolling device running in tracks on the table. Two men were walking up and down, rolling fabric from a large roll onto this table and creating what Steve thought looked like a sandwich of cloth. Further to the right was a caged area that seemed to contain rolls of fabric, cardboard boxes and odd bits of machinery. Steve thought this must be the store. Just in front of this store was the only part of the structure that might have been an office.

The detectives turned to the man with his cart, but he'd gone. Steve thought this vanishing act was to avoid getting into trouble with his employer.

The pair were about to walk towards the office when a middle-aged man, well dressed in a three-piece suit, called over the noise inside the building. "What do you want? This is private property so bugger off out of it."

The noise of machines sewing away was deafening. Steve was impressed that this obvious person of authority had the lung power to throw his voice loudly enough for Steve and Barry to hear him. The fact he was overweight might have helped his volume. His hair was slicked back to give his face a Dracula look.

Without trying to win a shouting match with the three-piece suit, Steve and Barry simply held up their warrant cards. The man approached them, scanned them and shouted: "You'd better come into the office."

The office was no more than a temporary structure made of wood and glass on two sides. The other two sides were the corner outside walls of the building. This wasn't a plush office.

The three-piece suit sat in a cheap chair behind a cheap desk. "How did you get in here? We don't encourage visitors."

"Well, sir, let's just say we're here. Can I have your name?" Barry had his notebook in his hand and the murder file under his arm.

"I don't see it's any of your business but if you must know I'm Mr Hodge. I own this company." This was said with pride and the Mr before his surname made him sound a bit pompous.

Steve didn't take to this man. "And your Christian name, sir? Just for the record," he asked.

"It's Norman."

"Thank you, Norman." Steve carried on after formally introducing himself and Barry. "We're led to believe that there are a number of businesses in this area involved in garment making and they all use the dumpsters in the adjoining alley to dispose of their waste. We're investigating a murder that took place in that alley on the 2nd November. We have reason to believe the victim may have been in contact with your type of business."

"Well, Detective Chief Inspector, I don't know who gave you the information." Mr Hodge puffed out his chest. "But I bought up all the other manufacturers years ago. We're now the only garment manufacturing company in Hackney." This was music to Steve's ears. Life had just gotten simpler.

Barry produced a photograph of the first victim and asked: "Have you ever seen this lady?" Norman Hodge glanced at the photograph and shook his head.

"No, I've never seen her."

"She didn't work here? Maybe in sales or in the office?" Steve was clutching at straws.

"For a couple of detectives, you're not too observant. Have you looked outside? All of our operators are either Asian or from the Far East. This woman would stand out like a sore thumb so I might just remember her."

"Yes. I see that. What about say in your accounts department?"

"Nope, we outsource all our admin. All we do here is manufacture."

Steve decided to change tack.

"Is there any way someone could get hold of one of the carts you use to dispose of your waste?"

"Not that I know of. I mean who'd want one of our dirty old carts?" Mr Hodge sniggered.

"Have you had any stolen or lost any over the past few weeks? Maybe a broken one you might have disposed of?"

"Hang on." Mr Hodge picked up the telephone on his desk, pressed two numbers and replaced the receiver. "Salaman Khan's my foreman. He'll know better than me if any of our carts are missing or broken."

The door to the office opened within fifteen seconds of Norman replacing his receiver. "Salaman, these gents are from the police. Have we had any of our trash carts stolen recently?"

Salaman was unusually tall, standing around six feet. He was slim with a full beard and wore a white warehouse coat. "No, Mr Hodge, nothing's been stolen."

Steve decided to take over. "Mr Khan, how many trash carts do you have?"

"Oh! I'm not sure. Maybe around ten."

"Have any of them been scrapped recently? You know, broken and not worth fixing?"

"No. Nothing like that." Steve felt he was barking up the wrong tree with this line of thought.

"Thank you, Mr Khan." The foreman nodded and prepared to leave. As he was leaving, he turned back into the room. "There was one funny thing about three weeks ago. I don't know if it's relevant but one of our carts was borrowed. Some guy stopped one of our sweepers and asked to borrow his cart for half an hour. He gave the guy ten quid. It was around the lunch break. Our sweeper took the tenner and the guy delivered the cart back and left it outside the front door."

"When exactly was this?"

"I'm not sure. At least a couple of weeks ago... No, wait, it was the same day they found that lady opposite our waste bins."

Steve and Barry looked quickly at each other. "Didn't anyone from the police question you about this?"

"No, I've not spoken to a policeman for years and if you don't mind, I'd like to keep it that way."

Mr Hodge chirped up. "Which sweeper was it?"

"It was Rashid. He didn't think he'd done anything wrong. He told me about it, he got his ten quid and we got the cart back. It was all done over his lunch break, Mr Hodge, and he didn't have any down time."

Steve thought Norman Hodge probably ran a tight ship.

"Right, we'll need to see this Rashid and his cart right now. I'm afraid there may be some down time, Norman." This last remark was to upset Mr Hodge.

They met Rashid and his cart outside the front door of the building. It was quieter and they could hear one another. Steve told Barry to get a forensic team to the factory urgently — the cart might have trace evidence that could be useful. Rashid confirmed to the detectives exactly what Salaman had already passed on. Rashid couldn't exactly remember the man so it was arranged he would go to the Yard and sit with an identikit technician and try and put together a picture of the man who rented the cart.

"Barry, get in touch with Andy. Bring him up to speed and I want him to sit in when Rashid's with the ID technician."

Barry pulled out his phone and made the call.

Once Forensics had removed the cart and a car had whisked Rashid off to Scotland Yard, Steve and Barry adjourned to a café on the main road that was nothing like Davie Robertson's favoured venue.

Both men discussed this latest turn of events over coffee. "You see what I mean, Steve. DI Chalmers could have had this weeks ago but was either too lazy or too incompetent to realise there must have been witnesses."

"Yes, I see that, and your frustration. Let's not get carried away."

Steve smiled at his DS. "Still, we have it now but what does it mean?"

"Well. This guy Rashid is emptying his waste just before his lunch break. That would have been around twelve fifteen. Someone gives him ten quid to use his cart. If this renter is our killer, then he must have returned the cart around one o'clock. Rashid said it was at the front door of the factory when he started his shift again after his break. Remember the post-mortem confirmed time of death at around twelve noon. Give or take the usual caveats, he kills the girl before or after he gets the cart, uses the cart to transport her, thinking he can get her into the larger bins, but he's disturbed. He hangs about pretending to be emptying the cart until the coast's clear, dumps the body in the alley in a panic, and walks back to the factory just as Rashid does every day. Nobody's paying him any attention. Quite clever really."

"Mm, could be." Steve wasn't convinced, although he thought Barry was close with his appraisal. "We need to know if our victim was dead before or after our man got the cart. But just think about it — if he's just

54

had sex with her and intends on killing her, he's not about to dust himself down, go outside looking for Rashid and return to kill her. No, it's not likely, it doesn't fit."

Steve was on a roll, his brain working overtime. "It's more likely he had his fun, killed her, and then went looking for Rashid or one of his mates from the factory. He must have planned it. If I'm right and the dumping of the body was planned, it means our murder was deliberate. Not just a passionate get-together gone wrong. It also means she was killed locally. She appears to have been alive within fifteen or twenty minutes of Rashid renting his cart. The timeline supports it."

Steve was as intense as Barry had seen him during their brief working relationship. "Victim killed around noon; Rashid does his deal around twelve fifteen. If pathology's right, she has to be already dead. Rashid gets his cart back around one p.m. and our killer disappears into the crowd. Also remember the forensics, thread and dust, probably from a garment factory."

"Well, it makes sense. What now?" Barry sipped the last of his coffee.

"Get on the phone to Andy. Tell him what we've just worked out and ask him to update the file. I'm going to wander over to Beecham Park and have a nosey. Join me once you're finished with Andy."

"Will do."

Steve left the café and on his short walk to the site of the second killing he wondered why a thirty-three-year-old woman from Peckham was deliberately murdered in Hackney. What had brought her here of all places? It was a mystery, especially as it seemed the other two victims must have been killed by the same man. Steve was also aware that they only had five days to prevent a fourth murder.

Chapter Seven

David Graham sat in the back of the same black Audi that had taken him from Heathrow Airport to the Mayflower Hotel. He was nervous and worried. He'd never worked with Hans on his experiment and somehow felt uncomfortable following his friend's work, knowing it was Hans' legacy and that he had murdered his friend merely to pay off his debts. He quickly dismissed this line of thinking; he knew he had murdered his friend in order to survive. Now perhaps it was all for nothing. He didn't trust these UK gangsters any more than their American counterparts.

The journey took over an hour. It was dark and traffic was heavy. Frankie sat beside David in the rear and the other large man drove.

From his position in the rear, David noted that they were approaching an industrial unit that was fenced and gated. A uniformed guard with a brute of an Alsatian dog by his side opened one side of the gate. This was just wide enough to allow the Audi passage beyond the gate and into the industrial site. The Audi drove on and turned left, heading for what looked like an aircraft hangar.

The car came to a halt outside a plain metal door and everyone got out. Frankie and the driver quickly took up positions either side of their charge. Frankie unlocked the door and all three entered the building.

David's initial assessment had been correct. This was a vast, empty, hangar-sized space. It was dark except for an area halfway down the right-hand side. This was brightly lit and looked cleaner than the rest of the building. Someone had erected laboratory-style work benches and had apparently installed a water and electric supply as evidenced by several sinks and taps and bright overhead neon tubes. The benches were set in a square and on each bench was a series of glass laboratory equipment and receptacles. There were expensive analytical machines including spectrometers and auto analysers. David was looking at an almost fully equipped laboratory. The scene was completed by two laptop computers positioned side by side on the only bench that didn't have any lab equipment on it.

Working at one of the benches was a tall, thin man dressed in a white lab coat. He had no hair on top of his head but thick grey hair either side. The glasses perched on the end of his nose gave him the look of an eccentric professor. David put his age at around sixty-five.

Frankie gave David a slight nudge in the back towards the laboratory.

"This is where you'll work. Let me know if you need anything." Frankie was clearly a man of few words. He nodded towards the white-coated man. "This is your assistant." was all he said before disappearing into the gloom of the hangar.

David approached the academic-looking stranger and introduced himself. It struck him that given the circumstances this was perhaps a bit too formal and unnecessary, but it was his way.

"I'm Peter Small, ex-Professor of Molecular Engineering at The Bernall Institute in Zurich. It's nice to meet you, Dr Graham." The professor looked around before taking David's arm and ushering him to the furthest away part of their laboratory. "What are we doing here?"

David was taken aback. He thought this tall man worked for either the brothers St John or Gregory Anderson. "What do you mean? I thought you were fully briefed and are here to help and keep an eye on me?" David's voice was pleading.

"Well, the second part's right. I've been told to follow your work and make sure everything you do is legitimate. They gave me a memory stick this morning, drove me here and said to get set up. I've been reading the stuff on the stick but it's nonsense. Maybe I'm missing something, but I can't make any sense of the formula or the notes. I hope you're on the level with these guys. If you're not, then believe me you're a dead man walking."

David stood frozen to the spot. He was trying to regroup his thoughts. The MIT graduate in New York had told Gregory Anderson the formula should work. He had praised Hans' brilliance. This professor was now saying that having spent the day with the same data he didn't understand it. David tried to hide his confusion. "Well, it's a formula for a super fuel based on water. We have to produce a sample to prove that the fuel will ignite upon contact with heat. All we have to do is replicate the work of my colleague at MIT, show these people it works, and we'll be free to go."

"You don't really believe that, do you?"

"Yes, it's what I've been promised." The professor smiled, shrugged his shoulders and walked towards the two laptop computers, thinking Dr Graham was bit naive.

"OK, let's make a start."

The two boffins worked diligently through the next three hours following Hans' formula and notes. They synthesised compounds they had made up; they replicated the molecular count and structure of various formulae; and they condensed and re-condensed various potions, until eventually they mixed everything into one container. The formula called for this concoction of specific molecularly adjusted chemicals to be mixed with a higher volume of purified water at pH7. This larger mixed volume was placed in a pressure vessel and pumped up to just under 10 bar pressure for a period not stipulated in Hans' notes. They had been provided with a basic hand pump for this purpose, it wasn't ideal but would have to do. They decided to leave the liquid under pressure for fifteen minutes.

Despite the rather formal and stiff start to their relationship, both academics worked well together and were forming a bond even though it would only be temporary.

The two men talked to each other as Peter made two cups of instant coffee. In an attempt to make conversation, David asked how Peter Small came to be here. "It's a long story but the shortened version can be described in one word, greed. I had my place at Bernall, I was successful and had published some work in major scientific journals, but that wasn't enough.

The Bernall Institute is a truly remarkable place. Those of us with tenure were allowed free rein to pursue our own work. All the Institute's directors wanted was recognition and twenty-five per cent of royalties that came from our research. Of course most of us were working on theoretical projects — nothing that would ever result in Bernall ever seeing any royalties. But they didn't mind, they just kept funding our projects. I suppose having a theoretical scientific faculty helped with the recruitment of the best students."

"Sounds like the kind of set-up I wish I'd had at MIT."

"Yes, quite so. Anyway, a colleague and I stumbled on something that was outside pure research. We produced an oil that worked across all temperature ranges but more importantly never needed renewing. It self-recharged its molecular structure. The harder it was worked, the better it became. No matter what you had to keep lubricated our oil did it. One product for all uses." Peter Small was looking into the distance and smiling as he recounted his success.

"We perfected it to a point where it could replace any oil on the market. It was one product for everything. Car engines, aircraft engines, marine engines, even the space shuttle. We offered it to an oil company and the next thing we know The Bernall Institute is being showered with money and I'm given a whole load of legal papers to sign. My colleague, who was part of our discovery, was given a handsome pay-off and signed the papers. I wasn't sure. After all, I could see the commercial application." Peter Small stopped to sip his now cold and not very good coffee. David remained silent. He didn't want to interrupt the story.

"Then the St John brothers arrived at the Institute. They wanted to know why I hadn't signed the papers. I'd had them checked by a lawyer and basically, I'd be giving up all rights to future royalties in exchange for a few million dollars. They were very insistent, saying that if I signed, they would work around the contracts and ensure I had everything I'd ever dreamed of." Peter paused to gather his thoughts. "Anyway, to cut to the chase, I didn't sign them. They wined and dined me, paid for extravagant holidays, trips on luxury yachts, the works. I was introduced to girls and, I'm ashamed to say, recreational drugs. They completely took over my life and of course I didn't object. I'd never lived like this in my entire life. Then the time came when I had to be made to pay." David was sure he could see a tear developing in this man's left eye.

"After a particularly wild night, I woke up next to one of the girls. I had no recollection of the night before, but it was obvious the girl was dead. She was covered in blood and so was I. The brothers had pictures and promised to make it go away. All I had to do was sign the papers, take my money and live happily ever after as though nothing had happened. Well, of course, once they have you, you're theirs." Peter wiped the tear away.

"I've had to live with the threat of those pictures being published for years. They said it was their insurance. I'd be well looked after and all I had to do was perform little favours for them from time to time. This is one of those favours. I don't know how you've finished up here, but my advice is be very careful."

David heard the story but couldn't quite take it in. A leading academic being corrupted by gangsters? It was like a movie. "What happened to your discovery?"

"The brothers call themselves facilitators. I found out afterwards that they negotiated with the oil company to acquire the rights to the formulation. They apparently sold the rights onto a Middle Eastern country whose economy and wealth were oil-based. Our discovery was shelved and never developed. You see, if it had been produced and sold it had the potential to upset the balance of power."

"Yes, I see that." David looked at his watch. The clock alarm had sounded while Peter was telling his story. "We've been pressurising for seventeen minutes now — shall we see what we've got?"

David switched on the hot plate and adjusted the thermostat to maximum while Peter decanted the liquid from the pressure vessel into a beaker. Both men noted that the liquid was now pale yellow and had a noticeably thicker viscosity than water.

David had the honour. After filling a syringe with the liquid, he dropped a small amount onto the hot plate. The liquid fizzed and spluttered but didn't ignite. He tried again with the same result. It was a failure.

The pair looked at each other in anticipation that the other would say something. Neither man did. They just stood rooted to the spot.

David was the first to speak. "I wonder if it's the pressurisation? Hans didn't say how long he left the solution under pressure. It could be that the ninth molecule in the spiral chain didn't have time to bond properly with the next helix."

"Could be, but I wonder if we increase the pressure at the same time. The notes said 10 bar, but this hand pump gauge may not be too accurate. Let's put together another batch. Leave it under pressure for say thirty minutes and increase the gauge pressure to say 14 bar. What do you think?"

"We've nothing else. We followed the formula exactly for the ancillary compounds. Let's do it and pray."

The two set to work as before and produced enough liquid to place in the pressure vessel and, as they'd decided, they pumped the pressure up to 14 bar as indicated on the dial attached to the pump. They set an alarm clock for thirty minutes and waited.

Unbeknown to the scientist, Ruby had arrived several hours previously and had been studying events as they unfolded. She now knew the formula didn't work. It was no surprise to her, but she had to keep Gregory's interest alive at least for another few days. She approached the laboratory; David saw her appear into the light from the surrounding gloom like a phantom. "Well, gentlemen, do we have success?"

Peter Small had no idea who this lovely looking creature was, and David didn't bother to introduce them. Not that he could have. He was suddenly totally tongue-tied in the presence of this woman. It was Peter who answered.

"We've just completed our first batch trial. We're now waiting for the second batch. Eh… Miss…" Ruby just grunted and returned to the chair she had been sitting in within the gloom.

David explained as best he could who she was but that he didn't know her name.

After what seemed a long thirty minutes, the pressure vessel was once again cracked open and the liquid decanted. Both men observed that the liquid was about the same viscosity as last time but was considerably darker. This time Peter had the honour. With the syringe filled and an air of anticipation and a little excitement, Peter let the first few drops leave the syringe. The drops immediately burst into flames upon contact with the heated surface of the hot plate. As before, both men stared at each other, willing the other to speak. Peter repeated the drops and again the liquid burst into flames.

"It works! My god, I don't understand how, but it bloody well works!" Peter was delighted and ready to dance but just stood holding the syringe.

Ruby had been looking from her chair and heard the excitement coming from the laboratory area. Before she could move, Frankie walked quickly towards the scientists. "Is that it? You've proven that the formula is kosher? It actually works?" This was addressed to Peter.

"Yes, my boy. You can tell Julian and his brother that it works." Peter had a satisfied grin on his face.

Frankie pulled his mobile phone from his pocket and as he walked back into the gloom, he could be heard talking excitedly to whoever he was calling.

Unknown to anyone in the hangar, Ruby was also making a call. Seated by herself in the gloom, the call clicked into life. She whispered into the speaker. "It's OK, the thing worked. We've just got to keep things moving. How about your end?" The voice replied, saying that all was well and going according to plan. "Great. This'll soon be over, and we'll be free. Just think of our future." She hung up.

David was exhausted but elated. Not so much because the experiment worked but because now, he might be free and escape from the clutches of the brothers.

Obviously in response to Frankie's call, the St John brothers arrived some thirty minutes later. David had no idea what the time was but presumed it was late. Both brothers were dressed in exactly the same black overcoats with black fur collars. The hangar space was cold and neither removed their coat.

"Well, Dr Graham, it seems you have delivered us everything Gregory Anderson said you would. Just to be sure, can we see a demonstration together with an explanation as to how it works?"

Julian St John smiled and held up a gloved hand. "Nothing too technical, of course. My brother and I are mere mortals."

David did as requested, pointing to Peter and the hot plate. The drops from the syringe burst into flames every time Peter allowed a few to come into contact with the hot plate. "There you are. Proof positive that the formula works." David gave a very superficial explanation of the science. As he was explaining he noticed that Peter Small was looking at Julian and confirming everything he said with a nod. David felt that Professor Peter Small might be closer to the brothers than he had indicated.

Sebastian St John, who appeared to be the thinker of the brothers, walked towards David and put his arm round his shoulder. "Dr Graham, thank you for bringing this to us. Now…" He paused. "Why don't you go back to your hotel with Ruby? I know she fancies men with brains, and after tonight you must be top of her list."

He looked straight into David Graham's eyes without smiling. Still locked onto his eyes, he called out: "Ruby — your client wants to go back to his hotel. There's a good girl." David Graham was very, very afraid of this man. "Frankie, get the car and drive the lovely couple to the Mayflower."

Frankie appeared and gave David a gentle push towards the gloom and the door where Ruby stood waiting.

Whatever the remainder of the night held in store for Dr David Graham, he was sure it didn't involve a romp with Ruby. Although he admitted to himself that, despite his lack of knowledge of women, he'd surely rise to the occasion.

Chapter Eight

Steve was sitting on a bench in Beecham Park when Barry disturbed his thoughts. The DCI had walked around the park. It wasn't big, maybe only the size of a football pitch. It was the same shape and was enclosed by metal railings along the long sides. The shorter ends were closed in by buildings. There was a lake to one side, surrounded by a path, and there were various planted areas that weren't flowering due to the time of year. Several walking paths had been laid throughout the park and large areas of bushes had been allowed to grow around the perimeter. Steve noticed that people appeared to use the park as a shortcut, although it wasn't busy.

Barry sat down next to his boss. "That Andy is something else. I told him what we were thinking. The cheeky sod said he'd have something worked out by the time we got back." Both detectives laughed.

"I've looked around this place but for the life of me I can't figure it out." Steve was allowing depression to set in. "Look at this place. It's open. How do you strangle someone here in broad daylight? Or… if you've done the deed somewhere else, how do you get the body in here without being seen? Stacey Mathews was found mid-afternoon in broad daylight for goodness' sake. How the hell did he do it?"

"I don't know, Steve. We've got a theory for the first one, maybe that will lead us to the other two." Barry was trying to be positive, but he also saw the impossibility of the case. "Andy's pulling all the CCTV from all three crime scenes. You never know, we might get something."

"Good. Our child from the 1950s is developing into a half-decent cop. Look, I'm not sure we'll learn more here, let's put out a public…" Steve's phone rang. With some annoyance he looked at the screen and his body language immediately changed.

"Hello, you."

Barry was surprised by the sudden change in his boss and decided to listen in to this side of the conversation.

"Yes, I'm not forgetting and yes, I'm remembering the wine." Barry noted that Steve was talking quietly, and his voice had risen an octave. He surmised it had to be a woman on the other end.

"No, I won't be late, around seven. Yes, I know, and I'll be there before it spoils. No, not having a good day but I've got to go. See you tonight." Steve put his phone back in his pocket.

Barry was waiting for Steve to explain but he was disappointed. The DCI carried on. "Let's put out a public request for witnesses. You know, anyone in or around the park, etc. etc. Get onto the Public Relations boys and have them try local papers, radio, and local TV if they can get it. If they get TV, you'll have to front it, so you'd better wear your best suit."

"Thanks, boss! A star is born."

Both detectives set off for the third murder site. As they walked, Barry spoke with Public Relations at Scotland Yard. He put his phone away. "It's all possible, Steve, but it'll have to be tomorrow. Can you write the press release and let them have it first thing tomorrow?"

"Yes, I'm sure you can, you know more about these cases than anyone, remember." Steve walked on, leaving Barry trailing in his wake with his jaw dropping.

The site of the third murder was similar to that of the first. The alley off Hackney High Road differed only in that it was a dead end. There were buildings each side with various doors opening onto the alley. The road surface looked as though it had recently been re-laid and there were again large bins on wheels down one side. The body of Barbara James was discovered approximately one third of the way down.

Armed with the scene of crime photographs, both detectives struggled to locate the exact spot where the body had been found.

"You know, Barry, it doesn't matter if we can't get the exact site. There's nothing here. The road's smooth and Forensics have been all over it. We're not suddenly going to find something they've missed. Now, all I want is to figure out how our killer got a body in here without attracting anybody's attention."

"Well, that's our problem with all of them. If we're right and the killings took place somewhere else, and the bodies were dumped, then all we've achieved is a working theory about the first murder but nothing at all about the other two."

"Not quite." Steve stood in the middle of the alley with the murder file in his hands. "The puzzle is there are no forensics. Most murderers leave something behind, but this guy is scrupulous." Steve thought through what they'd learned since leaving Scotland Yard, then started to share his thoughts with Barry, who was obviously a bit depressed.

"Right, stay with me. Number one, we've established that the killings couldn't realistically have taken place where the bodies were found. Ergo… they were dumped. Number two, we know or we suspect that the first one was transported into the alley in a cart used to move material waste, and that it's likely the killer intended to hide the body in one of the big bins, but it was too busy and he was disturbed. Number three, we haven't a clue how he moved the other two bodies but it's odds on he used something similar to the waste cart. We just have to figure out what. And number four…" Steve paused and allowed a grin to take over his face. "We've got your press conference and media debut."

Barry smiled back at Steve, his feeling of gloom lifted. Steve continued talking as they started to walk up the alley towards the entrance to Hackney High Road.

"We didn't have any of that a couple of hours ago, did we?"

"No, that's true, boss, but if we're right about the first one, how the hell did our boy get the next two bodies moved and dumped without being seen?"

"Well, after your media show tomorrow, we might have a better idea. You'd better include both murders in your press release but don't say we think they are linked. We don't want to start a panic. What's getting to me is we're running out of time if our murderer is sticking to his ten-day timetable. If he is, we've only got four days to catch the son of a bitch."

***

The pair arrived back at Steve's office to find Andy busy sticking an enlarged map of Hackney onto the wall. It wasn't pretty as he seemed to be using brown packing tape to secure the four corners.

"What's all this, Andy? Planning a trip?"

"No, sir." Andy seemed in a serious frame of mind.

"How did you get on with DI Chalmers and the Harding thing?"

"He wasn't too pleased, but I didn't put it to him quite like you said."

Steve sat at his desk. "Well, DC Miller, you may prove to be a better diplomat than me. Now, what's with the map? You've obviously been busy, so let's hear what you've got. Take a seat."

Andy sat on the visitor's side of Steve's desk. Barry sat beside him. He opened his laptop and placed it on the desk.

"Right, first I pulled the details of the owners of the sex clubs and the like on the list you've seen. I wondered if there might be some connection. Well, there is."

Andy waited for a reaction from his colleagues but all he got from Steve was "OK, carry on."

"First, all the strip clubs are owned by one company. It seems over the past few years this company 'PLEASURE HOLDINGS' has been buying them up one by one, and now they own every strip club in Hackney. The ownership of the business is a bit vague but there's a Mrs Ann Strange listed as the managing director. I did a bit more digging and Mrs Strange is South African. She and her husband arrived in the UK ten years ago. There's nothing on the police computer about them but a lot of suspicion. Seems they've been pulled a few times for living off immoral earnings but never charged."

Andy stopped talking while he stabbed a few keys on his laptop. "The gentlemen's clubs are a different story. One is called The Pink Warehouse. It's owned by one James Milne, late of her Majesty's pleasure. He did six years for drug dealing and prostitution. He was released four years ago and it seems he bought the club from the previous owner the day he got out. The licences are in his wife's name."

"Now that's something we didn't know." Steve was thoughtful and had his hands steepled in front of his face as he sat back in his chair. "I know you've got more."

Andy was warming up. "Oh yes, sir. Milne was investigated not long after he took over the club in connection with the beating of one of his hostesses. She was given a good going over and said Milne had done it. She later recanted her story and said it was a punter and that Milne had saved her from a worse fate. Then eighteen months ago there was a similar report, but again the victim recanted. Both incidents took place in the club. There's a note on the files saying that if the beatings had carried on it was likely both women would have been killed."

Andy sat back looking pleased with himself. "Before you ask, sir, I've tracked down both women and their names and addresses are in the file."

Steve was mightily impressed with his detective constable.

"Good job, Andy, but I've a feeling you're not finished."

"No, sir. The other gentleman's club is called The Fortress Club. It's a members' only club and is a hundred per cent owned by a Mr Alistair Ramsay."

Andy again sat back in expectation. He was enjoying the moment and stayed silent. The silence went on for several long seconds. No one spoke until Barry chirped up. "All right, Alistair Ramsay who?"

Ignoring Barry, Andy asked: "Doesn't ring a bell, sir?"

"No, I can't say it does."

"Alistair Ramsay was, until seven years ago, known as Commander Ramsay of the Metropolitan Police. He left to become Deputy Chief Constable of Kent and retired three years ago under a bit of a cloud. He bought The Fortress Club as soon as he retired. The Land Registry shows he paid over two million for it."

"Bloody hell!" was all Barry could manage.

Steve said nothing but was mentally weighing up this latest information. "This is good stuff, Andy. I presume you've logged everything onto the files?"

"Yes, sir. I also thought of what other ways our killer might have lured these women to Hackney so I looked up newspaper adverts for the weeks before the killings. You know the sort of thing, 'man seeks partner', etc. I've added a couple of the more interesting ones to the list of clubs just in case — you never know. I've also called for the CCTV from the areas where the bodies were found but can I show you the maps?"

"Please do. This is getting better by the minute."

Andy stood and went to the wall where he'd stuck the map. He turned and addressed his two colleagues as if giving a formal lecture.

"When Barry called in with your thoughts about the first victim and the timeline, I started thinking. If our murderer was in the first alley renting the cart at twelve fifteen and the pathologist confirmed death around twelve noon, and if the killing didn't happen in the alley, then he had to have killed Marjory Pearson close by. Given the lack of forensic evidence, I'm assuming she was killed in either a building or a house. If our killer's planning these murders, he's probably quite smart and most probably prepares for these murders, plus, remember the victim had had sex just before she died. Her clothes weren't dishevelled and she was properly dressed therefore it's safe to assume she must have dressed herself after her romp. I double-checked the post-mortem report and she had recently applied lipstick, probably after she had re-dressed herself. If we believe the killer was her sex partner, then it's possible they both had to get dressed after the event and then he killed her."

"Right, Andy, I'm following all this but where's it going?"

"I'm coming to that, sir. We have the timeline, so I took it and expanded it to give an allowance for errors. Say they climbed out of bed at eleven thirty, were dressed by 11.35, and she was strangled at 11.37. Our killer had to have a car or van. Let's say he needs four minutes to get the body into a vehicle. That takes us till 11.41. We know where he is at twelve fifteen but he doesn't have the body. It must still be in his vehicle. Let's assume he parked close by but needs five minutes to park and walk to the alley. Are we agreed so far?"

Both Steve and Barry were spellbound and could only nod.

Andy carried on. "We have a time frame from 11.41 when he could have started his journey with the body until say 12.10 when he parked his vehicle before walking to the alley. Give or take, call it thirty minutes' travel time. I checked with Traffic Division and the average speed of traffic around central Hackney on the 2nd November was only eight miles an hour. That means if we're right then the killer could only have travelled four miles." With an air of triumph, Andy declared: "Our killing took place no more than four miles from the first alley. Traffic said that on the date of the second killing, that's the 12thNovember, the traffic speed was only just under six miles an hour. Apparently, a bus had broken down on the High Road and traffic was chaotic. That means our man could only have travelled three miles on that day, if our assumptions are correct. It's a similar story for the last murder. Traffic was backed up all around Hackney. BT had dug up half of Smiley Road so you can imagine."

Andy continued before his audience could interrupt with questions. "I think our man must live in a house within a maximum four-mile radius and the house probably has a garage attached. I don't see him taking a body to a car in an open car park within a block of flats. I think it's also likely he can get into his garage from the house without going outside."

Leaving his colleagues to think that through, he turned to his map.

"I've marked the first killing on the map here." He pointed. "Then I've drawn a four-mile circle using this as the centre. I believe our killer lives, or at least the killing took place, somewhere within this area." Andy pointed to the circle. "I've marked the second and third site in the same way and drawn the four-mile circle. The traffic speeds for the second and third murders mean four miles is the maximum distance."

Andy was now definitely giving a lecture using a wooden ruler as a pointer. "If you look, you'll see the circles cross over each other. I've marked the outside edge of the left and right circles and drawn a line across the top and bottom of each circle." To emphasise this, Andy took a marker pen and re-drew the outline of an ellipse shape surrounding the circles. Somewhere in this area is our killer. I've marked the locations of the massage parlours with green spots, strip clubs have red spots, and the two gentlemen's clubs have yellow. I've also marked the addresses of the two newspaper adverts in orange. You'll see that all these sites are within the area so this data may not help too much."

With a flourish Andy returned to his seat in front of Steve's desk.

Once again, silence fell on the room. To fill the void, Andy started up again. With a shy tone to his voice, he declared: "I think we're looking for a small, dark-coloured van, make and registration unknown."

"What, do you have a sixth sense or something? How can you possibly know that?" Steve was excited but couldn't work out how his DC had come up with this information. He admitted that so far Andy had been brilliant in his deductions, but this was a stretch.

"Well, sir, you asked me to sit in on your witnesses photofit session with Mr Rashid. By the way, the identikit's in the file. After it was over, I arranged to have this Rashid's elimination fingerprints taken and I took his statement. I was thinking about the timeline even before I sat down with the maps. Our killer had to have parked close by. Rashid said he remembered a dark-coloured van parked at the opposite end of the alley. He said he noticed it because the guy who rented his cart came from that direction and then walked back that way with the cart. He said it's unusual for anyone to park there and that's why he noticed it. It's a bit narrow and the parking attendant on that beat is a bit keen. Without thinking, Rashid thought the man was headed for the van, but he went for his lunch and didn't see the renter get into the van nor get anything out."

"Bloody hell," Barry exploded. "We had Rashid with us but didn't ask the right question — what a fool." Barry realised Steve had been with him. "Sorry, Steve, no criticism of you. It's me, I slipped up."

"No, we both did. This is excellent work, Andy. Let's get some coffee and review everything." Steve looked at his watch. It was 5.55 p.m. He had to be in Knightsbridge by seven p.m. and stop to buy wine on his way. It would take a good hour to get there at this time of night. "On second thoughts, let's leave it there and we'll sleep on it. I've got to go now, anyway. See you both at eight thirty tomorrow morning. I think we might be getting somewhere.

Andy — chase up those two DCs we've had seconded to help with the Harding case. Remind them that they've not been stood down and I want them here at nine o'clock sharp tomorrow morning. Also chase Forensics. We need anything they find on that cart, OK?"

"Yes, sir, no problem."

With a wave goodbye the DCI was gone.

Barry looked at Andy. "Andy, are you old enough to drink?" he joked. "I'd like to stand you a beer. The boss has a heavy date tonight so we're free. What about it?"

Andy was nervous. He'd only been in a few pubs before and didn't really like beer, but he agreed so as not to offend his new-found friend and colleague. "I've only got to text the two DCs the boss wants in tomorrow and then we can go."

"Great, and while we're in the pub you can help me write the press release, I've got to send to Public Relations first thing tomorrow morning."

Barry patted Andy on the shoulder and closed the door to Steve's office.

Chapter Nine

The DCI arrived at the home and medical practice of Dr Alison Mills at exactly 7.07 p.m. He'd used a combination of modes of transport he felt were necessary not only to get there on time but also to collect the wine he had been instructed to bring.

The taxi dropped him off outside a Georgian terraced house in Knightsbridge with stone steps leading up to a highly varnished red front door. At the top of the steps, to the right-hand side of the door, was a highly polished brass plate proudly stating that this was the surgery of Dr Alison Mills. There was an intercom system and Steve pressed the button marked 'Alison Mills'. This connected him to her private apartment above her workspace. The other button said 'Surgery' and he knew this connected to the desk of the receptionist who managed the doctor's patient load.

"I could say you're late." The disconnected voice came from the intercom. "But you're not too bad. Come on up, but only if you've brought wine." Steve held the wine in front of the integrated camera and the door buzzed open.

When Steve entered the living quarters, he found Alison standing over the stove on the far side of the open-plan kitchen and breakfast bar. She was dressed in a casual baggy top and jeans and was wearing a comedy apron suggesting she was naked. She held up her hand in acknowledgement. "Just at a tricky bit. The table's laid but can you put out the wine glasses and open the wine?"

"Yes, ma'am," Steve laughed. As he set about following Alison's instructions, she said: "I hope you got decent plonk. That last red you brought was awful."

"I selected this merlot specially for the occasion and it cost me over ten quid," he joked.

"Wow, last of the big spenders," she responded. "I'm almost ready. Have a seat and pour me a small one."

Steve Burt had met Dr Mills eight months previously when he was working on what appeared to be an impossible case. He'd gone to interview a WW2 veteran who was living in a care home in Rye, West Sussex. Alison was the doctor who looked after the residents' ongoing medical needs on a voluntary basis. She attended two Saturdays a month when her workload allowed. He'd instantly liked her and felt there was a chemistry between them that he couldn't explain. Since their first meeting they'd been on a few dinner dates and had slowly begun to spend more time in each other's company. Steve was no stranger to female companionship but hadn't rushed things with Alison. It was almost as though he was afraid of losing her.

Alison set the timer on the cooker and joined Steve on a stool at the breakfast bar. She took a sip of her wine. "That's better, Detective Chief Inspector. I do believe your taste in wine is improving." She smiled, leaned over and lightly kissed Steve on the cheek. "How was your day?"

"It's difficult to say. We've got a new case. It's a triple murder." Steve had decided that if he and Alison were to ever get serious then he would include her in his work as best as he was able. She was, after all, a medical professional.

"But the strange thing is I may have discovered the new Sherlock Holmes."

"You're not serious?"

"Oh yes." Steve proceeded to fill Alison in on the deductions that Andy had made and presented earlier. "He seems to have a unique way of looking at events and analysing them from a completely different perspective. I think he could be a genius." This was said in a mocking tone.

"Has this Sherlock solved your triple murder then?"

"Well, no. Not yet, but he's certainly opened up a few lines of enquiry."

The bell sounded on the oven. "Let's eat. You can tell me all about your genius over dinner."

Alison served up a delicious steak that had been fried and allowed to simmer in an onion gravy. Over dinner, Steve explained about Hackney and their calculations of the timeline. They talked as they enjoyed the meal. Alison explained that her niece had won a musical scholarship to a prestigious private school, then the conversation turned to cars when Alison said she was thinking of buying a new car. The time raced by and Alison rose from the table to make coffee.

"Let's do the dishes while the coffee sorts itself out." Steve felt he was becoming domesticated and quite liked it.

Once everything had been tidied up and the coffee made, they sat on a sofa on the living room side of the open-plan room. Opposite the sofa was a wall-mounted television.

"Do you mind if we watch *Panorama*? I've been persuaded to take on the shelter for beaten women in Notting Hill and *Panorama* are doing a programme that's supposed to be related. I thought it might be useful research."

"No problem, I don't mind what we watch." With the empty coffee cups on the coffee table in front of the sofa, the pair sat comfortably in each other's arms. A serious amount of kissing was the order of the day. Steve was a happy man. He asked Alison how her day had gone. She told him about her first three patients who had come for test results; none of them were happy with the results nor the prognoses. "Sometimes I really don't like my job. All three are younger than me and I had to tell one she would never have children, one her facial disfigurement couldn't be treated by plastic surgery, and the other that she needed an operation to replace her knee, so my morning was a bit grotty."

Steve knew just how she felt and gave her a comforting hug.

"After lunch things picked up though. I was reading up on a batch of new drugs when I decided to phone this detective I know, but he was too busy to talk to me." She stabbed Steve in the chest with her index finger. "Then I had a three o'clock referral from a colleague. A four o'clock patient with a heart condition and then into the kitchen to prepare tonight's feast. Just an ordinary day in the life of a busy doctor."

Steve pulled back to examine this woman more closely. She wasn't what most people would call classically beautiful, but she had a quality that he found very attractive.

"Sounds like we both have had pretty grotty days. Come here."

"Oh, look, *Panorama* is about to start." They settled back to watch the programme. Steve wasn't interested but sat and watched as the interviewer went on about how men lure women with all kinds of different promises, and how most eventually seek the sanctuary of a home or institution. They cited several examples from the States and most of the programme had an American bias. Steve didn't mind as he was with Alison.

Alison switched the television off and went into the kitchen, returning with the wine bottle and two glasses. They discussed the programme briefly, but Alison didn't feel it had helped her, and she'd just have to take things as they came when she was working at the shelter. The pair sat side by side sipping their wine. Alison tucked her feet under her and put her head on Steve's shoulder.

"Steve... I'm going down to Rye this weekend to the care home. I wondered if you'd like to come?"

Steve was pleasantly surprised at the suggestion.

"We could stay at The Bull and even have a double room," she suggested.

Steve had been very cautious with this new relationship and hadn't attempted to suggest he would welcome a more physical relationship, but here was the woman he cared about suggesting just that. The DCI had a dilemma.

"Alison, that would be fantastic."

"I feel a 'but' coming on." She pulled back just a fraction.

"It's this case, the triple homicide. I didn't tell you, but we think our killer is operating on a ten-day kill cycle. The first three murders were exactly ten days apart. If we're right, then he's due to strike four days from now, and today's over as far as the investigation's concerned. Tomorrow is Thursday, so it's likely that if we don't get him before that, he'll kill again on Saturday." Steve was almost pleading. "You do see, don't you?"

Alison sat back and considered the man sitting next to her. She knew he had feelings for her just as she did for him. Subconsciously she'd decided to test his and her resolve. She made a decision.

"Well, if you can't come to Rye, maybe Rye could come to you." She was deliberately teasing him. She put on what she hoped was a cockney voice. "I've a perfectly nice bedroom next door and if the gentleman were interested, he could stay the night. This is a one-time offer with no commitment." She smiled at him.

Steve was surprised but pleased that this amazing lady had taken the initiative in developing their relationship. In what he equally hoped was a reasonable cockney accent, he replied: "Well, I'm not interested in a one-night stand, but..." Steve became serious, as did Alison.

"Steve, my darling, let's see where we go. I'd hoped we could enjoy Rye this weekend but of course you have to be here. I'm not interested in a one-off either but, if it leads to more, then I'm willing to give it a chance."

Steve reached out for the woman he hoped he would spend the rest of his life with.

Chapter Ten

Alison made breakfast, and after a shower and a farewell kiss Steve set out for Scotland Yard. He knew he had to accelerate the investigation if he were to prevent another murder.

His night spent with Alison had been beyond his wildest expectations. He felt ready for any challenge.

As he entered his office, both Andy and Barry were there. When Barry saw Steve, he immediately pushed an A4 sheet of paper into his hands. "That's a copy of the press release I've sent up to Public Relations. I got a text last night saying BBC South would interview me outside the building at ten o'clock this morning."

Steve scanned the press release and looked Barry up and down. It was clear Barry was wearing his best suit. "You might have dressed for the cameras." Barry just grunted.

The DCI turned to Andy. "Anything overnight, Andy?"

"No, sir. I've had a text back from the two DCs. They'll be here at nine o'clock. Forensics haven't finished with the cart and I've asked Tech to get onto the CCTV and to look for any small, dark-coloured vans. I thought that when we're finished here, I'd go up and give them a hand."

"Good thinking. How about some coffee and we'll make a start?"

Barry looked at Steve and felt confident enough to comment. "Is that the same shirt you were wearing yesterday, boss?"

Steve remembered that Barry had been with him yesterday when Alison had called. "Are you trying to prove you're a detective? Yes, I admit it. It's the same shirt, and before you ask, I'm saying nothing. Clear?" Steve and Barry grinned at each other.

"Just thought I'd ask."

With coffee in hand, Steve stood in front of the whiteboard and Andy's map. "Let's look at what we know as opposed to what we think we know. We have three murders, all women, all dressed for a night out, but could be sex workers, and all murdered around twelve noon. They were all discovered in Hackney no more than half a mile from each other. None of them lived anywhere near Hackney and their bodies were left in the open. Do we agree that's all we actually know?"

"It's not much but we have Andy's analysis to top down on what we know."

"Andy — from your map, what is the total area we might have to look at?"

"Obviously a four-mile circumference means eight miles across. So that's eight miles top to bottom. The circles centred where the bodies were found are only half a mile or so apart. That gives us nine and a half miles. I've marked the map area to be ten miles by eight miles, so eighty square miles."

"What we're theorising is that our killer lives in an eighty square mile area as per the map, he lives in a house, as opposed to a flat, and the house has an attached garage. We think he drives a small, dark-coloured van and is meticulous in his planning, given the lack of any trace evidence on the bodies. Also, we think he might strike again in three days. Is that about it?"

"What if the killings are linked to these clubs and massage parlours in Hackney? It's only the lack of forensics that suggests the murder scene is prepared. It could be that these clubs have side rooms that are cleaned or areas where nobody goes." Barry was exploring other theories.

"Good point, except if the killings are carried out in something like a business, then surely there would be staff or other people around. I'm inclined to go with Andy that our murderer has his own quiet space. But how the hell does he get these women to go to him?"

Andy chipped in. "All these clubs are within the eighty square mile area so should be easy to check. What if I start looking at houses with attached garages inside our area?"

"That's a lot of area, Andy, but if it's a realistic theory I suppose we have to. How will you…" There was a tap on the office door. Two young men stood awkwardly in the doorway. Steve looked in their direction.

"Good morning, DC Fairchild and DC Brooks." Steve looked at his watch. "And on time, well done." Steve stood up and approached the two detective constables. "I've got a little job for you. Andy, can you get pictures of our dead girls out and give our colleagues here a full set? Also, the list of sex joints you put together."

"Yes, no problem." Andy stood and left Steve's office for his own desk in the outer room.

"We're working on a triple murder centred on Hackney. It's possible that our victims might be known to various clubs in Hackney that cater for punters looking for a bit of excitement. I want you to visit each establishment on the list and show the photographs around. I want to know if any of these girls were known, if anyone remembers seeing them, and if anyone who uses these places has a particular sexual fantasy, even if these girls aren't known in the establishment. Anything that might show us where these three girls have been and if any individual has been acting suspiciously in any of these places. Got it?"

"Yes, sir. Do we take a pool car?" Steve smiled at the question.

"Yes, we don't expect you to walk. Don't visit The Pink Warehouse or The Fortress gentlemen's clubs. I'll do that with DS Gibson. I want you back here at six o'clock tonight for a debrief. Clear?"

Both detectives nodded.

"Good lads. Off you go and if you come across anything that you think is urgent, phone me."

The two young detectives set off with promises that they would do as Steve had instructed.

"Boss, I'll have to go and meet the people from the BBC."

"Right. Try not to milk it and get back as soon as. We're heading to Hackney when you're finished."

Steve and Andy were left alone in Steve's office. After the comings and goings of the past few minutes it felt very tranquil.

"What were you saying, Andy, before we were interrupted?"

"I thought I might look at properties in our search area with garages and I think you were asking how we could do it."

"Yes, but there must be thousands of properties."

"I suppose so, but we can discount flats, commercial buildings, industrial estates, care homes and student accommodation. I could start taking each borough's housing register and see how I get on. I might be able to develop an algorithm that would make the search quicker. If we can discount certain profile types living in these houses, we might be able to narrow them down."

"Are you suggesting we need a profiler?"

Andy looked a bit nervous but was becoming more confident when he was on a one-to-one with Steve. "Yes, if we had an idea of the type of person we're looking for, then it would be easier to spot if a particular owner or tenant living in the correct type of property might be our man."

"Interesting." Steve stroked his chin. Profiling was expensive and he knew budgets were tight but still… Andy had a point. "Right, Andy, I'll set it up, but you'll have to work with the profiler. I'll try and get it set up this morning."

Steve spent the next twenty minutes talking with the Metropolitan Police's commander for serious crimes persuading her that he needed the input of a profiler. The commander wasn't keen on incurring the cost until Steve reminded her of his belief that this individual might strike again in three days. Reluctantly, the commander agreed and said she would organise someone to be in touch with Steve within the hour.

Ten minutes later, Steve's phone rang. "Is this DCI Burt?" The voice was female, obviously educated with a home counties accent and speaking from a handsfree phone.

"Speaking. Who's calling?"

"My name's Samantha Burns. Please call me Sam. I'm a freelance profiler often employed by the Met. I had a message to call you. It seems you have something I can help with."

"Yes. One of my colleagues thinks the input of a profiler might help him narrow down any likely suspects that come our way on a case we're working on. Miss Burns, you…"

"Please, Sam."

"Sam. You should be aware that the case is a triple murder and that we believe our killer may strike again within days, so there's a bit of pressure on this one."

"Fine. I can be there in an hour and make a start if that suits you?"

"Yes, it suits me fine, but you'll be working with Detective Constable Andy Miller. Please ask for him when you arrive. I'll be out most of the day but should be back late afternoon, so I'll see you then if you're still here."

"Very good, I look forward to it, and I'll see your Andy in an hour. Goodbye." The profiler was gone, and the line went dead.

Steve told Andy to expect Samantha to be known as Sam and to give her as much information and theories as she needed. He reminded Andy that Sam was expensive and charged by the hour.

Just as Steve had finished briefing Andy, Barry arrived back. He looked smart in his new suit and had obviously had some facial make-up applied for the cameras. Steve decided to get his own back after Barry's reference to his shirt and his prying into Steve's love life. "I think you look better with the make-up. It's a big improvement. If I were you, I'd keep the look. What do you think, Andy?" Steve was grinning.

Forever the diplomat, Andy simply said: "Anything you say, sir."

***

They set off for Hackney in another pool car. This one had a satnav system so finding The Pink Warehouse was simple. They pulled into a large car park that was barrier-controlled. The barrier was up and there was no sign of any security. The building itself had obviously been a warehouse with large roller doors still in place. A new extension had been built over what had once been a loading bay. This was clearly the main entrance and was basically a glass box with steps leading to double glass doors.

Steve and Barry climbed the steps and entered the world of The Pink Warehouse. It was quiet and the whole atmosphere was of a seedy establishment. This feeling was enhanced by the low-level pink lighting that was everywhere, plus the faint music playing in the background. "Maybe there's no one here. It's only eleven thirty. Could be it's just cleaners." Barry was apprehensive.

As the detective's eyes adjusted to the low light, they saw a large dance floor surrounded by round tables and chairs. Everywhere they looked they saw the colour pink. Pink walls, pink tablecloths, pink chairs and pink drapes hanging from the walls. Even the large bar at the far end of the space had a pink countertop.

The pair ventured further into the cavern of pink. They saw a woman mopping the floor area around the stage. There were vertical metal poles in various positions on the stage, which was also washed in low, pink lighting. "Excuse me? We're looking for the owner, Mr James Milne."

"Oh yeah? Who're you then?"

"We're police. From Scotland Yard," Steve added for no obvious reason. Neither detective produced their warrant card for this woman to inspect.

"He's in the back but he'll not want to talk to you. He's busy auditioning."

"Just tell us where to find him."

The woman gave a sly grin as she pointed. "There's a door behind that curtain in the corner. If you open it, his office is the second on the right, but like I said he'll not see you."

The detectives did as instructed, and as they walked towards the curtain Barry noted that a large man was working behind the long bar that ran down one side of the room. He appeared to be polishing glasses. They found the office door of James Milne, owner of The Pink Warehouse. Steve knocked loudly and without waiting for a response opened the door and entered. James Milne was indeed auditioning a young woman, but Steve knew it wasn't an audition for a singing job at the club.

"What the... Who the hell are you? Get out!" James Milne was frantically pulling his shirt on while the woman picked up her clothes and ran past the detectives.

Steve was amused and somehow pleased he'd interrupted this club owner. "Mr Milne? I'm DCI Steve Burt, and this DS Gibson. We'd like a word."

Both detectives produced their warrant cards for James Milne to inspect, although from his position on a sofa at the far end of his windowless office he wouldn't see much.

"I don't care if you're from the Salvation Army. Bugger off out of it or I'll call my solicitor." Milne continued to dress himself but was struggling to pull his trousers up while still seated.

"As you wish, sir, but we'd like to ask you questions in connection with the murders of Marjory Pearson, Stacey Mathews and Barbara James. We can ask our questions here or down at the local nick. It's up to you."

"What're you talking about?" James Milne was now almost fully dressed and sitting upright on the sofa. "I don't know nothing about murders. You've got the wrong fella. I run a professional club. We've never had no trouble."

"Mr Milne, we'd like you to look at some photographs and tell us if you've ever 'auditioned' these girls." Steve smiled to himself.

Without looking at the photos, Milne shouted: "No, I've never seen any of them."

"You need to take a proper look, sir, but that can wait." Steve knew this sleazy guy wouldn't admit to knowing the girls even if he did.

"Mr Milne, we believe the victims had sex before they died, and they were killed around midday." Steve ignored the Barbara James case. He looked at his watch. "It's now exactly 11.53 and we have just discovered you in a similar situation with the young lady who rushed out. The bodies were found round the corner from this establishment." Again, Steve was economical with the truth. "You might wonder why we want to talk to you."

James Milne saw exactly why this policeman would want to talk to him. "Now listen here, I employ a lot of girls and sometimes one or two of them are keener than others to make sure I give them a job. Nothing wrong with it, it's just the perks of being a successful businessman." Milne sat back as though this answer would satisfy the detective.

"Now, Mr. Milne, you know the drill. We put two and two together and sometimes come up with four. Where were you on Wednesday 22nd November at twelve noon?" Both detectives were now standing directly in front of the seated James Milne.

"How the hell should I know? I must have been here." Milne was visibly shaken by events.

"Were you auditioning again, maybe with Barbara James?"

"No, no, I don't know." Milne was panicking. Steve pressed on.

"Can you tell us where you were on the 12th November at twelve noon? That's the day Stacey Mathews was murdered. It was a Sunday."

"I'd have to check with my secretary. It's possible I was here, or I might have been playing golf." Milne looked at the detectives with a surprised look on his face. He smiled. "That's right. I was playing golf in a charity event at Royal Berkshire. I was there from around ten until after four in the afternoon. There were masses of people who'll tell you." James Milne stood up and walked past the detectives towards the door. "So there you are. I'm in the clear. Now bugger off." He pointed to the door. Neither detective moved.

Steve carried on: "What about the 2nd November? Where were you, again around noon?"

"Look, I've told you — I don't know. I'm a busy man. I run a reputable business so if you've anything else, contact my solicitor." Milne produced a business card from his back pocket and threw it at Barry. The DS picked it up. It was the business card of a solicitor.

Steve changed tack. "Does the name Penny Smith mean anything to you?"

"No, should it?"

"Well, roughly six years ago you beat her up while having sex with her."

"That was never taken to court. The tart made the whole thing up. Now, like I said, just get out." James Milne's voice was now very loud, and he was obviously very angry.

"What about Olivia Clarkson? You did the same to her about eighteen months ago — beat her up while in the act. I think even an uneducated thug like you might see it doesn't look good for you. You might be our prime suspect in these murders."

James Milne was sweating and became very red in the face. Almost screaming, again he said: "Nothing went to court!". Without warning he launched himself at Steve with his fists flying. Steve saw it coming as he'd been aware that Milne was getting worked up into a state. He sidestepped the on-rushing suspect, who met Barry standing just behind Steve. Barry met Milne full on, pushed him away to one side, and then turned and landed a precise rabbit punch on the back of his neck.

Barry looked pleased. "He'll not get up from that."

"Good lad. Call Davie Robertson. Get him to get some uniforms over here and get this piece of trash into a cell at Hackney nick."

Barry made the arrangements and handcuffed the comatose James Milne. It only took five minutes for the cavalry to arrive and Milne was whisked away, still unconscious.

Steve spoke with Davie Robertson and instructed that a doctor should be called and reminded Robertson that their prisoner hadn't been read his rights nor charged. Steve and Barry would be at Hackney Police Station later to interview James Milne.

They showed the pictures of the dead girls to the cleaner and the barman but neither recognised them.

"Better get on to Andy and ask him to check out Milne's golf club alibi for the second murder. The Royal Berkshire sounds a posh place so maybe they have CCTV. Andy knows what to do."

Both detectives exited the pink-shrouded building and drew long breaths. They were glad to be out of the stifling, downmarket atmosphere of The Pink Warehouse.

"Do you think this guy's our man?"

"Not sure, Barry. We could make a case, but if his alibi checks out for Stacey Mathews' murder, he's probably off the hook. Let's get over to the next one, but only after we've eaten. I'm starving."

Chapter Eleven

Sir Timothy Head was seated on a Chesterfield sofa that was one of a pair. Sitting opposite him, resting in the corner of the other Chesterfield sofa, was Sir Patrick Bond. They were seated in a room that was part of Westminster and the House of Commons. However, this room was not used much these days as it was remote from the main parliamentary buildings.

The room dated back to when Westminster was originally built and had been used by many great and good politicians over the years. It was said that the Duke of Wellington had used this room to meet with his mistress Lady Hamilton on many occasions.

The walls boasted several portraits of previous important government ministers and a portrait of Queen Elizabeth II was located to one side of the large window that allowed natural light into the room, while a portrait of the Duke of Edinburgh was hung on the other side.

Both men had known each other since university; both had achieved first-class honours degrees from Cambridge and had joined the civil service immediately after university. They looked exactly what they were. Career civil servants: well fed, affluent and wearing the dark blue three-piece suits favoured by Whitehall mandarins. Both men stood five feet, nine inches tall, and both had thinning hair, but only Sir Patrick needed the glasses that were perched on the end of his nose.

Sir Timothy Head had remained a career civil servant and had risen to be head of the civil service. He was fifty-nine years old, married to the daughter of a Duke, and was well thought of by most politicians.

Sir Patrick Bond's career had taken a different direction. After five years working as a civil servant, he transferred to MI6 and was now head of the UK's spy network. Sir Patrick was sixty years old and was unknown outside Westminster.

"What time did you ask the foreign secretary to join us?"

Sir Timothy looked at his pocket watch. "Eleven o'clock but you know he's always late. It's now 11.06. I'll wager he gets here around eleven fifteen."

"You know what I think of our minister. He's not too smart and always has an excuse for everything. He's one of a type who don't know what they don't know, but always try to impress with their knowledge. He's always trying to appear important. What's the bet that when he arrives, he says he was held up by another meeting. The man's a bit of a waste of space."

"I'm sure you're right but we have to work with him — he is the foreign secretary after all. I appointed Peter Border as his main civil servant. Peter's a brilliant administrator and so far, has kept our minister out of trouble. We'll just have to see how things develop but the prime minister knows the foreign secretary's shortcomings."

Sir Timothy Head sat back and sighed. He carried on: "Patrick, are you sure about briefing our foreign secretary? Couldn't you handle the liaison with the CIA on the side?"

"Not really. This..." The door opened and a flustered foreign secretary entered carrying a bunch of papers clutched to his chest. This was Robert Cliff, MP for Peterborough and the UK Government's foreign minister. He was forty-eight years old, married with three children, and had been a member of parliament for fourteen years.

Robert Cliff sat on the same Chesterfield sofa as Sir Patrick Bond. He was clearly flustered as he laid his papers beside him. "Sorry I'm a bit late but my previous meeting ran on a bit." Timothy and Patrick looked at each other and smiled.

"No problem, Minister, we appreciate you're very busy and we're grateful that you can spare us some of your time." Sir Timothy Head was a smooth operator and managed to tell politicians what they wanted to hear.

"Yes, I'm busy, especially with what's going on in Yemen. My people are exploring our options so I really must get back as soon as we're finished. I got your note, Sir Timothy. It's a bit cloak-and-dagger and meeting here isn't ideal. It's well away from the Foreign Office."

"Yes, Minister, I appreciate it, but Sir Patrick has something to discuss with you, and we both feel that the fewer people who know about our meeting the better. That's why I asked you to come alone and to this room."

"Fine, but can we get on please." The foreign secretary was known not to have a long attention span and quickly lost interest in topics that didn't directly affect him.

"Minister…" Knowing the minister's deficiencies, Sir Patrick spoke up. "We've had a note from the deputy head of the American CIA telling us about a murder that took place a few days ago in the States. It seems that the suspected murderer arrived at Heathrow twenty-four hours or so after the murder. The murdered man was a scientist at the Massachusetts Institute of Technology. The CIA believe the murdered man was working on something revolutionary and are linking his murder and the theft of his computer to a possible scientific breakthrough." Sir Patrick paused in the hope the minister was following.

"Go on."

"This murdered scientist, a Dr Hans Raga, was secretive about his work but a few of his colleagues think he was close to a major breakthrough in connection with a super fuel. He'd referred to his work on a few occasions to other scientists without telling them what exactly he was working on. Unfortunately, the only person who might have known was a colleague who is believed to be the murderer and is now in London together with the stolen data. The CIA have asked us to track down this person, a Dr David Graham.

"I don't see what this has to do with me." The minister looked at his watch.

"Please bear with me, Minister. Whether or not this murder has any bearing on events, GCHQ has been picking up chatter between various oil-producing countries and an unknown source in the UK. They've also seen evidence that Discovery Oil has been in touch with this UK source. The CIA believe our Dr Graham may have murdered the scientist and is working for an organisation based in New York led by a Gregory Anderson. They believe that, if this Anderson is involved, he may already have sold on the formula to the highest bidder. If this does concern a super fuel, it could have national interest implications and the Americans want to know."

"Mm, I'm not seeing where you're going."

"GCHQ have been monitoring this Anderson's chatter plus the oil-producing countries and this unknown UK source. We don't know what the scientific breakthrough is, but we believe something is being sold on the open market to the highest bidder, and given the chatter it's probably something to do with oil. We've picked up messages talking about millions of dollars, even hundreds of millions of dollars."

The head of MI6 drew breath and looked at the minister, who appeared lost in his thoughts.

Sir Patrick carried on. "The American government believe it could be Hans Raga's research that's up for sale, and given the apparent interest being shown by oil interests, it could be this super fuel. If so, it could have a significant and revolutionary impact on the world economy. They want whatever it is back."

"I see that, but I still don't see where we come in other than the murder suspect is in the UK."

Sir Patrick sighed and delivered the final summary. "GCHQ confirmed yesterday that the oil ministers from several countries are headed to London in ten days' time. They're not travelling on diplomatic passports but as private individuals. It seems that vast sums of money have been moved around over the past few days without any explanation. We've picked up encrypted messages between Discovery Oil and our unknown UK source. Discovery Oil may be taking the lead in an auction and will be leading this meeting. We've been asked to investigate and infiltrate this meeting. The CIA have asked us to intervene and stop the sale of whatever's being auctioned. They are not asking for our help officially but want to send their own operatives over here."

The minister appeared to be having difficulty following Sir Patrick's explanation. "What are you advising?" This was addressed to the head of the civil service.

"Well, Minister, it boils down to whether we allow the American CIA to operate within the UK officially or whether we let them come but turn a blind eye. I don't believe we can stop them. Also, do we believe the arrival here of so many oil ministers from oil-producing countries is in some way connected to a murder in the States and the auction of a super fuel? We don't know, but the Americans are concerned that national security interests could be involved."

"Sir Patrick, do you think this story is real? And if so, can MI6 crack this thing without the CIA's help?"

"I don't know if the story is true. All I know is there was a murder and the suspect is here. Add GCHQ's contribution and I'd have to think it could be a real situation. As Sir Timothy says, if the CIA want to come, we can't stop them. If we agree and they come officially then at least we'd be able to keep an eye on them. As to unearthing what's going on, I don't know, but if there's something to investigate then I'm confident we'd get to the bottom of it."

"Gentlemen, thank you. I've got my in tray full as it is. I'll leave this to you to sort out, but I cannot sanction CIA activity in this country. Is that clear?"

"Yes, Minister," Sir Timothy replied. All three men stood as the foreign secretary took his leave and hurried off.

"As predicted, Patrick, you're on your own. Our minister is a politician first and an intellect second. What will you do?"

"Keep my head down. Work with our American cousins and tell them not to send people here but give them our direct number at our Washington embassy. That way we can use our secure lines of communication and I'll get a team onto finding out what the hell is going on."

Both men started to leave the room. Sir Timothy put his hand on Sir Patrick's shoulder. "Good luck, I think you'll need it!"

Chapter Twelve

After a quick snack, Steve and Barry walked the fifteen minutes to The Fortress gentlemen's club. From outside it was like night and day compared to The Pink Warehouse. The building fronted the main road and boasted a discreet plaque stating it was the registered office of The Fortress Club. It was obviously a converted grand Victorian manor house and was one of three such properties making up a terrace.

The front double doors were open to the street to show a vestibule that had a glass door leading into an inner hallway. The glass door was locked so Barry rang the bell. After a few minutes, a man dressed as a butler appeared and opened the door. Without asking any questions he ushered the pair into the hall and closed the door.

"Gentlemen, how may we help you?"

If this was a butler, he must have gone to either Eton or Harrow. He was tall, distinguished and held an air of authority. Looking around this inner hall, Barry noted a desk in front of a cupboard with a very pretty young woman seated at it. The sign on the desk said 'Coat check'. Barry was impressed. He'd only seen such a thing in films. His gaze continued and took in a grand staircase that seemed to spiral to the heavens and a modern board on a stand at the base of the staircase. The board had the day and date written on the top in pre-prepared plastic letters. Below were a series of five names of companies written in the same plastic letters with what looked like room numbers recorded against each.

Steve introduced himself and his colleague. "We'd like to see Mr Alistair Ramsay."

"I see, perhaps you could tell me why you need to speak to my employer?"

Steve took an instant dislike to this upper crust dummy. "No, I can't tell you anything. Our business is with your employer." The DCI enjoyed feeding this upstart's words back to him. The butler appeared not to flinch.

"Perhaps you'd care to wait in the lounge?" The butler raised his left arm towards a door leading off the hall. "Mandy's on duty and will be happy to serve you drinks of your choice. In the meantime, I'll check with Mr Ramsey to see if he's free." Without any further word or waiting for confirmation he walked off.

On entering the lounge, Steve and Barry found a wonderfully exotic room decorated with flourishes of the East. Elegant leather chairs — each with a side table — were scattered around the room with a large open fire and ornate plasterwork around the ceiling. Everything said money and quality. Even the carpet was luxurious and both detectives felt their feet sinking into the lush pile.

As they stood taking in this grand room, a lady dressed in a full evening gown that certainly didn't hide her figure approached the pair. "Good day. Please have a seat and I'll get you a drink. What would you like?" Steve assumed this was Mandy. Barry didn't assume anything — he'd never seen a woman like this in real life. His mouth hung open. From her accent she was Australian, and she had very long legs and an outstanding figure.

Barry eventually returned to the real world and ordered a black coffee; Steve asked for a tea and both men chose two chairs by the window. There were around six or seven guests scattered around the room, all reading something and drinking various beverages. Steve felt he was in an upmarket city club.

Before Mandy returned with their drinks, the superior butler appeared and almost bowed to the detectives. "Mr Ramsay's compliments, gentlemen, he asks you to bear with him. He is just finalising something and will join you shortly. In the meantime, I hope Mandy is looking after you." Again, without waiting for confirmation the butler turned and left.

Once Mandy had set out their drinks and Barry had stopped staring at her, he said: "You know, boss, I could get used to this. Especially Mandy. I think I could be in love."

"More likely in lust." Steve smiled at his colleague. "But I agree, this is some posh set-up. Wonder what it costs to be a member?"

"Whatever it is it's outside our pay scale."

The pair sat in silence and enjoyed the ambience of the room whilst sipping their drinks.

After about five minutes a figure appeared in front of the detectives. He was an imposing man of around six feet, slim with a full head of silvery-grey hair. He was dressed in a light grey suit that Steve suspected costed more than he earned in a month.

"Gentlemen, I understand you wish to see me, I'm Alistair Ramsay."

Both detectives stood and exchanged handshakes with the owner of The Fortress Club. They introduced themselves and showed their warrant cards.

"We're looking into three deaths that have all occurred around Hackney over the past few weeks." Steve was trying some mental gymnastics searching for something that wouldn't refer to this establishment as a sex club. "Our enquiries have led us to interview the proprietors of various leisure establishments in the hope of tracking the victims' movements prior to their deaths." Steve was proud of his choice of words.

"I see, and you think I can help you how exactly?"

Barry produced the photographs of the three dead girls and Steve said: "I wonder if you would mind looking at these pictures to see if you recognise any of the victims?"

The proprietor took the photographs and studied them for a long time. "Poor bitches, were they on the game?"

"Not that we've established. Do you recognise any of them? Maybe they've worked here?"

"Gentlemen, please take a seat." Alistair Ramsay sat opposite the detectives. "Let me explain something. This is a high-class establishment. We host corporate events for national companies, banks, even the police. You've met Mandy. Do you think she would dress as these poor girls are in those photographs? Those tarts wouldn't get over the door never mind work here as a hostess."

It was clear to Steve that the ex-commander still had a lot of copper in him given his choice of language.

"We employ only high-class women to act as our hostesses. We even have a titled girl and some out-of-work actresses. All ladies who dress well, know about fine wines, and know which knives to use. They can hold a conversation with our members over a drink, or even dinner if invited. So, you see, Chief Inspector, those poor unfortunates would never be employed in this establishment."

"Yes, I can see that. Well, thank you, sir, for your help. What exactly do you offer your members?" For some reason Steve didn't totally trust Alistair Ramsay.

"We're a members-only club. We have a full kitchen and dining room, a pleasant lounge bar, a fully equipped gymnasium, steam rooms, and even a few letting bedrooms. Everything is available to our members. As I told you, we employ top-drawer hostesses who meet and greet our members and entertain them. Most men like to see a pretty face after a hard day at the office. We aim for an all-inclusive atmosphere in the club."

Barry chipped in. "Do any of the girls offer more than having a meal or a few drinks with your members?"

The retired commander suddenly sat up his chair. "We're not a knocking shop, Sergeant! We select only the best applicants from the hundreds we get in response to our advertisements in *Country Life* and such." Mr. Ramsay sat back again.

"I appreciate that, sir, but could you please answer the question?"

"Look, I don't know where you're coming from, but I have some very good friends at the Yard, so you'd better watch what you imply. All I'll say is that if any of our hostesses wish to entertain any of our members upstairs then it is nothing to do with me. We pay our ladies a handsome salary and any extra money they get by way of tips is theirs to keep."

Barry persisted while Steve sat back, impressed by his sergeant.

"Thank you, sir, I appreciate your candour. Have any of your members who've taken any of your hostesses upstairs been reported to you as having any unnatural sexual habits?"

"Certainly not. Our members are all respectable businessmen and pillars of the community. This is their refuge. Their home-from-home, so to speak."

"Nonetheless, would your ladies report it to you if one of your clients was a bit kinky?"

The ex-commander was on his feet.

"Sergeant, that's enough. This interview is at an end. Chief Inspector, unless things have changed since my day, you should not let a junior officer speak to an interviewee like that. I reiterate this is not a knocking shop. I shall be having words with your senior officer. Now please get out!"

Both officers stood and walked towards the door. Halfway there, Steve stopped and turned to Alistair Ramsay. "It would be useful to have a list of your members in order for us to rule them out of having any possible involvement in these deaths."

"Our members value their privacy. Unless you get a court order, I will not allow you sight of our members list. Now please go before I do something I might regret."

***

The two detectives were now outside The Fortress Club with their imaginary tails between their legs.

"That went well." Both men smiled at each other. "Do you think he'll turn us in?"

Steve considered this. "Nah, if he did, and it was official, he'd have to explain the upstairs bedrooms and the hostesses. Your line of questioning was a bit off-the-wall, but you got the sex angle from him. Pillars of society as members who go there for a romp with a hostess before going home. No, our commander has too much to keep hidden."

"Why'd you ask for the members list? You surely don't suspect anybody from there?"

"No, but I'd sure as hell like to see who his members are, and where he got the money to start that club. It could be that he's not as white as he pretends. What's the bet, he's got the odd gang boss as a member? Let's get Andy on to looking into The Fortress Club's affairs: company accounts, bank records, the works. Let's see if our ex-commander is the saint he's pretending to be."

As they started to walk back towards Hackney Police Station and their prisoner from The Pink Warehouse, Barry's phone went. He stopped and took the call. "That was Andy. He's confirmed with The Royal Berkshire Golf Club that James Milne was at a golf do on the 12th

March. Andy's asked for CCTV, but he's spoken to two of Milne's playing partners from that day and they confirmed that they teed off at 10.27 and Milne was with them for the whole eighteen holes. They finished at around two o'clock so Milne couldn't have murdered the second victim."

"Mm, it was a long shot. I had hoped we'd gotten lucky."

Both men carried on walking. Steve was in deep thought, so Barry stayed quiet. He already knew the signs. His DCI would return to the world once he'd worked through what was on his mind.

"Barry, there's something bothering me, and for the life of me I can't get it to the surface. It was something Andy said, then Milne, and then back there just now. I just can't get it."

"My mum always said that if you know something and can't remember it, try and put it out of your mind and it'll just appear when you least expect it."

"Probably good advice." The pair walked on. "Listen, Barry. What do you think if I ask for a swamp operation for Saturday? If we're right and chummy sticks to his ten-day cycle then he's due another one this Saturday. We're no nearer catching him, and I'm worried he'll kill again."

"The last swamp operation I was on was a waste of time, boss. I don't like them. All those bobbies trying to mix with the crowds hoping to spot a needle in a haystack. Just a waste of overtime if you ask me. Also, Andy's theory is that the killings take place in a house. The best we could hope for is to catch him with his next victim's body, and even that's a long shot."

"What else do we have? I hear what you say but isn't it worth a try?"

The two detectives were approaching the entrance to the police station.

"It's your budget, Steve. If you want to do it, I'm up for it, but I hope it's not a waste of time."

As both men entered, they were met by a rather brash peroxide blonde woman sitting on the wooden bench. As soon as she saw the outside door open, she was on her feet and marching towards Steve as the obviously older and more senior of the two.

"Are you the inspector who's jailed my man?"

Steve looked towards the counter and the same desk sergeant he had seen on his last visit. The sergeant called out: "It's Mrs Milne, sir. Wants to see her husband."

Steve looked at this, five feet, six inch, slightly rounded woman with her dark roots and fake leopard skin coat. He noticed she had more make-up on her face than the average actor used in a month, plus she stank of cigarette smoke and her teeth were yellow.

"Mrs Milne, your husband is under arrest for attacking a police officer. Until he's charged you cannot see him."

"Look, I'm not bothered about a punch, but one of the staff at the club said you were asking about them murders. My Jimmy wouldn't have anything to do with them. He's not a violent man."

Steve might take a different view having seen her Jimmy charging towards him. He decided on a different tack. He wasn't too concerned about seeing James Milne done for assault.

"Mrs Milne, do you know where your husband was on the 2nd and 22nd of this month, around twelve noon?"

"Why?"

"It would help him be released if you could answer the question."

The peroxide head tilted to one side and suddenly Mrs Milne was searching her handbag. She produced a pocket diary and started looking up dates and entries.

"Right, on the 2nd, Jimmy was at the wholesalers. We'd ordered in a load of extra snacky things for a private party organised for that night. He got back around eleven thirty and was with me and the bar staff setting everything up until around two o'clock. I'm sure Tony our barman will tell you.

"Thank you, Mrs Milne, and what about the 22nd?"

Again, the lady flicked pages. "Jimmy was interviewing for new strippers all day; the girls would remember."

Steve and Barry both held back grins.

"Thank you, Mrs Milne." He turned to the desk sergeant. "Has Mr Milne seen a doctor?"

"Yes, sir — just like you asked. Apart from a bruise on the side of his neck and a headache he's as fit as a fiddle."

"Sergeant, please release Mr Milne." He turned to Mrs Milne. "Tell your Jimmy he's been very lucky. Next time he attacks anyone, and I hear about it, I'll throw the book at him. Understand?"

"Yes, Inspector. Thank you, Inspector. I'll make sure Jimmy behaves himself." Mrs Milne was almost bowing.

After waving goodbye to the desk sergeant and asking to be remembered to Davie Robertson, the detectives left the police station for their car and the return journey to New Scotland Yard.

"We'd better get the local boys to check out Jimmy Milne's alibi but I'm sure he's in the clear."

The DCI still couldn't bring whatever was nagging away at him to the front of his mind. He somehow knew it was important.

Chapter Thirteen

While Barry returned the pool car, Steve went back to his office. He noted that Andy had taken over the end nearest the whiteboard and his map. Seated next to him was a lady that Steve thought must be Samantha Burns. Both stood and Andy shyly introduced Miss Burns to his boss.

Sam Burns was a thin lady in her late twenties. She had an old-fashioned haircut similar to those the girls at Steve's primary school had worn. She was dressed simply in a one-piece shapeless dress and Steve noted thick woollen stockings and flat, very sensible shoes. This lady could never be confused with a fashion statement.

Steve shook her hand. "How are you getting on?"

"Andy's been very helpful," she gushed. It seemed the more she gushed the more Andy looked embarrassed. "He's given me access to the files and crime scene data. He's also updated me on your present working hypothesis that your killer is operating from a house approximately four miles from central Hackney."

Before Sam Burns could carry on, and to spare his own blushes, Andy spoke up, interrupting Sam's flow. "Sir, there are two messages, both urgent. First, you're to go and see Commander Southgate as soon as you get back. Then Superintendent Dobson asked if you could go and see him again as soon as possible."

"I'd better see the commander first." Steve was looking for a cup of coffee but of course Andy was busy with Miss Burns. "Andy, that club we visited earlier, The Fortress. When you get a chance, can you call up all you can about the place. You know, company accounts, bank records, shareholders, any other business interests, that sort of thing. I don't trust our ex-commander Ramsay."

"Will do, sir."

"OK, I'm off." As Steve was exiting his office, he turned. "Any word from our two DCs?"

"They called in about an hour ago with a couple of questions. They'll come back for the six o'clock briefing."

***

Steve knocked on the inner door of Commander Sheila Southgate's office. He entered to find the woman seated at a large, efficient-looking desk. As usual, she was dressed in her uniform that to Steve's eyes seemed to be getting a little tight for her.

"Ah, DCI Burt, come in, have a seat." She pointed to a pair of comfortable-looking armchairs positioned to one side of her office. A glass-topped coffee table sat between the two chairs. "Can I get you coffee or something else?" she asked as she moved from her desk to take one of the proffered chairs.

"Coffee would be great. Thank you, ma'am."

Sheila Southgate called out in a clipped, no-nonsense voice. "Two black coffees at the double." She smiled sweetly at Steve. "Saves using the phone."

"How are you getting on with the triple Hackney case?"

Steve explained everything they had discovered and their working theories in detail. He was careful to give Andy Miller credit for his logical thinking and contribution to the team.

The coffee arrived served by a rather harassed-looking uniformed police constable.

"Mm, do you think he'll strike again this weekend?"

"Yes, ma'am, I do. I've discussed with my DS the possibility of a swamp operation but he's against it and I tend to agree with him."

"Good for him." The commander became serious. "We've no budget for a deal like swamp. If you'd brought it upstairs, I'm sure it would have been rejected, so your DS has saved you a lot of unnecessary paperwork."

"Yes, ma'am."

"Steve, I'm retiring in a few weeks, so it's time to call me Sheila, at least in here. Ma'am makes me sound ancient."

Steve just nodded. So far, he had no idea why he was here and being treated to coffee and first names.

"Steve, as you've only got one case on at the moment, I thought I might give you another, but it's not straightforward. What I'm about to tell you is in the strictest confidence — is that clear?"

"Of course."

"I've had a government department on to us asking specifically to look into a murder that took place yesterday. At least, the body was discovered yesterday. It was washed up out of the Thames by Tower Bridge.

This request in itself is a pretty rare occurrence. To the best of my knowledge, we've only ever had one other such request coming straight from Whitehall. I've done a bit of snooping and it looks like this could have MI6's DNA all over it. That means there's some international connection. If it were purely domestic then MI5 would be involved." The commander was obviously choosing her words carefully.

"We're almost certain the request is MI6-inspired, but we don't know why, and that's a concern. The government bod who called me made it very clear they didn't want Special Branch involved. They just want the murder investigated by the Yard and brought to a conclusion." Again, the commander stopped to think how best to continue.

"We've no information on who the body is or why the spooks are interested. That's all we have. A body washed up by the river and a government interest with an implied instruction to keep a lid on the investigation."

Sheila looked across at Steve. She had an enquiring stare and her left eyebrow was higher than her right. She was obviously expecting a response.

"It all sounds very mysterious. What do you want me to do?"

The commander's mood lightened. She had her man.

"Steve, you proved earlier this year that you can be discreet. The Clark case proved that. I've no idea what's going on, but you can bet it's political. I want you to investigate this by the book but be aware that there's probably a sub-plot, so you should be careful who you trust and how much you record in the official records. Do you understand?"

"Sheila, you are asking me to investigate another murder when I've got three bodies already and maybe a fourth by the weekend? You are asking me to deliberately omit information from an official file, if I think it somehow compromises the investigation, but I don't know what I'm looking for? I'm to work the case almost in secret and not discuss it outside my team. Is that a pretty fair assessment?"

"You see…" Sheila was smiling and had opened her arms towards the DCI. "You've got it first time. I knew you were smart!"

The commander became more serious. "Look, Steve, there may be nothing here so treat it as a normal case, but given the interest from Whitehall and MI6, I'm sure this is far from straightforward. As you get into it, you're bound to sort out what's going on and know what's important and what's not. Just be suspicious of anyone who approaches you about the case who wouldn't normally. It could be another officer or a civilian. I've no one else to give this to that I can trust. I'll have your back and hopefully you'll solve it before I retire."

"Well, Sheila, it's certainly different. I presume you want me on it right away?"

"Yes, and before you ask about additional manpower, Chief Superintendent Charles of Human Resources has been to see me. He's got a newly transferred DI going spare." The commander had a glint in her eye. "And for some reason he's asked to be assigned to Special Resources. His name is Detective Inspector Abul Ishmal." Sheila sat back grinning.

"Commander, that's the best news you've given me since I walked in here."

"He will report in tomorrow morning. Steve, I know you've worked with this DI before and I'm not going to tell you how to deploy your resources, but I want you full-time on this body in the Thames. A DI on your team should free you up."

"Thanks, Sheila, I've got it." Steve stood up but before leaving asked the commander: "Superintendent Dobson has asked to see me. It's nothing to do with this new case, is it?"

"No, it can't be. He probably wants an update on the Hackney situation."

Steve left Sheila's office and decided to take the stairs down to the office of Detective Superintendent Frank Dobson. Halfway down, he stopped in thought, and almost dropped the file Sheila had given him on the latest murder. That thing he was trying to remember was trying to get out but still he couldn't bring it forward. He knew it was important and was becoming frustrated with himself. He started once more down the flight of stairs.

Steve was surprised by the amount of activity taking place in the Murder Room. Various plain-clothed officers were dashing around, carrying stacks of paper and calling out to each other as they navigated their way around desks and other pieces of furniture. Frank Dobson was standing beside an incident board looking like a traffic cop directing operations. Clearly something big was happening and Steve felt his presence would not be appreciated.

He turned to leave but heard the loud and not too cultured voice of the superintendent call him back.

"Steve, over here." Frank Dobson was waving his arm in a motion that said he wanted the DCI to go towards him.

Steve obeyed. "Thanks for coming, Steve. We're a bit manic here just now. One of our teams has just lifted our prime suspect in a double shooting. Seems he's coughed to the lot so we're trying to get everything in order before the DPP gets it and his brief turns up and spoils all our fun. It was worse an hour ago but we're a bit calmer now." The superintendent smiled benevolently at Steve while giving off a superior, 'look how clever I am' air. "Let's go into the office. Get a bit of space to breathe."

Superintendent Dobson's office was surprisingly small, especially given his reputation as the best murder detective at the Yard. His desk was chaotic with paper scattered everywhere and he only had two chairs, the one behind his desk and the other in front. The one in front didn't look too comfortable. Steve assumed most of Dobson's work was carried out in interview rooms, not here.

"So how have you been? Getting on with the Hackney triple?"

"You know, making progress. What can I do for you, sir?"

Steve didn't want to be here. He had another case to get started and was trying to prevent a fourth murder in Hackney. He was in an impatient mood.

"Well, Steve, it's a bit awkward. You see I've had a call from an old boss of mine, retired Commander Ramsay. He left a while ago to take over as ACC in Kent. I think you saw him this afternoon?"

"Yes, I did, and before you carry on, sir, it's my enquiry and I hope you're not about to pull rank."

"Good heavens, no. Whatever gave you that thought? No! No! Alistair Ramsay called to ask if I could have a word in your shell-like ear. He's a bit concerned that he may have gotten off on the wrong foot with you but he did say your DS was a bit rude."

Steve felt there was more to come so sat saying nothing.

"The thing is that club is Alistair's baby. He's sunk every penny he has into it and doesn't want any aggro from us. He didn't like the line of questioning and I understand you asked for his members list. You must have known he couldn't give you that? It's confidential."

Steve still remained silent. This tactic was beginning to annoy the superintendent.

"Look, man, are The Fortress Club or Alistair Ramsay featuring in any way in your enquiry? That's all we want to know."

"With respect, sir, you know I can't answer that. Our investigation is ongoing, and no member of the public, including an ex-copper, is entitled to that information."

"Damn it, man, you're not making this easy. Are you going to subpoena his members list?"

"Probably."

"Steve…" The superintendent was trying a more friendly and considered approach. "If you do, it could be a career bust. I happen to know there are a lot of very influential people who are members at The Fortress. People a DCI in the Met doesn't want to cross. My advice is to drop all reference to Alistair Ramsay and his club."

"Frank — may I call you Frank? After all, you've just threatened me." Although this wasn't something Steve sought, he was up for the challenge and wouldn't be bullied.

"Let me tell you." Superintendent Frank Dobson was red with rage but was smart enough to hear his colleague out. "I don't think the club or its owner are involved in my murder cases. I do think he's running an upmarket brothel however and is possibly involved with some unsavoury characters. I've asked for a deep background search of his financials. I will be seeking a court order to examine his membership list and finally

I intend handing the file over to the Vice Squad. He may have all his money in that business now, but I suspect not for much longer!"

The superintendent smiled a sad smile that barely extended his lips. "Steve, some of the most senior officers in the Met together with High Court judges are on that list. Hell, I'm even a member. I can't stop you ruining your career but think long and hard. The members of The Fortress won't appreciate being outed by a DCI with a chequered past."

"Well, thanks for the advice. You've just convinced me to not only involve Vice but also Anti-Corruption. If there is one gangster on that list, together with the people you say, then Anti-Corruption will be more than interested and perhaps a few others need to look out for their careers. I'm no boy scout but I can't let this pass. Sorry, sir."

Steve rose to leave the small office.

"Steve — before you go, do me a favour. Give me 'til Monday next week before you press any buttons. Let me sort Alistair out. He'll need time to organise for an investigation."

Steve just nodded and left. He knew he couldn't do anything before next week anyway, so it was a meaningless gesture.

Chapter Fourteen

Sebastian and Julian St John were seated on the sofas in their vast open-plan penthouse in Central London. With them was Ruby, who was dressed in an impossibly tight black cocktail dress that covered up very little of her magnificent body. Julian St John told himself that one day she would give in to his requests and give him a private viewing. Then he remembered the Derringer pistol and that took him on another flight of fancy trying to work out where she had it on her tonight. It certainly wasn't obvious.

Sitting beside Julian was a largish man wearing a cowboy-style jacket, jeans and cowboy boots — even the casual observer would take him to be American. The only thing missing was the ten-gallon hat. A large cigar sticking out of one corner of his mouth completed the picture.

This was Mr Desmond Cutter, CEO and major shareholder in Olympic Oil. Not only was Desmond officially the major shareholder but he owned 100% of the stock through shady nominee accounts, offshore nominee directors, paid puppets on oil company boards, and often the not-too-subtle use of onshore muscle. He was a man who got what he wanted.

Mr Cutter was more than the owner of Olympic Oil. Through various deals done over the years, he now controlled almost all of the world's refining capacity and oil exploration companies, including the large multinationals. He had gotten away with his illegal financial activities by bypassing the American Securities and Exchange Commission rules on corporate ownership. Desmond Cutter ruled the world of oil, but few people knew who he was. He'd similarly gotten around the London Stock Exchange rules for years and held sway over all European, Middle East and other OPEC countries' oil. He was the world's most influential oil man, and probably the world's richest if anyone could follow the complicated trail left by his dummy corporations and secret bank accounts.

In a heavy Texas accent, Desmond asked: "Where are we with this formula? You guys are sure it works?"

Julian was beaming as he sipped his forty-year-old brandy. "Oh! Yes. We've had it tested and it does everything we've told you it does."

"And it came from Gregory Anderson out of New York?"

"Yes. It was, let's say, in payment of a debt he was owed by a scientist who knew of the work being carried out on synthetic fuels based on water."

"It all sounds a bit science fiction, but I suppose if you're convinced it does the job then I'd better have it. How much are you paying Anderson for the formula?"

"The agreed fee was one hundred million dollars."

"That's a lot for a piece of paper. I suppose you guys have double-crossed him by now?" Desmond was joking but there was purpose to his question.

Julian looked shocked but it was theatrical. He even put his hands up. "No, no, we're men of our word, and we've done business with Gregory before. He trusts us and we trust him. Besides, we like to breathe, and double-crossing Gregory Anderson isn't good for your health."

Everyone including Ruby laughed at Julian's attempt to lightly dismiss this very real possibility of Gregory Anderson feeling slighted.

As usual, Sebastian St John had been quiet, drinking his brandy at a faster rate than the others. "The New Yorker sent his emissary here to keep tabs on us. Isn't that right, Miss Ruby?" Sebastian was getting drunk.

"You know it is, Sebastian." Ruby was drinking still water. "I work for Gregory and he asked me to be here to help you to help him. I'm only the hired help, but while we're talking about my boss, he says he hasn't received his fee and wants to know when he'll get it?"

Desmond, who was drinking malt whiskey, spoke up. "What! You haven't paid New York and you're trying to sell it to me?" The Texan had raised his voice just a bit too loudly.

"Calm down, dear boy. Gregory Anderson will get his money just as soon as we've concluded our business." Julian St John had slipped into his most convincing tone of voice. He thought he sounded very persuasive. This was his sales and negotiating voice.

"Listen, Julian. In my world you honour your liabilities and don't sell the other guy short. I won't give you a penny until I'm convinced you own this formula, otherwise I might as well deal directly with Anderson."

Julian hadn't seen this coming. "Now, now!" He needed his smoothest voice now. "No need to get upset. Gregory Anderson will get his money once we have yours. It's standard business practice in our world."

"Look, if you guys have a cash flow problem then I can help, but it will come at a price."

"Nothing like that, Desmond. We just prefer to spend other people's money — in this case, yours. You know what's at stake. We can manipulate the possession of this formula to make us all rich and at the same time keep Olympic Oil top of the international tree. You can see everyone wins under our little plan!"

Julian refreshed everyone's drinks but lingered over pouring Ruby's water as he admired her well-proportioned chest.

"Let's cut to the chase here. I've got to be in Norway tomorrow morning, so we need to wrap this up. Give it to me again, but slowly. I don't want to miss anything."

Sebastian was approaching a semi-comatose state so would be no further use to his brother. Julian soldiered on. "Gregory Anderson in New York is selling us a super fuel formula that has the ability to put you and the oil producers out of business. If no one needs refined oil then you're all finished, consigned to history. We're buying the formula for this super synthetic fuel from Anderson for one hundred million dollars. Given its potential, that's a snip." Julian paused to gauge the reaction of his American guest.

"We're offering you as Olympic Oil the first chance to purchase the formula for a very modest ten billion dollars. We know we could get more but we're facilitators. We make a little from each deal. We're not in the business of only ever doing one deal; we leave such transactions to you. By owning the formula, you can sell it on to the highest bidder, who will certainly want it destroyed. You see the beauty of our plan is that by dealing with us now, you get to sell the formula to someone who has no interest in developing it, and that also serves your purpose." Desmond was looking pensive.

"Once our initial transaction has been completed, we will, for a modest fee of a further fifty million dollars, arrange for you to meet the oil ministers of all OPEC countries and other leaders of foreign governments with an interest in our plan at a secret location so that you may sell them the formula. We propose that the sale be by auction, with the highest bid winning the right to bury this formula so that it will never see the light of day. We expect the bidding to be in excess of five hundred billion dollars. After all, the entire future of the oil-producing economies is at stake. Of course, it's possible they may all agree to jointly fund the purchase and avoid an auction. That's a matter for them but you finish up still in business and significantly richer regardless."

Julian stopped to observe if Desmond Cutter had absorbed the plan and the amounts involved. It appeared he did. He was seated, his head was nodding and a conspiratorial grin was on his face.

"So, you see," Julian continued. "You really can't turn our proposal down. Everybody wins. We've already put in motion events that will see the auction taking place on Saturday 9thDecember. All those invited have accepted. The meeting and auction are very secret and only those invited, and now you, know it is taking place. The exact venue is still secret and security will be tight."

"You seem to have it all worked out but I'm worried. I like the money and the idea of burying this formula. I agree it could put oil as a commodity out of business but only if it works. Can I see a demonstration?"

"I'm sure that can be arranged. My dear Ruby, where did you leave Dr Graham?" Julian leered at Ruby before adding: "He's no doubt exhausted after your ministrations."

"He's at his hotel. He's booked in for another four nights. He said he needed time to think."

"Desmond, I'm sure there's no time like the present." Julian stood up, and as he did so he called out: "Frankie."

As if by magic, the faithful Frankie appeared at the front door and stepped into the open-plan apartment. "Go and collect Dr Graham from the Mayflower and take him to Redbridge. Have Micky get hold of Professor Small — get him over to Redbridge too. Say we're doing the experiment again for a guest. I want to be ready in two hours."

A man of few words, Frankie simply nodded and left.

"Shall we all have another drink?" Julian was again re-filling glasses but ignored the slumped figure of Sebastian. "Now, Desmond, what do you think of our little plan? Assuming we can show you the experiment working a little later, when will you transfer our hundred billion dollars?" Julian was excited at the prospect of all this money. "We'll give you the bank details before you leave."

"Gee, you guys are smooth. I'm being stitched up here, but I feel like I want to be. If this works then I'm in. I'll get the money moving within the next thirty-six hours. That amount has to be moved slowly and in lesser amounts, but don't worry, we've done it before. But what about Anderson? I'm still concerned that he hasn't been paid."

"Fear not, Desmond. As soon as your funds hit our bank, Gregory Anderson will be paid. After all, we have Ruby here to make sure we do."

Ruby just glared at Julian. She would be reporting in later this evening, but not to Gregory.

***

The Audi containing Julian St John, Desmond Cutter, Ruby and Frankie arrived at the Redbridge warehouse exactly two hours after Frankie was despatched to get David Graham. Inside the warehouse everything looked as before. The scientists were in conversation dressed in their white lab coats, the bright lights were illuminating the laboratory area, and everything seemed organised and ready.

Desmond approached the scientists. "You guys ready to show that this formula actually makes fuel from water?"

Not knowing who Desmond was but spying Julian hanging back by the door, David Graham thought he'd better answer this obvious American.

"It's not quite as simple but yes, the formula allows water under certain pressure and with various additives to be converted into high-performance fuel."

"Wow! This I've got to see. Fire away, boys."

Professor Small and Dr Graham once again demonstrated that the water-based fuel did in fact still explode upon contact with the hot plate. They repeated it several times for Desmond's benefit. "And you're sure this can be scaled up to produce enough fuel for the world?"

"The science suggests it can and the notes from the original researcher certainly say he believed it could."

"Amazing. And that little bang when the fuel hit the hot plate, that's what'll happen in a normal car engine when this fuel hits the hot spark plug?"

Peter Small hadn't spoken to Desmond but thought he'd answer. "We believe so, yes. And of course, that's what happens now in a normal petrol engine. All we have to do is use this synthetic fuel instead of an oil-based product."

Desmond Cutter was impressed, not only with the demonstration but with the brothers St John. They had a plan and something to sell. If he went along with it, he'd be even wealthier but, more importantly, he'd make sure this new fuel would be killed off before the green do-good brigade got to hear of it.

He walked towards Julian. "I'm in. E-mail me your bank details and I'll transfer the first hundred million dollars, but I want to see this amount transferred to Anderson in New York before I send the rest. I'm not getting involved in any dispute. Everything has to be done right, even if it's a bit below the radar. If you agree then we have a deal."

Julian wasn't happy, and would have preferred more money in the first payment, but agreed. "Remember, after we've paid off Anderson, we expect the total balance within twenty-four hours. If it doesn't arrive, the deal's off and we'll deal with the auction ourselves."

"Understood. Now I have to get to that little airport we came in at. My jet's there and I have to get to Norway."

"I'll have my driver take you. Micky, please take Mr Cutter to Biggin Hill in Kent."

Just as Desmond Cutter was leaving, he turned to Julian St John. "Julian, just so you know, the last guy who tried to fool me isn't breathing. Nor are any of his nearest and dearest. I like money as much as the next man but if you're playing with me then there will be retribution. Do you understand?" The Texan had a hard focus in his eyes that left Julian in no doubt that this apparently amiable businessman was not a man to be crossed. Julian felt a bowel movement coming on.

Desmond Cutter left a happy man, dreaming of an auction that would make him even richer.

Julian approached Ruby; David Graham walked behind; Desmond Cutter's words were still ringing in his ears. "Ruby, my dear, you'd better take our good doctor here back to his hotel and tuck him in as only you can. Dr Graham, thank you once again. I fear we may need your services one more time but not for a week or so. We'll keep in touch and keep you safe. Go out and enjoy the sights of London. Ruby — Frankie will drive you. I'll stay here for a while."

Frankie dropped Ruby and David Graham off outside the Mayflower Hotel. It was just after one o'clock in the morning. Once in David's room, Ruby took a whiskey from the minibar and offered him one. He declined. Ruby had already thrown her coat onto the chair in the window and sat on the other one opposite. David was mesmerised by her beauty and her apparent availability, but he had something more pressing on his mind than a possible romp with Ruby.

Ruby could sense that David wasn't really with her. "What's wrong? The experiment worked again and you're almost free of Gregory Anderson and the St John brothers. Another two weeks, maximum and you'll be free. Meantime you've got first class protection."

"It's not that, the whole thing's getting crazy. That's twice now that grown men have been fooled by a party trick a first-year chemistry student could perform. I've been keeping quiet just to get away from these horrible men, but now I think that if I don't tell them it's a trick they'll keep after me for misleading them." David was almost in tears.

Sitting with her whiskey in her hand, Ruby looked horrified. "David, they simply would not understand. Your life would be in greater danger. You can't say anything!"

"I have to, Ruby. I'll call St John tomorrow and explain. At least he'll know before he spends all that money. I heard the driver saying millions are involved. Don't you see? If they think this formula works and I know it doesn't then they'll blame me if they lose a lot of money. I'll be dead."

"David." Ruby rose from her seat and went to him. She'd used her womanly charms on better men than David Graham. "I'm worried about you." She stroked his hair at the side. "You know the police are probably looking for you here in London? They must know you are staying at a hotel, and it wasn't smart of Gregory to book you in under your own name. I'm surprised you've not been arrested already."

"What can I do? I have to get away." David was pleading.

Ruby put her arm around his shoulders and pulled him towards her. "Look, I can help. Pack a bag now and come and stay at my place. I'm not a bad cook and there could be fringe benefits." She smiled and lightly kissed David on the lips. He was putty in her hands.

David had brought a small rucksack for exploring London and used that to pack a few personal items. Although he was nervous and afraid, he trusted Ruby. Who wouldn't? She was speaking sense and it would be good to be somewhere away from the brothers.

Once outside, Ruby hailed a taxi and the pair disappeared into the night. Ruby knew Julian St John didn't have anyone watching the hotel. They were clear.

Chapter Fifteen

Steve headed back to his office, still seething from his confrontation with Frank Dobson. Barry was at his desk; Andy was typing away on his computer; and Samantha Burns seemed to be working on an iPad.

Steve went straight to his office to try and cool down. After a few minutes he went outside and over to Andy's desk. "Anything back from Forensics on that waste material cart?"

"Yes, sir. It's in the file but they didn't get much. They said there was too much contamination and there was nothing they could find of the girl."

"Thanks, Andy. How about nipping off and getting coffees all round? It's almost six so our two wandering DCs should be here soon. Better get them cups as well." Without waiting for a response, Steve called to Samantha: "Sam, are you staying for the briefing and giving us your insight into our killer?"

"Wilco."

Steve smiled. "Who says "Wilco" today?" The choice of word matched her appearance. The DCI hoped her profiling skills were better than her packaging and first impressions.

Detective Constables Fairchild and Brooks arrived in a bit of a flap. Fairchild, the taller of the two, stuttered out: "So sorry, we thought we were late. The traffic from Hackney was manic."

"You're not late — settle down and catch your breath, compose yourselves. After all, we're only dealing with a triple murder." Steve was pleased by his gentle put-down of the young constables.

Andy appeared with coffee. Barry returned from the garage and everyone was standing in Steve's office awaiting some sort of announcement from their boss.

"I'm concerned that our man is likely to strike again within the next thirty-six hours. So far, he's stuck to a ten-day interval between murders, and there's nothing we've learnt so far to suggest he'll change this timeline. If we're going to avoid another death, we've got to apply ourselves and catch this guy now. We need inspiration."

Steve moved to the whiteboard and leaned against the wall with his coffee cup in hand.

"Sam, you first. Everyone, this is Sam Burns. She's a Met profiler and Andy asked to have her join the team." Steve knew this would make Andy blush and it did. Samantha Burns stood forward.

"Andy has given me access to all the files. Given the times the murders are carried out, I don't think our killer is employed. Allowing for the sexual nature of the murders, I'd say he's probably been sexually repressed since childhood. He's new to women and sex. Andy's explained about his theory that the killings take place in a private house and then the bodies are dumped afterwards. I think it's a sound theory, especially as I am suggesting he's only recently found his sexual appetite." Sam paused and sipped her coffee. The room was spellbound.

"I believe he's in his forties, doesn't possess a high IQ, is unemployed and has been living with one or both of his parents since he left school. He may have had an odd job on and off but is certainly controlled by his parents. I believe he's socially awkward and hasn't mixed with many people. He's been a virgin until recently, probably due to the controlling influence of his parents. They almost certainly have controlled every aspect of his life for years. It's possible that his father died a few years ago and he's been controlled by his mother. It's a classic situation — when the mother is widowed, the son becomes a surrogate husband. If the son's already a mummy's boy, the psychological damage can be immense. He's probably had fantasies about his mother most of his life. Plus, he's a storyteller probably living in his own world. He'd be able to spin a plausible tale to anyone, if required." Samantha's audience was still spellbound.

"Let's think what might happen if the mother were to die, leaving a sexually aware but unfulfilled son in the family house, now on his own for the first time in his life. It's a classic situation for sexual transference. He sets off to have sex thinking it's with his mother, only to realise after the event it's some woman he doesn't know. He feels betrayed and wants revenge on his mother. She's let him down. He's killing these women to cleanse himself of the shame. The killings are for his mother. It's significant that from the post-mortem reports all three victims were strangled from behind. Again, classic behaviour. He doesn't want to look at their faces. If his mother had died first and he'd spent time just with his father, I'm not sure we'd be looking at the same outcome."

Samantha sipped more coffee. "So, without making one theory fit another, I believe you're looking for a man in his forties who has been living with his parents. His father probably passed away some time ago, and his mother died recently, probably a few weeks before the first killing. He's sexually frustrated and only had sex for the first time with your first victim. The use of a condom indicates he's been planning for a sexual encounter for some time. He's probably living on benefits and is a loner. I support Andy's theory about the house and garage. This is exactly the type of property our killer would be living in as it would have been his family home. As to the location, again, I can find nothing to fault Andy's logic." Sam looked around the room, shrugged her shoulders and said: "Well, there you have it, for what it's worth." She'd finished but added: "This is one very sick individual. I don't believe he has any sense of what he's doing."

The room was silent. Nobody moved or hardly breathed. This little poorly-dressed, young-looking girl had just given the detectives more to think about in the last five minutes than they had had in the last five hours.

Steve was about to resume control of the meeting, but Andy spoke up first. "Sir, you remember I said I might be able to look for detached or semi-detached houses in our search area?" He pointed to the map. "Well, after Miss Burns explained her theories to me earlier, I got to thinking. Suppose I take the land registry for the postcodes in our search area and flush out only houses with garages? I agree the area is too big. But if I get Somerset House records for deaths of ladies over, say, sixty-five in the same postcodes who have died within the past six to eight weeks and then…" Andy was on a roll. Steve thought it was a wonderful sight. "… and then I got the census for the same postcodes and sifted out only addresses where parents lived with a thirty-five to forty-five-year-old son then we might pinpoint our house. If Sam's correct, we've got all the bits to build a profile and a map." Andy paused for effect. "We would have a man who lived with his mother who has recently died and is living in the family house with a garage in our perceived search area. If we narrow it down to a manageable number, then a DVLA search of vehicles at the addresses might throw up a dark-coloured van." Andy was triumphant. Steve told himself that this lad was a genius.

"How soon can you put this together?"

"I didn't think you'd mind, so after Sam and I discussed things, I called up all the records. They've arrived and are on my computer. The thing is the programme to allow for all the variables and writing a suitable algorithm is beyond my skills. The coding alone to compare all our data is a huge task. I've specified the parameters and I've asked a pal in Technical Support to put a software and coding package together, but it'll take time."

"How much time, Andy? I think you're onto something."

"Thanks, sir, but unless he's given a specific instruction, he'll only be able to work part-time."

"Barry, get the internal number for Tech Support. What's your pal's name, Andy?"

"Brian Somerset."

Barry left the office to make the call and returned holding a phone out towards Steve. "I've got an Inspector Harvey. He's the senior man in the department." Steve took the phone, and after explaining the importance of getting the software written and working, the Inspector agreed to assign Constable Brian Somerset to the task full-time, starting now. Steve agreed to fund any overtime and was promised a passable version of what Andy needed by the morning.

Steve looked around the room. "Now then, Mr Fairchild and Mr Brooks, what do you have to tell us?"

Neither detective was keen to speak, especially after Andy's brilliance. Brooks decided to bite the bullet. "Well, sir, we visited every address on the list. We showed the photographs of the dead girls to everyone who was in each establishment." Brooks sniggered. "Even the customers." The room erupted in laughter.

"We had no joy in the massage parlours. The strip clubs were mostly closed except for cleaning but no one recognised the girls. We had a bit of luck with the striptease pubs. One of the regulars in The Black Swan

117

said he thought he recognised our third victim, Barbara James." DC Brooks was now looking up his notes. "A bloke called Terry Smith says he thinks she was in the pub a couple of weeks ago. He thought it was a Thursday because that's the gala stripper lunch." Again, the DC smiled. "He saw her talking to the pub manager and thought she was asking for directions. He said she looked like a tart and didn't pay any attention. He says whatever the manager said she left in a hurry."

"Detective Constable, please tell me you spoke to the manager?"

"No, sir. He's on holiday in Portugal, some place in the Algarve."

"Don't tell me he's just left?"

"Afraid so, sir. He flew out yesterday morning. He's not due back for two weeks. Seems he's on a winter golf break." DC Brooks appeared not to recognise the importance of this information.

Steve hid his exacerbation. "Write it up, Andy. Make sure it's in the file. Did this witness say anything else?" Steve acknowledged that there was little else they could have done.

DC Fairchild answered. "All he said was that she had a piece of paper in her hand. That's why he thought she was asking for directions. He thought it was an address."

"Andy, get onto Exhibits. I want everything found on Barbara Brooks. Tell them it's urgent and we need it first thing tomorrow."

"Yes, sir."

Steve addressed his two DCs. "Anything else?"

"Not really, sir, but we had a strange encounter. When DC Miller gave us the lists, he'd added a couple of private addresses from the lonely-hearts section of a newspaper." Brookes was reading from his notes.

"Yes…"

"Well, we followed those up as well. There are a lot of strange people out there. The two men we interviewed didn't recognise the girls. One asked where he could advertise for ones like them. Really spooky, but not killers." DC Brooks closed his notebook.

"You two are to return to general duties with the Murder Squad. DI Chalmers is expecting you first thing tomorrow morning. Make sure everything is written up and thank you for your help. We couldn't have covered the ground without you."

Both constables were smiling as they left the office, but both were grateful to be away from such an intense atmosphere. They preferred the slower pace of the Murder Squad under Detective Inspector Chalmers.

When the DCs had gone, Steve moved to sit behind his desk. Barry took a chair and Andy brought two chairs from the outer office for himself and Samantha. All four felt washed out.

"Anything from the TV or press?"

"No, nothing, sir. We had one call, but it was a dead end."

"Anything from the CCTV around the body dump sites?"

Barry thought his boss was relentless. He seemed in a hurry to move these murders on.

Andy brightened up. "Yes, sir. We got a hit on a van at the second dump site. It's saved on my laptop. Hang on, I'll get it." Andy left and returned holding his computer.

As he set it up, Steve turned to Samantha Burns. "Sam, how sure are you about your profile?"

"It's never an exact science but given your analysis and what I've read in the files I'd be surprised if it's too far off."

"So, we're looking for the right type of suspect and can use your profile?"

"I believe so, yes."

Andy had set his machine up so everyone could see the screen. He pressed play and took up the narrative. He pointed at the screen. "There, that's the van. It looks like a small Renault Kangoo. We don't get the registration number." The screen carries on showing. "This is our man. Look, he gets out and goes to the back of the van. We can't see his face because he's got the hood of his parka pulled up." Everyone was spellbound watching the screen and listening to Andy's descriptions. "The thing he's pulled from the back of the van looks like a folded-down wheelchair and there... look... He's pulled it up so it can be used... Now look. He opens the passenger door and lifts out a woman and puts her in the wheelchair." Andy froze the picture. All ten eyes were staring at the screen trying to identify the disabled woman. Nobody could, so Andy started the film again. "Now look, the woman's in a bad way. She's slumped in the chair and her head is on her chest. She's wrapped in a blanket, so we don't have any idea of her size or age." The film kept moving forward. Andy pointed again. "There. He's wheeling her into the park and out of CCTV range. Look at the time — 2.29 p.m."

"Now if I fast forward to just before 2.41 p.m…" Andy pressed a few keys on his laptop. The film ran forward and stopped just as Andy had intended. "At 2.41… wait… there! You see the same man re-appears but there's no wheelchair. I've checked with the council parks department and no wheelchair has been reported lost or stolen. Now, look, he gets back into his van and drives off."

Andy was triumphant. "I think that's our second victim being dumped. Who looks twice at someone in a wheelchair?"

Steve was impressed. "Have Tech tried to enhance the shot of the man and the van?"

"Yes, but no joy. He kept his face covered and there wasn't a clear shot of the registration number of the van."

Everyone tried to talk at once except Steve, who was deep in thought. Recognising the signs, Barry held up a hand to quell the noise.

"Barry, tomorrow get a team to dredge that pond in the park. If our killer has left it behind and no one has found it, then the only logical place to hide it is underwater. Who'd look for a wheelchair there?"

"Bloody hell — we were right there. I'll get onto it first thing. We might get lucky and get some forensics off of it."

"If it's there, but I can't think where else it might be."

Steve felt washed out. "Good work, everybody. We've only got tomorrow to get this perp before he does another girl."

I've got…" Steve's phone rang. He looked at the screen and instantly his body language softened. "I've got to take this. Hang on here a few minutes, we're not finished."

Barry looked at Andy and mouthed: "It's a woman."

In the corridor Steve spoke to Alison Mills. "Are you coming round later?" she enquired.

"I'd love to, darling, but I'm up to my neck. We've only got tomorrow to find our Hackney killer, and on top of that I've been given another case that apparently only I can handle. Plus, I want to be in here by six o'clock tomorrow, and my head's spinning with information I can't make sense of."

"So that's a no, is it, Detective Chief Inspector? You take advantage of a girl one night and dump her the next?"

"You know it's not like that. Tell you what, why not book us a nice restaurant for tomorrow night? I'll pick you up at, say, eight o'clock in case I'm held up. If things get a bit hairy and I can't make it, it'll be because we've had a success and I'll be free to come down to Rye on Saturday afternoon. How's that? You know I want to see you."

"Well, if that's the best offer an abandoned girl can get, I suppose it'll have to do, but you don't know what you're missing."

"Dr Mills, you're a very naughty doctor. I'll have to go, the team's waiting. See you tomorrow, or if not, I'll call."

"You'd better. Stay safe." Alison was gone.

Steve returned to his office and took his seat. He looked at Barry. "Don't ask and don't second guess." This was said with a grin.

"Andy, you seem to have the lion's share of the workload. You've got the Tech guys delivering this super programme to you tomorrow. How long before it throws out any information?"

"Hard to say, sir. I'd hope, if the coding's finished and I can input the parameters of the search, then early afternoon if we're lucky. But remember, we think we're looking for a Renault Kangoo van, so that'll tighten up our search even further." Andy was in his element.

"Good, you're also going to receive the contents of Barbara James' effects. See if anything with an address is there — we might get lucky. If not, we'll have to consider asking the Portuguese police to track down our pub manager in the Algarve and hope he can remember the address our victim was looking for. It's a long shot but we've got to try."

Steve sat back. "I don't suppose you've had a chance to chase up the records for The Fortress, Andy?"

"Yes — I've filed the request. Everything'll be here tomorrow but to be honest, sir, I don't know when I'll get round to looking at the data."

"Don't worry. It's got a low priority. Your first task is the computer programme and the Hackney case."

"Barry, you're chasing up the lake search, but I want you to do that late morning."

Barry was a bit bewildered but agreed.

Steve stood so as to have everyone's undivided attention. "Sam, I think we're done, so if you want to go, we'll carry on."

"If you don't mind, Inspector, I'd like to stay and help. I might contribute something more, and Andy... I mean DC Miller might need an extra pair of hands tomorrow."

"If you're sure then we're glad of your help. So, as of tomorrow, a new DI is joining the team on full-time status. His name is Abul Ishmal. I've worked with him before and he's a good lad. Also, I've been given another case, so it'll mean splitting our resources. Andy, you'll carry on as is. Barry, I know you're seconded only for the Hackney murders, but I want you with me on this other case. But you'll help out DI Ishmal as well. I'll get around everyone as best I can. Sam, you'll make your own job up and help out where you see fit. Does everyone follow?"

Barry put his hand up. "What's the new case, Steve?"

"I'll fill you in later." From Steve's body language it was clear that this was not a topic for conversation.

"We've had a long and — we hope — productive day. Let's call it quits now and start fresh again tomorrow. You know I can't help thinking we're close on Hackney. We're missing something." It was as though the DCI was talking to himself. "Oh well, it will come, it usually does, but let's hope it's not too late."

The team started to file out. "Andy, can you wait a minute?" To Steve's surprise, Andy blushed and looked over at Samantha.

"Well sir... I suppose, it's just Miss Burns and I are going for a meal."

Steve smiled inwardly. "It'll only take a minute."

Andy closed the office door. "Andy, I want you to get another laptop from central stores tomorrow morning. No one should know you have it. This new case is very hush-hush and is for our eyes only. I don't want you discussing any of the details with anyone, and if anyone asks you about it you tell me immediately. Is that clear?"

"Yes, sir."

"Good. I don't want any paper copies of anything to do with the case. It's to be only on your new laptop and I want you to make sure you have all the security known to man on it. Now have you got that?"

"Yes, sir."

"And Andy, you're doing a great job, but on this new case, trust no one. Not even our team. Oh, and just to rub salt in can you get in here at seven o'clock tomorrow morning?"

Andy smiled. He liked being at the centre of things.

"Of course, Steve."

Steve watched this awkward but gifted detective leave. Using his Christian name was a big step forward for Andy. He belonged.

Steve sat back, still trying to bring forward whatever was eating away at his subconscious. He knew his team lacked headcount, but he also knew the Hackney murders would be solved by brain power, not by the number of officers on the case. This was the Special Resolutions Unit. For some strange and unexplained reason, Steve felt pride. Maybe tomorrow whatever was stuck in his brain would come forward, and Andy's programme would work, and maybe tomorrow they'd catch a killer. If not, then another girl would surely die.

Chapter Sixteen

Steve arrived in his office at precisely 6.51 a.m., and to his surprise Andy was already at his desk.

"What time did you get in, Andy?"

"Oh! Just a few minutes ago. You said you wanted an early meet and I've got a lot on today. I've put a coffee on your desk, and I've got mine." Andy pointed to a Costa cardboard cup on his desk.

"Good man. Come on in." Steve pointed to his inner office.

Steve was sitting behind his desk while Andy pulled up a chair and sat on the opposite side.

"I told you last night we've got another case, do you remember?"

"Yes, sir."

"Andy, it was 'Steve' last night. Unless something traumatic happened last night with Miss Burns, can we keep it informal?" Steve wasn't smiling. "I think we work better if we can speak up without rank getting in the way, OK?"

Andy was blushing. Steve thought it was probably the earliest he'd blushed in his life. The mention of Sam Burns had triggered the reaction.

"Yes, Steve, sorry."

"No problem, Andy. You know we all value your input." Steve gave a smile. "Right, our new case…"

"Steve, if I can interrupt…" Andy didn't wait for permission and carried on. "I took it from last night that this new case is a bit sensitive and potentially a bit secret. I know you wanted me to requisition a new laptop, but I thought if this case is so hush-hush it might be better not to use a police issue machine, so I've brought my own one. I cleared everything off it last night so it's completely clean. I also reinstalled all the security protocols so it should be secure, especially if I keep online activity to a minimum. I hope that's OK?"

Steve sat back and sipped his excellent coffee. This detective constable had the power to surprise him at every turn.

"Andy, you are amazing. That's good thinking. I don't want anybody, and I mean anybody, not even Sam, to have access to your laptop. Use it only for this new case and nothing else. I hope you follow that?"

"Yes, I do, Steve, and I'm sure you'll fill me in when you're ready."

"Andy, the reason I asked you to come in early is to fill you in."

"I'm all ears." Andy was up for a challenge and sensed within himself that he enjoyed being at the centre of the action. He produced his notebook expecting to take notes. When he looked up, he saw his boss's expression and instantly remembered the conversation from the previous night. There were to be no paper copies of anything. Andy put his notebook away.

Steve explained what he'd been told about the body and the likely involvement of the Government and MI6. He'd been thinking about this new case on and off overnight and had come up with a few thoughts that he now shared with Andy. He produced the initial incident report from his inside jacket pocket and passed it to Andy.

"That's the first piece of paper. Scan it into your laptop and then shred it. We clearly don't know who the body belongs to or any identity. The post-mortem's set for ten o'clock this morning and the body is in St Thomas's mortuary. It seems the pathologist is to be Sir Humphrey Campbell, so we're honoured. He's the top Home Office man. But why use an eminent pathologist if the body's just another drowning?" Steve drank his coffee and threw the empty cup into his waste bin.

Andy sat and listened. He was fascinated.

"The fact Sir Humphrey is involved tells us something about what's going on. This isn't just a body from the river. Somebody in high places knows who our body is but isn't sharing. Why? Strings are obviously being pulled and we're the puppets."

Steve was thinking out loud — something he did a lot of. "If this were an ordinary body fished out from the Thames then the local police pathologist would do the post. This body means something to somebody, but we don't know who."

Andy was about to speak but Steve held up a hand. "We don't know anything beyond what I've told you, Andy. We need an identity to start with, then we'll follow procedure. But like I said last night, trust no one.

Be suspicious. People like Barry, Sam and DI Ishmal have all recently joined us. Although I don't believe any of them have been planted on us ahead of this case, we can't be sure."

Andy sat dumbfounded but said nothing.

Steve carried on. "I'll be on this more or less solo, but I'll use Barry as I need to. You're the data man so keep the files up to date. I'll feed you everything I learn but all reports will be verbal. It may mean updating what we know after work. I hope that's OK, Andy?"

"Yes, of course, Steve. It all sounds a bit cloak-and-dagger. What about Hackney?"

"We keep at it. I've been told to concentrate on our river man, but our focus for the next thirty-six hours has to be Hackney."

Steve and Andy were wrapping up when there was a rap on the door. It was opened by a youngish man. He was in his shirt sleeves with his tie pulled down from the collar. "DCI Burt?" The newcomer took a few paces into Steve's office.

"Yes?"

"I'm Inspector Harvey from Tech Support. We spoke yesterday evening about a programme you need writing."

"Yes, come in. I hope you've got something for us."

Steve was on his feet with his hand outstretched. He noted that this inspector was a bit short for a policeman at about five feet, eight inches tall. He had a largish beer belly, and his hair was going grey at the sides. He had a round face with a ready smile. Andy also stood. After the usual introductions, Inspector Harvey spoke.

"I know how important this is and I said I'd get something to DC Miller here this morning." He pointed towards Andy. "The reason I'm here is to apologise. I've had two lads at it all night and I've been on it as well. The thing is we're not finished — it'll be another four to five hours. Some things you can't rush, I'm sorry."

Steve was clearly disappointed but tried not to show it. "I appreciate your help. I'm sure you're doing the best you can. Will you let Andy know the moment you've finished?"

"Yes, but it won't have been fully tested."

"No matter, we'll just be glad to get it."

Inspector Harvey was about to leave before Andy spoke.

"Excuse me, sir." This was addressed to the man from Tech Support. "We've had a breakthrough from the CCTV. I'd like to add a field for vehicles. I'm getting a file from the DVLA showing all Renault Kangoo vans in our postcodes and I want to run our programme over that file also."

"You blokes don't ask for much, do you?" Inspector Harvey was rubbing his chin in thought. "Tell you what — if you get everything you want inputted, I'll have a team get onto it. We've got a good OCR suite of programmes that I've been dying to use on a big job. We've also got spare time on our mainframe. If we upload everything once the coding has been done, the mainframe should get you your results a lot faster than using laptops."

"I know it's a lot to ask but anything you can do might help save another girl being killed."

Steve thought this was worth mentioning although he could see the inspector was ready to help.

"Leave it with me," he said to Andy. "Forward the DVLA stuff as soon as you get it plus every other database you want scrutinised. I'll have Brian input it all and with luck we'll get there sooner."

Steve stepped in again. "We appreciate what you're doing, and we know you'll do your best."

"Well, let's see. I'll be in touch. By the way, your overtime budget has taken a hit for all the overtime last night. Must be well into four figures." With a wave and a smile, Inspector Harvey left and returned to his computers.

Andy stood up. "I'll just get the data from all the agencies up to Tech now."

"Right, Andy, remember about our new case. No paper and only verbal reports — mum's the word."

Andy set off to pull all the data together. It was a big job but he was organised and made light work of it. He was just finishing off sending the last file when a man arrived looking very happy. "Good morning. I presume you're Andy Miller?"

"Yes." Andy wasn't sure who this was but was suddenly struck by the fact an Inspector Ishmal was joining the team today. Andy stood up and extended his hand. "You must be Inspector Ishmal." Then he remembered that the inspector had visited a few days earlier when he was in uniform. Both men shook hands. "Please call me Cap. It's a long story and our leader might explain it to you one day when he's ready. Is he in?"

"Yes."

Steve had heard the exchange through his open office door and called out: "Cap, get yourself in here."

The Cap entered and shook hands with his old and now current boss. "It's good to have you here, Cap. You're early."

"Well, you know me, Steve, always keen." Both men laughed.

"Andy, can you hold the fort for half an hour? When the effects for Barbara James arrive, get Barry to start going through them. The Cap and I are off to the canteen for a coffee and a briefing. Remember to tell Barry we're looking…" Steve stopped in his tracks. Something occurred to him like a bolt from the blue. "Andy, get in here!"

Steve went back to his desk, leaving his new inspector stranded in the middle of his office. Andy bustled in. Steve realised that Abul was still standing looking lost. "Sorry, Cap, I'll explain as we go." The DCI was excited. The thing he'd been trying to get from his subconscious had just arrived at the front of his brain.

"Andy, take a seat. You too, Cap."

The Cap giggled out loud. "Sorry, Steve. It's just Andy and Cap. I'm surprised you didn't see it."

Steve also laughed. "No, I missed it, but I'm sure we'll use it in the future." Steve became serious. "Andy, do you remember you added a couple of lonely-hearts ads to the canvas list we gave those two DCs from the Murder Squad?"

"Yes."

"What publications did you get them from?"

"Just the local newspapers, why?"

"I've had this thing buzzing around in my brain. You'd mentioned adverts earlier: The Pink Warehouse advertises for strippers, The Fortress advertises for hostesses. Everybody who wants to meet someone advertises. It's just where and the type of person you want to meet. The Fortress uses *Country Life*. The Pink Warehouse probably uses the free publications or even postcards in post office windows, and your lonely hearts use the local press. Do you see?" "Steve was animated, his brain running ahead of his mouth.

"Not really, boss."

"Our victims all travelled some distance to get to Hackney but what brought them there? I don't mean transport but what event? They were all looking for something better. They all enjoyed themselves and were all dressed up in what they thought was their best. Why?"

Steve waited for comments but got none. The Cap had seen Steve like this before and suspected he was about to crack whatever case they were working on.

"You were on to something with the adverts, Andy, just not the right ones. What if our victims answered an advert placed by the killer, but not for a lonely heart? What about a glamorous job that someone like them could never hope to get? Alistair Ramsay of The Fortress took one look at the pictures of the dead girls and immediately dismissed them. They were too much like tarts to work in an upmarket brothel like his. Besides, I doubt if any of the victims knew what *Country Life* was."

"I see where you're going, I think."

"We need to get all London provincial papers, starting with those distributed as free press in Peckham, Mile End and Stepney. That's where our victims lived. Then the more popular, London-wide papers — the *Evening Standard* and such like. Any newspaper these normal, ambitious, working-class girls might have picked up and seen an advert in that looked like a great opportunity for them. Start with a couple of weeks before the first murder. Scan every advert for something asking young girls to apply for some kind of exotic job. You know, something like hostesses for a luxury private yacht. Let's see if the same advert appears in successive weeks. Something out of the normal took these girls to Hackney and I bet we'll find it in the newspaper adverts."

Steve sat back exhausted.

"Wow! That's some deduction, boss. I'll ask Sam to help with it and I'll chase up the press office for their archive files. They keep copies of all London newspapers going back years. It should be simple enough to get them." Andy was impressed with his boss.

"Steve, I've no idea what that was all about, but I think you're ready for that coffee. Come on, boss, I'll buy." The Cap stood and waited for

Steve to stand and follow him out. As they left, Andy was already on the phone to the press office.

Over some coffee, Steve brought Abul up to speed on the Hackney murders and the fact that they felt the killer would strike again, possibly within the next twenty-four hours. He explained about the fabric waste cart to move the first body and how they were stumped to see how a body could be moved without any comment. "You see, Cap, we've got a lot of lines of enquiry. Andy's next to brilliant. Barry's useful but is better at following than leading. We've got this profiler attached and she seems competent. I'm sorry to dump this on you on your first day but I've got another matter to deal with, so you'll have to lead. I'll back you up of course and be around when this other thing allows."

"I guess that's why I'm here, Steve."

The pair then exchanged news of their private lives. Abul's family were doing well. Steve told Abul about Alison Mills. They chatted about cases and Steve told The Cap about his intentions towards The Fortress Club and its owner, ex-commander Alistair Ramsay. They soon returned to the Hackney murders.

"Andy's putting together a programme with the help of Tech Support that, once everything is loaded, should spit out a list of suspects to match our theories and the profile put together by Sam Burns. We got lucky with CCTV at the second dump site. We believe our killer is using a dark van, probably a Renault Kangoo. Andy feels we have enough parameters to break down to a small list of suspects, especially with the van info." Both detectives drank their coffee. Inspector Abul Ishmal was glad to be back working for this DCI. They'd already shared a lot on a previous case.

"Andy will give you the files. They are up to date and immaculate. I've never seen such precise information in a Metropolitan Police file."

"This Andy sounds one of a kind. I guess you'll be keeping him?"

"Oh yes. Let's get back, Barry should be in. You can meet him and get started."

The pair left the canteen and headed for the eighth floor, happy to be working together again. But given the Thames river body, could Steve fully trust Detective Inspector Abul Ishmal?

Chapter Seventeen

The St John brothers were finishing their breakfast when the phone rang. The ever-vigilant Frankie answered it, and after a brief conversation hung up and entered the open-plan penthouse lounge. The kitchen was designed to eat in and was located in the rear corner. "That was Mr Cutter's secretary. She says Mr Cutter has invited you for lunch today. He'll send a car at twelve noon sharp."

Julian was alarmed. "Is that all she said? Desmond Cutter wasn't there?"

"I don't know, boss, that's all she said." With that, Frankie once again vanished.

The St John brothers had been having sleepless nights since Desmond Cutter agreed to be part of their plan. There had been no word from him, and the hundred million dollars had not arrived in their account. They told themselves that this was normal, and that Desmond was busy with his main business, like flying off to Norway. Julian was the worrier of the pair while Sebastian told him not to fret. Everything would work out.

Still, Julian had a horrible feeling that things weren't going to plan. And now this invitation to lunch. Julian St John wasn't a happy man.

"Is everything arranged for the auction?" Julian decided to keep busy and soldier on.

"Yes, we've had confirmations from everybody. The Argentinian guy was the last to accept. The hotel's all booked up, and I've got a security team already there searching for listening bugs and doing ground searches. We've forked out over forty grand so far, and the hotel bill alone will be around ninety big ones."

"We're on the hook now I suppose so there's no going back. What about Dr Graham?" Julian was still not happy. Something wasn't right. He could sense it.

"Haven't heard. Micky's at his hotel every day. He hasn't seen the doctor, but he hasn't checked out."

"Good. I've a feeling we're going to need him again."

"Did you see the e-mail from Gregory Anderson? He's getting anxious and wants his money."

Sebastian finished a piece of toast. "Thought he might. We'll just have to keep him interested until Desmond comes through. It's all we can do. We don't have the hundred million dollars."

"No, Sebastian — that's what's worrying me. If Desmond Cutter pulls out, we'll have to emigrate and change our names. Gregory Anderson doesn't know we don't have the money."

Julian carried on in a weak voice. "You don't think we're in over our heads, brother? I liked the original idea, and the money looks incredible, but can we pull it off? Our piggy bank's a bit empty."

"Don't worry, we've got the formula. That's all that matters. Anderson was a fool to let it go before he was paid. We're in the driving seat. The plan's good and we hold all the aces. If we hold our nerve, we'll be fine, so don't worry."

Julian said nothing but carried on worrying.

***

At 11.55, the buzzer to the penthouse apartment sounded, signalling the arrival of the car to take the brothers to lunch. As always, Frankie went with them. The car was a top-of-the-range BMW. Frankie sat in the front while the two brothers climbed into the back.

Julian asked the driver: "Where are we going?"

The driver didn't answer but looked straight ahead at the lunchtime traffic.

Julian spoke again. "Frankie, ask the driver where we're going."

Frankie turned in his seat to face the driver. "My boss asked you a question and he'd like an answer."

The driver was unfazed and carried on looking forward.

Frankie stirred and leant in towards the driver. "Unless you're deaf, you'd better have a good reason for ignoring me." Frankie opened his coat to reveal a Glock pistol in a shoulder holster. As he stared hard, he

132

could swear the driver smiled. Frankie turned around to face the rear to look for instructions.

"Just leave it, Frankie, we'll know soon enough." Julian was now very nervous.

The journey took approximately forty-five minutes. The car pulled up outside a club in Hackney and the brothers plus Frankie exited the car. The brass plaque outside the front door read 'The Fortress Club'. All three climbed the stairs to the main glass doors and were met by the same gentleman who had greeted the Scotland Yard detectives only the day before.

"You're expected, gentlemen. Unfortunately, your man (Frankie) isn't invited but he can wait in the lounge once he's checked his firearm. It'll be perfectly safe with us." The butler pointed to the coat check desk and the girl who'd heard the conversation simply put out her hand to accept the Glock. Without waiting for confirmation, this superior doorman started to walk towards the staircase. "Please follow me, gentlemen. Lunch is being served in our Lagoon Room."

The brothers entered the dining room. Everywhere they looked they saw good taste and luxurious fittings. The room was big, and in its centre stood an antique table laid out with silver cutlery and crystal goblets. A silver ice bucket had been placed in the middle of the table and a bottle of unopened champagne stood at its centre.

Two men stood chatting by the window. One was Desmond Cutter but neither brother recognised the other man.

Desmond saw the door open and called out. "Ah, you got my invitation. Glad you could come. Come on, let's sit down. The lunches here are fantastic and the young ladies who serve the food are not bad either." Julian noted that Desmond seemed nervous and over-friendly. He also noted that Desmond had not introduced his companion. At around five feet, seven inches, the stranger was not tall, but looked solid. Not fat but all muscle. Julian couldn't remember seeing a broader pair of shoulders. The man's face was scarred on the left cheek and his hair was unnaturally black.

All four men sat down, and a male waiter immediately served chilled white wine before retiring.

"This is very kind of you, Desmond." Julian was trying to be brave and act confidently.

"No, no, it's my pleasure. I wanted you to meet a business associate of mine, James Rushdie."

Desmond pointed to his companion. "Jim's in the import business and over the years we've had a few successful joint ventures. I wanted you to meet because Jim might come in with us."

Julian wasn't sure if this made him feel any easier. At least Cutter seemed to be confirming he was going ahead — this eased Julian's mind a little. To make conversation, Julian asked: "What sort of imports are you in, Jim?"

The look James Rushdie gave Julian was menacing. The more Julian looked across the table at this man the more certain he was that he was witnessing pure evil. Threats seemed to come from his pores and the air around him seemed devoid of oxygen.

James Rushdie drank his wine and picked up a fork that he pointed at Julian. In a tortured New York accent, he said: "My name's James. Only my friends call me 'Jim', got it?"

Julian didn't know how to react. Sebastian stepped in.

"OK, James, no need to get off on the wrong foot. We're all here to make money. We only have to work together. We're not getting married." Sebastian laughed at his joke, trying to lighten the atmosphere.

"You're right there. Like Des said, we've worked together before. Unfortunately, Des isn't as sharp as he thinks he is." James put up a hand. "Sorry, Des, but you know it's true. You're the master of the international oil markets and sharp as a knife in the board room, but when it comes to getting down and dirty and working with non-corporate types, you're not the man. That's why I'm here." Julian saw why Desmond Cutter might need someone like this on his side. He didn't like it.

James Rushdie continued to drink his wine. As he drained his glass, the male waiter appeared from nowhere and refilled it. He topped up the other three although Julian had only sipped his.

James continued. "You see, when Des told me about this deal, I started to ask him questions. Guess what? He couldn't answer them, so I thought to myself, 'is my buddy being ripped off?' The more I realised he didn't know, the more convinced I became that you two carpetbaggers aren't on the level. I've advised Des not to pay a penny until I check this out."

With a sneer and a shrug of his huge shoulders, he continued: "Being legitimate businessmen, you'll appreciate our position."

Julian and Sebastian didn't appreciate his or their position. It was as though they were back at the beginning. Julian was about to speak up when the door opened, and a lunch trolley was pushed in by one of the club's hostesses.

Business talk stopped while Julian admired the waitress, and she set to work, simultaneously serving food and obliging Julian by showing him her assets. Eating formed a secondary part to lunch. They enjoyed excellent food and wine, and after coffee Julian was feeling mellow and very aroused by the hostess. She slipped a card into his breast pocket as she left the room pushing the trolley. However, even the sight of this temptress couldn't completely keep Julian comfortably confident about the future, and he nervously finished his wine.

While all four men sat back enjoying fine forty-year-old brandy, Julian came to from his fantasies about what he'd do with the hostess, but this daydream had calmed his nerves.

"Look, James, I understand your concern, but believe me this is fool proof. Desmond has seen the experiment, so he knows the formula works. What is it you need to know?"

"I understand this formula was stolen from a dead professor at MIT?"

"Yes, he was killed by another professor who used the formula to pay off his gambling debts."

"Yeah, that's Gregory Anderson. Greg and myself have history so I know how he operates."

Julian wasn't so anxious now. Maybe it was the lunch or the girl. Sebastian was as always getting lost in brandy fumes and contributed nothing.

"We have the scientist here in London who stole the formula and murdered the inventor. Desmond has met him and, as we said, he's been shown that the experiment works."

"Yeah. All well and good, but Des says all he saw was a flash when some liquid hit a hot plate. It's not much for billions of dollars. You guys could have used regular gasoline for all we know."

"No, no. The mixture was made from water in our laboratory. The flash is the only way to show it'll ignite. I'm not technical but in a normal engine, fuel gets injected into a cylinder then there's a spark that is hot and ignites the fuel. Just like our experiment."

"How do you know it'll work in the real world? It's only got a value if it can be produced commercially and then only by Olympic Oil, and they don't want to produce it. Your scheme seems a bit weak."

"Look, James, we know it works, and according to the inventor's notes it can be scaled up in next to no time. We know if that happened then the oil nations would go bankrupt. If you guys bought it, we know Olympic Oil would control the supply, but somebody could get their hands on the formula and soon every petro plant in the world would be producing it. Nobody wins. But if the oil countries see it as a threat, and believe me right now they do, then they'll pay handsomely to have the formula destroyed."

"I hear you, but it's only a piece of paper. I'd be happy to see something else."

"James — we've got the world's oil nations arriving here within the week. They aren't coming for a winter break in darkest Kent; they're taking it seriously. If we could fund it ourselves then we would but we can't. We have to pay Anderson in New York but only from the deposit agreed with Desmond. We're not greedy and only want a reasonable cut. We'll let you guys make the big money."

James Rushdie sat back and placed his empty brandy goblet on the table. He was deep in thought and stared at Desmond, who had sat quietly throughout the recent exchange. James stood up from the table and picked up the telephone in the corner of the room. He spoke quietly but firmly and returned to the table. No one spoke.

A well-dressed man entered the room without knocking. James remained seated but pointed to the brothers and made the introductions. "This is Alistair Ramsay. He works for me and looks after this place." Without pausing, James carried on. "Alistair, would you take our guests downstairs? Introduce them to the delights of the lounge for half an hour. Des and I need to discuss a few things."

The brothers were dismissed and followed Alistair out.

The two business colleagues heaved huge sighs. "Well…" Desmond spoke first. "What do you think? You always tell me you're smarter." This was said with a slight smile.

"I don't trust them, but they do have a plan. There might be something in this for us, but the deal will have to be structured our way."

"What do you mean?"

"Well, first off, they can't pay New York. Gregory Anderson isn't known for his goodwill. These two are in a heap of trouble and only we can get them out of it, but at a price."

James loved scheming. "All they have is the formula and this murdering scientist. Anderson was a mug to let the thing go on a promise but that works for us. So first, we agree to take care of New York."

"I'm listening."

"Second, they've got the formula. We need to get our hands on it. Short of stealing it we'll have to sweeten the pot. Say we give them ten million as a deposit? I'm pretty sure these two are starving and trying to play with the big boys to get a one-off payday. Agreed? We do five million each."

"If they go for it, then, yeah, I'm in."

"Third…" James held up his fingers. "We help them set up the meet with these oil guys. There'll be no auction. Once these people get together and we explain the reality that they could be bankrupt in say five to ten years, I'm pretty sure they'll collectively put up and pay us to destroy it. I've no idea how much we'll get, but it'll be a hell of a lot more than the ten million we're giving these two shmucks."

"What about New York? He's going to want his money."

"Leave Gregory Anderson to me. I've got something on him. He'll settle for ten million after we've sold it."

"What about the brothers after we've sold it?"

"We'll tell them we've saved their lives by paying off New York. We'll give them another ten million after the sale, that's it. What do you think?"

"I think it's a better plan than mine if the two will buy it."

"Oh, I think they will. We need to get this murdering scientist locked away to make sure he doesn't do a runner. We'll need him for the big meeting, and I want to see a demonstration."

"Fine by me, let's get it agreed."

Alistair Ramsay brought the brothers back to the Lagoon Room. It was clear they'd both enjoyed the delights of the lounge and both had applied for membership. Alistair remained in the room and took a chair at the table when all those present sat down.

James Rushdie sat opposite Julian. Once again, Julian was afraid. This man had an air of violence surrounding him. Julian felt like one word out of place and James would reach over the table and strangle him. All of a sudden there was a weird and frightening atmosphere in the room.

James opened the debate. "Des and I have come up with our own plan. You see, I think you two are smelling the main chance, but you need our money to take advantage of it. So here's what we're going to do." He held up his hand and counted on his fingers.

"One — we'll take care of Gregory Anderson in New York. That's a hundred million dollars, according to you. Gregory's not a man to cross, and I sense he's a bit fed up with you two just now. If you don't pay him, you're dead. I think you know that, so there's our first contribution. As of now, you're off the hook with New York and can sleep safely in your beds, or whichever of our hostesses' beds you finish up in."

Julian was about to speak but James cut him off with a simple look and carried on. "That means we own the formula, so when you leave here, Alistair will go with you and collect it."

"Second…" Another finger was raised. "We'll pay you ten million dollars within twenty-four hours to reward you for your work in putting this thing together."

Julian jumped in. "No, no! We've worked on this and have already spent millions!" he lied. "Ten million dollars is not nearly enough. The formula's worth billions."

"You haven't heard me out. Don't interrupt again." The violence and evil were back. "If you don't take our generous offer, you'll certainly be dead by tomorrow night and you know it, so listen!" Julian listened.

"Third…" Another finger appeared. "You get ten million and you carry on with the meeting, except it won't be an auction. We'll take collective bids from all the delegates but only to destroy the formula. Whatever we get, we get. You'll get another ten million for your troubles." James sat back and stared Julian down. He couldn't maintain eye contact.

"There you have it. You'll be twenty million up, you'll be clear of New York, and you can become members here and spend some of your dollars on the ladies and some of my white powder.

Just one other thing — your scientist. I want a demonstration and I want him in a secure location. We'll need him at the meeting just to show our oil friends that it works." James Rushdie was finished. He'd taken away their dream.

Just as they were leaving, he added: "Alistair, make sure you get everything, any copies and notes. After all, we wouldn't like to have to come looking for the brothers if we found out they hadn't been honest with us."

Alistair Ramsay looked smug as he showed the crestfallen brothers out. "Gentlemen, I have a car waiting if you'd follow me?"

The meeting was over. Julian and Sebastian's dreams of billions were shattered. They'd have to console themselves that their lives were safe, and they had a twenty-million-dollar payday. The bonus was membership of an exclusive knocking shop.

Frankie was waiting in the hallway, having been paged by a hostess five minutes earlier. The coat check girl held a box containing his Glock. As the brothers and Alistair Ramsay approached, she handed the box to Frankie. "The bullets have been removed and the magazine is out."

Frankie followed his dejected bosses out.

Chapter Eighteen

Steve and The Cap returned to find the office awash with excitement. Barry was present, as was Sam Burns. Together with Andy, all three were grouped around a desk in the outer office.

Andy was excited, bubbling with enthusiasm. "Boss, I think we've got him!"

Steve looked at Barry, who nodded his head in confirmation.

"Right, who's going to explain?"

As the senior of the three, Barry took the lead. "It's all down to you, Steve. You said to get Barbara James' effects but to look for an advert or something with an address. Remember, we were getting all the newspaper adverts to see if there was some exotic job advertised that these girls would never normally dream of applying for."

Steve nodded.

"Well, you were right. Even before we started looking through the newspapers, we found an advert that'd been cut out of a local rag. It was stuck in the lining of her handbag." Barry lifted a piece of newsprint from the table. It was now in a clear plastic evidence bag. He handed it to Steve.

Andy couldn't contain himself. He had to speak. "It's asking girls between twenty-one and thirty-five to apply for vacancies as flight attendants. See, it says 'no experience necessary', just 'average size and weight and must be good socially'."

"Yes, I see that, Andy."

"But look further down, the phone number. It's a Hackney exchange number. I've traced it and it's registered to a Richard Bale. He lives at 45 Bracewell Avenue, Hackney. And guess what, it's a detached house with a garage, and he fits Sam's profile — age, no job, everything."

"You're sure about this?" Steve was addressing Barry.

"It's all there, Steve. Why don't we pick him up?"

Steve looked at his watch. It was 9.23. He had to be at St Thomas's for ten o'clock. "Right, Cap, in at the deep end." Steve introduced DI Ishmal as The Cap to Barry. "Grab a couple of uniforms and you go and interview this Richard Bale. Andy will fill you in before you go and give you the file. Barry and I have to be somewhere else now but a simple lift for questioning, shouldn't be a problem if you sense he's our man."

"No problem, Steve." The Cap was back.

Steve turned to Andy and Samantha Burns. "Just in case this isn't our man, I want you to get on with the newspaper ads. I can see there's a pile on the other desk."

"Yes, they were delivered by a guy from the press office." Andy smiled. "He wasn't very happy. He said they weighed a ton."

"Sam will help you. Also, can you chase up Inspector Harvey in Tech Support? See how he's doing with the programme."

Steve turned to Barry. The atmosphere in the office was electric. "Have you arranged for a team to search that lake in Beecham Park for the wheelchair?"

"First thing. They know it's evidence and has to go straight to Forensics. When we're done, I'm going over there to make sure, just like you said."

"Good, I think that's everything. Cap, if you bring this bloke in, I'll be back around noon to help with the interview. If anybody needs me for anything, I'll be on the mobile. Right, Barry, let's go."

Both detectives left to start the investigation into a body washed up by Tower Bridge, a body that someone in authority knew all about but hadn't told CID.

On the drive to St Thomas's, Steve briefed Barry on the case. He was careful not to alert his sergeant to the political nature of the enquiry, preferring that it be treated like any other murder enquiry. "There's been a bit of politics from the twelfth floor so I've asked Andy to keep the file ultra-confidential, and once our notes are recorded, we should destroy them. I don't want any paper lying around on this one, just in case. Is that clear, Barry?"

"Sure, Steve, but it's a bit cloak-and-dagger."

"Yeah, well, that's how the commander wants it. With any luck we'll have it cracked before anything comes back to bite us. Hackney's still our priority. I hope The Cap's interviewing the right man but somehow it's all a bit too easy."

"Well, no one can say we haven't pulled out all the stops. We've got the computer programme and the newspaper ads. We've got the profile from Samantha. We know how he moved the first body and with luck we'll get something off the wheelchair, so I'm hoping we're done and Inspector Ishmal has our man. Oh! And if that's not enough, Andy got a load of financial stuff about The Fortress Club this morning. He was asking if you want him to get a court order for the membership list?"

Barry drove into the hospital car park and parked in a reserved space. He left a cardboard notice saying 'Police on Duty' on the dashboard. As the detectives walked towards the main building, Steve replied: "We've got enough on so we'll leave it just now and pick it up again once we're a bit clearer."

They arrived outside the mortuary of St Thomas's hospital at exactly09.56. They rang the bell and the double rubber doors swung open to reveal a semi-sterile changing area. A young girl dressed in green hospital scrubs and oversized white rubber boots entered from the far side of the room. As soon as the detectives were in the room, the double rubber doors closed behind them.

"You must be DCI Burt?"

"Yes, and this is DS Gibson."

"Professor Campbell is expecting you. If you wouldn't mind gowning up and putting on these plastic overshoes and the hated head covering, I'll take you through."

They did as instructed. Steve looked at this girl, who seemed very efficient and had a ready smile. She wasn't tall, and in her hospital gear it was difficult to see her shape, but at first glance she was a bit plain.

Once the two detectives were suited up, she said: "Please follow me, gentlemen. Once we go through, there are face masks by the door. Please put one on."

They entered the world of dead bodies and peculiar smells, not all of them pleasant. Professor Sir Humphrey Campbell was already cutting into a body on a steel table. He looked up as the three figures approached him. Steve was aware that Sir Humphrey was the leading Home Office pathologist. He had carried out thousands of post-mortems and given evidence for the prosecution in dozens of murder cases.

Steve took a few seconds to ponder this conundrum. The professor was very eminent in his field so why was he here, cutting into an unknown body that perhaps wasn't so unknown.

"Gentlemen, you're just in time, splendid." Sir Humphrey was a large man, probably over six feet, two inches tall, and weighing at least two hundred and fifty pounds. He had the loud, commanding voice of someone at the top of their profession who was used to being obeyed.

"Now the first thing you'll want to know is 'how did this poor fellow die?' Am I not correct?" The atmosphere within the theatre was light-hearted.

"That would be useful, sir."

"Just so! You know he was fished out of the Thames so you might think he drowned." The pathologist was enjoying himself. "Well, you'd be wrong. Come over here."

The detectives moved forward and rounded the table to look at what Sir Humphrey was pointing at.

"You see, that's a bullet hole. Even a first-year medical student might think a bullet between the eyes was enough to kill someone, and you know..." The professor gave a huge belly laugh. "They'd be spot on." Professor Campbell became serious. "You see the stippling around the wound? That's a powder burn. This poor fellow was shot up close and personal. It's a .22 round, and see here..." He again pointed directly to the wound. "You can see the bullet, so it didn't enter the brain very far. What does that tell us, gentlemen?"

Both Steve and Barry just looked on.

"Nothing to say. Well, given the close range and the fact that the bullet didn't enter far into the skull tells us that the killer didn't use a powerful handgun. Any decent weapon even firing .22 rounds would have pushed the round deeper inside the skull, so I can tell you you're looking for a small .22 pistol."

Without waiting for comments, the professor turned to the girl who had escorted the two detectives in. "Mary, my dear, can you hand me the long forceps? I think I can get this round out without cutting into the skull."

143

After a few minutes in which Steve thought the professor looked like a dentist extracting a tooth, Sir Humphrey stood to his full height, and with a flourish he held the bullet between the two arms of his forceps.

"There, just as I thought. It's a .22 but your Ballistics people will have to verify it."

He looked around again. "Mary, a specimen jar if you please." He dropped the piece of metal into a glass jar with a screw top lid. "Please mark it up." He handed the jar to the girl.

"Now we need to delve deeper into this poor soul. Mary, can you wheel over the full PM kit? Our cadaver looks healthy enough, but once I start rooting around his insides you never know what I'll find."

The two detectives spent the next hour watching Sir Humphrey skilfully dissect their victim. Mary was always on hand with the correct instrument or specimen container. She took whole organs from the pathologist to weigh them and she took pieces of organs and cut into them at a separate bench, all while Sir Humphrey dictated into an overhead microphone.

"There we are then, all done. Your man was mid-fifties, healthy except for an inflamed prostate, and well-nourished with good bone density and muscle development. I can tell by his hands that he wasn't a manual worker and he had not been very sexually active throughout his life. That's all I can tell you. I'll put it in my report."

Steve needed fresh air and Barry was late for his appointment with the search team at Hackney. "Barry, you'd better push off. We've done our duty to satisfy the coroner."

"Thanks, Steve. Can I keep the car?"

"Yes, I'll get back to the Yard by myself."

Barry was relieved to be out of the mortuary and leaving Sir Humphrey's world behind.

It suited Steve to be alone with the professor and his assistant. "Do we have his effects? Clothes and so on?"

"Yes, and that's interesting. I think your corpse is American." Sir Humphrey walked to another table having removed his surgical gown, mask and gloves and deposited them in a sanitised bin.

"Look here, the label in his jacket says 'Macy's'. His shirt is from Saks and his shoes are not a brand I've come across."

"What about his pockets?"

"Mary has everything in neat bags for you. She'll bag up the clothes and get them to your exhibits officer. You can take the stuff from his pockets."

"Thank you, sir. You've been very helpful. I know I don't have to ask but will we get his fingerprints this morning?"

"Already done. Mary's forwarded them to your fingerprint unit for comparison. If they get anything you should know within the next few hours."

"Once again, thank you, sir."

"Not at all, it's a pleasure." Neither man shook hands, which was a relief for Steve given where he had seen the professor put his. Steve was heading for the exit but stopped and turned.

"Sir Humphrey, can I ask you who asked you to do this post-mortem?"

Without thinking, the pathologist answered. "It was Sir Tim Head. He's the head of the civil service and an old friend of mine. I suppose thinking about it it's a bit unusual, but not unknown for one friend to help another. Why do you ask?"

"Oh, no reason, just a policeman's curiosity. You don't have a name for our corpse?"

"What a very funny question. No, I have no idea who he is, other than what I have discussed with you. If Sir Timothy knows who he is, he didn't tell me."

"Again, thank you, sir." Steve left, placing his plastic overalls in a marked bin.

***

Steve had just exited the main hospital entrance when his phone rang. It was The Cap. "Sorry, Steve, but the guy from the adverts isn't our man. Turns out it's legit. They only reply to the advert by phone to his house, but he interviews the girls at an employment exchange. It depends how many he gets from one area. The interviews from the advert our victim answered were held out in Putney."

"And you're sure he's clean?"

"Yeah. He's a bit of a con artist. It seems he gets girls with ambition and arranges loans for them to attend his training courses. He pockets the money, and the girls are left with the debt. He says he gets them jobs with the big airlines, but I doubt it. Anyway, I'll check his alibi, but he says he was teaching his classes on the dates of the murders. Oh, and he doesn't have a van!"

"Fair enough, Cap, check him out, but it seems it's a dead end. Can you get back to the office? I'll be there in about thirty minutes."

As Steve walked to the Yard, he called Alison Mills. Her phone went to answer phone so she must have been busy. He left a brief message reminding her that he was still remembering their dinner date, and that he'd do everything he could to make it.

When Steve walked into his office, he found everyone seated and eating sandwiches. "It's lunch, boss. We thought we would have a quick snack before we crack on." Andy had his mouth full.

"Very sensible, Andy, but let's have a review of Hackney. Barry, did they find the wheelchair?"

"Sure did, just like you said. Forensics have it. I've told them it's top priority. They said they'd get anything they find to us later today."

"Good. Have you had a chance to go through the adverts?" Realising his boss was back, Andy accepted that his lunch break was now up. It was back to business.

Andy stood and went to the map that was still stuck to the wall with brown tape. "We started going through the ads as you said. We took the first victim's address in Peckham and sorted out the local and free press papers that covered the area. We then looked at the two weeks before the killing, so from mid-October. There are a lot of adverts and it took most of the morning." Andy looked in the direction of Samantha Burns. "Sam's been a great help. Anyway, we finished looking at all the ads, but nothing jumped out. So we went back to the beginning of October, and again nothing. Sorry, Steve. That's as far as we got when we thought we'd have a break."

"There was nothing?"

"No, but we've got the main London papers to look through. That's our next job."

Steve was disappointed but knew his team had done their best. Somehow, he was convinced that the solution was in the adverts in these papers. "OK, carry on with that. Concentrate on the first murder. Everything started there."

Sam and Andy left to take up their positions at a desk in the outer office covered with old newspapers. Andy opened his computer and feverishly typed. After a few minutes, he called out. "Steve — can you come here a minute, please?"

Andy was typing away and grinning.

"I realised that the main London papers are online and have an archive. The small local and free papers usually aren't so sophisticated. I've called up the issues two weeks before the murder and bingo, look!" Andy pointed to the screen. Steve had to bend down and look over his constable's shoulder. The Cap and Barry crowded round.

Andy was pointing to an advertisement asking for young, unattached ladies between twenty-five and thirty-five who were interested in working in films to contact a telephone number. It said that no experience was necessary but that they must be prepared to relocate to Hollywood.

"What date was that published?"

"Ten days before the first murder. I recognise the…"

The office phone was ringing. The Cap picked it up and listened. A great grin filled his face. "Thank you, I'll tell him." He carefully replaced the receiver while the assembled audience stared at him in expectation.

"That was DI Harvey of Tech Support. He's ready for us."

The atmosphere was once again electric, but Steve had to maintain the workflow and not just drop everything. "Great." Everyone was smiling and feeling almost light-headed.

"Barry, you and The Cap go over there. If Andy's right, we should get a list of names and addresses fitting Samantha's profile, plus they should drive a Renault van. I'll be over as soon as Andy's done his stuff. Sam, maybe you'd better go as well. You know as much of what we're trying to do as anybody."

The two detectives and the civilian profiler left in a hurry and with much anticipation.

Steve sat beside Andy. "Right, Andy, where were we?"

"Well, I've found this advert in the *Standard*. It was placed only once, ten days before the first murder. I've run a day before and a day after and it's not there, and it's definitely a Hackney exchange number."

"Let's not get ahead of ourselves. Look up the 2nd November, that's ten days before the second murder."

Andy began typing and after a few minutes looked up in triumph. "The same advert, but it was run on the 3rd November. The second murder was on the 2nd, so if this is our guy, he has murdered on the 2nd and was fishing for his next victim the day after."

"Keep your fingers crossed, Andy. Try the 13th November?"

After what seemed an hour to Steve, Andy looked up. There's an advert on the 17th November. The same one but quite a few days later than we thought."

"Never mind. Check out the phone number. Let's get an address for that phone." Andy set to work both on his laptop and on the phone. Steve was impressed by Andy's multi-tasking skills.

While Andy was checking the phone number, Steve went to his desk and took out the effects of the man in the Thames. His mind was in three places and he found it difficult to concentrate. First Andy, second the computer programme now running, and third this new case. He forced himself to concentrate. He emptied the contents of the plastic bags onto his desk. He spread out the assorted rubbish that everyone seems to accumulate in their pockets. The first thing that struck Steve was that there was no wallet, no watch and no other form of identity. Whoever had killed this man had tried to conceal his identity. Using the tip of a pen, Steve started to sift through the items on his desk. He flicked through the water damaged tickets for the London Eye and the Tower of London, together with odd London Underground tickets. None of this helped. There were various other papers too damaged to read but there was a plastic card with the address of The Mayflower Hotel.

"Bingo!" Whoever had tried to conceal the identity of the victim, they'd missed this card. Steve realised that as the John Doe was staying at the Mayflower, someone must know him, and this was a room key card, so maybe he was still registered?

Steve packed the items back into the plastic bags but kept the electronic room key for the Mayflower Hotel. This he put into a separate, smaller bag. He kept the key and locked the other plastic bags in a drawer in his desk. He'd move them later.

Steve was living with an adrenaline rush after his discovery of the room key card, but his mind was on what was going on with the Hackney cases. He went into the outer office to find Andy finishing a phone call. He seemed very pleased with himself.

"The phone line is registered to 63 Minton Mews and was paid for by a Mrs Ryder, but get this, Mrs Ryder is now deceased, and her son Neil Ryder took over the account six weeks ago." Andy had a thought. "Hold on, Steve, let me check something else." Andy was back typing furiously. After a few minutes of impressive multi-figure keyboard work, he stopped, looked at Steve, pumped the air with his fist and yelled "YES!"

"Our Mr Ryder owns a grey Renault Kangoo van."

Steve sat beside Andy. Neither man spoke but each looked smug. In a low voice, Steve said: "We've got him." In a louder, more animated show of emotion, he repeated, "We've bloody well got him!"

Andy was sitting quietly, trying to understand his emotions. He was close to tears.

Steve was the professional and senior officer. "Let's you and I go see what Inspector Harvey has. It was your brainchild so you should be there to see the results." With a mischievous glint in his eyes, Steve told Andy: "Let's keep this to ourselves until we see the computer printouts."

Steve and Andy arrived at the offices of Technical Support just as Inspector Harvey was ripping a large piece of computer stationery from an oversized printer. "Ah, DCI Burt, you're just in time. We've only just completed our run, and we now have your list of potential suspects."

Everyone crowded around a large, plain table while the inspector laid out the printout. He read from the summary box at the foot of the almost four-foot-long paper. "It seems we have twenty-seven matches from your original profile. All with at least one recently departed parent and all living within your area in houses with garages. Your profile was helpful, if it's correct, in as much as we added 'unemployed' to the criteria." Inspector Harvey looked at Samantha, who smiled sweetly back.

"It gets more interesting when we add the van. Only seven people have a Kangoo van but a further five have a van of some sort. So, there you have it. It was a mountain of work, but we did it. You have twenty-seven suspects by name, address and age. This goes down to twelve with vans, and then seven if you're right about the Renault van. All in all, folks, I'm pretty proud of my lads. This has been twenty hours of non-stop work. I hope your man's there after all that."

Steve admitted that Inspector Harvey and the three technicians present looked to be out on their feet.

"Cap, can you take the seven names first?"

The Cap separated the sheet with the seven names by tearing it along a pre-perforated tear line.

"Everybody's done remarkably well, so congratulations and thanks."

"Andy, would you like to ask The Cap to confirm a name on his list?"

Andy had a wicked sparkle in his eyes that everyone around the table noticed. His body language told of something special as he produced a piece of folded paper with a flourish. "Inspector Ishmal, is the name Neil Ryder, of 63 Minton Mews, on the list?"

The Cap examined the names and as he looked up his jaw dropped. "How the hell did you get that?"

Steve took command. "Never mind. We've got two separate confirmations that this is our man. Let's get back to the office." He turned to The Cap. "Can you bring all of this with you?" He pointed to the reams of printout paper.

"Yes, no problem. Can I just say that that was impressive, I'm glad I'm back?"

"So am I." Steve patted Abul on the back.

Chapter Nineteen

Once everyone was seated, Steve stood by the whiteboard with a marker pen in hand. "I'd like to thank Sam for her input. I'm sure without her profile we couldn't have achieved what we think we have." Steve looked directly at Samantha Burns. "Sam, I asked you to stay and help, and I'm sure Andy has benefited from your assistance. Unfortunately, I'll have to say goodbye with our thanks. I'll make sure your bill is paid but now we're moving on to operational police matters and I can't have a civilian present."

Sam stood up and shyly looked at Andy. "I understand, sir. It's been a pleasure, and if you ever need a profiler then remember me." With an obvious tear in her eye, she left the office without looking back.

All four detectives sat around Steve's desk. "First, we're only part way there. We think we've got him but without firm evidence the CPS won't entertain a charge." The DCI was firmly in charge. "So now we need evidence. First, we need to bring him in on suspicion. Cap, that's up to you. With any luck we'll get a confession, but somehow, I doubt we'll get that lucky. And remember, by the book, OK?" Steve looked directly at his detective inspector.

"Yes, sir, understood."

"Right. It's just coming up to three o'clock. I want this done and dusted before six o'clock tonight." Steve was too professional to let his date with Alison Mills interfere with his decisions, but he conceded that it would be nice to get a result, and then enjoy his evening.

"I want this coordinated properly. Cap, like I said, you'll take the lead. Get a search warrant for the house, garage, garden and van."

"Will do."

"Barry, get on to Forensics and the Search Unit. I want them both available as we go in."

"Got it."

"It'll take, say, ninety minutes to get the search warrant, and, say, two hours to get forensics and search lined up, including travel time. I make it we go in at five o'clock. Any questions?"

"Where do we rendezvous?" The Cap was now in charge.

"Andy, from your map, where should the squads meet up, do you think?"

Andy stood and studied his wall map. "If they want to be out of sight, I'd say the corner of Milton Mews and Blackwood Road. Blackwood Road's a dead end so there should be no parking problems."

"Good. So that's it — Milton Mews and Blackwood Road."

"Where do I take him? Here or the local nick?"

"Good point, Cap. We've got room here, and better facilities, so let's bring him here."

"Anything else?" Steve waited but silence descended. "Right, Cap, you're in command. You and Barry round up the teams and get a few local uniforms to help out. Barry — give Hackney nick a buzz. Tell them what's going down and to have, say, four uniforms at the RV point at four thirty. We don't think he's likely to be armed but be careful. Don't take any chances. I've got something else I have to do so if I'm not at the RV on time, go in anyway. All clear?"

There were nods all round.

"If I don't make it to Hackney, I'll be back here by six o'clock. Cap, you should have this Ryder character in an interview room by then, so I'll join you. Barry, you'll be senior man at the site. Remember, we think it's a crime scene, so make sure everyone knows the drill."

Barry nodded his understanding and was keen to get on with it, as was The Cap.

Steve looked at his two detectives. He could see that they were impatient to get on with it and his schoolteacher lecture, although necessary, wasn't what they wanted. "It's what we've been working for, so let's go catch a killer."

Both The Cap, and Barry were fully fired up. Now full of purpose, they almost ran from the office.

Steve noted that Andy was quiet and had a dejected look on his face.

"What's up, Andy? Sorry that Sam's gone?" Steve tried a light-hearted approach with his office administrator.

152

"No, nothing like that, although we have been on a few dates." Andy was blushing again.

"Andy, I'm a detective. I'd worked out you liked her, so good on you. She's a nice girl but what's bothering you?"

"Well, it's just that I'd hoped to be in on the arrest, not sitting here."

Steve should have seen this coming. "Andy, the job you do here is more important than putting handcuffs on bad guys. If we don't keep records, and if you hadn't analysed the data, and incidentally brilliantly deduced the postcode areas, we'd be nowhere near catching this guy."

Andy looked embarrassed and was blushing again. "Thank you, Steve. It's only just once I'd like to be there."

"Here's a deal — on our next bust you'll come with us. How's that?"

Andy smiled. "I'll hold you to that. Now I know you've got something for me to do."

Steve was relieved that his prime asset was back on board. He went into his office and returned with the exhibits bags containing the John Doe's effects.

"We're back on our second case now, Andy. By the way, has the post-mortem report come in?"

"Yes, it was here by lunchtime. I've got it in my drawer, and I made sure nobody got a look at it."

Steve nodded a 'well done'.

"I want you to load the findings onto your laptop and scan the pictures. Let me have the pictures now, and once you're finished, shred the lot, remember. No paper."

Andy retrieved the file and extracted the post-mortem photographs. Steve quickly looked through them and picked out the facial shots. "I'll need these now, so I'll give them to you to scan later. Meantime, you can scan the rest of the pics." He handed the remaining photographs back to Andy.

"Steve, are you sure about shredding these files? It's not normal."

"Yes, I know, but provided you've got everything on your laptop and there'll be a copy somewhere in the system, we won't have lost any information."

Andy just nodded. "Now, Andy, I've had a look through the effects of our John Doe. I want to record my statements on the file. Remember, verbal statements only, so I hope your memory's up to it."

The DCI looked at Andy and smiled. Andy shrugged back with a smile. "We'll soon find out."

"Our victim is almost certainly American from his clothes. You'll see from the PM report he was shot at close range by a small .22 pistol. Everything else is in the PM report. In his effects I've found what I believe to be a room key from the Mayflower Hotel." Steve produced the piece of white plastic, still in the small forensic evidence bag, from his jacket pocket. I'm going there now to see what's what." He paused to consider if he needed to add any more to his statement.

"That's it for now. Have you got that?"

"Yes, that's not going to overload my memory banks." Andy was fascinated by what was going on.

"Now, I want you to sift through and record what's in these bags of effects. I know it's a bugger of a job but it's necessary. When you've done that, get them down to the evidence room but give the reference as something unrelated to our case."

"Got it. Do you think you'll ever be able to tell me what's going on?"

Steve stood and gathered up the facial photographs. "Yes, but I might have to shoot you." Both men laughed.

As Steve was leaving, he turned to Andy. "Oh, Andy, can you get the fingerprint boys on to our victim's prints. See if he's in the system — you never know."

Andy was now alone. He had enough to get on with and would do as his DCI had ordered but he allowed himself a few moments to daydream about the day when he would be DCI Andy Miller.

***

DCI Steve Burt entered the vast foyer of the Mayflower Hotel. He went straight to the reception desk and asked to speak to the general manager while showing his warrant card. He was asked to wait, and it was suggested that he take a seat in the lounge area of the foyer — the general manager would be down shortly.

Steve knew not to rush things and, although he needed to be in Hackney, this case was important. Besides, The Cap and Barry could handle things if he didn't make it.

While he was waiting, he decided to call Alison Mills. With his phone to his ear, he scanned his fellow citizens enjoying a peaceful break in their armchairs within this luxurious hotel. His call went to voicemail. He left a short message saying that it was looking good for their date later and that he would call again.

As he put his phone away, he continued to look around, and then he spotted a face he knew. This was another occasion when he knew something but it remained firmly locked at the back of his brain. He knew the face but couldn't place it.

The DCI was sitting trying to solve his problem when a small, very dapper man dressed in pinstripe trousers, a grey waistcoat and a morning jacket entered his field of vision. Steve instantly knew this was the general manager of the Mayflower Hotel.

Steve pre-empted the meeting and stood before this man arrived. Both men met a few feet from the chair Steve had been occupying. The newcomer held out his hand and in a low voice said: "I take it you're Mr Burt? I'm Guy North, General Manager. I understand you need to talk to me."

"Yes, sir, nothing serious. I'm trying to identify someone I think may have been a guest recently in the hotel."

"You'd better come to my office. It's more private and we can get you all the information you need." Guy North ushered Steve away from the seating area and guided him to a door behind the reception area.

Mr North offered coffee and biscuits and Steve accepted. He suddenly realised he hadn't eaten all day. The general manager sat behind a grand desk on which stood a computer terminal, a printer, a phone and a desk lamp. It looked very empty, as though Guy North was either very efficient or didn't have a lot to do. Steve reserved judgement, but based on first impressions, he thought this five feet, seven inch tall man, who weighed no more than a hundred and fifty pounds, was probably very efficient. His full head of black hair was neatly trimmed, as was his small, thin moustache.

"Now, how can I help you?"

"A body has been recovered from the Thames." Steve produced what he thought was a room key from this hotel. "We found this on him. We believe it's a room key for this hotel. As you can see, it has your name and address printed on it. I'd be interested to learn which of your guests was last in that room."

"Mm, I see. May I see the card?"

Steve handed the plastic card inside the evidence bag over. "Please don't remove it from the bag, sir."

"Well, it's certainly one of our room keys. Just a moment." The general manager lifted his phone and asked for someone to come to his office.

While they waited, Steve produced the photographs of the head taken at the autopsy. "These are not very pleasant, sir, but do you think any of your staff might recognise our victim?"

Guy North took the photographs and pulled a face as he looked at the coloured pictures. "Oh my, this is terrible." He looked as though he might be sick.

A knock on the door brought Guy North back from the brink of nausea. "Come in."

A woman of about forty entered, dressed in the hotel uniform for front of house staff. "This is Mrs Williamson. She's our manager for front of house."

Steve stood and shook hands and Mrs Williamson took a chair next to Steve in front of the general manager's desk. Guy North invited Steve to repeat what he'd been told and show her the photographs.

Mrs Williamson looked shocked but quickly regained her composure. "It's certainly our key. I can scan it and tell you the room number, but I think I recognise the person in the pictures."

This was music to Steve's ears. "Go on, please, Mrs Williamson."

Mrs Williamson bravely took a second look at the face of the John Doe. In a gentle but cultured voice, she said: "I can't be one hundred per cent sure, but I think it's Dr Graham. He's an American gentleman. From memory, he was checked in by an outside party for two nights, but he

156

extended it by another four nights. As far as I know, he's still checked in. He's due to leave tomorrow."

Guy North spoke up. "Thank you, Mrs Williamson." He handed her the key he'd received from Steve.

Steve interrupted. "I'm sorry, sir, that's evidence. If Mrs Williamson takes the key from this office, I'll have to accompany her. We have something called 'chain of evidence'. I can't let that key out of my sight."

"Ah! I see. I was simply going to ask Mrs Williamson to scan the key to confirm the room number. But we can all go outside and have the key scanned in your presence."

The party of three exited to the reception desk, where Mrs Williamson confirmed the key was for Room 1202 and it was indeed still occupied by Dr David Graham.

"Tell me, Mrs Williamson, when overseas visitors check in, do you take extra details from them that a UK resident wouldn't give?"

"Yes. We ask for details of their home address and country, plus we scan their passport."

Steve couldn't believe his luck. "Can I have a copy of the record for this Dr Graham? And I'd also like to see his room."

Guy North became a bit prickly. "Well, our client's information is confidential, and showing a stranger, even a policeman, a guest's room without their permission is highly irregular."

This was something Steve had heard before. "Excuse me, sir, I think you are missing the point. In all likelihood, we fished your guest out of the Thames yesterday. This is a murder enquiry, and the niceties of customer confidentiality don't apply. We usually find honest citizens are keen to assist us without asking us to crawl through yards of red tape." Steve noted that Mrs Williamson was trying to smother a giggle. Clearly Guy North was a bit of a stuffed shirt.

"Of course, Inspector, we'll help in any way we can. It's just that this is an unusual situation for us. Can I ask you to keep the name of the hotel secret? Murdered guests won't encourage our repeat patrons."

"I can't promise but with this case it may be possible. Now can I have the records and see the room?"

"Mrs Williamson, will you please make up a file of Dr Graham's information and have it ready for when he leaves? I'll show the inspector the room. Can you please give me a pass key?"

Everything was friendly and polite. Guy North showed Steve into the lift and they zoomed to the twelfth floor and Room 1202.

The general manager used his pass key and they entered the room that had been used by Dr Graham. It was neat and tidy and had obviously been cleaned recently. It was a typical upmarket hotel room featuring a king-size bed with cupboards either side of the padded headboard; a large, wall-mounted plasma television; a writing desk; and a free-standing cupboard that Steve assumed contained the minibar. Two small chairs stood in the window recess. Steve noted a door to what must be the en suite bathroom and a bank of sliding doors behind which must be wardrobe storage.

"This is one of our finer rooms. It's on the twelfth floor in order to give views…" Steve interrupted the sales brochure speech.

"Thank you, Mr North. I'd like you to leave now. I'll close the door when I'm finished. In the meantime, as well as our victim's details I'd like to take copies of your CCTV discs from every camera — both inside and out — from the time Dr Graham checked in. I believe that would be Monday 27th November, if your Mrs Williamson is correct about the days booked." Steve was waiting for a response but quickly added: "And I'll need details of whoever made the original two-night booking, including credit card."

"Very well, Inspector. Please call in on me as you leave." With that Guy North left, closing the door to Room 1202 behind him.

Steve sat in one of the window chairs. He thought about what he was doing here. It was against all known police procedure for a senior investigating officer to carry out any search without either another colleague or a search team. Still, this wasn't an ordinary case, so it called for the 'procedures manual' to be forgotten.

The DCI learnt nothing by surveying the room so he got up and started opening drawers, looking under the bed and generally exploring every corner of the room. He found nothing. He moved towards the bathroom and the wardrobes. Dr Graham had travelled light. Apart from a jacket, there were only two shirts and some underwear.

Steve mulled this over, looking for what it meant. After a few brain-churning minutes, he gave up, but the face of the man in the foyer came back to him. Again, the information wouldn't come but deep down he felt it was important.

He went into the bathroom. There was a bath with a shower over it. The walls were tiled and a bathroom cabinet was fixed to the wall above the sink. Examination of the cabinet yielded little that was obviously helpful. Steve went back into the bedroom and put everything into a large evidence bag.

He returned to his seat by the window and decided to call Andy.

"Andy, it's me. Any news from Hackney?"

"Not yet, they'll only be assembling. We got the search warrant and the search team's on standby. They don't want to hang about, but their DS said that if it's worth their while they'll be on site within fifteen minutes of getting the call. Forensics had a team on standby, so they're on their way."

"Good. Andy, I need you to do something for me. Our victim is a Dr David Graham, an American. He checked in at the Mayflower on Monday 27th November. I'm thinking he probably arrived the day he checked in, so get on to Immigration. Let's get his entry details and see if we can get CCTV of all arriving passengers from flights from the USA as they exit onto landside. We might see him coming in."

"Right. What are you doing?"

"I've got a bag of effects for you to look through and I've to collect some information from the general manager of the hotel. It sounds as though things are pretty much under control at Hackney, so I'll come back to the office. I should be there just before five. The Cap should be back around five thirty with our suspect, if all goes to plan."

Steve hung up and immediately called The Cap. The detective inspector answered on the first ring. "Hi, Steve. I wondered how long you'd take to check up on us." The Cap wasn't serious and Steve knew it.

"Just checking in. What's going on?"

"We're all set. Just waiting for the uniforms from Hackney nick. Forensics are here and the search team say that if they are needed, they'll be here within fifteen minutes. We got the search warrant and I've done a drive-by of the house. His van's in the driveway so we're assuming he's in. I've got Barry keeping watch on the house in case he goes out. Barry will stop him and bring him in. I don't want to take a chance." The Cap laughed over the phone. "After all, I've got a very demanding DCI to answer to."

Steve smiled. "Yeah, you have. Listen, I'm not going to join you. I'll meet you in the interview suite with chummy. Remember, he's only helping with enquiries, but if you have to, arrest him on suspicion. We don't want him reaching out for a solicitor until we've had a go at him, so gently does it."

"Understood. We're ready this end. See you at the Yard."

Next, Steve called Alison again. This time she picked up.

"Well, hello, Detective Chief Inspector. I've seen your missed call and voice message. A girl might think a policeman was stalking her." She was happy at the prospect of a late dinner and the possibility that Steve would stay the night.

"This policeman would certainly stalk you if he thought it would improve his chances. Mind you, he already knows you're a very wicked doctor."

They chatted for five minutes, talking about nothing in particular. Both were just happy to hear the other's voice.

"Did you book the table for nine?"

"Yes, sir, as instructed, but not the place you suggested. The restaurant is coming to us. I've ordered a home delivery from the Italian bistro round the corner. The whole nine yards, so don't be late. The table will be set, the wine open and breathing, and I'll be wearing something light and feminine. If you're late, you'll get nothing and see even less, but if you're on time, a night of pleasure and high living awaits."

"Well, if you put it that way I'd better be on time. Now, hang up, otherwise I'll not get off this phone and I'll be late."

After the usual goodbyes, they hung up.

Steve knew he had to move but talking with Alison had done nothing to clear his brain. He took his bag of exhibits and returned to the general manager's office as agreed. The man was behind his desk drinking coffee. He offered Steve a cup and poured it from a pre-prepared coffee pot.

"I've got everything you requested. The CCTV tapes are the originals. We don't have an adequate copying machine that could copy that many hours that quickly, so I'd appreciate their return." Without waiting for a reply, Guy North carried on. "There's the file of Dr Graham's check-in records, plus the original reservation, made by Brothers International Inc. The credit card information has been printed from our records. I'm sure you know that we don't use paper copies for credit card transactions any more."

As Steve drank his coffee, he had another thought. "Can I have a copy of Dr Graham's bill? I presume it will show any phone calls he made?"

"Yes, but not incoming calls. We log all calls, of course, but once a call is received into our system it's intercepted manually and connected to the appropriate room. One moment please." The general manager lifted his telephone and asked someone to bring in the up-to-date bill for Room 1202.

"Thank you, sir. You've been very helpful. I'll make sure your CCTV records are returned as soon as we're finished with them."

Both men walked to the door, but just as Guy North pulled the handle to open it, a woman came in holding the final bill for Dr Graham's room at the Mayflower Hotel.

***

Steve arrived back at his office clutching the data from the hotel. He asked Andy to join him in his office and to bring his personal laptop.

"So, Andy, we now know who our John Doe is. Did his fingerprints show anything?"

"No, nothing on our system, but as you said American, I've asked for a search of the FBI and State fingerprint systems."

Steve thought that Andy was thorough as usual. "Here's the key card from the hotel. Make sure you put it with the other effects." Steve handed over the key together with the head photographs from the post-mortem. "Scan the head shots in and shred the pictures. OK?"

A nod of the head was all the confirmation the DCI needed.

161

"Report time — are you ready?" Steve carried on. "I met the general manager of the Mayflower Hotel. He confirmed our victim's identity. I have CCTV records for all hotel cameras both inside and out from the date our victim checked in. I want you to go over them. See if anything pops up. Professor Campbell said he'd been dead for about twenty-four hours and hadn't been long in the water, so we're looking between his arrival on the 27th and, say, the 30th. OK, Andy?"

"Yes. I was thinking of coming in tomorrow, so I'll do it then, and you don't have to tell me — no snoopers allowed."

"Good man. Now, I've got his bill and he's made a few phone calls. Check them out. Let's see who he knew in London." Steve didn't wait for Andy's response. "And then we know that the original booking was made by a company called Brothers International Inc. Find out who they are and what they do, and pull their company accounts." Andy was feverishly typing away on his laptop.

"Got it, Steve."

"Just a thought, Andy. Get on to the American Embassy. See if they know a Dr David Graham."

"Right, Steve. Is that it?"

"No." Steve handed over the evidence bag containing everything he'd taken from Room 1202. "Go through that lot and log everything into your laptop. It's evidence, so get it to the evidence locker when you've done. There might be something there, but remember: scan and shred all paper, scan and shred. I'm not sure where this is going, but I've got something going round in my head again. We're not going to like the outcome unless we're very careful."

Chapter Twenty

The Fortress Club was quiet; Friday evenings weren't busy. Most members usually went home to their wives and families immediately after work. They liked to go back to their normal suburban lives with their 2.4 children and respectability. What they did in The Fortress Club midweek was another world. A world they hoped no one would ever see.

A few of the upstairs rooms were occupied, mostly by members who'd drunk too much with their lunch, or lonely, elderly bachelors or widowers just looking to start their weekend off with a bang. It didn't matter to the hostesses. They charged the same regardless of the clients' circumstances.

James Rushdie was seated in a comfortable armchair in the office of Alistair Ramsay. Ramsay had returned a few minutes earlier with two memory sticks, a folder of printed paper copies, and the date, time and location for a demonstration of the formula. He now sat in another chair opposite Desmond Cutter, who occupied the third.

"Any trouble from those two clowns?" Rushdie asked in his heavily accented New York voice. In this quiet room, Alistair Ramsay felt the menace his voice contained, even in normal conversation.

"No, good as gold. When I told them I wanted the copies, they denied having any, but the mention of retributions if they were lying seemed to have an effect, and they coughed up the second memory stick."

All three men were sipping forty-year-old brandy.

"Alistair, I've got a big shipment coming in through Ramsgate on Sunday. I need you to arrange for police and customs to look the other way. They'll get the usual fee."

"Jim, it's getting more difficult. I've been out of the job too long now. The pals I greased before have moved on — I don't have the same access to the new faces. You might want to look at other ways of bringing the stuff in."

James Rushdie was outwardly calm, but the menace was always there. He looked at Alistair Ramsay with a fatherly stare although the two men were about the same age. "Alistair, remember I own you." This was said in a low, deliberate voice. "When I own someone, they do what I tell them. No excuses. I've got five tonnes of the finest Colombian white powder arriving Sunday and you'll see it gets through customs and into my warehouse at Faversham. No ifs, no buts, just a job well done. Do you understand?"

"I understand, Jim, but can you not see what I'm saying?"

"I hope I'm wrong, but I think you're telling me that all those millions of dollars I've spent on this place and given you over the past few years have been wasted." James Rushdie's voice was increasing in volume. "I think you're telling me you're no longer any use to me and therefore not worth having around." Rushdie glared at Alistair. "Am I right or wrong?" Alistair Ramsay thought this conversation could end badly for him until Desmond Cutter intervened.

"Gentlemen, gentlemen, please. Let's not fall out. I think what Alistair is saying, Jim, is that the guys previously on the payroll aren't there now, and he'll have to sort out a new bunch of bent officials and police. Isn't that all, Alistair? I'm sure your contribution to our organisation isn't over. You just need to re-group, that's all."

Alistair Ramsay was grateful for Desmond's intervention. He had no idea how to answer James Rushdie.

"Always the diplomat, Des, but I need to hear it from Alistair. Tell me my merchandise will get safely through on Sunday?"

Alistair didn't know, but he still had a few people within customs that he'd paid off handsomely over the years, although they weren't based at Ramsgate. He'd have to rely on their continued greed.

"Yes, of course, Jim. It'll get through. It's just that such a big shipment might cause a few eyebrows to be raised and the bribes might be bigger, but we'll get it to Faversham."

"Right, let's have another drink." As the junior member and the most under threat, Alistair obliged and refilled two glasses. He didn't top his up.

"What about this experiment? Where and when?"

Alistair felt on more solid ground. "They've set up a laboratory at Redbridge. I've got the address. We're set for five o'clock Monday afternoon. Their expert, this Dr Graham, will be there to explain how it works and give a demonstration."

"This is the guy that killed to get it to pay off his gambling debts and get Gregory Anderson off his back. What a shmuck. He's probably got every law enforcement unit in the States and Europe looking for him. Do we know where he's holed up?"

"No, but he was staying in a hotel under his own name. The brothers didn't book him in under a false one, but he hasn't been picked up as far as we know."

"I don't like it. Get on to them and tell them to bring him here, now, tonight. He can enjoy one of the girls until we're done with him."

Alistair went to his desk and called Julian St John.

"What about the cops who were here yesterday? Anything to worry about there?" This was addressed to Desmond Cutter.

"No, not as far as Alistair is concerned. They're investigating the murders of some tarts around here. Not the type of flesh we get involved with, way too low rent. The only thing was, this detective wanted the membership list. Alistair refused and had one of his contacts at Scotland Yard put the squeeze on. Seems this guy's a bit of a boy scout but it should all be taken care of."

"Des, we don't want the cops sneaking around here, especially with the Ramsgate shipment and this auction coming up. I don't want to be looking over my shoulder while all that's going on."

"Relax. Alistair says it's under control."

"Yeah! Why don't I feel reassured?"

Alistair Ramsay returned to his chair having spoken to Julian St John.

"All fixed. They'll get hold of him and get him here later tonight."

"Well, that's something. Alistair — call for my car! Des, I suppose you want a ride?"

"Yeah, I'm off now. Alistair, you'd better make arrangements for this scientist to be taken care of when he gets here."

Monday was the start of a new and hopefully very profitable week.

Julian St John replaced the receiver. He looked across to his brother.

"That was Alistair Ramsay. That mobster from New York wants a demonstration of the formula on Monday and he wants Dr Graham housed at their place for, as he said, 'safe keeping'."

Julian returned to his sofa and sat opposite his brother.

Sebastian seemed to be thinking before he spoke. "Well, there's no reason why they shouldn't have him. He's no bloody use to us. It's just another loose end hanging out there. Where do they want him?"

"That swanky club of theirs, The Fortress Club. They want him tonight."

"No problem. Micky's still there. Call him and tell him to get the doctor out of his room and over to the club. I wish I were going to be looked after in that place." Both brothers smiled.

Micky Russ was still sitting in the foyer of the Mayflower Hotel. Each morning he'd arrive, and apart from toilet breaks and going to buy the odd sandwich, he'd sat at his post as instructed until 6 p.m. His job was to look out for Dr Graham and follow him each time he went out. Unfortunately, it seemed the good doctor didn't go out much, and so Micky Russ had been sitting about for almost three days, just doing as he'd been told. Even Micky would admit he wasn't a great thinker. Give him a task and there was no one better, only don't expect initiative. He'd work for anyone who needed his muscle and that's exactly what they got.

Micky's phone vibrated in his jacket pocket.

"Micky, it's Julian. Are you still at the hotel?"

"Yeah, boss."

"Has Dr Graham moved today?"

"No. My backside has lumps on it from sitting all day. He's not shifted for days."

"Now listen carefully, Micky. I want you to go to reception and ask to speak to Dr Graham in Room 1202. Got that?"

"Yes."

"Good. When you speak to him tell him to pack everything up and to come down to meet you in reception. Understood?"

"Yeah! In reception."

"Tell him he's moving to another hotel and to hurry. Have you got that?"

"Yes, I've got it — I'm not stupid!"

"Frankie will be there with the car in about thirty minutes. Keep the doctor with you until Frankie arrives and then you can knock off."

"Right. Do you want me to call you when all that's done?"

"No, Micky. Frankie will keep us posted. Off you go now and we'll be in touch."

Both Julian and Micky hung up.

Julian shouted for Frankie and told him to go to the Mayflower Hotel and meet Micky with Dr Graham. He was to take him to The Fortress Club and leave him there. No need to hang around. Just hand Dr Graham over and leave.

As always, the silent Frankie left to obey his employers' wishes.

Chapter Twenty-One

Steve was sitting at his desk listening to Andy working away. He knew there weren't many like Detective Constable Andrew Miller in the Metropolitan Police Force. The DCI felt somehow responsible for this thin, shy but brilliant young man. He didn't know how, but he promised himself to look after Andy going forwards.

He was just thinking of going down to the interview suite when his phone rang. The screen told him it was Barry.

"Hi, Steve, just reporting in. The Cap's left with our suspect. I'd have thought he'd be there now unless the traffic is bad."

"I'm just on my way down. How's it going there?"

"We're making progress, but I tell you, our suspect's a funny bugger. He didn't say a word, so The Cap arrested him on suspicion and read him his rights. He didn't bat an eyelid. I think he's a bit spooky. Anyway, you'll see for yourself." Barry paused and then carried on.

"Forensics are all over the house. Nothing yet but it's early. I called the search team and they're in there as well."

"Good, keep them at it. Barry — I'm designating you Scene of Crime Commander so it's yours until everyone's finished. I want a twenty-four-hour guard. Get Hackney nick to help out with uniforms. You can tell them the overtime will come from my budget. When you're satisfied we've got everything, then, and only then, close the site down. Everything now depends on us getting evidence and you're the man on the ground."

"Understood, Steve. You know it's amazing, we'd only just put the tapes up when a car drove past at about five miles an hour, rubbernecking. The same car's been past three times. We've got a bunch of lookers and an old dear offering everyone a cup of tea. They seem to think it's a circus and I'm the ringmaster. I'm thinking if that car goes past again any slower, I'll give out a parking ticket." Both men laughed.

"Well after your TV performance the other day it might be a fan. Keep me posted, and if you need more manpower just shout."

Both men hung up.

Before Steve could gather his thoughts for the upcoming interview, Andy entered. "Steve, I've been thinking. First, maybe the River Police could give us an idea where our victim went into the river. The post-mortem said the body hadn't been in the water for more than twelve hours. If we take that as a maximum time and the river boys give us a location, we could work back to Tower Bridge. There can't be many places you can chuck a body into the busiest stretch of the river."

"Yes, could work."

"Also, our body didn't have a mobile phone. If he did, it was most likely an American number because he'd have brought it with him. I could ask the providers with masts close to the Mayflower Hotel to give me a list of American numbers using their masts. All these companies have reciprocal international agreements. If we got one close to a mast beside the hotel, we might get access to our man's call history since he arrived. What do you think?"

"Bloody brilliant, Andy. Do it."

Andy left with a big smile on his face.

He was back inside thirty seconds. "Oh, Steve... Forensics came through with the wheelchair in the lake at Hackney. They said there's nothing usable by way of trace evidence due to submersion, but they've got a partial print. I've asked them to get it to the Fingerprint Search Unit and let me have a copy. Sorry it's not good news."

"Oh, it is. If our suspect's prints match the partial it could be our first piece of firm evidence."

***

The DCI entered the area below ground known as 'the dungeon'. This was where the interview rooms were housed. Each of the six rooms were exactly the same. The Cap had been allocated Room 3. The light above the door was on, telling everyone that a suspect was being interviewed. The uniformed sergeant had told Steve this was the room The Cap was using. Steve didn't knock but opened the door and entered.

169

The Cap nodded to Steve and introduced him to the suspect. Steve sat next to The Cap on the opposite side of a small table that was screwed to the floor.

"I haven't started yet, sir. We've been waiting for you, so Mr Ryder and I have been having a chat. Or should I say I've been talking to myself. Mr Ryder isn't very talkative."

"Really? Well, Mr Ryder, or can I call you 'Neil'? We can't make you talk but we find people with nothing to hide usually don't mind answering a few questions. Have you something to hide, Neil? Is that why you won't talk to us?"

The suspect just looked straight at Steve and appeared to be sneering. He just sat with this expression on his face and had his arms folded over his chest. Steve put him at mid-thirties, although he knew from Andy that Neil Ryder was forty-one years old. He was a bit overweight with a prominent belly hanging over his too-tight trousers. He had a full head of dark hair that looked as though it was dyed.

Steve nodded to The Cap and in the direction of the recorder that was fixed to one end of the table. This was the standard police voice recorder that not only recorded everything that was said but made a simultaneous copy, too. The Cap switched it on and waited for the audible alarm to switch off.

Steve started things off. "For the benefit of the tape, Mr Neil Ryder, aged forty-one, of 63 Milton Mews, Hackney, is being interviewed under caution by Detective Chief Inspector Steven Burt and Detective Inspector Abul Ishmal, in connection with the deaths of Marjory Pearson, Stacey Mathews and Barbara James. All three deaths have been designated as unlawful and took place in and around Hackney between 2nd November and 22nd November this year. The suspect was read his rights by DI Ishmal before being transported to New Scotland Yard where this interview is taking place."

Steve looked at his watch. "Interview commencing at 18.12 hours."

Steve studied the suspect and noted that he had a dark, heavy growth suggesting he hadn't shaved for a few days.

"Mr Ryder — is there anything you want to tell us about the deaths of these three women?"

Silence.

"Mr Ryder — if you don't talk to us, we can't clear you of involvement in these deaths."

Silence.

"Neil — we have a whole team of forensic scientists and a search team going over your property inch by inch. If they find as much as a pubic hair from one of these girls, you're done for. You know we have enough on you to bring you in. You know our teams will find something so you better tell us before we tell you. Just admit you murdered these girls and we can all have a nice cup of tea."

Silence.

"Well, Neil, if you don't want to help us, then we can't help you. If you save us a lot of time by telling us what happened, we could put in a word with the judge. Maybe get you into a softer prison. What do you say?"

Silence.

"OK. Have it your way. Let's start with Marjory Pearson. She was a pretty little thing. Tell us what you did to her."

Silence.

"What about Stacey Mathews? We've seen the pictures of her naked at the post-mortem. What was it like having sex with her?"

Silence.

"You didn't have your way with Barbara James? Why was that? She was a bit older? Did she kick you in the nuts or wouldn't she play your game? Which was it?"

Silence.

Steve had come across this type of behaviour before in suspects, but it didn't make it easy. He was about to try a new approach when Neil Ryder spoke.

"I don't know what you're talking about. For the first and last time, I didn't kill anybody. I'm saying no more but I would like a cup of tea and maybe a ham sandwich."

"Well at least we know you can talk. If you tell us how you murdered these three girls, all sort of good things like a cup of tea and a sandwich will be yours. Just tell us. Get it off your chest."

Silence.

Neil Ryder gave a huge sigh and stared at Steve with something approaching contempt.

"Listen, Neil. You know we can hold you, but I only want to do that if you're guilty. You've said you didn't kill these girls, so tell us where you were on Sunday 2nd November. That's when Marjory Pearson was killed."

Silence.

"You see, Neil, if you don't talk to us, we'll have to assume you killed these girls, but if you tell us where you were then that's called an alibi."

Silence.

Assisted by The Cap from time to time, Steve kept asking the suspect questions. No matter how outrageous the question, Neil Ryder didn't talk. He appeared unfazed and looked to be enjoying the efforts of the two detectives to get him to talk.

Just before eight o'clock Steve gave up and had Neil Ryder sent to a cell. They would continue in the morning.

Steve and The Cap returned to Steve's office. Neither man had spoken on the journey from the interview suite. The Cap could see that his boss had a well-known look on his face. He was deep in thought.

"There's something not right, Cap. Our suspect's far too cocksure of himself. He's arrogant and doesn't seem worried that we've got him locked up."

"I agree but what's the problem? We've both had suspects like that over the years. They all fold eventually."

"No, that's not what I mean. Samantha Burns' profile said we're looking for a mummy's boy. Someone who's not worldly wise. That guy is just the opposite of her profile. It doesn't feel right."

"Maybe the profile's wrong. These people aren't perfect."

"Yeah, that's true, but she seemed so sure. Tell you what, get on to her and get her here tomorrow morning. I'd like her to sit in. Her details are on Andy's desk." As The Cap was leaving, Steve called out: "Has Neil Ryder been fingerprinted?"

"Yes, as part of processing."

"Forensics got a partial from the wheelchair. Can you chase up the comparison unit? Let's see if we have a match."

The Cap went to search Andy's desk for Sam Burns' details while he picked up his mobile phone to speak with the fingerprint comparison unit. Steve phoned Alison Mills to announce that he was leaving and would be at her place on time.

Chapter Twenty-Two

The phone rang in the penthouse of Julian and Sebastian St John. This was slightly unusual. The brothers didn't get a lot of calls and when they did Frankie was always available to answer them. Julian reluctantly rose from his comfortable chair to answer the ringing machine.

As soon as he picked up the receiver, he wished he hadn't.

"Boss, it's Frankie. Graham's gone. He's not here."

"What!" Julian was apoplectic. "What do you mean 'gone'? He can't have. Micky's been keeping an eye on him."

"Yes, boss, but he's not here." Frankie knew how to handle Julian. He just kept repeating what he knew and never ventured an opinion.

"That slapper Ruby was keeping him company; she must know where he is."

"Yes, boss, but there's no sign of her here either."

"You're sure he's gone?" Julian was having palpitations, his blood pressure was up and he was sweating. "Get round to Ruby's place. She's maybe got him there. And tell Micky he's sacked."

"Yes, boss." Frankie hung up and Julian went back to his chair more worried about this latest development than his impending heart attack.

Frankie knew Julian was all bluster so he took Micky with him to Ruby's apartment. He'd been to her address before when the brothers had first come across the delicious American. She lived in a mews flat in Chelsea that Frankie estimated to be worth a fortune.

When they got there, Frankie left Micky in the car and went to the main door of the flat. After one ring, Ruby answered the door. She really was a very attractive woman. If Frankie hadn't been the hired help, he thought he'd enjoy a tumble with Ruby.

"The brothers want to see you."

"Really? Well, they'll have to wait — I've got plans."

Frankie suddenly hoped she'd be awkward and that he'd have to manhandle her into the car. He thought he'd enjoy even that contact.

"It's important. Julian says you must come."

"Don't you listen? Tell Julian St John I don't work for him and that he can't push me around." Ruby was secretly afraid of what the brothers might want her for.

"I'll have to carry you to the car if you won't come."

Ruby knew men and saw the lust in Frankie's eyes. It was better to give in and avoid being nearly raped by this monster. "OK, let me get my coat." Ruby was closing the door when Frankie's large foot wedged itself against the open door. Ruby knew when she was beaten.

Ruby arrived at the penthouse with more than a little trepidation. She had her Derringer just in case.

Julian, who hadn't had a heart attack, but was still sweating and annoyed, watched her enter.

He stood up with his arms outstretched hoping Ruby would walk into them and that he could give her a hug. It hadn't happened before, but he lived in hope.

"What's this all about, Julian? I had plans for tonight."

Julian was feeling better. "Well, my dear, it seems we've lost our American scientist and we wondered if you knew where he was?"

"Why would I? You asked me to get him back to his hotel. That's what I did."

"Yes, but I suggested you might give him a few extras to keep him sweet. I'm sure after a night with you he'd never leave."

"Julian, I'm not a whore. I took him to his hotel. I went to his room. He was tired so I left. That's all I know."

"That's a pity, my dear. You see, we have a new partner in the formula enterprise, and he wants to meet our doctor and have him show the experiment." Julian suddenly realised the trouble they were in if they couldn't find Dr Graham.

"This gentleman is from your country and, I suspect, is a very cruel man. For the sake of the enterprise, it's vital that we find Dr Graham. You must have some idea where he might be. You were the last one to be with him. He must have said something." There was a pleading tone to Julian's voice.

Ruby sat down on one of the sofas. Sebastian was seated on the other and had been listening to their conversation.

Again, Ruby said that she had no idea where Dr Graham was. Julian sat and all three stared at each other in silence.

Sebastian was the first to speak. "What do we do? Let's assume we've lost him. What do we tell that American thug, and how do we handle the demonstration on Monday?"

Julian stood up again and paced around the sofas. "I don't know. Christ, what a mess. Our plan to get rich is up in smoke. If we can't find David Graham and get the demonstration done then even our twenty million is gone, and we'll be lucky to be alive by Monday. We've got to think. Somehow we have to stall for time."

Sebastian spoke again. "Neither Desmond Cutter nor that horrible James Rushdie have met Dr Graham. We've still got our tame scientist on the books. You know, the one who helped out at the last demonstration. If we sent him, would anybody be any wiser? He talks the talk, he's a real scientist. It's just that he likes little boys, but that apart, we might get away with it."

"Bloody brilliant, brother." Julian was relieved. They had a plan. He called for Frankie, and as if by magic, Frankie appeared again. "Get hold of that Professor Small guy. You know, the one who helped out down at Redbridge with the American scientist. Go and collect him and bring him here, and tell him to pack a bag. He's going on a trip."

Frankie disappeared.

Ruby had been listening. "Who's this other guy you're mixed up with now, Julian?"

She seemed to be taking an interest in Julian's affairs. He liked it.

"One guy called Desmond Cutter. He's head of Olympic Oil. We had a deal with him but he brought in another American called James Rushdie. He's a nasty piece of work."

Julian went on to explain to Ruby, who was now sitting on the sofa with her legs tucked under herself and showing a lot of thigh, that their deal had been usurped by James Rushdie, and he now had the formula. He told a sad tale of being cut out of the deal, and that all he and Sebastian would get out of it, after all their hard work, was a miserable twenty million dollars. Julian had moved to sit beside Ruby. She was very sympathetic.

"You poor baby. Is that all you'll get? $20 million?"

"Yes." Julian was playing the hurt schoolboy in the hope of getting more than sympathy from Ruby.

Ruby took his hand and allowed it to rest in hers, but her hand rested on her thigh. Julian couldn't believe his luck. This was the closest he'd ever been to Ruby.

"Olympic Oil I've heard of, but who's this other character, Rushdie? Does he have a company? Where's he from?"

"That's a lot of questions, my dear." Julian thought he was on a winning streak. "Once we've dealt with our little problem, maybe we could have a late supper somewhere nice? We don't have to talk about business." He positively leered at her.

"Well, Julian, that would be nice." Ruby let his hand go and allowed it to brush her thigh. She uncurled her legs and her skirt stuck around her bottom, revealing almost all of her beautiful legs. She quickly squirmed her body inside her dress and pushed her skirt down.

Julian was mesmerised.

"What's the new deal with this James Rushdie? Is he going to sell the formula just as you planned?"

"That's the annoying thing. He's taken the formula. He's taken our plan. He's taken our hard work setting up the auction and we're only getting twenty million. It's just not fair. He knows it's worth billions and he wants to get all the people attending our little auction to club together and buy the formula so he can destroy it for them. I have to admit it's a better plan than ours, but we had the original idea."

Julian was now looking at Ruby as a conquest.

"Can I get you a drink before our supper, my dear?"

"No, thank you, Julian."

Julian was about to try again with Ruby when Frankie appeared with Professor Peter Small.

"Professor, thank you for coming. We have a little problem that you can sort for us. Shall we say a retainer of ten thousand pounds?"

Julian went on to outline Sebastian's plan. Peter Small would be taken to The Fortress Club by Frankie and would stay there as Dr David Graham. He'd meet a few people there and travel with them on Monday to the laboratory at Redbridge where he'd assisted the real Dr Graham, to repeat the same experiment.

"It's likely that these other gentlemen will want you to stay at the club until you go down to Kent next week to repeat the experiment again for the benefit of our oil rich buyers. If that's what they ask, then that's what you'll do. Understand?"

"Yes, but I'll have to make up batches of the additives, and the papers are at Redbridge."

"Don't tell me, tell your new best friends. They have the formula now." Julian called Frankie, who silently appeared again.

"Frankie — take our new Dr David Graham to The Fortress Club. He's expected."

Being a man of few words, Frankie simply nodded.

"And remember, you're now David Graham until I tell you you're not. For God's sake don't cock this up or we'll all be floating face down in the Thames by next week."

Ruby got a shock at hearing Julian's last statement. Surely, he couldn't know? It was only a figure of speech. She stood up, collected her coat from a chair and walked towards Frankie and Peter Small.

"I'll just get a lift back to my apartment with Frankie. After all, he dragged me here. It's the least he can do."

Julian was lost for words. He had plans for Ruby.

"But, Ruby, our supper date?"

"Another time, Julian. I've already eaten." With a wave of her hand, she followed Frankie and the new David Graham out of the penthouse.

Unknown to Julian and Sebastian, Ruby used her feminine wiles on Frankie and persuaded him to take her to The Fortress Club with the new Dr Graham. She said she'd never been to the club and that maybe she and Frankie could have a drink. They quickly realised it was a members' only club, but as Dr Graham was staying as a guest of the owner then they could have one drink in the lounge. Ruby had what she wanted. After finishing her fizzy water, she allowed Frankie to take her back to her flat in Chelsea, where she left him sitting in the car.

Chapter Twenty-Three

DCI Steve Burt arrived in his office to find Andy hard at work. He closed his office door after saying 'good morning' to Andy. He needed time to think this morning.

He and Alison had had an evening to remember. He'd stopped off on his way to her house to buy two bottles of an exceptionally fine claret. He'd added chocolates and flowers. After all, Alison had ordered in the food and would have gone to great lengths to make sure everything was perfect. And it was perfect. They'd had a fantastic meal, washed down by a bottle of wine Alison had bought specially, followed by a few glasses of Steve's claret. They'd found it difficult to keep their hands off each other once they were settled on Alison's sofa.

Steve thought back to last night and their pleasure at sharing a bed. He found Alison Mills easy to get along with. They shared the same interest in books, both liked good food and wine, and both were professionals who loved their work.

Over a cooked breakfast they'd discussed plans to go on holiday once Steve's caseload eased. They'd discussed moving in together but couldn't agree which house they should use, although Steve admitted that given Alison's medical practice was set up in her home, it would be more sensible for him to move in with her.

The DCI was in a happy place in his personal life. It was a warm, comfortable feeling knowing he had someone to share his life with, possibly on a permanent basis. This commitment, although willingly given, was a bit scary. He wasn't sure where his relationship with the lady doctor would finish up, but he'd decided that he didn't care.

Alison was going down to Rye in West Sussex later to fulfil her duties as volunteer doctor to the residents of the View Care Home. This was where Steve had first met Alison and he knew she'd be staying at the same hotel where they'd shared their first meal. He'd promised to try and get down to Rye in the evening and once again enjoy her company. It depended on work and she understood.

Steve realised he had a lot on today and opened his door to see Andy still hard at it. Andy looked up as he saw his boss's door open.

"I've had a fingerprint match from the States. It seems our dead body was wanted for murder in Massachusetts. An International Arrest Warrant was issued by the FBI less than a week ago. The e-mail I got from them didn't pull any punches. To say they're annoyed is too mild — they're bloody livid. They want to know why their man wasn't arrested using their warrant and why he was allowed to stay in a London hotel under his own name and using his own passport. They're not happy, Steve, and I must say I can't blame them."

"Who did our body kill?"

"Another scientist. Seems he not only killed the other bloke but stole his research. A laptop's missing and the Feds think he came over here to sell the contents."

"Interesting. If he was living at the Mayflower in open sight and we knew about the warrant, it's a good question. Why wasn't he picked up?"

Steve stood beside Andy's desk scratching his chin. "It must be that someone sat on it, but who? Who has that kind of muscle?"

"The Home Office or the spooks in MI5 or MI6 could suppress the warrant. Maybe they were following him to see who he was selling this other guy's research to."

"Remember that I was told to keep this case quiet and it was political? Well, it's just got a whole load more so. We'll have to figure this out, but only after our Hackney suspect's coughed to the killings."

Just as Steve was about to ask about the CCTV search from the Mayflower Hotel, Samantha Burns walked in. She was dressed exactly as before, leading Steve to wonder if she had any other clothes. Needless to say, Andy became obviously nervous and fidgety while he smiled at the profiler and said a shy 'hello'.

"Sam, welcome back. Are you OK for today?"

"Yes. I've nothing on so I'm all yours."

"Good. Come into my office please — I need to talk to you."

Andy chipped in. "Excuse me, Steve. You should know that the fingerprint comparison is back. There's not enough of the partial from the wheelchair to be conclusive. They only got a 40% match."

"Thanks, Andy."

Once the pair were comfortably seated, Steve explained himself.

"We have a suspect in custody, one Neil Ryder. You heard Andy say that we can't yet place him at any of the dump sites. We'd hoped the fingerprint we lifted from the wheelchair he used to move his second victim would get us closer, but no go."

Samantha said nothing but continued listening. "The thing is, Sam, the guy we have downstairs doesn't fit your profile. He's aggressive, full of himself and doesn't seem afraid of us or his situation. He's refusing to say much, but what he did he say was that it wasn't him." Steve paused.

"From your profile I thought we were looking for a mummy's boy. You indicated that he was sexually repressed, but this guy looks like he's put it about a bit."

Sam remained silent. "I'm not questioning your profile. We're pretty sure we've got our man, but something isn't sitting right. I want you to either sit in on the interviews or watch from the observation room. See what you think of Neil Ryder. See if you can form an opinion of him, especially whether you think he's capable of three murders. Maybe reassess your profile. Can you do that?"

"Of course I can. Remember profiling isn't an exact science but I was fairly sure based on what you'd concluded that my profile was accurate, but not to worry. I'm not too proud to admit I may have gotten it wrong." Samantha Burns smiled.

Steve was relieved that she appeared to be a sensible young woman.

As they entered the interview suite, The Cap was standing outside Room 6. This was their allocated interview room for the second round with Neil Ryder. Steve explained that Sam would be present, but The Cap suggested she observe from the one-way glass observation room instead. That way she'd hear and see everything without getting close to someone who might be a triple murderer.

The Cap could see she hadn't thought about that and she seemed relieved by the suggestion.

With Samantha Burns looking on, Steve and The Cap were once again sitting opposite their suspect. After the usual formalities for the tape machine, they started. It had been decided that The Cap would lead this session.

"So, Neil, you've had all night to think things over. What's it to be? Stony silence like yesterday, or are you going to help yourself?"

Instead of the expected silence, Neil Ryder simply said: "No comment and I want a lawyer. I know my rights. I'm saying nothing except that I didn't kill anybody, and you can't say that I did."

"Well, Neil, that's as much as you've said since we met. Why not carry on talking now and tell us what happened to the three girls?"

Silence.

"We told you yesterday that if you confess it'll go a lot easier on you in court."

Silence.

"Look, Neil, we've got our forensic and search teams going all over your house. We know you killed those girls there. Nobody can do what you've done and not leave any trace evidence. It's only a matter of time before we get enough to charge you. Come on." The Cap used his pleading voice. "Confess and let's get this over with."

Silence.

Steve and The Cap looked at each other. Steve nodded. It was his turn.

After an hour of similar questioning, the suspect only spoke once to ask for a lawyer. Both detectives were exasperated by this, and eventually Steve called an end to the interview. He promised Neil Ryder he'd get a solicitor for their next interview and again told him it would be easier if he admitted the murders.

The suspect smiled and shrugged his shoulders but remained silent.

The Cap, Sam and Steve adjourned to the canteen for coffee and a debrief. On the way, Steve called Barry at the crime scene.

"Nothing happening in a hurry here, Steve. The people in their white suits are dead slow but thorough. So far, they've not got much. They've started on the van so hopefully we'll get something from that."

"Any idea how long they'll take?"

"No, but all this hanging around isn't doing me any good. I think the old dear who keeps bringing cups of tea thinks that I'm a possible toy boy for her."

Steve just laughed. "I suppose someone has to. Think of all the tea."

"Very funny. I'll call you if we get anything."

Steve hung up.

With their coffee in front of them, Steve asked Samantha: "Well, what do you think?"

"I'm not sure. Based on our previous discussions and Andy's analysis, I'd say he's not your man. Based on his demeanour I believe he's probably capable of murder, but you're right, he's not a fit for my profile. I still think I'm right about the type of person we're looking for. That's not to say I'm pig-headed enough to not admit that I'm wrong. I just don't believe I am."

"What do you think, Cap?"

"I'm sure he's a bad lad. He knows something but is *he* our killer? I don't know. If we don't get any forensics and he doesn't talk, we don't have enough to hold him."

Steve just nodded and stared ahead. He drank his coffee and looked at his two colleagues. "We're running out of time to hold him without applying for an extension. If we…" Steve's phone rang. He saw it was Barry. Hoping for good news, he answered.

"Steve, we've got a problem. The DS from Hackney, that Scottish bloke Davie Robertson, has just called. They've found a body, same M.O. He's at the scene but wants our people there."

"What do you mean the same M.O.?"

"All I know is that a young woman dressed like a tart has been dumped behind the Tesco store on Hackney High Road. She's apparently been strangled."

"Right, Barry, you're nearest. Leave one of the local boys in charge and get yourself over to Tesco. We'll call out the circus and I'll meet you there as soon as I can."

"Right." Barry was gone.

Steve phoned the ever-reliable Andy and told him about his conversation with Barry. He told him to get the duty pathologist and another forensics team to the dump site as soon as. Andy sounded excited at the prospect of another murder, and as soon as Steve had hung up, he set everything in motion.

Steve explained to his coffee drinking partners what had happened.

"I know it's bloody obvious, but our man downstairs couldn't have killed this one."

"Yes, I'd worked that out. I'm a detective, remember."

Sam spoke up. "If the man in custody isn't your killer, then that supports my profile and your gut reaction, Steve. You're still looking for the killer."

"Yes, but who the hell is Neil Ryder?" Steve was getting annoyed, mainly with himself and this case. He was also annoyed that his other secret case wasn't getting the attention he knew the commander was expecting.

"Everything fits — the newspaper advert, the computer programme, the van, just everything. So where did we go wrong?"

All three sat in silence and finished their coffees, which, by now, were cold.

"Cap — check the guy downstairs out. Go back to his arrest. Check out his booking form with the custody sergeant. Go through his personal effects, everything, a full background check. We need to know who Neil Ryder is."

"Right."

"Sam — I'm not sure there's any more you can do but I know Andy's up to his neck. If you have the time, I think he'd appreciate some help. Don't worry about getting paid. This fourth murder means my budget has just become open-ended."

"I'd like to be around and see how this plays out. It's not always possible to see the end results or how an enquiry develops."

All three left the canteen. The DCI to attend a crime scene in Hackney, his DI to do a thorough background search on Neil Ryder, and Samantha to aid the 'sweet Andy', as she had started calling him.

Chapter Twenty-Four

Steve arrived at the dump site behind Tesco just as the pathologist was exiting the white pop-up tent used to cover the body. Barry and Davie Robertson were standing off to one side, obviously sharing a joke. Steve remembered back to his last meeting with Detective Sergeant Davie Robertson and was sure their topic of conversation would include food.

As he saw Steve arrive, Barry peeled away from the Hackney-based DS. The pathologist was peeling off her hood and face mask as the two detectives approached her. Neither knew this doctor, nor had worked with her before.

Steve showed the pathologist his warrant card and introduced Barry. "I'm Sophie Kendell, Duty Pathologist. I did the cutting on two of the previous victims so I'm familiar with your killer's M.O."

Steve thought that this was a bonus. He noted that Dr Kendell was a small, plump woman in her mid-thirties with short dark hair and a few extra chins.

"So, is it the same killer?"

"Well, yes and no. It's similar, but different. I know you want a straight answer but there are differences. First, she's been dead about eighteen hours. Some time yesterday between, say, five and seven in the evening. Second, she's not as sterile as the other two I saw. She's got bits of grass and leaves in her hair and on her clothes. She's also got bruising to her shoulders and a few of her nails are broken as though she tried to fend off her attacker. Lastly, she was strangled with a piece of rough rope, not a scarf or a belt." The pathologist paused.

"If you really pushed me, I'd say it's very possible that it's the same killer, but something happened to spoil his usual procedure. We might get lucky and get some DNA from under her fingernails where she likely scratched her attacker, but I'll know more when I get her back to the morgue."

"Thank you, Dr Kendell. The PM can wait till Monday."

"I know, I'm off for a dirty weekend with my boyfriend." She gave out a really dirty laugh. "See you Monday, say ten o'clock?" Dr Kendell turned without waiting for an answer and was off.

Steve and Barry entered the tent. The victim was lying there exactly like the other three; a young girl dressed in cheap, trashy clothes, ready for a night out. They left the tent and Steve asked Davie Robertson to organise getting the body to the morgue and to stay until the Scene of Crime Unit were finished. As expected, the Scotsman wasn't too keen to help, citing the lack of overtime at Hackney nick and the fact he hadn't had his lunch. An arrangement was made for Steve to authorise overtime for him and to add an expense claim for his lunch. Davie Robertson now wished he worked for DCI Burt instead of his present boss.

The two Scotland Yard men walked around the area behind the store and saw at least two CCTV cameras. They found the store manager and a uniformed man who was introduced as the store's head of security. All four men settled into a small room above the store which housed banks of TV monitors and a few CD players.

"We're only interested in the CCTV from the rear of the store. The body was discovered at 11.34 so we only need to look at, say, eleven o'clock until then."

The head of security loaded discs into two players and a grainy image from both cameras appeared and started to tick forward minute by minute. Barry was looking more closely than the others as he'd grabbed the chair directly in front of a monitor. The security man sat at the other while the store manager and Steve stood looking on.

As the time-lapsed images ticked forward, Barry noticed a Rover 75 arrive behind the store at 11.27. It stopped and reversed towards a piece of undeveloped land that adjoined the smooth surface of the road at the rear of the screen. A man got out, opened the rear door and appeared to pull something out, just letting it lie where it fell. The driver then got in his car and drove off. Barry could tell from his earlier encounter with the body that this was the same spot where the body had been discovered.

Only Barry had seen this as the others were concentrating on the other monitor. "Can you stop this one now please and rewind till 11.27? Sir, I think we might have something. Look!"

The scene was replayed. This was clearly the killer dumping the body, not from a Renault van but from an old car. The killer's face was obscured by his hooded jacket and the registration number of the car wasn't clear. The security man said he couldn't enhance the pictures.

"Right, I'll have to take that disk. Our technicians at the Yard might have some luck."

Steve noted that Barry wasn't as euphoric as he thought he might be. After all, they'd just seen the killer in action, and even if it wasn't the same one, they were well on their way to solving this murder. Steve said nothing to Barry but said that they should leave and get back to the Yard.

Driving back, Barry was quiet, obviously deep in thought. Just as Steve was about to open a conversation, Barry pulled the car to a stop by the kerb. He fished inside his jacket and produced his notebook. "Oh yes!"

Barry turned to Steve. "Remember I told you that a car had driven past our crime scene yesterday three or four times and it was going very slowly?"

"Yes. You said if it went past again at such a slow speed, you'd give it a parking ticket."

"Well, that car was a Rover 75, dark red. I'd swear that's the car on the CCTV."

"Are you sure? I know it's an old model but there must be hundreds still on the road."

"Well, the CCTV's in black and white and the car looked black but could have been dark red. Also..." Barry gave a grin. "I've got the registration number. We'll soon find out if it's important or not."

"OK. Call Andy and get him to do a PNC check."

Barry called Andy, gave him the number and asked to be called as soon as he got the information. The pair resumed their journey. On the way, Barry explained that the forensic and search of 63 Milton Mews would take time and that the senior forensics officer would call when they'd finished.

After about fifteen minutes, Andy called back. The hands-free phones in police pool cars aren't the best, but this one didn't have to be to hear the excitement and confusion in Andy Miller's voice.

"You won't believe this, but that car is registered to one Neil Ryder, the suspect we have downstairs."

Barry almost ran into the car in front.

"Never, Andy, it's not possible. You did a DVLA search."

"Yes, Steve, but only for Renault Kangoo vans. I didn't check to see if our name had another vehicle."

"Bloody hell, this gets worse. If we have Neil Ryder in custody, then who's driving his car and dumping bodies?" Steve felt at his wits' end.

"Andy — set up a meeting for everyone in my office in, say, forty-five minutes. We should be back by then. We need to brainstorm this; it's getting out of hand."

"Right. I'll get coffee. Do you want Sam there?"

"It's Saturday and she's given her day up for us, so yes, if she would like to be."

Everyone except The Cap was seated in Steve's office. He would be along shortly.

***

Back in his office, Steve stood at the whiteboard with a marker pen in one hand and his coffee in the other.

"I don't know what's going on. We have three now, maybe four murders. The first three followed the same M.O. exactly. All killed more or less at the same time of day and all dumped at around the same time. Our fourth victim seems to have been killed earlier, and not dumped until some eighteen hours after her death." Steve spoke as he wrote on the board. "Is it the same killer?"

"It can't be if our suspect downstairs was here all night, unless we've got the wrong man." Andy had been thinking.

"Right again. Everything points to this Neil Ryder as our killer, except he doesn't match Sam's profile, but it could be..."

The Cap arrived looking flushed and a bit sorry for himself. He immediately interrupted proceedings. "Sir, I'm sorry, and I've no idea how it happened, but our man downstairs isn't Neil Ryder."

"What!" Everyone in the room was initially shocked by this revelation.

"I'm sorry, Steve, it's down to me. We knocked on 63 Milton Mews yesterday, the home of Neil Ryder. This guy answered the door but didn't confirm or deny who he was. I just assumed it had to be our man. He was relaxed and looked at home, not like a visitor, so when I brought him in I told the custody sergeant to book him in as Neil Ryder. He didn't have many personal effects, so we just bagged them up and got him processed and into the interview room. I had no reason to think this wasn't Ryder. He's never admitted he's not, and he's not saying anything. I'm really sorry, Steve."

Steve looked at his DI with a mixture of anger and sympathy. He knew that such a mistake wasn't like The Cap, but also, he knew he couldn't let it slide. He'd have to deal with Detective Inspector Ishmal later.

Still standing by the whiteboard, Steve asked: "So, who've we got downstairs?"

The Cap looked at his notes and smiled a relieved smile. "He had his driving licence in his wallet. He's John Peter Saunders and, get this, he lives at 65 Milton Mews, next door to the real Neil Ryder."

Samantha raised her hand like a schoolgirl in class. "I'm not gloating, it's not my style, but this throws more light onto the fact that the person downstairs doesn't fit the profile but could still be involved." She looked shyly down at her hands.

Steve was mystified.

"Let's think this through. Everything we have points to Neil Ryder as our killer, but we don't have him. Barry — put out an all-points with the car registration number. Some of the traffic boys might pick him up. Now, what do we think of chummy downstairs?"

As usual, Andy was the first to venture an opinion. "Suppose they're in it together, houses next to one another. One a mummy's boy, the other a more streetwise person. One could lead the other on."

"Yes, it's possible, but we've nothing on our suspect downstairs."

"Couldn't we get a warrant?" The Cap was desperate to make amends and hopefully soften the reprimand he knew must be coming. "I remember a few years ago we got a joint search warrant based on suspicion two parties were jointly committing the crimes, even though all the evidence was in one location. We might get a search warrant for number sixty-five based on the warrant for sixty-three?"

"Yes, I've heard of it, but we'd need a hard-nosed judge."

"The original warrant was signed off by Mrs Justice Shambling. She signed off pretty quickly as soon as we mentioned the triple murders." Andy sat back and waited for instructions.

"I've come across her before. She's very pro-police. It's worth a shot. Cap, you get on to it. If we do get it, we'll go in this afternoon, so no one make plans for tonight." As he said it, he realised his weekend in Rye was not going to happen.

"Andy — chase up our fourth victim's identity. We'd better know who she is. The post-mortem is booked for Monday at ten o'clock. Put it in the file please."

Steve was still thinking about this case when suddenly the thing that had been tucked away at the back of his memory bank came rushing forward. He knew what had been bothering him but kept quiet about his eureka moment as it related to his other, secret case. He'd talk with Andy later.

"While The Cap's chasing the warrant, let's talk to our Mr John Peter Saunders. Has the duty solicitor arrived?"

"Yes, about an hour ago. I put them in Interview Room 6." As always, Andy was on the ball.

"Right, Andy, when you've got the identity of our fourth victim, come and join me in Room 6. It's about time you got your feet wet. Let's see if we can shake him up a bit. Barry — get back out to number sixty-three. See how the teams are doing. If by any chance we get the warrant, you'll be there and we won't waste time."

Steve wrote a name on a piece of paper and handed it to Andy once The Cap and Barry had left. "I know I said no paper on our other case, but when you get a chance, look this name up. But don't leave it lying around."

Andy took it, and with a conspiratorial grin, he put it in his trouser pocket.

The meeting was over, and a plan of sorts was developing.

***

Steve showed Samantha into the observation room attached to Interview Room 6. He then entered Room 6 to see their suspect now known as John Peter Saunders sitting next to a very young-looking man dressed in a professional suit. Steve introduced himself to this youthful-looking individual and learned in return that he was Christian Wellsley, the duty solicitor. Steve estimated that he'd only just started shaving and couldn't have been qualified for more than six months. "And they say policemen are getting younger," he thought.

After the usual formalities for the tapes, Steve began.

"Good afternoon, Neil." A pause for effect. "Or, is it John? Or Peter? Which do you prefer?"

Steve took satisfaction from seeing that the sneer that was present on his face when he'd entered was now completely gone, replaced by a look of total bewilderment.

"Yes, we know who you are. John Peter Saunders of 65 Milton Mews, Hackney. Right next door to the house of our main suspect, Neil Ryder of 63 Milton Mews, Hackney. A bit of a coincidence wouldn't you say, John or Peter?"

"So, you know who I am — big deal. I'll still sue for wrongful arrest. You've held me here as the wrong man. You can't do that."

Steve decided to be cool. But before he could form a response, there was a light tap at the door and Andy entered.

"For the tape, Detective Constable Andrew Miller has entered the room." Andy sat beside Steve. He felt important being in on the interview.

"You'll have to consult with your solicitor, but we still believe you're involved in the deaths of at least three girls. A fourth body was found today. Can you tell us what you know about it?"

"Nothing, how could I? You've had me locked up here." John Peter Saunders wasn't as confident as he'd been earlier.

"Whose idea was the newspaper adverts?"

Silence.

"The girls who replied... how did you decide which ones to kill?"

"We never killed none. You can't prove a thing."

"We're still going over number sixty-three with a fine-tooth comb, and we've got your partner on CCTV dumping the body of a young girl today. It will all tie back to you. Do yourself a favour and own up!"

Silence.

Andy touched Steve's arm. He wanted to say something.

"The girl we found today was called Mary Sumner. She was twenty-two years old and lived in Mile End, the same as your second victim, Stacey Mathews. Why were two of the four girls from the same place?"

"Listen, son, if you're a real cop you'll know you've got nothing on me and what you just said is slander." The suspect sat back and stared at Andy. "I'll get my brief here to sue you, and all the other old bill, so don't try and pin anything on me."

Andy persisted. "You see, I'm interested... the newspaper adverts were a brilliant idea — who thought of it?"

"Me, of... Good trick, son. I'm saying nothing."

Andy sat back while Steve resumed more conventional questioning, although Andy had yet again shown that he was nobody's fool.

"You should know that we've applied for a warrant to search your house. Care to tell us what we'll find?"

"You can't do that, you've got no evidence." He turned to his youthful solicitor. "Tell them they can't do that, it's not legal." The suspect was beginning to sweat, and Steve wondered what might be behind the door of 65 Milton Mews.

The solicitor spoke up. "Well, DCI Burt, under PACE regulations, you'll need reasonable doubt and firm evidence linking my client to a crime before a judge will sign off on a search warrant, so I'm afraid my client is correct. Based on what you've disclosed today, I doubt you'll get a warrant."

John Peter Saunders leaned forward with a look of triumph on his face, although he was still sweating heavily.

Steve addressed the solicitor in his most condescending tone. "We'll see, Mr Wellsley. You'll discover, as your career develops, that there are often different routes to the same end. We've made our application on the basis of shared crime."

The suspect again proclaimed his innocence. He said he wanted to be released and that he wanted a proper lawyer.

"Mr Saunders — we can keep you here for another twenty-four hours or so, and then a further thirty-six hours, if we deem it necessary, before we charge you. You're not going anywhere except back to your cell. For the tape, interview suspended at 6.37 p.m."

As they left the interview suite, Steve turned his mobile phone back on. It was standard procedure not to have live phones during an interview. It immediately sounded — a message was waiting. As Andy and Steve made their way to Steve's office, Andy peeled off to collect Sam. Steve listened to his message as he walked. It was Barry with an urgent plea to call him.

The DCI waited until he was behind his desk before calling Barry. Right from the start, Barry was on a high. If Steve didn't know any better, he'd accuse him of being drunk or on drugs.

"Steve, I know you'll not believe me, but I'm sitting in the lounge of 63 Milton Mews with the owner of the property, one Mr Neil Ryder."

"What! How? What's happened?"

"I was coming back and parked a few doors up was the Rover 75 I saw the other day... and maybe on the CCTV today. Sitting in the driver's seat was this man — he was in a terrible state. He'd been crying and had wet himself. I brought him here, got him a cup of tea and he's been telling me all about himself and his best mate from next door, Peter Saunders."

"Be careful, Barry. Have you arrested him? Told him his rights?"

"No, Steve, we've just had a man-to-man chat. Neil likes that. He's invited me to go next door and see their film studio. It seems that Peter's a great filmmaker. Hang on a second..." Steve could hear movement at the other end of the phone.

"I'm out of his earshot now, Steve. This guy's definitely weird. I think we'll need a doctor to confirm he's fit to be questioned. It could be that he's nuts and unfit to plead. I haven't heard from The Cap about the warrant, but if this guy has got a key and is happy to show me around, I think I'll do it, just in case we don't get the warrant."

"It's good thinking, but I'm not sure. If your man's not sane enough, it could be argued that we took advantage and entered into an illegal search." Steve stopped to think. "On the other hand, if you haven't told me anything about him, and he invited you next door, go in, but don't touch anything. I'm sure we'll be OK. Tell you what, I'll come over and we can both have a look. I'll be there in forty-five minutes."

"Right. I'll make Neil a nice cup of tea and get him cleaned up while we're waiting."

Steve heard Andy and Sam talking in the outer office.

"I'm off to Hackney — Barry's got a lead. You two can call it a day. It's been a long one. Before you go, Andy, can you get hold of The Cap? Find out what's happening with the search warrant for number sixty-five and ask him to meet us there. And Andy, I don't want to see you in here tomorrow. It's Sunday."

Steve left the two young people together and could only smile at what their evening ahead would be like.

***

The DCI made good time to Hackney despite Saturday evening traffic. He found Barry and Neil Ryder seated on a settee in the lounge of number sixty-three.

On first impressions, Neil Ryder looked like a large schoolboy. He was clearly overweight, with a mass of thick black hair growing wildly on top of his head. His face was round with red cheeks, but his eyes were sad — like a puppy dog looking for attention. Without pre-empting anything, the DCI got the feeling that this suspect was maybe a little simple in his thoughts.

After Barry had introduced them, Steve sat on the other side of Neil on the settee. "Neil, do you have anything to tell us about what you got up to with Mr Saunders and the girls?"

"Yes, I told Barry all about it, but would you like to see the film studio?"

"I'd love to, but can you please tell me about the first girl? You remember Marjory…" Steve produced a pocket recorder and set it up.

"Oh! She was the first. It was just after my mummy died. Peter became my best friend. He said as my mummy wasn't there to stop me, I could do anything I wanted to, even have girls."

"So what happened, Neil?"

"Peter put an advert in a newspaper. He said he was looking for future film stars. He even set up the studio next door so he could do proper screen tests. He said it'd be better if he used my address because he didn't want people turning up at his studio without appointments."

"I see." Steve was having to take things slowly.

"The first girl came around ten o'clock on the first day. She was pretty. Peter took her next door and I went as well. He has a big bed there and he asked the girl to take off all her clothes." Neil was beginning to foam a little at the mouth, obviously visualising past events.

"I remember she only took some off, and Peter asked her to pose for the camera. I think he called them 'calendar shots'. It was all very sexy."

Neil stopped talking. His body shook as he remembered. "It was my fault. She was so beautiful. I only wanted to touch her. I'd never seen an almost naked girl before. She pushed me off and screamed. Peter pushed her onto the bed and told me to take off all my clothes. Everything just went blank. Peter got her to lie back and said something to her. She was very gentle. I'd never had a woman before."

"What happened when it was all over?"

"We put our clothes back on. I got to kiss her on the lips then Peter put a belt round her neck. He pushed her onto the floor and gave me the ends of the belt and told me to pull. He said it was part of what I'd done, and she'd deserved it, so I pulled with all my strength."

"Was she dead, Neil?"

"Yes — just like mummy."

"What happened after that?"

"Peter told me to get my van and drive it into his garage, so I did. We then carried the girl out and put her in the back of the van. Peter said I'd been good, and that we'd do it again, but he'd take her away so that we wouldn't get into trouble. I never saw her again."

Steve looked at Barry, who shrugged. Both detectives knew that Neil was telling the truth, but neither had heard such a tale of depravity in their careers.

"What about the second girl, Neil? That was Stacey. What happened with her?"

"Oh! She was great. When we got to the studio, she took off all her clothes. Peter said she was a natural actress and that she'd definitely be in demand in Hollywood."

Again, Neil was getting excited by his memories.

"Go on, Neil."

"It was easy. Peter told me to climb on her and do what I'd done before, and she let me. I think I enjoyed it." Neil looked shyly at Steve. "Then when we'd finished and put our clothes back on, Peter said something to her and she laid on the floor with a scarf around her neck. She was on her tummy. Peter gave me the ends again and I pulled really hard."

"Neil, why do you think she laid down and let you strangle her?"

"I don't know. Peter said it was for the film, and she wanted to be an actress."

"What film?"

"Next door. Peter filmed everything, even me enjoying myself. He said he had to so that there was a record."

Steve couldn't believe it, and neither could Barry. They looked at each other, knowing what this meant.

"Did Peter take the girl away in your van again?"

"Yes, and he took mummy's wheelchair."

Steve wanted to get next door and see the films Neil had said were there. He was just about to patiently ask about the third victim when The Cap arrived. He held up a search warrant.

"Neil, you've been very helpful. Now I know you want to show us the film studio. Can we take a break from your story and go next door to the studio?"

"Yes. I'll show you."

All three detectives and Neil entered 65 Milton Mews using Neil's key. "Neil — please wait here by the front door with Barry. We won't be a minute," said Steve.

Steve and The Cap carried out a cursory search of what was the conventional downstairs of a 1930s detached house. They could see nothing out of the ordinary, so they returned to the inner hallway and climbed the stairs.

To their surprise, the upper floor was completely open-plan — every wall had been removed. In the centre of the space was a king-sized bed covered in plastic sheeting. What looked like a professional lighting system had been set up around the bed and two cameras on tripods were trained on the bed. The floor was carpeted and covered with plastic sheeting. The only other item in the room was a desk, with a large monitor to one side and what looked like a bank of CD recorders.

Both detectives stood still, not venturing into this open space. The Cap tugged Steve's sleeve. "Look, boxes of DVDs or CDs. If those are the recordings, we've got them."

The two men stood for several long seconds, taking in what they were seeing, until Steve broke the spell. "Let's go back down."

Outside the front door, Steve officially arrested Neil Ryder for the murders of Marjory Pearson and Stacey Mathews. He also arrested him in connection with the deaths of Barbara James and Mary Summer. "We'll firm up the charges tomorrow and put the lot on one indictment," he told Barry and The Cap.

The DCI turned to Neil. "Neil — Barry here is going to take you to Scotland Yard, and I'll see you tomorrow. Do you understand what's happening and what I've said?"

"Yes."

Barry set off with the prisoner. Steve spoke to The Cap. "Get the full circus out here tomorrow morning." He looked at his watch. "It's too late now. I want full Scene of Crime, Forensics, Search and a couple of officers from Tech Support to go through those CDs. When it's clear, I want those CDs in the office, pronto. Get Hackney nick to post a constable on this door overnight and I want everybody here at seven o'clock sharp — got it?"

"Yes, boss."

Abul was about to apologise for his slip-up about booking John Peter Saunders but Steve got in first. "You're site commander here until further notice. Consider it punishment for your cock-up and consider yourself lucky that both parties are guilty. No more foul-ups, Abul. Are we clear?"

Abul could see a slight smile on his DCI's face but knew that he'd been gently reprimanded when it could have been a lot worse. All he could say was "Yes, boss. It won't happen again."

Steve set off home while The Cap sorted out the overnight guard for 65 Milton Mews.

Chapter Twenty-Five

By seven o'clock on Sunday morning, the circus of professional police scientists had arrived at 65 Milton Mews. Detective Inspector Abul Ishmal had been on site twenty minutes early. After his lapse in processing the owner of this property, he didn't want to be found failing on this case again.

The DCI arrived at seven thirty carrying three cardboard cups of strong black coffee. He spotted The Cap and offered him one of the three coffees. "How's it going?" He noted the yards of blue and white police tape cordoning off the house down to the road.

"Everyone was keen to get started. Even the Tech team were here on time. I double-checked the search warrant for next door and although we asked for it to cover the van, the lawyers worded it as 'vehicles', so we're covered for the Rover. I've had a couple of forensics techs on it, and so far, they're telling me it's a goldmine of trace evidence. Chummy has a wool blanket in the back and the back seat's down, so hopefully we'll have no problem proving he did for our fourth victim."

"Good. When will the techs finish with the CDs?"

"Scene of Crime said they could bag them straight away and we could have them, but the techs wanted a look. They're up there now."

Just as Steve was about to answer, Barry arrived looking a bit dishevelled.

"Late night, Barry?"

"Not really, boss. My bloody alarm didn't go off." He eyed the two cups of coffee in the DCI's hands. "I don't suppose one of those is for me?"

Steve handed the third cup over and The Cap brought Barry up to speed on events to date.

"We're just going in to see how the techs are doing with the movies. Come on — blue plastic on, and no touching." Steve knew that his officers knew the drill but wanted to lighten the mood.

Two figures dressed in all-in-one white paper suits were seated at the desk with the large monitor and DVD player. Even before the three detectives got close enough to see clearly what was showing on the screen, it was obviously pornographic.

One of the techs paused the film when he realised, they had company. Steve made the introductions and thanked the two officers for working on a Sunday.

With the pleasantries over, they asked about the movies.

The more senior technician spoke for himself and his colleague. "I've been in this job for ten years and thought I'd seen it all, but this is something else. Your perpetrators are in full view before, during and after the killings, so if you've got them, then it's a slam dunk certain conviction. The content's horrific, even for me. It's as though they've tried to make snuff movies of the most violent kind. Do you want to see them? We're just cataloguing for the report."

"Not especially, but I suppose we'd better."

The technician pressed the start button and the images appeared. It was more or less as Neil Ryder had described it, but more violent, especially the murders. The senior tech was correct. Both men were clearly seen on the film and couldn't argue their innocence. Despite the horror of what he was looking at, the DCI knew the case was solved.

"Can you finish up here? I thought I'd take these back to our office and we'd review them ourselves, but I think I'd be happy for your team to review them and give us a report. Not sure I'd want any of this on general distribution within the Yard. The CPS are usually OK with third party evidence in cases like this. We'll simply say that we've seen them, and your team will fully review and give evidence at the trial. Is that, OK?"

The senior tech, who'd introduced himself as Constable Alex Lesley, nodded his approval. "I've done it before, so no problem. If we see anything we're not expecting, I'll give you a shout. Oh! We'll need mug shots of the two prisoners. We have to confirm they are the ones on the film for the court."

After the mix-up with the identity of Neil Ryder, Steve thought this was a very good idea. "I'll get them over to you."

When the three detectives were once again outside and had removed their protective blue plastic, no one spoke. Each was dealing with the horror of what they'd just seen on the monitor.

"I need another coffee and a greasy bacon roll. Don't ask why — I just do." Barry looked worse than when he'd arrived.

"I know a nice restaurant favoured by Scottish detectives working out of Hackney nick. Let's go there and fill up. I'll pay."

The three set off for DS Davie Robertson's favoured café.

***

It was after ten o'clock when Steve and Barry arrived back at Steve's office. The Cap was still in command at 65 Milton Mews and would be there most of the day.

As they entered, Steve saw Andy busily typing away on a laptop.

"I thought I told you to stay away today? You need your beauty sleep."

Barry smiled at this, envisaging the evening Andy and Samantha Burns probably had together.

"I know you did, but I've got a lot to enter, and I need an hour or so with you quietly, sir, about another matter."

Steve appreciated that Andy was talking in code.

"My office — both of you."

Steve was in his control mode. "We've got two suspects downstairs. One's been arrested but not charged and one's about to be arrested. That's our first item — to officially arrest John Peter Saunders for the first three Hackney murders. The statement from Neil Ryder is enough, but the films clinch it. I'll do that and, Barry, you'll be with me."

"Right."

"Second, we need to continue to interview Neil Ryder about the third and fourth murders. I think number four is exclusively down to him. Then, we need to push Saunders to at least admit it's him on the films. If we can get all the ends tied up today, we'll get it upstairs to the CPS to confirm the charges. I want them charged today.

Andy — you haven't seen the films, and I hope you never do, but both guys downstairs are on film killing these women."

"Wow, actually on camera? They must be mad."

"You could be right. Barry — let's get started. Andy — you carry on with what you're doing, and once I get finished downstairs, we'll have that chat."

Steve and Barry entered Interview Room 2. Neil Ryder was sitting at the desk. There was an elderly-looking woman sitting beside him who Steve knew was a duty solicitor. Her name was Moira Stubbs and she'd been a solicitor for a long time but had never ventured into private practice. She'd been content supporting prisoners. Steve knew that she was very good at her job.

After the usual formalities, Steve asked if Neil had seen a doctor. He had. Barry handed the medical report to Steve. He'd been handed it by the custody sergeant as they entered the interview suite. It stated that the prisoner was fit to be interviewed but any questions as to his mental faculties would be for a specialist to answer.

"Neil — yesterday you told us about what happened to the first two girls, Marjory and Stacey. Can you tell us again just so we understand?"

Neil Ryder repeated exactly what he had said the previous evening.

"Now, Neil, what about the third girl, Barbara Jones?"

"She wasn't any good. She wouldn't let me touch her or anything. When Peter told her to get ready for the camera she didn't. She kept saying she wanted to leave and that we'd tricked her. She wasn't very nice."

"What happened, Neil?"

"Peter was angry, so we missed out the bit where I got to do it, and instead Peter put a belt around her neck from the back and held her standing, like. She must've fainted or something because he put her on the ground just like the others and I pulled the belt tight."

"Did Peter take the girl away like before?"

"Yes. I got the van and put it in Peter's garage."

"Listen very carefully, Neil. Your solicitor will help you. Are you confessing to these murders and did John Peter Saunders help you?"

Steve looked at Moira Stubbs for confirmation that she was happy. She gave a slight nod in return.

"Now, Neil, tell us about Mary Sumner. She was different, wasn't she?"

Neil became a bit restless and started to wring his hands. "Yes, she was different. She didn't obey the rules. The girls were told to come at ten o'clock in the morning but this one came at three o'clock in the afternoon. She made everything bad."

"What do you mean, Neil?"

"Well, you came and took Peter away. Peter told me to take her to the studio and wait for him. I'd not been alone in the studio with a girl before, so we just sat on the bed and waited. Then all these police came, and I saw Peter leaving. I didn't know what to do with the girl."

"So, what did you do?"

"She thought all the police were part of the film, so I told her we had to go. My car was in the road, so we went in that and left."

"Did you drive past your house?"

"Yes, a few times. The girl said it was exciting being in a film and that she'd do anything to get a part. I don't know how, but we finished up on the common. She said she wanted to go home because there was no film crew on the common."

"Go on…"

"I don't know how, but I got her to get out of the car. I had a rope in the back and the next thing I know she's on the grass face down just like the others and I'm pulling hard on the rope."

"You're saying you killed her?"

"Yes. I put her in the car and took her to Tesco in Hackney. Peter told me where he'd dumped the other girls so I thought Tesco would be a good place."

Steve had what he needed. He stood up. Barry followed. "Barry — please charge Mr Neil Ryder with the four murders he's confessed to."

Steve left after stopping the tape. He felt unclean having listened to this simple-minded man explain how callously he'd committed four murders.

Now for the leader, John Peter Saunders, but before taking him on, Steve needed to relax. He headed for the canteen and a coffee. He knew Barry would find him.

With a strong coffee in hand, he called Alison on her mobile. She'd had a good trip down to Rye and had heard all the stories of the residents of the View Care Home for the hundredth time. She was disappointed he'd not made it down to Rye the previous evening, but Steve explained about the case and they then talked about getting away for a few days within the next two weeks. She promised to call Steve when she returned from Rye and they made a tentative arrangement to see each other later that evening.

After speaking with Alison, Steve felt better.

Barry joined him and explained that Neil Ryder was now "bound up like a kipper" — a sure guilty verdict. They joked that even the greenest member of the Crown Prosecution Service couldn't argue with the thoroughness of the investigation.

As they sat, The Cap arrived full of smiles. He got himself a coffee and explained. "All done in Hackney. The plastic sheeting didn't give up much so that's why there was no trace on the first three victims. The car's thrown up a lot and it's now all bagged and at the lab. We'll get a report tomorrow. They found fingerprints all over the place and it's a certainty that some will belong to the victims. I watched a few more of the films with the techs. That stuff's pure snuff movie land but very amateurish. The good news is, our prisoners are all over the film, so we've got them."

All three sat back and sighed. It was almost choreographed. They each felt satisfaction in their own way.

Steve was pleased to see The Cap back. "You two can do the interview with Saunders. I bet he's not so cocky when you ask him to explain what we've got, plus Neil Ryder's confession. It's up to you. I'm going to do some real police work now — that's shovelling paper, to you." All three smiled at what they knew was true in today's police force.

"Get them charged and locked up. Express the paperwork to the CPS and let's get a hearing early next week if we can."

Steve stood up and left with a wave. He stopped after a few steps and turned. "I've had an idea…"

His idea was to introduce Dr Alison Mills to his colleagues and success in the Hackney case was just the excuse he needed.

"Everybody down The Frog tonight at, say, eight o'clock. I'll buy the first round. Bring your partners or wives. I'll tell Andy and see who he turns up with."

All three laughed. "I'll bet you a fiver it's Samantha Burns."

"Well, if it's not her it'll be his mother," Barry explained. "The bet's on."

Chapter Twenty-Six

When Steve got back to his office, Andy was pacing around, obviously in an agitated state.

"Come in, Andy, and close the door." Once both detectives were seated, Steve asked Andy what was bothering him.

"I've been working on the other case and it's a bit weird. Can I take you through what we've got, but slowly? I don't want to miss anything."

"Of course. Carry on, I'm all ears."

Andy had his laptop set up, remembering his boss's instruction that there was to be no paper left lying around.

"First, we've got our victim, one Dr David Graham, an American. We've got him on CCTV arriving at Heathrow last Sunday morning. He's wanted in the States for the murder of a fellow scientist and is suspected of stealing whatever research this other boffin was working on." Andy paused and Steve nodded.

"We know that an International Arrest Warrant was issued for this Dr Graham, but it wasn't actioned in this country, despite Graham having flown here on a commercial flight using his real name. He checks into the Mayflower Hotel, again under his real name, but is allowed to move around and he's not arrested. I've gone through the CCTV from the hotel." Andy turned his laptop so Steve had a view of the screen.

Andy pointed at the screen. "There he is checking in. He's handing over his passport and so on. Now, there he is heading for the lift." Andy had something else. "Ten minutes after he's checked in, a girl goes to the reception desk, asks something and then walks towards the lifts."

"I see that, Andy, but where does she fit in?"

"I'm coming to that, Steve. Bear with me." Andy pressed keys on his computer at lightning speed. "Now look, the time clock's 5.03 on the evening Dr Graham arrived. See the girl standing with the largish man? I'm certain that's the same girl. Watch... One minute later, our Dr Graham arrives and all three leave the hotel."

Andy ejected the disc they'd been looking at and inserted another.

"This is the CCTV from outside the hotel. All three get into a car and drive off. I was able to read the registration plate of the car."

Andy sat back. "I know it's a bit boring, but it gets better."

"No, no, Andy, carry on."

"The hotel told you that the room for Graham was booked by Brothers International Inc. Well, there's no such company registered. I thought we'd get lucky with the credit card used to pay for the booking, but it's issued by a funny bank based in Zurich. But I got lucky with the car. It's registered to a Julian St. John I've got the address and phone number. So this Julian St John character pays for our victim to stay at a swanky hotel in London. Why?"

"Good question. Do you have an answer?"

"Not at the moment." Andy looked disappointed.

"Now, remember I said I'd talk to the River Police? Well, they estimate that the body might have gone in near Chelsea." Andy held up his hand and grinned at his boss. He was enjoying this. "Hold that thought. You also remember that I was going to check out his mobile phone, or rather his lack of a mobile phone? It seems he did have a USA registered phone. AT&T were the provider over there and they work with O2 in this country. All I had to do was ask O2 for details of any USA registered phone that had pinged a mast near the Mayflower Hotel. I only got one hit so it's odds on that it's his. The police in Massachusetts have pulled his phone records as part of their case so we know it's a match."

"Hang on, Andy. How did you get O2 to cooperate without a warrant?"

Andy just smiled. "Let's just say I may have over exaggerated my importance to this case. A murder case seems to get a lot of sympathetic help and a bit of, let's say, secret hacking never does any harm."

"For your sake I hope you don't get caught but you're saying most of the information was given freely?"

"Yes, of course." Andy just smiled.

Steve admired the initiative so said nothing. "Is there anything of interest from the records?"

"Yes, but it's a bit disturbing. He called another American number using his O2 connection, so it was made here. I got the number and O2 confirmed that it was also an original AT&T phone. Now, here's the bit you'll not like. I asked the police in Massachusetts to search the records for this other American phone. It seems over there they can legally hack into anyone's account. Anyway, it came back totally redacted. Every call was blanked out. The only thing that wasn't was the payee's address." Andy stopped to make sure he had Steve's attention.

"Well go on..."

"The company that pays the bill is the CIA out of Langley, Virginia."

Steve was shell-shocked; he appeared to be struck dumb. Both men sat in silence and tried to digest this piece of information. Eventually, Steve made some sense of Andy's revelation.

"Our victim was in touch with a CIA operative in London before his death?" Steve was incredulous.

"Looks like it."

"Do we know who this agent might be?"

"No, but on a hunch, I asked O2 to check masts in Chelsea to see if this second American phone had pinged any of them. Remember, the body could have gone in at Chelsea, so I thought it was worth a look."

"Tell me you got something."

Andy was looking pleased with himself but was still wearing his serious face. "I got the O2 records, and the second phone did ping in Chelsea. It's been used several times during the last week, always connecting to the same Chelsea mast. Whoever it is has phoned the same number I got from telecoms for this Julian St John, plus, and here's the kicker, that club you asked me to get the records for earlier on this week. You remember The Fortress Club in Hackney? Well the number for the club is on the call records for the second phone as well. Also, according to O2, given the number of mast pings they've had, it's likely that the CIA agent lives somewhere in Chelsea."

Again, Steve sat back admiring the brain of DC Andrew Miller. This was a lot of data to take in and Steve needed time to digest it all.

"Andy, is all this on file now?"

"Yes, no paper."

"So, we know we have a CIA agent operating around our case. We know that somehow the victim, this St John character and the club owned by an ex-police commander at Scotland Yard all seem connected. Plus, we know that an International Arrest Warrant was squashed and that our victim was himself a murderer who may have stolen something valuable from his victim. Does that more or less sum things up?"

"I'd say so, Steve, except we don't know who the girl is who was at the Mayflower the morning Graham checked in and got into the car with him on his first night. I've checked all the discs. She's in a few but look at this one." Andy set to work on his laptop again. "There they are getting back to the hotel together at 11.07 on Tuesday night." Andy run the film forwards. "Now look. There they are leaving at 00.37 Wednesday morning and the doctor's got a bag with him. The outside camera shows them getting into a taxi. I've got a partial plate, so I'll try and run it down. But this is the last we see of Dr Graham on any hotel CCTV images." Andy closed his laptop lid with a gentle click. "Also, I checked the calls Graham made from his room. Most were looking for tickets for shows or museums, but one was to the States. I'm waiting to hear back who the number belongs to, but it's a New York prefix."

"First thing tomorrow, get me an appointment with Sir Timothy Head. He's the main civil servant in the Government. I'm sure he won't like it, but the pathologist Professor Campbell let slip that our Sir Timothy had asked him personally to do the post-mortem on Dr Graham. With everything that's going on, I want to know why. I'll also see this Julian St John tomorrow and see what he's got to say. Will you remind The Cap that he's to be at the post-mortem for our fourth Hackney victim tomorrow at ten, sharp? I don't think Dr Sophie Kendell suffers fools gladly and we need to get all the files up to date ready for the lawyers."

"Got it. Now, I checked on that name you gave me — Micky Russ. He's been in and out of prison most of his life — always for violence. It seems he's been involved with a few gangs over the years but now seems to be freelance. He'll work for anybody who pays him. At the moment he's clean, with no warrants out for him. I got his file and he's on the CCTV from the hotel foyer. Is that where you saw him?"

"Yes, but what's a heavy like Russ doing in the same hotel as our murder victim? It's just too much of a coincidence, don't you think?"

"I agree but I don't have an answer."

"Good work, Andy. Let's put all this to bed and we'll get into it first thing tomorrow. The Cap and Barry can finish up the Hackney case and hopefully we'll concentrate on this one."

Steve stood up with a flourish. "Right, Andy. You and a partner of your choice are invited to a celebration tonight. The Frog at eight o'clock. We're due a bit of light relief after the Hackney business. I'll see you there."

"Great, thanks. Can I bring anyone?"

"Anyone you want, but don't be late. I'll see you there."

***

In The Fortress Club, ex-police commander Alistair Ramsay took a phone call from a member of Customs and Excise based in Ramsgate. He'd been anticipating this call all day. The voice on the end of the telephone confirmed that James Rushdie's shipment had cleared successfully through Ramsgate and was now on its way to a warehouse in Faversham. The voice said that there had been a problem but he'd dealt with it. However, to solve the problem he'd had to increase the bribe money he'd paid to his colleagues and now he was out of pocket — a state of affairs he was decidedly unhappy with. Everyone concerned needed more money and so did he.

Alistair Ramsay had dealt with such money-grabbing, corrupt individuals before and knew how to handle them.

"Listen. You've been paid, so don't give me some cock and bull story about something happening that's cost you more money. You've had all you're getting."

The official at the other end of the line was quiet. Ramsay didn't like that. He preferred dealing with crooks who got excited and said things without thinking.

"Commander, it's up to you. There's no proof of the money you say you've paid me, and the boys here certainly aren't going to admit to passing through a container full of Colombia's finest. All I have to do is alert Kent Constabulary to my suspicions that a load of drugs has just slipped through the port, and put them on to the truck. It's probably just now on the Thanet Way heading to the warehouse, so, easy to stop."

"Now listen here. I've looked after you long enough. This is a favour I've asked for but one I've paid for. There's no more money."

"Well, that's a shame. I'll try and keep your name out of the statements we'll have to give. After all, we're not admitting anything, are we?"

"Don't think you can blackmail me. I've still got connections you know nothing about."

"Please. You're a has-been, in over your head. Now be sensible. Another ten grand and we're done. Usual procedure so it's not traceable. That shipment's worth millions and you know it. Another ten grand's nothing."

Alistair Ramsay knew this customs officer was right. The shipment was big, and if James Rushdie didn't get it through, Alistair Ramsay was a dead man walking. Reluctantly, he agreed to the extra payment.

As he sat in his office, he contemplated how he'd arrived at this point. He'd had a glittering police career, even reaching dizzily high rank. He'd been well-regarded but he did like the white powder similar to that on its way to Faversham. At first it was just recreational. He and his fellow senior officers had partied a lot, and there were always girls, booze and drugs. Everyone seemed to enjoy themselves, so he saw nothing unusual. He knew after a while that he was becoming more addicted to the powder and the girls that came with it. He'd transferred to the Kent force to try and escape, but it followed him. Because the county of Kent housed so many ports, he was soon being asked to arrange for officials to turn a blind eye to small-time smuggling operations.

Then, at one party in London, he'd met James Rushdie. His recollection was a bit vague, but he knew that he was stoned and had agreed to help get Rushdie's stuff into the country.

He thought back and realised that this was when he'd gotten in too deep. James Rushdie had set him up in The Fortress Club as a cover for drugs and prostitution. He'd recruited senior police officers and members of the judiciary as members. They still ran the type of parties that had gotten him hooked in the first place, so James Rushdie had some kind of hold over some very prominent people.

Alistair Ramsay considered his options. He'd made money over the years and saved some of it. He was coming under ever-increasing pressure to be Rushdie's puppet and fixer. He didn't like his role. He determined that the last shipment he had just been blackmailed into paying extra bribe money for was his last. He still used the powder but not as much; he was getting too old for the girls. He now knew his time was up. He'd escape when he could.

Or so he thought.

Chapter Twenty-Seven

The DCI was up and out of the door of his apartment by six thirty. It looked like being one of those cold, clear, crisp December mornings. He had a spring in his step despite the cold air. He'd decided to walk to his office this morning. One reason was that he wanted to reminisce about last night's social gathering. The other was to consider the case and to try and digest the information Andy had given him.

The pub had been a great success. He'd called Alison just as she was arriving back from Rye. He explained what he'd arranged, and she'd instantly agreed to meet him at the pub at eight o'clock. The Cap was there with his wife, a very pretty, petite lady with a ready smile and a good sense of humour. She'd said she needed it living with Abul. As a couple they looked made for each other. Barry was with his latest girlfriend, a good-looking girl of about thirty who had huge brown eyes offsetting her sallow skin type, giving her an almost mystical air. She was as tall as Barry, was drinking orange juice and, according to Barry, would be his ex-girlfriend within the week. He explained that she was becoming too much like his mother.

Andy was there with Samantha Burns. Steve had noticed that the two were a bit shy and didn't mix readily, but after a few glasses they'd both opened up and were soon involved in the conversations that ran from politics to the royal family. Everyone seemed to enjoy it and Steve was particularly happy to see Alison talking to everybody and answering the obvious questions about their relationship. Steve felt she batted such questions away with skill.

This had been their first social event and Steve was determined it wouldn't be the last.

As he walked, his mind turned to the case. Andy had proven a link between this mysterious American CIA agent, their murder victim, this Julian St John character and The Fortress Club, and possibly ex-Commander Alistair Ramsay. He was worried about the hired muscle

Micky Russ and his appearance at the Mayflower Hotel. He thought about the girl from the hotel CCTV leaving with David Graham on his first night and possibly his last, and why was the most senior Home Office pathologist being asked by the head of the civil service to do him a favour. And there was the question of the suppressed International Arrest Warrant.

His mind was spinning. What did it all mean? He didn't have a clue, but with all this information and unanswered questions something had to break.

He arrived at the Yard refreshed and eager to get going. He'd bought a coffee on his walk and was finishing it when his internal phone rang. It was Superintendent Frank Dobson asking if Steve could visit him in his office now.

"What's it about, sir? Our last meeting didn't end too well as I recall."

"Don't be smart. Just get up here now, I didn't come in early to be mucked about." Steve didn't like the tone in the superintendent's voice but as his junior he had to do as requested.

Frank Dobson, the Yard's number one murder detective, was pacing in his small office and clearly upset. On seeing Steve approach, he waved him in and took his place behind his desk.

"Close the door."

"What's this about, sir?"

"Cut out the 'sir'! You're still looking into The Fortress Club. I got the search warrants granted list for last week this morning and your boy applied for and got one on Friday."

Andy had been his usual efficient self but with the Hackney thing going down he must have forgotten to mention it. As Steve recalled, they'd established a link to this club so the warrant would be useful.

"And your point is?"

"I told you to lay off. You were only going for their financials and I told you not to go after the membership list. I had hoped to persuade Alistair Ramsay to cooperate but he's adamant you'll not see the list. Is there nothing I can say that'll persuade you to call the dogs off?"

"Listen, Frank, I'm working on another murder case, and we've got a link between the victim and The Fortress Club, so the answer's no. This place could be front and centre to my enquiries."

"What murder case? I don't know anything about you being allocated another case?"

"Sorry, but that wasn't my decision. We'll execute the warrant later today or tomorrow morning, so tell your buddy not to do anything stupid as far as his records are concerned."

"Steve — you're a bloody good detective but you need to stand back and look at what you're getting into. The owner of The Fortress isn't Alistair. It's some American bloke, and he's not nice. I've only met him once and he scared me by just being in the room. People could get hurt, you included, if you pursue this."

"Is that a threat?"

"I'm afraid it is. I won't lie to you. I told Alistair about the search warrant this morning. Within five minutes he was back relaying instructions to me from his boss to make sure you were warned off or you'd face the consequences. I'm sorry, Steve, but there it is."

"How deep are you into this set-up? I thought you were a good, decent, clean cop, but now this!"

"Don't look too deep. I made a mistake and I'm paying for it. They own me but don't think this is an idle threat. They will come after you and yours if you carry on."

"Why wouldn't I go straight to professional standards and report you threatening me?"

"You could, but by the time they got their act together, we might both be in the ground or in wheelchairs."

"You can tell whoever they are that I'm not giving up, but I will pursue the club, only in as much as I need to, in connection with my murder case. I'll hold off on the warrant, but I'll use it if I have to. That's the best I can do for now, but we will talk about this later. Is that clear, SIR?"

Superintendent Frank Dobson remained seated and silent as Steve stormed out.

***

DCI Steve Burt sat in his office with the door closed; he needed time to calm down after his meeting with Frank Dobson. He worked through as many scenarios as he could think of as to how some obviously criminal organisation might get to him. Clearly Frank Dobson was in the pocket of whoever owned this club, but Steve wasn't sure if sight of the members list would necessarily help his enquiries into the murder of David Graham. He argued with himself that he hadn't been weak and given in. He genuinely felt that unless his investigation needed sight of the list then he'd let it go.

Satisfied that he'd made the right judgement call, Steve opened his door to see Andy at his desk. He had two cups of coffee and clearly one was for his boss.

"Thanks, Andy. Come on in."

Both men were seated on the visitor's side of Steve's desk.

"You said you'd pulled the company accounts for The Fortress Club. Have you had a look at them yet?"

"No. I'm sorry, Steve, but I'm not an accountant. I got their last three years' filings, plus a list of directors listed at Companies House. I've also got a list of their shareholders, and I got the search warrant, but that's it."

"Let's look at the directors list."

Andy opened his laptop and set to work. "There." He swung the machine so both men could see the screen.

Steve wasn't sure what he was looking for. At the top of the list was Alistair Ramsay as Managing Director. Then came James Rushdie as Executive Chairman, and a Desmond Cutter as Non-Executive Director. Mrs Desmond Cutter was also listed as a Non-Executive Director.

"Not sure this tells us anything."

"Check the shareholder's roll." Andy obliged.

"Here it is. Almost all the shares are held by this bloke Rushdie. Mr Cutter has 10%, Mrs Cutter has 5%. Rushdie holds the rest."

"Alistair Ramsay doesn't have any shares?"

"Not according to Companies House."

"Interesting." Steve became all business. "Write this up. It's interesting but might not mean anything. Send all the financial stuff over to the Financial Crimes Unit. Ask them to take a look, and to report anything they find back to us, certainly in the beginning." Steve didn't wait for an answer. "Now, have you asked for my meeting with Sir Timothy Head?"

"I e-mailed yesterday so they'd have it first thing. There was no reply so I phoned. Have you ever tried to get through the Whitehall switchboard? It's a nightmare and almost impossible. Anyway, I eventually got some jumped-up undersecretary or something who said he'd check with Sir Timothy and phone back. I'm still waiting."

"Keep at it, Andy. I want to have a face-to-face with this guy today."

"Right."

"Have you put out an all-points to lift Micky Russ? He's another one I'd like to talk to today."

"I put it out last night but so far no sightings."

"Let me know the minute we find him. Any luck with the taxi number from the Mayflower CCTV?"

"No. It's on my list, as is the USA phone number David Graham phoned from his hotel room."

"Sounds like you've got enough on. I'll go and see this Julian St John now. Shouldn't take long. I'll be back by lunchtime unless this guy has got something to tell me."

***

Julian and Sebastian St John were sitting discussing recent events. Both still felt hard done by as a result of James Rushdie's actions. Both secretly harboured thoughts of revenge but the twenty million dollars they were expecting was a big incentive to do nothing. Still, if they could secure their money and get revenge…

"I've had an e-mail from Gregory Anderson in New York. He's still banging on that we owe him the money. It seems your James Rushdie has stiffed him, and he doesn't like it. Rushdie told us he'd take care of the money owed to Anderson, but he hasn't. He's got some hold over him and apparently has said he won't go to the authorities in exchange for Anderson forgetting about the formula." Julian looked over at his brother.

"It's surely not our problem now. Rushdie's got the formula and all the headaches that seem to go with it."

"Not so, brother." Julian was the more astute of the pair. "Anderson still wants his cash. He's threatening to send someone over from the States to collect. My idea that we might have to disappear looks even more interesting now, don't you think?"

"Yes, but we'll have to get our money first. Has the first ten million arrived yet?"

"No, and we're getting more demands from Kent. The security team have swept the place clean, so they want more money to keep their operatives on site, and the hotel now wants another fifty grand, to keep all its rooms vacant until after the auction."

Sebastian amazed himself by suggesting: "We should ask Desmond Cutter and his pal Rushdie to pay for the auction — lock, stock and barrel. After all, we did all the hard work putting the venue on notice and getting the delegates to come."

Julian suddenly became more interested. "Do you think he would?"

"No reason why not. No venue, no auction; no auction, no money. We need to get the venue sorted now. The auction's on Friday."

"I'll phone him, but you have a look round. We can disappear after the auction. Somewhere nice. Our twenty million won't last long but we can set up somewhere else. We've still got our contacts, and as long as Gregory Anderson doesn't find us, we'll be home-free and back in business." Suddenly Julian felt more positive.

Desmond Cutter was in the lounge of The Fortress Club reading a newspaper and drinking tea. When his phone vibrated, he answered it without looking at the caller ID. It was Julian St John.

Julian explained his predicament. He laid it on thickly, maybe too thickly. "The auction's on Friday, Desmond. The delegates are arriving from Wednesday — that's the day after tomorrow. If we don't pay security and the hotel, the people coming with the money won't get a room, and the whole thing will be a disaster. So, you see, we need two hundred grand now, to keep things moving."

"Why didn't you tell us sooner?"

"We thought we could cover it, but now your buddy James has come along and changed our deal, we find we're a little short."

"Send me a text with the hotel name, address and contact number." Just as he asked, Desmond Cutter suddenly realised that they didn't know the venue or any details of the auction. "On second thoughts, I'll send a car. You both come here and bring everything with you. We'll take care of the hotel, and you bring the details of everyone who is attending. Have you got that?"

"Yes, but why can't we just e-mail it to you?"

"Never mind — just be ready. James isn't here right now but he will be for lunch. I'll have you picked up just before twelve. Be ready and don't bring that goon with the Glock."

The line went dead.

Desmond Cutter sighed a great sigh of relief. This was the one area they'd not screwed down. Julian was right — without the auction there'd be no payday. Desmond smiled, thinking they'd dodged a bullet. Now they would have everything tied down with no loose ends. They couldn't have the brothers involved in the final show.

Julian hung up. He was depressed again. It struck him that these days his emotions were all over the place. Every bit of news brought a different problem. This deal wasn't what he'd planned.

He was about to inform Sebastian of his phone call when Ruby arrived, looking gorgeous as always. Julian brightened up. This woman had a hypnotic effect on him, but he couldn't see how to persuade her into his bed.

"My dear, what a pleasant surprise. What can we do for you?"

"You can do nothing, but I might do something for you."

Julian deliberately misunderstood this statement. Lust swelled up in his chest and other parts of his anatomy. Ruby saw the signs and aimed a warning glance at Julian.

"I had a call from Gregory late last night. He's sending over his tech guy to be at the auction. He says that if you don't pay up, his tech guy will stand up and tell the meeting the formula doesn't work."

Julian and Sebastian stood in unison. Sebastian was the first to speak. "He can't do that. That guy Rushdie will kill him. He's off his rocker if he thinks a blackmail tactic like that will get him his money."

Ruby sat on one of the sofas and removed her coat. "He clearly thinks it will. I'm to tell your Desmond Cutter and James Rushdie just that, but I thought I'd tell you first."

Julian had slumped into a depression again. "I need a drink. What are we going to do, brother?"

"I don't know what we'll do, but what will the other two do? That's the question."

Julian poured himself a small scotch. "When's this tech bloke arriving?"

"I don't know," Ruby lied. He was in fact at her apartment in Chelsea and had been for several days.

Sebastian had returned to his seat. "I suppose Gregory Anderson's not too bothered about what Rushdie thinks he's got over him. The only way to keep everything going is for Rushdie to pay Anderson out of the sale proceeds. If they could agree a deal then everyone except us would win." Sebastian was wearing a dark, thoughtful expression. "Brother, how can we take advantage of this?"

"I'm sorry, I don't understand."

"No, neither do I, but there must be a way we can turn this to our advantage. I'm not sure how, but there has to be a way."

Ruby asked if she could have a coffee. "If you're planning some kind of double cross, remember that both sides are not easy to deal with, and are more likely to have you wiped out than pay you."

Julian thought Ruby's American accent was straight out of Hollywood. He handed Ruby her coffee and sat beside her, ever hopeful. He outlined for his brother what Desmond Cutter had told him. Sebastian started to pull together the various invoices and quotations from Ridge Securities and The Bell Tower Hotel just outside Maidstone.

An air of gloom descended on the penthouse. Ruby was deliberately quiet but didn't encourage either brother to speak. The mood wasn't helped when Frankie appeared. "There's a Detective Chief Inspector Burt to see you."

"To see us? Tell him to get lost. We've nothing to say to the police."

Frankie disappeared as Ruby put her coat on, preparing to leave.

Obviously, Sebastian's message to Steve was relayed by Frankie and wasn't received very favourably because Steve pushed past the faithful servant and was now front and centre in their open-plan apartment. Steve noted that the servant didn't try to stop him pushing past. He made a mental note.

"Good morning. Thank you for agreeing to see me." He knew this wasn't true but it was better to take charge right from the beginning.

Steve pointed to Julian. "You, sir, would be who?"

Julian didn't know how to react to this, so he answered: "I am Julian St John. This other gentleman is my brother, Sebastian."

Sebastian had been sitting at their long table but stood up upon being introduced to the detective.

"Thank you, sir." He turned to Ruby, who he recognised from the CCTV as being with Dr Graham in the Mayflower Hotel. "And you are, miss?"

"I'm just visiting and I'm leaving."

Steve outstretched an arm, effectively corralling Ruby and making it obvious that he wasn't allowing her to leave.

"This is just routine, miss, so please just answer my question. Once again, you are?" Steve noted Ruby's American accent.

"Oh! All right, I'm Ruby Thomas."

"And where do you live, Miss Thomas?" Ruby looked a little startled but gave her address as a flat in Chelsea. Steve noted the address in his notebook.

"Thank you. Can I suggest we all sit down? This won't take long."

Ruby removed her coat and the brothers sat. Steve positioned himself in front of his audience.

"I'm investigating the murder of a Dr David Graham, someone I think you are all acquainted with?"

"No, I don't think I know anyone of that name," Julian lied. "What about you, Sebastian?"

Sebastian just sat and scowled at Steve, shaking his head.

"What about you, Miss Thomas? Do you know a Dr Graham?"

"No, I don't think I do. The name's not familiar."

Steve knew they were lying but didn't know why.

"Dr Graham was staying at the Mayflower Hotel until a few days ago. His initial reservation was made by a company called Brothers International Inc. Does this ring any bells with anyone?"

No one answered but Steve noted that Julian was flushing up. The DCI had been in this position before and knew he had to take things step by step.

Looking straight at Julian, Steve went for a question he knew would get a reaction. "Can you explain why we have a CCTV recording of Dr Graham…" Steve turned to look at Ruby. "And you, Miss Thomas, getting into a car that's registered to you, sir, Julian St John?"

Steve sat back.

All three looked at each other with shocked expressions. Ruby was the first to speak. She tried to make light of this revelation. "Oh! Of course! I remember. Julian, you asked me to collect a business associate from the Mayflower and take him to dinner, you remember?"

"Yes, of course. Was that this doctor fellow you're investigating, Inspector?"

"Yes, sir." Steve decided on a little deception to try and bring something like the truth to the fore. "What was the name of the restaurant, Miss Thomas? And why did you, Mr St John, reserve and pay for someone, whose name you don't know, to stay two nights at the Mayflower?"

Steve waited to see if his lie would work. While he suspected his statement was true, Andy hadn't been able to prove it.

"Well, you see…" Julian was now openly sweating. "We sometimes have overseas visitors that we're required to accommodate for short business trips to London. This was just one of them."

Ruby eyed Steve with her most alluring and sexy stare, hoping he could be distracted as easily as Julian. "I really can't remember the restaurant." She hitched her skirt higher and brushed down her hair. She instantly saw that this detective wasn't interested in what she might offer.

"I see. Why was Dr Graham in London?"

"I really don't know. As I said, it was a business arrangement."

"Who asked you to accommodate Dr Graham?"

Steve had backed Julian into a corner. In a panic and without thinking, he blurted out: "A Gregory Anderson of New York."

Steve noted this. It was clear to him that these three were up to something and were probably involved somehow in the murder. He decided to leave things for a while, but to keep them off guard he turned to Ruby. "Do you have a mobile phone, Miss Thomas?"

Ruby was relieved at the change of questioning. "Of course I do, Inspector. Doesn't everyone?"

"May I see it?"

"Well, I can let you look at it, but even a simple girl like me knows you'll need a court order to look at what's on it."

She handed Steve her phone. It was inside a leather cover that looked like a book. Steve opened it and was rewarded with what he'd hoped for. On the inside flap, Ruby had written a number that Steve took to be the number of this phone. He knew it was a common thing for people to do when they travelled a lot.

He memorised the number and handed the phone back. With stealth, he immediately wrote the number in his notebook before he forgot it.

"Inspector — time is getting on and we've a luncheon appointment in ten minutes. Is there anything else?"

"Yes, I'm afraid there is." The DCI studied each person before dropping his deliberate bombshell. "Which one of you killed Dr Graham?"

There was close to uproar — even Sebastian was talking. All three talked over each other. Julian was in a state of panic. He was calling the lovely Ruby some nasty things, suggesting that if she hadn't been so much of a whore then none of this would be happening. Sebastian was on his feet, shouting at Julian about getting them into this mess, and Ruby was screaming at both brothers to stay calm and shut up.

Eventually, all three calmed down and it seemed that Ruby took charge. She didn't panic easily and knew how to divert attention away from both herself and the immediate problem.

"Inspector, you're wrong. Dr Graham isn't dead. In fact, he's alive and well and has just changed where he's staying."

This caused Steve to now be at a momentary loss. What was this woman saying? Of course Dr Graham was dead — he was in a freezer box in a London mortuary. Steve quickly regained his composure.

"Interesting, Miss Thomas. Care to tell me where I might find him?" With more than a hint of sarcasm, he added: "Just so we can ask him how he'd managed his resurrection."

Ruby realised she'd opened the door and couldn't back out. "He's staying at The Fortress Club in Hackney, if you must know."

Steve hadn't been expecting this. Once again, he needed to re-group and shuffle his thoughts into some semblance of order.

"How long has he been there?"

"A few days. From just before the weekend, I think. I'm sure if you call, they'll confirm he's there. So you see, Inspector, if he's at The Fortress then no one here could have murdered him because he's not dead." Ruby was a bit smug but deep down hoped she'd not started something.

Frankie appeared to announce that a car had arrived to take his employers to lunch.

"If you don't mind, Inspector, we have a luncheon appointment." Julian looked calmer.

Steve walked around the sofas and chairs. He'd spotted a small pile of papers on the large table and nonchalantly positioned himself so that he could read the headings on some of the papers. He noted that they were invoices from The Bell Tower Hotel and from Ridge Securities. He committed both to memory. There also seemed to be a report from Ridge Securities but he couldn't read it without drawing attention to himself.

"Just before you go, Miss Thomas — how long have you been in the UK?"

"I arrived a couple of weeks ago. You can check my passport if you like."

"Thank you, we might just do that."

As Steve prepared to leave, the ever-faithful Frankie arrived to escort him to the lift and then to the street below.

Once outside, Steve held back and witnessed a large black BMW waiting by the kerb. He noted the registration number and observed the brothers and Ruby leaving the apartment block and getting into the car.

***

The DCI returned to his office with his head full of new information and more questions. As he entered, Andy was in the middle of a large sandwich and Barry was reading something while drinking coffee from a plastic cup.

"Andy — be a good lad and grab me a coffee, please. I'm desperate. Then come into my office. You too, Barry."

"Will do boss." Just as Andy was leaving, he said: "I've sent all the financial stuff over to Financial Crimes like you asked. They said they were busy but would take a look when they could. I told them it wasn't top priority."

Armed with his coffee, and with his two colleagues seated opposite him, Steve updated both of them on his previous meeting. He'd decided on his way back that he needed more boots on the ground and would bring Barry in on the case.

"Barry — I know you're not up to speed, and Andy will brief you, but remember this is very sensitive. Not even The Cap knows about this case. Orders from the top. I'm not even sure I should bring you in, but there you go. I'm doing it, so no blabbing. Understood?"

"Yes, I've got it, Steve."

"Andy — first, this is the registration of the car that picked the brothers up. Check it out with DVLA. I want to know who it belongs to. Barry — second, there were invoices from The Bell Tower Hotel and Ridge Securities in that apartment. Track them down. Let's see what they can tell us."

Both detectives nodded. Barry was about to take notes but saw Steve's expression. "Sorry, no paper, I forgot."

"Right. If you need to put anything on paper, make it in code, and once you've had Andy enter anything onto the file, shred your notes. OK?"

"Andy — have you heard from this Timothy Head character?"

"No, Steve, and no one's phoned back."

"Let me have the phone number. I'm getting a bit fed up with all this high-powered cloak-and-dagger. Anything else?"

Andy opened his laptop. "Yes. I ran that partial plate from the taxi that took that girl and our doctor away from the Mayflower. I tracked it down to three cabs and got lucky with my second call. The driver remembers them because they were both American and the girl was a stunner." With a smile, Andy added: "He thought it was unusual that a hooker was taking a John away from a hotel. He said it was usually the other way round."

All three relaxed a little at the taxi driver's observation. Andy continued. "He took them to a mews apartment in Chelsea."

Before Andy could continue, Steve held up his hand. He opened his notebook and read off the address Ruby Thomas had given him as hers. They matched. Steve removed the page from his notebook and gave it to Andy to place on file and then shred.

Steve sat back and put his hands together under his chin as though he were praying. "We now know that this Ruby Thomas, an American, was the last person, we know of, to see our victim alive. What do we think? We believe there's a CIA agent living in Chelsea and this Ruby lives in Chelsea." Steve handed the telephone number he'd lifted from Ruby's phone to Andy. Andy consulted his laptop and smiled.

"I got the data from O2. It's the same number. This is the phone that's paid for by the CIA. She must be their agent."

"So why did she tell me Dr Graham isn't dead but is living at The Fortress Club? She must know we'd check?"

Barry, who'd been listening but not taking part in the discussion due to his lack of knowledge of the case, chipped in. "What if there's more to this agent? We don't know her mission. It would be nice to find out what she's doing here and with these men."

"Good point, but I bet we'll get blanked if we go directly to the CIA and ask what one of their agents is doing in London."

Steve again referred to his notebook and removed a page. "Julian St John let slip that he was asked to arrange the Mayflower Hotel for our victim by a Gregory Anderson."

Andy put his hand up like a schoolboy trying to attract his teacher's attention. It was his turn to say what Steve was about to ask.

"Gregory Anderson lives in New York and it was his number that Dr Graham called from his hotel room phone."

All three sat back in silence.

"Let's recap. Our victim is a scientist, who apparently stole something from another American scientist, and then killed him. There's an International Arrest Warrant issued for his arrest, but it's not actioned. The St John brothers arrange his hotel in London and an American CIA agent arrives, according to her, just days before our victim, and latches onto the brothers. There seems to be a connection with The Fortress Club. It's run by an ex-assistant chief constable of Kent Constabulary, but we know it's owned by James Rushdie. The muscle for hire Micky Russ was in the foyer of the hotel our victim was staying at."

Steve broke off. "By the way, Andy — any sightings of Micky Russ yet?"

"No, nothing. It's as though he's disappeared."

"Well, keep the pressure on our all-points. I want to speak to him. And check with Immigration. Let's find out when exactly Ruby Thomas arrived in this country. Oh, and do a full background check on the directors of The Fortress Club, especially James Rushdie."

Steve knew that he was putting a lot of pressure onto Andy but he had no choice. "Right. Any thoughts on what we have so far?"

Andy spoke up. "I think your summary is spot on, but I can't see where we are going. We've chased down every lead and there are definitely connections, but it's not taking us to our murderer."

Silence descended again, as well as a certain amount of gloom.

"Andy — get everything written up and shred the paper. Follow up with DVLA and give me that civil servant's number. Barry — check out those invoices and then you and I will go to meet this Dr Graham who's living at The Fortress Club."

The meeting was over. Progress was being made, and a lot of coincidences were emerging, but they still didn't have a clue as to what it all meant.

That was about to change.

Chapter Twenty-Eight

The brothers and Ruby arrived at The Fortress Club in good time for lunch thanks to the efficiency of James Rushdie's driver.

They were escorted to a private room where the table was set out. James Rushdie greeted everyone and looked quizzically at Ruby. Desmond Cutter looked on and welcomed everyone, as did Alistair Ramsay. To Ruby's surprise, the stand-in Dr Graham was also present. Julian was a bit uncomfortable, believing that the reason for this meeting was that they'd discovered their ruse.

After the introductions, a hostess arrived with drinks and everyone seated themselves at the table. As always, Julian sat next to Ruby. Because lunch was clearly not going to be served for some time, everyone placed their chairs well away from the edge of the table in what appeared to be a more relaxed atmosphere.

"Did you bring those invoices?" Desmond Cutter took the lead.

Holding the file, Sebastian replied: "Yes, they're in here." He handed over the slim, buff-bound file.

Looking a bit aggressive, James Rushdie asked Julian: "Is everything laid on for Friday?"

"Well, if you pay those invoices, and the final balance, then yes. We're good to go, but we still haven't had the initial ten million you promised."

"Never mind that, you'll get it. Now did you bring the list of delegates?"

"Yes, this is the list," Sebastian answered, handing Rushdie a sheet of A4 paper. "It's got the name each delegate is using, when and where they arrive, and who they represent. The first one arrives on Wednesday. He's flying into Biggin Hill by private jet under the name of 'Smith'. He's actually the Kuwaiti deputy oil minister. You'll see their times of arrival and they expect a car to meet them. That's part of the contract with Ridge Securities."

James Rushdie looked pleased. "Well done. This is a good job. We'll pick up these costs, but it'll come off your final payment." He sat back looking at the brothers, expecting a reaction; he got none. The brothers knew what Ruby was about to say.

Ruby cleared her throat. "That sounds great, but there's one thing you're overlooking, Jimmy." James Rushdie looked surprised. Everyone knew not to call him anything other than James. He suppressed his natural anger and was about to speak when Ruby carried on. "You're forgetting about Gregory Anderson. He's owed a hundred million and has a contract with the brothers. They say that you've taken over the contract, so he's looking to you for the money."

James Rushdie was about to speak, but Ruby held up her hand to silence him and carried on. "He says to tell you that your efforts at blackmail didn't work, and that unless he gets some kind of agreement today, he'll have somebody at the auction on Friday to denounce the whole scheme as a sham."

Rushdie was red in the face, his fists clenched. He wasn't going to take this from some American gangster's girlfriend. He stood up full of fury, his chair flying behind him. He almost ran towards Ruby, intent on doing her harm. The rest of the guests just looked on in shock.

As James Rushdie approached Ruby, his arms reaching for her throat, she produced her Derringer 0.22 pistol and pointed it between his legs. "Unless you want to sing soprano for the rest of your life, you'll stop right there."

Rushdie looked at the gun, looked down to where she was pointing it and stopped his advance.

"Good. Now go sit down and let's see if we can find a way out of this mess, shall we?" Ruby continued to hold the gun.

"I presume you don't have one hundred million dollars ready in cash. We understand about cash flow, so Mr Anderson has a proposal."

"I thought he might. Let's hear it."

"He owes you for the last shipment of Colombian best, a bill of some thirty million dollars, which is due to be paid within the next week. He is also expecting a similar shipment from your English factory within the fortnight, of a similar value. Mr Anderson proposes that you write off the outstanding thirty-five million and double the size of his next shipment.

That means you'd be owed a hundred and thirty-five million dollars, which Mr Anderson will not pay. He regards your treatment of him as shoddy, and the extra thirty-five million as his bonus."

James Rushdie was once again apoplectic; he wasn't used to being dictated to and did not like not being in control. He felt boxed in. If he didn't agree, it was likely that Gregory Anderson would do as this woman was saying. If he gave in, it was a sign of weakness and his competitors would likely hear about it and take advantage. On the other hand, giving three shipments of Colombian without charge wasn't too much of a price to pay, given the size of the payday he was expecting from the formula. He also thought he could renege on the agreement after Friday. All he had to do was buy time.

"OK, Miss Thomas. Gregory seems to be holding all the cards. Put that peashooter away. You know you're not going to use it."

Ruby did as instructed, but in doing so showed Julian where she kept it, and a bit more besides. Julian's eyes almost popped out of their sockets.

"Now, let's get lunch ordered and move on, shall we?"

Ruby, now sitting with her legs crossed, spoke up. "And remember, Jimmy, the next two batches better be up to the usual quality. Don't try cutting it before shipping, and don't try to welch on this deal. Mr Anderson isn't known for his forgiving nature."

James Rushdie just looked at Ruby but didn't answer. It was as though she'd read his mind.

While all this was going on, Alistair Ramsay had been listening to the debate. He hadn't been sure he wanted out, but he was now. He had to get away from these mad criminals who spoke in dollar amounts he couldn't even envisage and who appeared to be capable of doing whatever it took to maintain their positions.

Chapter Twenty-Nine

DCI Steve Burt dialled the number Andy gave him for Sir Timothy Head. He'd been put on hold exactly eight minutes ago and was sick of listening to canned music; he hadn't spoken to a human being in those eight minutes. After a further seven minutes holding on, and just at the point where he was going to hang up, a human voice spoke to him down the telephone line.

"This is the office of Sir Timothy Head. How can I help you?"

Steve, with steam coming out of his ears having been left on hold for so long, was not in the mood to be civil. However, he calmed himself down and tried not to be too aggressive with what sounded like a very young man on the other end of the phone. "My name is Detective Chief Inspector Steve Burt. I'm with New Scotland Yard and I need to speak with Sir Timothy today in connection with a murder I'm investigating."

Steve found that using his full title and adding a connection to a murder usually got results.

"I'm sorry, Chief Inspector. Sir Timothy's in conference and cannot be disturbed."

"Who am I talking to?" Steve put on his most formal and demanding voice.

"I'm Sir Timothy's secretary, Percival Barlow."

"Well, Mr Percival Barlow, please look up Sir Timothy's diary and give me a time this afternoon when he has a free half hour to see me. It's very important."

"I'm sorry, sir, but Sir Timothy is busy all day."

Steve was prepared to bully this individual to get an appointment.

"Listen, Percival. If you don't give me an appointment, I'm prepared to involve our commissioner, the home secretary and anyone else in authority, and I don't think your boss would want these heavyweights bearing down on him. So again, give me a time."

Percival Barlow may have sounded young, but he had some steel in his character. "As I said, Sir Timothy cannot possibly see anyone who doesn't yet have an appointment today. I suggest that you e-mail asking for an appointment. Good day, sir." The line went dead.

Steve stood up. He was furious, and very frustrated. He knew he couldn't just barge his way into Whitehall — the place was a fortress and all the cops were armed. He'd have to try another route, and maybe they could solve the case without speaking to Sir Timothy anyway. Somehow Steve knew this would not be the case. He was getting organised to visit The Fortress Club and the mysterious Dr Graham when Andy knocked and entered.

"I've checked that licence plate you gave me, Steve. You'll not believe it, but it's registered to James Rushdie."

"Well, well, this is getting more interesting."

At that moment, Barry appeared. He'd overheard their conversation and, although not fully familiar with the case, he knew who James Rushdie was. "I've got something else to confuse you, boss. I phoned The Bell Tower Hotel — it's just outside Maidstone. I pretended to be a punter looking for a room. The girl on reception said they weren't taking any bookings until after Friday. I used my charm and she admitted that the hotel was empty, and that some corporation had booked all the rooms for two weeks, but guests weren't expected to start arriving until this Wednesday. That's all I could get out of her without blowing my cover."

Steve was rubbing his chin again. A sure sign, he was thinking.

Barry carried on. "I checked out Ridge Security. It's owned and run by an ex-cop, used to be a uniformed inspector, his name is Toby Break. Nothing on file. He's got all the correct licences and an office in Surbiton. I phoned them saying who I was. I got a stroppy individual who said he was the principal investigator. I asked about The Bell Tower Hotel. He said it was confidential, but when I became a bit heavier, he admitted they were providing security for an event taking place there this Friday. He said it wasn't confidential, just another job, so he wasn't betraying any confidences."

Barry looked at his colleagues. "I'm not too sure what ex-inspector Toby Break would say about that. Anyway, I asked him who was funding the event as we might be getting involved. I told him the local police were worried about traffic congestion, and that part of the licence for the event meant they may have to provide uniforms, and so they needed to speak to the organisers."

"You know, Barry, I had you marked down as a straight shooter, not a lying bugger, but I think some of Andy's flair must be rubbing off on you. Good man." It was clear that Steve was impressed. "So, no doubt you're going to enlighten us — who's paying for this gathering?" All three detectives smiled at each other, but Steve and Andy looked expectantly at Barry, who milked his moment in the spotlight.

After an extended pause, he announced with a flourish: "A company called Brothers International Inc."

Because he wasn't up to speed with the case, this meant nothing to him, but it did to Steve and Andy.

Andy spoke first. "That's the St John brothers. Why the hell are they hosting any kind of event? And why book the place for two weeks before the event?"

Steve was thinking the same thing but felt pride in Andy, who was slowly losing his reserved personality.

"Maybe we'd better take a trip to Kent, but have the locals visit this hotel first. Andy — ask them for a report. You can dress up the request. Tell them it's a serious enquiry, and that we suspect something may be going down at the hotel on Friday, but not to take any action. We need to know more before we move. It may have nothing to do with our murder, but you know what? I've got a hunch that this is all about the same thing — whatever Dr Graham stole."

***

Steve and Barry arrived at The Fortress Club at just after two o'clock. The usual greeter was there to welcome them but told the detectives that all the management were at lunch with guests. In no mood to be reasonable, Steve asked which room they were using. When the lackey refused to say, Steve told Barry to arrest him for obstruction. As Barry produced the handcuffs and the greeter realised that Steve meant it, he gave up the information that the luncheon was taking place in the side room off the main dining room.

The detectives went in search of this room and quickly found it. Without knocking, both entered to be greeted by a sea of surprised faces.

Steve and Barry introduced themselves and produced their warrant cards.

"This is a very happy little gathering, don't you think, sergeant?"

"Yes, I do, sir."

Steve recognised the St John brothers and Ruby. He also recognised Alistair Ramsay, the one-time police commander who was now apparently the manager of this club. There were three other men present that Steve didn't recognise.

One of the unknown men spoke. "Alistair — use your authority and get these clowns out of my club."

Being a detective, Steve surmised that this was James Rushdie and he was American.

"DCI Burt, I've told you before. There's nothing here for you to investigate. This is a private club and you're trespassing, so kindly leave now or I shall have you thrown out. You've no right to be here."

"A very pretty speech, Mr Ramsay, but wrong. I'm sure your henchman Frank Dobson has told you of our recent conversation. You'll know we have a warrant and you'll know I agreed to hold off on it unless we found this club was in some way involved in our murder case. So guess what? We think it is, and if you insist, I can have the warrant here in twenty minutes, together with a whole bunch of policemen in uniforms. Is that what you want?"

Alistair Ramsay looked flushed but held his ground. "Of course not. But I'm not without influence either, remember. One phone call and you'll be back on point duty."

Steve was at his silky smoothest, or so he hoped. It was a technique that really annoyed people, such as those he was looking at. "Does that sound like a threat to you, sergeant?"

"I'd say so, sir."

"Exactly what I thought. I'm sure everyone here knows it's a criminal offence to threaten a police officer in pursuance of his duties. The penalty, I believe, is up to five years in jail. Better get on to Hackney Police Station and have them send a van and a multiple arrest team."

Barry knew that Steve was bluffing but he produced his mobile phone and pretended to prepare to make the call.

The man Steve had worked out to be James Rushdie stood up. His face was flushed, he was angry and he didn't look to be totally in control of himself. "Now look, you jumped-up little shit. You're not going to arrest us or any such thing. No one here's done anything wrong, so you've no reason to be here." During the speech, Steve thought this American was calming down. "Ask your questions and get the hell out." James Rushdie sat down again.

Steve retained his silky, very annoying persona. "Well, thank you, sir. I believe you are James Rushdie, the owner of this club?"

"Yes — what of it?"

Steve ignored the question.

"And you, sir, seated next to Mr Rushdie. Who are you?"

"I'm Desmond Cutter. I'm CEO and owner of Olympic Oil, so if you think you can bully me, you're very mistaken. I've got lawyers who will eat you for breakfast."

"Just so, sir. I take it that's another threat?"

"Take it as you want, but I don't threaten, I do."

Steve noted Mr Cutter's American accent. They suddenly seemed to be all over this case.

Sitting next to Julian St John was the third man Steve didn't know. He looked directly at him. "And you, sir. You are...?"

This man wasn't as arrogant as his two American companions and seemed a little out of his depth in this company.

"I'm Dr David Graham."

"Oh. Dr Graham. Well, I'm sorry to say, you're under arrest for the murder of Dr Hans Raga, pursuant to an International Arrest Warrant issued in the United States of America. Sergeant, please."

Steve pointed to their new prisoner and Barry obligingly asked him to stand while he handcuffed his hands behind his back.

"This is all a terrible mistake. You've got it all wrong."

Julian was afraid the fake Dr Graham was about to admit he was an imposter, so he stood and announced: "Doctor — I'll get you the very best legal brain in the country. Please go with these officers and don't cause a scene. I'll look after you."

Professor Peter Small, AKA Dr Graham, didn't seem to understand that Julian wanted him to keep quiet. He struggled against the handcuffs, meaning that Barry had to push and shove him towards the door.

"This is all wrong. I'm only supposed to repeat the experiment."

"Be quiet, man." This was James Rushdie. "You'll be well looked after but keep your mouth shut." It was clear to Julian that the deception had worked so far. There was no way he or Sebastian could be faulted for the arrest of Dr David Graham. The brothers were in the clear, at least on this. The bogus doctor had achieved their aim.

After the detectives left, the atmosphere inside The Fortress Club was decidedly frosty. James Rushdie and Desmond Cutter were on their feet, standing by the window. The brothers and Ruby continued to sit at the table. Alistair Ramsay had left immediately after the detectives to, in the words of James Rushdie, "Sort it out". He knew there was nothing he could do but he had to be seen to try. This really was the last straw. He was getting out.

Alistair returned to report that his contacts would speak with someone in the CPS and try and have the warrant squashed so that Dr Graham could be freed. This was of course a lie, but it told Rushdie what he wanted to hear.

"Alistair — I want that detective brought to his knees. I want him hurt. Who does he think he is? He's interfered in our plans and is causing me to get acid reflux. I want him and his nearest and dearest hurt, and I want it done now."

"James, this is England. We don't hurt senior police officers for doing their job."

"I don't care. He has put our entire enterprise at risk. It was supposed to be easy. We have the formula, we had the doctor, and the venue's all set. We've got the delegates but now that interfering excuse for a policeman is screwing us over. We're too close to Friday to let this guy near to us. Julian — you've got a bit of muscle, haven't you?"

"Well yes, but he's no killer."

"I'm not talking killing; I'm talking sending a message. What's your guy's name?"

"It's Micky Russ."

"Call him. I think he's worked for us before, but I'll speak to him and get this sorted. These kind of low life hoodlums work for money."

James Rushdie spoke to Micky for five minutes while standing in the far corner of the room, making it difficult to hear what was said.

"That's sorted." He came back into the centre of the room rubbing his hands. "Let's see how your Inspector Burt likes having his world turned upside down."

He looked at Julian and Ruby. "You've created this mess, so you'll have to get us out." He pointed at Ruby. "*You* can tell Gregory Anderson his deal is in the balance. No auction, no powder. Got it?"

Rushdie reached for the brandy bottle and poured himself a large one.

***

Outside, the professor was put in the back of the pool car and the two detectives set off for the interview suite at the Yard. Neither spoke, for fear of admitting they knew this wasn't Dr Graham. They chose to let their prisoner sweat it out.

Interview Room 3 was the interview room of choice. The prisoner was locked in while Steve and Barry went to the office to review strategy and have Andy update the files.

Before they could begin, Andy announced: "Ruby Thomas arrived at Heathrow on the 26th November, just one day before Dr Graham."

"Right. Thanks, Andy. That's a bit too close just to be a coincidence. She's up to her neck in this."

Steve explained to Barry how, after each interview or action, he gave a verbal statement to Andy, who put it on the case file without anything being written down. As usual, Andy had questions. "Why did you leave Ruby Thomas behind? If she's the one who told you this bloke downstairs is our victim, then, clearly, she lied."

"I thought about it, but, by the expression on her and Julian St John's faces, there was something pleading there. I don't think their hosts know that the guy downstairs isn't Dr Graham. Besides, we know where she lives."

The discussion carried on until Steve and Barry left to visit Interview Room 3. Just as they were leaving, The Cap arrived looking flustered. "It's OK for you to leave me to tidy up the Hackney cases, but I've spent this morning at the fourth victim's PM, then the DPP. Then I had to explain to the commander for serious crimes how we caught the guys and arrange a full medical for Neil Ryder on instructions from the CPP, and now I've got another four hours of form-filling before I can go home."

"Cap, are you finished?" Steve was gentle.

"Yes. I'm just blowing off steam. I'm not very good with all the admin once a case is over."

As Steve and Barry left, and as a throwaway line, Barry, who'd enjoyed The Cap's discomfort, said: "I suppose a pint at five o'clock is out of the question?"

Both men ran before The Cap threw something at them, but all four detectives were laughing.

***

Interview Room 3 was identical to the ones the detectives had used so far when interviewing the people connected to the Hackney cases. The suspect was seated at the now familiar table screwed to the floor and the black recording machines were in place but not switched on.

Steve and Barry sat in front of this unknown man. As was usual, Steve, as the senior officer, took the lead.

"Who are you?"

"I'm saying nothing until my lawyer arrives. Mr St. John is arranging it."

"You know we didn't really arrest you? That little performance was for the benefit of your luncheon partners. Look, we haven't even switched the recorder on."

"Then I'm free to go?"

"Well, not exactly." Steve had a twinkle in his eye and a feeling in his gut. He was going to play this imposter until he got what he wanted.

"We know who you're not. You're not Dr David Graham, because he's lying in a cold box in our mortuary. The thing is, he was murdered."

"That has nothing to do with me."

"Maybe not, but you can see why we're just a little suspicious. Here you are impersonating a dead scientist, who himself is wanted for murder. So far, you're the only link, so unless we can eliminate you from our enquiries, we'll have to assume that you killed our victim and then we will charge you."

"I have nothing to say."

"That's your privilege. We've taken your fingerprints so if you're in the system we'll get a match. In the meantime, if you're refusing to co-operate, we'll have to charge you with murder." Steve looked at Barry. "Sergeant — please prepare the tapes." Barry stood and switched on the recording machine.

"No, wait, there's no need for that. If I co-operate, you'll have to give me protection. Some of the people I'm involved with are dangerous, and if they ever found out that I'd talked, or that I'm not the real Dr Graham, then my life is over."

Steve sat back. He was now this man's new best friend. Barry switched off the machine.

"Firstly, my name is Professor Peter Small. I was Professor of Molecular Engineering at the Bernall Institute in Zurich for many years until I retired. When you said you were checking my fingerprints, I knew it was only a matter of time before you found me. You see I was arrested for liking small boys too much. Nothing sordid or sexual — I just like having them around as friends. Unfortunately, a parent or two didn't see it as just friendship. I was arrested for molesting, but the case was dropped." Professor Small was looking shaken at having to confess his past.

Steve just sat saying nothing and making no judgemental comments.

"So, we now know who you are. What are you doing pretending to be a dead American scientist?"

Peter Small explained that the brothers knew of his past. He'd found it impossible to get a job and the brothers had a small project they'd asked him to oversee. "This was about two years ago," he said.

Steve interrupted. "What kind of project and what do the St John brothers do?"

"Ha! That's a question. They call themselves facilitators. They find somebody who has something to sell, then they find somebody who

239

wants or needs to buy it, and they put the two parties together for a fee. In my case it was a new accelerant for airbags in cars. Someone had devised a powder that expanded at an incredibly fast speed to inflate an airbag upon impact. Current technology uses air, and in certain crash scenarios the air line can be cut, plus the airbag material has to be more brittle to hold the air. With this powder the material can be softer, so that means fewer facial injuries and the powder can never fail."

The professor leaned back. "Could I have a drink of something please? Coffee — black, if it's going."

Barry left the room and returned within fifteen seconds having placed the order for three coffees.

Peter Small carried on. "I think they must have successfully dealt with the powder because they called me up and said they'd keep me on retainer and pay me each time I helped out. That's the way it's been until this time."

"Go on..."

"They sent for me and told me they were doing the biggest deal of their lives. Julian kept saying that this is 'the big one'. They'd been contacted by a fellow in New York saying he was about to get his hands on a formula that would put the oil companies and oil producers out of business, unless they paid huge sums to have it buried. The formula was based on water as the basic ingredient with a few cleverly engineered additives. You can see that, if it worked, it would be a clean fuel, and easy and cheap to manufacture. It would have the potential to replace oil, and the brothers were banking on the oil giants not wanting to see this water-based fuel produced."

"I see that, but how did they know about it?"

The professor was about to answer when the coffee arrived. Steve was pleased to see that Barry had disregarded his instruction about paper notes. He seemed to have filled half of his notebook already. After a few minutes of silence while the coffee was being drunk, Steve started again.

"So, what happened?" He was fascinated by this story.

"I was told to set up a laboratory in one of their warehouses at Redbridge and be available to work alongside an American academic who was to demonstrate the formula to the brothers. I was sent for one morning and given a memory stick. This had the formula on it, and I was to set up ready for everyone to come to Redbridge in the evening, and be prepared to assist this American."

"Go on…"

Professor Peter Small explained the events of the first demonstration and then the second. He told Steve and Barry how the demonstrations were received and confirmed that the girl known as 'Ruby' was present at all times.

He told the detectives he'd been summoned when they couldn't find David Graham and how he'd been told to impersonate the doctor. He explained that there was to have been another demonstration that evening and again at a hotel in Maidstone. The professor explained how he'd been forced to pretend to be Dr Graham and stay at The Fortress Club. He knew he was more or less a prisoner until the Maidstone experiment was concluded.

"So how did everyone fit in? There seems to be a lot of people involved. How much money are we talking about?" Steve was intrigued and trying to assemble this information alongside what they already knew.

"You're talking billions of dollars. From what I know, and what I'd guessed, it started with the fellow in New York. The brothers have put together a consortium of interested parties and they're meeting on Friday in Maidstone. I get the impression James Rushdie's taken the deal away from the brothers and they don't like it. That's all I can tell you."

"One final question — does this formula work?"

Professor Peter Small looked Steve squarely in the eyes. "No."

Steve and Barry stood outside Interview Room 3. "Steve, we'll never be able to use any of that in court. You've broken every PACE rule. No recording, no solicitor and no re-reading him his rights. We'll get crucified."

"You're not wrong, Barry, but remember, this is off the books. Besides, we can't charge him with anything. He's done nothing. This sounds like a great big fraud, and our murder victim's in the middle of it." Steve was stroking his chin. "In the normal course of events we'd hand the whole lot over to the Fraud Squad, but we can't. This is all unofficial and it's not taking us any nearer to our murderer."

241

Barry went home from the interview suite after arranging for Professor Peter Small to spend the night in the cells.

Steve went back to his office and, of course, Andy was still hard at it. Steve felt exhausted but had to de-brief Andy so that he could update the file. He explained that Barry had taken notes and that he would update Andy from these notes. Steve reminded Andy, although he knew he had no need to, that Barry's notes should be shredded.

They got everything covered and were just about to leave when Steve's phone rang.

"Steve? It's Commander Southgate. Be in my office tomorrow morning, nine o'clock sharp. Don't be late." The line went dead.

Andy, who'd heard some of the one-sided conversation due to Steve not fully holding the earpiece to his ear, looked surprised. "Trouble?"

"I hope not. Sheila Southgate's the one who gave me the Graham case. Did you e-mail that civil servant again? I still want to talk to him."

"Yes — I've sent two. One this morning and another one about two hours ago. Still, nothing's come back."

Steve stood up ready to leave. "Send another one tomorrow first thing. If we still don't get a reply, I'll take it upstairs."

Steve was at his office door. "Oh, Steve, by the way, I know it's late, but I got the background checks on the shareholders of The Fortress Club. It's not pretty reading. There are some nasty people involved. The Criminal Intelligence Unit called when they heard we were looking at these people. They want to see you tomorrow."

"Looks like I'm a popular detective all of a sudden." Steve gave a weary smile.

"Let's look at everything tomorrow. I'm bushed, but one question, Andy. If these are bad guys, how did Assistant Chief Constable and one-time Commander Alistair Ramsay get mixed up with them?"

The pair left for the night. Steve was off to see Alison for a drink, a quiet supper and, he hoped, an early bed.

He'd get all that, but tomorrow everything would change, and he had no idea how popular, or otherwise, he would be.

Chapter Thirty

When Steve arrived at his office in New Scotland Yard, a pleasant surprise was there to greet him. Sitting in his office was one of the largest women he knew. It had been almost nine months since he'd last seen Florance Rough. She was a detective constable, and like Steve and Abul Ishmal, it had been intended that she would join the ranks of the unemployed. Destiny had taken a hand and all three had saved their careers and moved on to better things. Steve moved to his current role as head of Special Resolutions, which was now a permanent appointment; Abul — AKA The Cap — was now a detective inspector working for Steve; and Florance — AKA Twiggy — had left the force to join the Treasury team seconded to the Metropolitan Police's Financial Crimes Squad, with the honorary rank of inspector. Steve knew she'd been away on several forensic accountancy courses sponsored by the Government and was now working within the financial teams.

"Well look at you! What on earth are you doing here?"

Twiggy gave a lopsided grin. "You mean you're not pleased to see me? Can't a girl visit her old boss without a reason?"

"Yes, of course. But I know you, there'll be a reason, but it's good to see you."

"And you, Steve. I've missed our chats. You and The Cap saved me. Without your recommendation and encouragement giving me my head to investigate the Clark thing, I'm sure I'd be out on the street by now."

"Let's not go there. You're here on merit, and an inspector, but can I say you're still taking up a fair bit of real estate." Both laughed. Twiggy knew she was large, and it was her size that had almost got her sacked.

"Your man Andy handed over a file on this Fortress Club. Normally I wouldn't be involved." She looked at her old boss with a sweet smile and a shrug of her shoulders. "I'm far too important these days!"

"Go on, I know there's something coming."

"Well, when I saw it had this unit's name as the referral, I took a look and grabbed the file. I'm now the investigating officer so we'll be working together again."

"Not sure I follow you, Twiggy. I'm investigating a murder not a financial crime."

"Just remember the last case. We dug up a lot of financial wrongdoing and that was what got us to the killer. This could be the same. I've spent a day going over their filed accounts with Companies House plus the tax returns for the owners and senior staff. So far, everything points to a front for drugs and maybe prostitution."

Steve looked at her. "I'm sure about the prostitution — I've been inside the place — but how do you make a drugs connection?"

"The main man's called James Rushdie. He's an American gangster with known connections to Colombian drug lords and the cartels. The FBI have tried to nail him for years without success, mainly because he doesn't file taxes anywhere. According to my contact, this Rushdie's like a ghost." Twiggy paused.

She carried on. "It seems this is the only country in which he's tried to look legitimate. From the accounts, The Fortress Club is a legal and legitimate business. It's the only tangible asset we can find anywhere in the world that he's ever been shown to own. The Feds have been tracking him for years, so they know where he's vulnerable, and that's right here. They want a joint task force to look into his whole business empire."

"All very encouraging, and I don't mind if he gets life, but I'm not clear where we fit in."

"You've met him. From what I hear, he's not pleased with you for arresting his scientist yesterday. If he's angry, he might slip up. We want you to keep pushing his buttons. We'll dig up every transaction he's ever made in this country and put them to him, but only after you've wound him up."

Steve looked at his watch. "Twiggy — is this anything to do with me being called to a meeting at nine o'clock this morning?"

"No. Nothing's been agreed or set up yet."

"Look, can we leave this just now? I'm not too sure what you're asking me to do, but I've got to go. Talk things over with Andy."

Steve paused and then called out to Andy, who was at his desk in the outer office. "This is Inspector Florance Rough, Andy, an ex-colleague of mine. Florance, this is DC Andy Miller." They shook hands and passed the expected pleasantries.

"Florance wants our help with something. Can you look after her and brief me later today? I've got to dash to the twelfth floor."

Steve left, straightening his tie as he went.

***

The DCI knocked on the office door of Commander Sheila Southgate and was called in. He'd been in this office before, so he knew the seating arrangements. Sheila Southgate had a reputation for being a cop's cop and operated a fairly informal regime. Today, however, Steve could feel the atmosphere was very formal.

Seated round a small table capable of seating six people sat the commander and three official-looking gentlemen. They were all dressed in similar three-piece suits made from a dark, striped material that looked as though it cost more than Steve's entire wardrobe. When Steve entered, the men didn't acknowledge his presence.

"DCI Burt, please be seated." The commander pointed to a chair next to her. To Steve's mind, it looked like the police against the suits.

Commander Southgate took charge.

"DCI Burt — these gentlemen asked for a meeting today in order to satisfy you that they have nothing to hide. This is a very unusual circumstance so I would ask you to remain silent and let them explain." From the tone of her voice, Steve knew that to say anything would be a mistake.

The commander opened her arms to the other side of the table, inviting them to speak. "Gentlemen…"

The man in the middle opened the meeting. "My name is Hendry De Ville. I am the senior partner in De Ville and Palmer based in the City of London."

Mr De Ville produced a business card and slid it over the table for Steve to collect. As instructed, Steve said nothing.

"I represent Sir Timothy Head, who, as you know, is head of Her Majesty's Civil Service." Mr De Ville lifted his hand and indicated the gentleman on his left.

Steve felt this solicitor must be getting paid by the hour. It was like watching paint dry. He was speaking so slowly and deliberately.

"My firm has also, and for the purposes of this meeting, been retained by Sir Patrick Bond, who you may not know is head of MI6, this country's overseas secret intelligence service." The solicitor lifted his hand to indicate that the gentleman sitting on his right was Sir Patrick Bond.

Both men stared at Steve and slid business cards towards him. Steve lined these cards up in front of him in the order they were sitting.

Steve wanted to ask a lot of questions, but a glance at the commander told him to stay silent.

The suit on the solicitor's left spoke first. "Detective Chief Inspector..." An instant pause for effect. This was a 'do you know who I am?' moment. The voice was silky smooth and obviously cultured. Steve thought that this pompous individual must go to the opera and the ballet.

"My solicitor has introduced us. I believe you have been making attempts to arrange a meeting with me concerning a murder case you are involved with?" Steve said nothing.

"You see, Inspector, there are many things that go on, both in government and internationally, that are best not broadcast. I fear you may have stumbled into such an event. I know you have not been positively vetted but nonetheless..." He looked at his solicitor who produced a document from a folder in front of him. "We require you to sign the Official Secrets Act before we can continue... apart from the phrase that you could be executed for divulging state secrets." All three men looked at each other and sniggered like schoolboys at Sir Timothy's joke. "You have nothing to fear by signing this document."

The solicitor provided a pen. Steve looked at Sheila Southgate who just shrugged but said nothing. Steve signed and the solicitor placed the document back in his folder.

"So, what you will hear from now on is ultra-secret, and you cannot divulge anything we say on pain of death."

Sir Timothy sat back looking satisfied.

"Some weeks ago, we were approached by our American cousins. They had invested in a scientist called Hans Raga, based at the MIT in Massachusetts. He was working on a fuel based on pure water. This would mean a pollution-free fuel that was easy to produce and cheap. It could solve the world's energy problems at a stroke and improve greenhouse gas emissions. Their Department of Defence part-funded the research, as did their Homeland Security. Everything was kept low-key for fear of other agencies or oil-producing governments hearing of it and trying to somehow prevent further experimentation."

Sir Timothy sipped from a glass of water he had beside him. Steve was fascinated. He wanted to hear more, but already saw how this could feed into the death of Dr David Graham.

"It appears the scientist working on this fuel was murdered by one of his colleagues, a Dr David Graham, the gentleman I believe we fished out of the Thames some days ago. The laptop on which the formula and notes were stored was a US Government-owned machine supplied to Dr Raga for security reasons. Given the sensitivity of the research, this is apparently standard procedure for the Americans. The reason I'm telling you this is that each American Government mobile electronic device is fitted with a GPS chip. When David Graham stole that Federal Government laptop, he was followed all the way via the tracking device." Another sip of water and still Steve was silent.

"The police department of Massachusetts of course knew nothing of this. All they had was a murder. The FBI were alerted by Homeland Security and told that a laptop with classified data had crossed the state line between Massachusetts and New York. They of course knew this because the GPS chip is monitored twenty-four hours a day. The FBI agent in charge apparently panicked a bit and issued an International Arrest Warrant for the main suspect, Dr Graham." Sir Timothy Head took another sip of water. He didn't look as though he was enjoying this experience.

"The laptop was traced to an expensive apartment block in New York. The only person of note living there was a certain Gregory Anderson. For once it appears the FBI and CIA were co-operating, and the FBI handed the case to the CIA. However, no one thought to cancel the International Arrest Warrant." The Whitehall mandarin looked across to Sir Patrick Bond.

Without being asked, Sir Patrick now took up the narrative. Steve thought this gentleman was well-named — a Bond working in the secret service. He smiled to himself.

"Once the CIA got notice of what was going on, they took over, just as Sir Timothy said. The reason was that they had been keeping a watch on this Anderson for some time and had planted one of their agents in deep cover within his organisation. I believe you are aware of a Ruby Thomas?"

Steve said nothing but nodded.

"Miss Thomas had been working undercover for some eighteen months when she started missing contact times with her handler. The CIA realised she had somehow gone rogue on them. They put her and Anderson under surveillance and followed her to JFK Airport. She boarded a flight to the UK on the 26th November. My department was notified, and we have had her under surveillance since she arrived."

Now Sir Patrick took a sip of water. "We were very impressed by your investigation, Chief Inspector. It seemed that everywhere my agents went, you had either been there or were just arriving. In many ways, your activities were beginning to alarm us, hence this meeting. But I digress. We were advised by our American colleagues that a Dr David Graham was responsible for stealing the laptop and was strongly suspected of the murder of Hans Raga. The Americans witnessed him being escorted from Gregory Anderson's building and their agents followed him to JFK. He was manifested on the evening British Airways flight to London, arriving the morning of the 27th November." Sir Patrick sat back, and without looking at his colleague, Sir Timothy took up the tale.

"I was advised by the US Embassy that this Dr Graham was en route to the UK and was made aware of the arrest warrant. I was requested to suppress the warrant and not have it activated. This was because the Americans were conducting a sensitive series of enquiries and they preferred to have Dr Graham free. I consulted with Sir Patrick and he agreed."

It was getting like a double act. Sir Timothy now sat back and Sir Patrick Bond once again took up the story. Steve could not look at him without wanting to call him James Bond.

"Just like Miss Thomas, we had one of our agents follow this doctor when he arrived at Heathrow. We followed him to his hotel and became aware of a link between him and Miss Thomas, plus of course the St John brothers. We've been working with MI5 and your colleagues in Serious Crimes for some time. The activities of the brothers have been closely monitored. I believe your head of serious crimes will fill you in if required. We are continuing to monitor the St Johns and their link to The Fortress Club. However, we noted your arrival yesterday and your arrest of a gentleman we are not familiar with. It's become clear to us that our national security might be under threat and that The Fortress Club is central to whatever criminal activities are going on there.

We learned late yesterday that you had requested the full financial records for this club and ordered deep background checks on the shareholders." Sir Patrick raised an eyebrow and looked at Steve, who remained silent. He wasn't sure what was going on, but he knew he didn't like it.

Sir Patrick carried on. "So, you see, Inspector, all our enquiries and efforts seem to be working somewhat at cross purposes. I understand from Commander Southgate here that she asked you to investigate the murder of Dr David Graham and only the murder of Dr David Graham. The fact you interrogated the Home Office pathologist Professor Campbell and learned that Sir Timothy had requested he carry out the post-mortem obviously led you to us.

Let me assure you, Chief Inspector — there is nothing here for you to get involved with. One of our agents followed Miss Thomas and Dr Graham when they left the Mayflower Hotel by taxi. They both entered Miss Thomas's apartment in Chelsea. Early the next morning, Miss Thomas and an unidentified man were seen carrying a body from the apartment and dumping it in the river by Chelsea Bridge. Miss Thomas is your murderer, Chief Inspector."

Now both Whitehall bosses had said their piece, Mr De Ville, the expensive lawyer, chipped in. "I believe that concludes this meeting. I think you'll agree that my clients have been very helpful and I trust they will not be bothered by anyone from the Metropolitan Police again. I'm happy to see their combined efforts have assisted you in solving your murder, Inspector."

All three started to rise. Steve held up his hand to indicate that they should remain seated. Commander Sheila Southgate looked sideways at Steve but said nothing.

"Gentlemen — first, I will decide when my murder, as you put it, is 'solved', based on the evidence.

Second, it is a criminal offence to suppress any arrest warrant." Steve looked directly at Sir Timothy. "No matter the reason nor the position of the person responsible." Sir Timothy looked at the commander.

"Third, had you not suppressed that warrant, Dr Graham would have been arrested at Heathrow and would still be alive. By your actions, you have caused the death of a human being. In case you didn't realise, we call it 'complicity in murder'." The over-priced lawyer's jaw dropped.

"Fourth, you have admitted withholding crucial evidence in a murder enquiry. You saw the body being dumped into the river, and you knew the identities of the victim and the person responsible, but you failed to come forward. That's called 'withholding'." No one moved, and breathing was shallow among the three gentlemen.

"And fifth and last, my enquiries have led me to various individuals you are investigating or have under surveillance. You have failed to follow protocol, informing all Metropolitan units of your involvement. Again, this is a criminal offence." Steve stopped for effect.

"In short, gentlemen, I believe I can arrest you both now on at least half a dozen charges, so please don't sit there and tell me I've cut across your enquiries or you've 'solved' my murder."

Steve had allowed himself to show his annoyance. He knew this was always a good tactic when dealing with people who he knew were untouchable, but he wanted to make a point. "I know it's unlikely I'll be allowed to arrest you, never mind charge you. Your type always hides behind national security and the like, but make no mistake, you are both on my radar…"

The commander interrupted. "Steve — that's enough. These are senior government servants. Please hold your tongue." Steve felt severely reprimanded but was glad he'd made his feelings known.

Commander Southgate carried on. "Gentlemen — my apologies for DCI Burt's outburst. While it may not have been politically correct, please be aware that I share his sentiments. Everything you have both admitted to today is incomprehensible. The charges DCI Burt referred to would, in normal circumstances, be laid before you, but given your privileged positions, we all know no charges will be brought. Let me say that I hope you sleep well with the blood of David Graham on your hands."

The men made no comment but didn't look suitably chastised. They made to rise for the second time, and for the second time Steve waved them down.

"How close are you to the details of these investigations?"

Sir Patrick Bond, as head of MI6, spoke. "I get daily reports and a full debrief each evening, so I believe I am current."

With a hint of irony, Steve sat back and almost sneered at the head of MI6. "In the interests of co-operation, are you aware that I was approached, just before this meeting, by a member of the Treasury Investigations Unit to assist them in their investigation of a Mr James Rushdie?"

"No, I was not aware of that."

"Have you heard of a meeting due to take place this Friday at The Bell Tower Hotel in Maidstone?"

"Again, no. I am unaware of that."

"You see, Sir Patrick…" The DCI almost said James. "Your agents may be very good at surveillance, but I suspect none of them are investigators. I have files on the activities of The Fortress Club that I intend handing to our Financial Crimes Unit, together with another to hand to our Vice Squad. If you're interested, I suggest you ask to see them. It might save your agents a lot of wasted time." Now Steve sat back.

Commander Southgate called the meeting to an end. "Thank you for coming, gentlemen. It's been very interesting. DCI Burt, please stay."

No one shook hands nor mouthed any pleasantries as they left.

The commander invited Steve to take a comfortable chair by her coffee table. "Well, that was interesting. I think I need a coffee. How about you?"

"Yes please, ma'am."

Coffee was ordered. Before Sheila Southgate could begin discussing the meeting with Steve, her phone rang. She answered it standing by her desk. She returned to her seat just as a WPC brought in the coffee.

"We have a visitor — I'd like you to stay. Let's leave the other meeting debate till later. I've a feeling our guest will have more to tell us."

The same WPC knocked on the office door and ushered in the commander's visitor.

It was Alistair Ramsay, ex-Metropolitan Police Commander and ex-Assistant Chief Constable of Kent. He didn't look well, nor did he look as though he'd slept much.

He entered holding out his hand and with a smile on his face. "Sheila, nice to see you again. It's been a long time." He looked at Steve and was obviously struggling to remember his name, although he knew the face. Sheila made the introductions.

"Sheila — I'm in a bit of a pickle and I'm hoping that if I come clean with you then you might help me out, for old times' sake."

"It depends what kind of a mess you're in and what you tell me. You know we can't make promises."

"Yes, I understand, but what I'm prepared to tell you might cost me my life. It's big, but I'll need protection."

"Let's hear it, Alistair. You're not under caution. We'll discuss things after you tell us why you're here."

Alistair Ramsay spelt it all out. He was like a schoolkid telling all the bad things he'd done at school. He started with his time in Kent and how James Rushdie had got him involved in bribing police units and customs officers to wave through certain shipments. He told them about the latest shipment and the warehouse in Faversham where the drugs were broken down into individual packs, and about The Fortress Club and the prostitution. He explained how James Rushdie and Desmond Cutter used Olympic Oil's distribution network to get the drugs to the dealers.

He then went on to the meetings with the St John brothers and how James Rushdie had taken over the deal to sell the formula. He explained about the warehouse at Redbridge and how Dr Graham had been sent by Gregory Anderson to prove the formula worked and to repeat Hans Raga's experiment. He detailed everything he knew about the auction on Friday at The Bell Tower Hotel, including some of the people who were attending under assumed names.

He opened up further and told how all of James Rushdie's plans were now uncertain because Steve had arrested the second Dr Graham, who was to conduct the experiment on Friday for the benefit of the visiting delegates. He said he knew that the Dr Graham sent by the brothers was a fraud because he had met the real doctor before. He explained how Rushdie wanted the bidding to go and how he'd destroy the formula once he had billions of dollars.

Alistair Ramsay was sweating badly and asked for a glass of water.

"When you left with the bogus Dr Graham, James Rushdie threw a fit of rage like I've never seen. The guy is a monster. I'll have nothing to do with guns or violence, plus he thinks that because of who I was, I can arrange things to suit him. He expects me to get the warrant for David Graham's arrest quashed so that he can be at Maidstone on Friday. The man's impossible, but Steve, he's put Micky Russ onto you with an instruction to do you and your nearest harm. I don't know what he means, but it's serious. I can't be part of that."

"When was that?"

"Last night."

"Ma'am, it's only me and my girlfriend. I know she was OK this morning. They won't come after me, but she might be in danger."

The commander agreed. "Steve — off you go. Do what you think, and call up armed response as you need them. Go! Sort it out but keep me posted."

DCI Steve Burt flew from the office and the building with only two thoughts: first, to protect Alison, and second, to get James Rushdie.

After Steve had left, Commander Sheila Southgate called several colleagues in to her office. Each was head of a specific unit within New Scotland Yard. Alistair Ramsay was seated where he had been when Steve rushed out.

"These gentlemen will arrange for you to be interviewed by each of their departments in turn, starting with Professional Standards and Corruption. You will give a full account to each officer who interviews you, detailing exactly what you told DCI Burt and myself earlier on. Firstly, however, when with Professional Standards, you will give a list of each and every police officer who accepted a bribe, as well as any other officers who have done you favours in the past." She looked a crestfallen Alistair Ramsay squarely in the face. "Is that understood?"

The reply was a muted "Yes".

"I don't know how you got yourself into this, but by God, before I retire, I'll have every bad apple you've corrupted out on the streets as a civilian or behind bars as a convict."

The commander was on her feet as she addressed the four senior officers who had responded to her telephone call. "Take him away. Everything by the book — no shortcuts. I want to know everything he knows. The drugs, the prostitution, the corruption, the beatings, and especially I want this American, James Rushdie, in custody before the week's out. Am I clear?"

She was rewarded with a collective nodding of heads. The chief superintendent in charge of Professional Standards advanced towards his prisoner and held his elbow as he rose from his chair. "Has he had his rights, ma'am?"

"No, and to be safe..." Sheila looked at all the officers present. "I want him processed as though he were a child, each time your department talks to him. I want reports from each unit. Goodness knows how many charges we can bring, so like I said, no slip-ups, and everything by the book."

After Alistair Ramsay and the department heads had left, Commander Sheila Southgate drank the rest of her cold coffee and wondered how Steve Burt was faring.

Chapter Thirty-One

Micky Russ got the call from James Rushdie but little detail. He was being well paid for a simple scare and rough-up job. He smiled to himself. Money for nothing.

He knew he was to hurt but not kill this DCI Burt, and he was also to hurt anyone close to him. He knew who Burt was. Burt had arrested him a few years ago on a GBH charge, but the brothers had paid for a smart lawyer and he had been given a suspended sentence. Micky had no idea who was close to the detective.

He got the call mid-afternoon on Tuesday and decided to stake out New Scotland Yard in the hope of seeing his target and maybe following him. He'd driven round for a few hours. He parked up and walked past the Yard for a few hours and was back in his car, illegally parked but with a view of the exit from the staff car park.

Micky wasn't bright but he was loyal if the money was right and he was thorough — he'd see the job through. Just as he was thinking of moving on and finding another car parking space, he saw his prey exiting the car park in a blue Toyota. Micky was lucky because the lighting wasn't too good but he was facing the same way as the Toyota turned, so it was easy to follow.

The Toyota headed straight for a private terraced house in Knightsbridge. Very expensive. He watched the car pull up and the driver, who he was now sure was DCI Burt, ring the bell of the house. A woman appeared and the pair hugged and kissed before closing the door on the outside world. Micky felt good. He'd been lucky and now knew someone close to the inspector he could hurt.

He considered doing it then but decided to take the woman first. He'd do it tomorrow.

Micky wasn't an early riser, so it was almost noon when he parked up, just along from the house he'd seen the inspector visit last night. He climbed the stairs to the front door and noted that it was a doctor's surgery. The woman must be Dr Alison Mills because that was the name on the brass plaque fixed to the wall.

Micky rung the bell and told the voice that responded that he had to see the doctor urgently, and no, he didn't have an appointment.

The door buzzed open and Micky entered. There was a nice-looking, motherly-type woman behind a reception desk. "I need to see Dr Mills urgently."

"I'm sorry, but without an appointment, it's not really possible, unless it's an emergency."

Micky liked how this lady talked. He thought she sounded like the voices he'd heard on the BBC.

"Oh! Right. But it's urgent. I've got to see her."

The receptionist phoned someone and told Micky he could go in. He should take the first door on the right. Dr Mills didn't have a patient at the moment and could see him.

Micky smiled to himself. People said he wasn't bright but just look at what he'd done. He'd show them.

Micky entered to see a lovely lady sitting behind a desk. She looked beautiful and Micky was sorry about what he was about to do, but orders were orders. He closed and locked the door behind him. Before he'd walked fully into the room, two men appeared from behind a hospital screen. Micky had seen them on TV hospital programmes.

"Hello, Micky. We've been looking for you."

It was his other target — the inspector. Having locked the door, he knew he couldn't just bolt. Besides, the other man was now standing in front of the door.

"I understand you've got something to say to Dr Mills and myself." The detective's voice was smooth but full of menace. Micky knew he was cornered, but he also knew that, so far, he hadn't done anything.

"No, Mr Burt, I came to see about my tonsils. They've been playing me up something rotten. I'd heard that the doctor was good at tonsils."

"Good try, Micky, but someone's already given you up."

The Cap moved forward and asked Micky to assume the standard search position. He found two knives — one of which was a flick knife — a small-bore Browning automatic pistol, a set of brass knuckledusters and a length of stiff rope.

"These your normal walking out effects, Micky? Or is this your 'I'm going to hurt someone' collection?"

"No, Mr Burt — honest. I've never seen them things before."

Alison, who was still sitting at her desk, gave a sharp laugh at this obvious lie.

Steve had wasted enough time. "Right, Cap — cuff him and take him in. I'll be along in a few minutes."

Steve and Alison were alone in her office. The excitement was over. "I don't know what I'd have done if Micky had arrived before me and had hurt you. I think I'd have killed him."

The pair held each other very tight. Alison was used to stressful situations but had never experienced anything like this before. "Do you really think he would have hurt me?"

"Yes, I do. You saw the armoury he had with him — that wasn't for show. He uses all of those things."

Alison clung to Steve and cried: "Oh! Steve. Is this your world? People like that, or even worse?"

"Yes, my darling, I'm afraid it is, but I promise I'll never let anything like this happen again. I won't even discuss my work unless you want me to." She stood back and kissed him on the lips.

Steve looked at this lovely creature he'd grown very fond of and from somewhere in his mind he heard himself say "Marry me?"

***

The DCI left Alison's surgery and phoned Barry. "Barry — meet me at Ruby Thomas' mews flat in Chelsea. Take a couple of uniforms. I'm on my way. She's now our main suspect for the murder of David Graham. See you there in half an hour. Blues and twos if you need them."

When Steve arrived, Barry was standing at the end of the mews talking to two uniformed officers. Steve parked on double yellow lines.

"There's definitely someone in. I walked past and saw a figure behind the net curtains. I've had a look round the back and there's no other way out except the front door."

"Thanks, Barry. Right, let's do this."

Ruby answered the door and was clearly surprised to see the number of police officers standing in front of her.

Steve took the lead. "Good afternoon, Miss Thomas. May we come in?"

"Do you have a warrant?"

"No, but as a CIA agent, you'll know we really don't need one for this visit."

Ruby was visibly shocked; Steve could see she that was thinking through her options. In the end, she just shrugged, turned her back on the officers and climbed the internal stairs leading to her apartment. Steve and his crew followed.

The apartment was small but neat. The living area also included the kitchen but there was no space for a table. Apart from a two-seater sofa, a television screwed to the wall, and the smell of cocaine having been recently used, the apartment was home to this American rogue agent.

"Ruby — tell me about Dr Graham?"

"Nothing much to tell. He was a nice guy, but he had a habit that Gregory Anderson cured him of."

"Why did you kill him?"

"Oh! I see. Just like the Feds, you've no proof, so you stitch up the nearest and weakest. Anything for a result. Well, not me, buster — I'm not guilty."

"Who was the man who helped you?"

"Don't know what you're talking about." Ruby was making eye contact with Barry. She sat on the sofa showing as much thigh as she had. Her dress was again skin-tight, showing the rest of her body to maximum advantage. Barry was impressed, but not enough to let Steve down.

"Where's the gun, Ruby?"

"Again, I don't know what you're on about. Sorry."

"Have it your way." Without speaking, Steve nodded to his colleagues, who started searching the room. One of the uniformed officers was about to open what he took to be the bedroom door. Before he could turn the handle, Ruby jumped to her feet.

"Don't go in there — that's my bedroom, you pervert. I'll have you up on charges for even thinking about looking through my underwear drawer." The PC blushed but Steve told him to carry on. He was impressed by Ruby's quick wit.

The PC disappeared into the room but immediately called out. He reappeared with a man who'd obviously been hiding in the bedroom.

"Well, well, what do have we here?"

Ruby ran to the newcomer. "Say nothing, Rory. They can't prove a thing."

"You may be right, Ruby, but just in case you're wrong, I'm arresting you both on suspicion of murder. Sergeant — cuff them."

The prisoners were taken to the now familiar interview suite, having been transported in separate cars and booked in by the custody sergeant. Ruby was in Interview Room 1 and the man called Rory was in Room 5. As was standard practice, both suspects were left to consider their situation individually and were guarded by a uniformed officer.

Micky Russ was in Room 2. The custody sergeant had joked with his colleagues that the DCI was taking over the custody suites.

Having transported Micky, The Cap was now officially interviewing him under caution. Micky was an old hand and knew that information could be traded. He offered to shop James Rushdie for either no charges or a lighter sentence in a softer prison.

"Micky — you know we can't do deals, but we can recommend things to the DPP. Any help you give us could certainly play well with the courts. At the moment we only have an attempted charge because we were there — that's not too serious. You help us and you might only get probation." The Cap knew that with Micky's record this was very unlikely, but Micky probably didn't know that.

"All right, Mr Ishmal, I'll be good. You see, I do freelance work for a few people in London. You know, the players. They usually pay me real good and the work's never too hard. I've worked for the St John brothers recently, and then James Rushdie, but that's what's got me here now."

Micky went on to tell everything. The Cap knew they had James Rushdie on conspiracy, and possibly attempted murder, or at least GBH.

He left Micky to find Steve.

When Steve returned to his office, The Cap was there. He reported that Micky was telling all and gave Steve a quick overview of Micky's statement.

Steve then phoned the commander to tell her that he'd arrested Micky Russ and it appeared he was already singing. She in turn told the DCI what actions she'd taken against Alistair Ramsay and how he too was singing. He was asking for protective custody and had been told it depended on how co-operative he was. Sheila said he was being very co-operative.

Andy appeared, full of concern for Alison. The Cap was still in the office and Barry arrived to confirm that both Ruby and her boyfriend had been processed and were ready for interview.

Steve looked at his team. "Let's go to the canteen first and have a decent cup of coffee. We need to quietly review where we are now. This is more than just a body in the Thames."

Chapter Thirty-Two

Over coffee, the four detectives discussed the various events of the day so far. Each had a feeling that things were reaching a crescendo and that the day was not done.

Before leaving his office, Steve had made two phone calls, both to ladies. The first arrived just as they started their coffee. It was Twiggy, AKA Honorary Inspector Florance Rough. Steve made the introductions, although Andy had met Twiggy before and she and The Cap were old friends. Barry looked at this large tent standing in front of him. He could see why she might be called Twiggy, but a two-hundred-and-fifty-pound version. She joined the men at their table, although she insisted on a chair without arms — she just wouldn't fit.

Before any conversation could begin, the second lady arrived in the form of Commander Sheila Southgate. She took a seat, refused coffee and asked Steve point-blank what was going on.

"Commander — we've got a lot of detail on something we don't fully understand. I haven't told the team here about Alistair Ramsay nor our meeting with the three suits, but neither do you know about the bogus Dr Graham, nor what the bruiser Micky Russ has told us. I'd like to pull everything together for you..." He was looking at Sheila. "And then make a suggestion. I hope that's OK, ma'am?"

"Fine, fire away."

"To begin at the beginning — one American scientist murders another and steals a laptop containing top secret data. The FBI are able to track the laptop to an American gangster in New York. This gangster sends a woman, who was originally implanted to spy on him, to London, the day before the second scientist, that's Dr David Graham, the one who stole the data, arrives. We know the St John brothers paid for Graham's hotel so there's a connection."

"Yes, go on."

"We know that the brothers are doing a deal with the American, a bloke called Gregory Anderson. We also know that the data that was stolen was a formula for a water-based fuel. The people involved think it's worth billions. It's too rich for the brothers to see through, so they involve a guy called Desmond Cutter. He in turn involves an American heavy called James Rushdie, who seems to have cut the brothers out of the deal. We know he owns The Fortress Club and that it's a front for prostitution and drug dealing. We also know that Rushdie has a drugs warehouse in Faversham in Kent and he's been bribing customs officers and police to look the other way when his drugs shipments arrive. Still, OK?"

"I'm not stupid, DCI Burt. Carry on."

"Yes, ma'am." Steve felt chastised. "We're getting more information all the time, but we know that the stolen formula is to be sold off at some form of auction on Friday at a hotel in Kent. There are a load of representatives from most of the oil-producing countries, supposedly turning up to buy the formula, with the intention that it doesn't ever get developed. These people are arriving using false identities and on false passports. But here's the kicker, the formula doesn't work — it's a scam."

Steve looked around ready for his big finish. "So, you see, we have potential for charges across a whole range of issues. I believe that unless we join all the elements up into one concerted investigation, we'll miss some of the big fish. We've got the vice angle, drugs on a huge scale, probable tax evasion, police corruption, attempted murder charges, international warrants, fraud and immigration. You see, ma'am, the way the Met's set up, these possible charges cover at least seven different units. My suggestion is that a task force be set up so that one team can tackle all these issues simultaneously and under one command. We know the whole thing will be over by Friday so there's not a lot of time."

"Yes, I take your point, Steve, but…" Steve's mobile rang but the commander carried on while Steve took the call. "That's a lot to put in place without someone who knows each element inside out. I'm not sure we have such a person unless…" She looked at Steve still on his phone. "You're volunteering?"

The commander was looking at Steve with an enquiring smile and wondering who was calling him.

Steve finished his call with a smile on his face. "Well, no, Ma'am. I was thinking that that command might best be given to a commander who's not far from retiring. Like I said, there's not long for this to play out, so it's unlikely to interfere with your retirement plans, plus we have DC Miller."

Andy's jaw dropped at the mention of his name. "What?"

Ignoring Andy's surprised expression, Steve addressed the group. "That call was from Frankie, the St John brothers' minder. He's just told me they are getting ready to do a runner. Once the auction's over on Friday, he says they are disappearing on false passports. He told me because he doesn't think he has been fairly dealt with by them." Steve laughed. "He says he's to take them to Heathrow and then he can keep the car. He thinks that years of loyal service deserves more. So, you see, ma'am, things are unravelling at a pace. We need to move."

Steve stopped to let things settle, but he was on a roll. "Back to DC Miller. Since you told me to trust no one, I've had Andy keep all the records safely stored on his own laptop. There are no paper reports, and Andy's been inputting everything, so he knows more about each element of this scam, and the players in it, than anyone else. He's more than capable of filling the role of controller for a joint task force."

"Interesting. So, you're saying I should set up a joint task force straight away, covering each discipline we're investigating, from fraud to false accounting to immigration offences, and that DC Miller here should be appointed controller?"

"Yes, ma'am. We don't have a lot of time to round up all the players, and DC Miller's best placed to pull all the pieces together."

The commander turned to Andy. "Well, Andy, do you think you can tell senior officers where to look for the bad guys?"

Andy blushed and temporarily reverted back to the Andy of a week ago. "Well, ma'am, if the DCI thinks I can, then I suppose I can."

Sheila looked pleased. "So, DC Miller is to be seconded to my task force for the duration. Anything else, Steve?"

"Yes, ma'am. Miss Rough here has already started looking into the accounts of The Fortress Club. I think it would save time if she was also seconded."

Commander Southgate was a lady of action. "Right, thank you, DCI Burt. I think your suggestions are sound, and I appreciate the time constraint. I'll pull in all the department heads and assistant heads we need, and, DC Miller — I want a full summary report of your proposed actions over the next forty-eight hours, together with full supporting back-up reports. You and Miss Rough — be in the main conference room tomorrow morning at seven a.m. sharp. We've got a lot to do in forty-eight hours."

The commander stood up, nodded to everyone and was about to leave. "Oh! And by the by, I've heard from Sir Timothy Head. He wanted you to know that the FBI arrested Gregory Anderson this morning, their time. So far, they are charging him with theft of government equipment, stealing government secrets, drug dealing and conspiracy to murder. He said other things, but as I'm a lady I won't repeat them. She left.

No one said anything but they all needed another coffee.

Steve looked at Barry. "Barry — you know you were only attached to us on a temporary assignment basis. The Murder Squad want you back at nine a.m. tomorrow, with Inspector Chalmers."

Barry looked slightly crestfallen. He sighed and shrugged his shoulders. "Well, Steve, I knew it had to come. I suppose I just hoped that Chalmers would forget about me and leave me here. Anyway, we got the result we wanted at Hackney, so we did more than DI Chalmers would ever have done. Remember me in future if you ever need an extra pair of hands."

Everyone stood and shook hands with Barry.

Steve turned to Twiggy. "I hope you're happy with this, Twiggy. Your comments this morning scared me a bit. It sounded like you wanted frontline duty again."

When Twiggy smiled she lit up a room. "No, Steve, it's fine. This way we all get a crack at them."

"Right, Barry — see you around. Andy — you and Twiggy have some work to do, and Andy — don't worry, you'll be great." Steve patted

Andy on the back. "Right, Cap, let's go and charge a couple of murderers. Then our job is done."

Andy wanted to say something but decided to wait.

Chapter Thirty-Three

"Who do you want to take first, Steve?" The Cap asked as they approached the interview suite.

"Let's take the bloke. He didn't seem as streetwise as our Ruby."

The man known as 'Rory' was sitting at the table. The Cap set things up with the recorder and Steve started the interview. "It's Rory, isn't it?"

"Yes, but you should know that Ruby had nothing to do with it." Steve thought this was a very promising start.

"With what, Rory? Maybe you'd better start at the beginning. What's your full name?"

The American looked like a scholar; he had a detached academic air about him. "My name's Rory Anderson, and I usually live in New York."

Steve broke one of his rules by breaking into the other man's train of thought. "Is your father Gregory Anderson?"

"Yes, he is." Steve didn't tell him that his father was now probably in a federal prison somewhere in New York.

"Carry on, Rory. From the beginning."

"I work for my father, but on the legitimate side of his businesses. I know he's no saint, and he's involved in a few shady deals at times, but on the legal side he is a good businessman. He owns car franchises and restaurant outlets all over New York. I graduated from MIT with a double PhD, but my dad wanted me in the business. A girl appeared one day to help out, setting up a big promotion for a new restaurant opening on 46th Street. It was Ruby." Rory's eyes lost focus. He stared into the distance as though seeing Ruby.

"So, when you met Ruby, what happened?"

"We happened. I hadn't had much to do with girls. I'm a bit of a nerd really, but Ruby was full of life. You've seen her, she's gorgeous. She stayed on working for the firm and dad moved her into her own apartment in our tower. It was right next to mine. After a couple of months, we more or less moved in together. It was great, then my father told us both about a big deal he was going to do —it was for a new formula for fuel that took water and turned it into usable fuel. He said he'd make at least a hundred million dollars. He didn't trust the guy who was bringing him the formula, so he wanted me to check it out. My double PhDs, you see. He told Ruby there was a contact in London and that she was to fly to London and await instructions. This was the night before she left."

"How much did you know about how your father was to get the formula?"

"Nothing. Just that someone was to deliver a laptop and I'd have to copy everything onto a firestick. Anyway, that night in bed, Ruby told me that she used to work for the CIA but since meeting me and my dad she now appreciated the big cars and the private jets. You know, the good things that only money can buy. She asked if I wanted to marry her." Rory was like a schoolboy who'd just had his first kiss.

"Well, I said yes, but I'd no money of my own. Ruby said that if my dad was really going to get all this money from this formula, maybe we could steal it and disappear to our own private Caribbean island. We spoke all night. I had access to all my father's bank accounts, so it would be simple to divert the cash, but he would kill me if we were caught.

Ruby said that we'd work on a plan but at all costs the formula had to work. The next evening, she left for London, and then in the early hours of the next day this Dr Graham turned up with the laptop. I did as I was asked but lied about the formula. It was a load of garbage and would never work, but I said it was great."

"Right, Rory — I think we know the rest. We've checked with Immigration and know when you arrived in London. What happened when you got here?"

"I told my dad I was going on vacation to the wilderness in Canada, but I came here to see Ruby. I'd been staying at her place and one night she arrived with Dr Graham, the guy I'd seen in New York with the laptop. Ruby said he was going to tell everyone that the formula was a fake and she'd brought him to stop him doing that. She pleaded and threatened him, but he was adamant — he was going to come clean. Ruby has a small two-shot pistol. She held it to this guy's head and threatened to shoot him. I can't be sure what happened, but I tried to stop her. I had the gun and all three of us were trying to get it when it went off. We'd shot Dr Graham."

"Just to be clear, Rory, and for the tape, you are admitting that you and Miss Thomas killed Dr Graham?"

Rory was in tears realising what he was admitting to. "Yes, yes, but I was holding the gun, not Ruby. She didn't pull the trigger."

Steve didn't comment but simply and quietly asked: "What happened next?"

"We waited until after midnight. We put the body in the car, drove to the side of Chelsea Bridge and threw the body in the river."

"Thank you, Rory, that's been very helpful. We'll get you something to drink in a minute. You'll be detained awaiting your first court appearance."

Steve and The Cap left a very dejected Rory Anderson sitting in the interview room. A uniformed constable stepped in as they left.

"Poor bugger. She's screwed her way to a fortune, or was trying to."

The Cap wasn't sympathetic towards Ruby after hearing Rory's confession.

"I agree. He's probably never been in trouble, but a girl who looks like Ruby might turn any young man's head, especially if he's a bit shy. Right — let's take on Ruby."

The detectives entered to see Ruby sitting coolly at the table. The same procedure was gone through, as was done with Rory, before Steve started.

"Ruby — your boyfriend, the son of the guy you were supposed to keep under surveillance, has just confessed to murder and has implicated you. Care to tell us about it?"

Ruby didn't seem surprised. "Look — it was an accident, OK? The gun doesn't have a safety catch and the trigger's a bit sensitive. All you've got is Rory on manslaughter and me as an accomplice. The CIA will have me out of here within twenty-four hours. All I've got to do is make a call."

"No, Ruby, I don't think so. It could be your best bet is to cough to the murder. I understand that your previous employers aren't too happy that an agent who'd gone rogue then became mixed up in a matter of national security. They're talking about espionage charges. I think in your country that's life in prison with no parole."

"Yeah, that's what *you* say." Ruby didn't look so confident.

"But you're right. If you admit to the murder, it's possible that a UK court might take a plea of manslaughter, but only if you confess."

At that moment, Steve saw something cross Ruby's mind. Her eyes refocused — she'd just hatched something. When she spoke, she sounded different, almost apologetic. She continued in a soft voice as she stared into the distance. "Rory's a sweet man, almost a boy. You know he'd never been with a girl before me? He is nothing like his father. In different circumstances I could get to love him for his love of nature and his intelligence. He's really a gentleman." She broke off and seemed to realise that she'd almost been talking to herself. "But, you're right, we're not going to beat this. I'll tell you how it happened."

Ruby detailed the events leading to the death of David Graham, matching Rory's statement almost word for word. When she'd finished, she said: "You know, I was a great agent. I could get men to tell me anything, but I was sick of working for a few bucks an hour, saving the world. I saw how Gregory Anderson lived, and what real money could give you. I knew I wanted that life no matter what." She sighed. "Oh well, I tried and here I am. I'll survive, I always have."

Steve repeated the statement he'd given to Rory at the end of his interview. They left the interview room as a WPC entered.

"Well, Steve, that's that, I think. Just the charging and the CPS and you've solved another one." The Cap patted Steve on the shoulder as they both climbed the stairs away from the interview suites.

When Steve got back to his office, Commander Southgate was waiting. She was dressed in civilian clothes and seemed to be ready to go home. "Steve — I thought you should hear it from me. Superintendent Frank Dobson resigned an hour ago. Alistair Ramsay's talking like there's no tomorrow. He's dished the dirt on Dobson, even the threats he made against you. It was James Rushdie who told Ramsay to put the squeeze on you. Ramsay told Dobson, who obliged. So, there you have it, another bad apple gone." Sheila looked tired but her eyes were bright. She shrugged as she made her way to the door. "I'm off home, but a lot of people will be working well into the night, including your boy, Andy." With a wave, she was off. "Good night."

Andy was indeed hard at it. The Cap had offered to help him so he too was typing away on a keyboard, but only gathering general data. Andy had all the statements safely on his own laptop and the regime of secrecy still applied, even though the case was now in the open.

Andy entered Steve's office. "Steve, this controller thing — what's it about?"

"Yes, sorry, Andy, I should have explained. In any joint task force, there's only one person who knows and sees the whole picture at any one time. That's the controller, meaning you." Steve smiled warmly at his junior officer. "In this case, I estimate that there'll be up to eight different departments all working on their own little bit of the puzzle. It's your job to make sure there's no duplication of effort and to brief each SIO on what needs to be done."

Andy didn't look too sure. "Sir, I'm a detective constable. How can I tell senior officers what to do?"

"Simple. It's a joint task force and Commander Southgate's in command. You report to her, and therefore anything you need doing you are speaking with her authority. Don't worry, Andy — you'll be brilliant and it's a great career opportunity. You'll be noticed by people who matter."

Steve thought he'd better not overload his DC. "Besides, it'll all be over, apart from the paperwork, by Friday night."

"I suppose you're right." With a smile and looking much more relaxed, Andy turned to leave, butthen stopped. "Steve — can I ask you a personal question?"

"Yes."

"Why didn't you go after James Rushdie yourself, instead of leaving it to the task force?"

"Before you came here, I had a problem with my temper and my vision of policing. I floored a senior officer in public and was suspended for three months. My vision of policing is still the same, but I've got something to live for now. If I'd gone after Rushdie, I think I'd be on another suspension right now."

"Thanks, boss. I'll get on."

Steve sat behind his desk thinking over the events of the day.

He was due to meet Alison for dinner but it looked like he would be late. He dialled her number, but before it could connect, the incident alarm sounded. This wasn't common and meant that a major problem was occurring somewhere in the building. He hung up his call to Alison just as The Cap rushed in. "Steve. The interview suite. We've got a problem."

Both men ran. At the entrance to the interview rooms was a small crowd of police officers. No one knew what was happening so Steve and The Cap went in. They didn't like what they found.

Ruby was standing in the middle of the assembly area for the six rooms holding a small Derringer pistol. Rory Anderson was beside her, looking pale and afraid. The PC and WPC who had been left to guard the two now stood against the wall with their hands raised above their heads. The DCI took all of this in in a split-second. He knew that Ruby was the key to resolving this stand-off.

"Ruby, what's going on?"

"We're getting out of here. Just open the doors, put us in a taxi and you'll never see us again. If you don't, I'll shoot either of these two." She was pointing to the uniformed officers. "Or you and your sidekick. I don't care who."

"Ruby — you know that's not going to happen. This is England, not the Wild West, and you're not playing a part in an old cowboy film. Put the gun on the floor and walk away."

"I'm sorry, detective, but I can't do that."

"Ruby — so far there's a chance you'll both get a light sentence. Neither of you planned to kill anyone, and the gun went off by accident. But this is different. If you go through with this, you'll never be free again, either of you. We'd charge Rory as an accessory. Think about it. Please put the gun down."

Ruby was obviously conflicted. She was intelligent enough to understand Steve's argument but rational enough to know what she had to do and why.

She continued to hold the gun and then turned to Rory. She put her arms around his neck and fired one shot directly into his brain.

Even before Rory had reached the floor, Ruby was back facing Steve and The Cap. Steve was shocked by the sudden change in events.

"Why, Ruby?" His voice was soft, almost pleading.

"Poor, sweet Rory wouldn't have lasted five minutes in prison. I realised earlier on that I really did love him. You see, I couldn't let him suffer. It's all been my fault."

Without looking at anyone, Ruby held the little gun to her head and fired.

Two dead Americans lay on the floor of the interview suite in New Scotland Yard.

Chapter Thirty-Four

Following events in the interview suite, everyone involved was locked down. Deaths in custody, no matter how they occurred, had to be investigated immediately by the Police Complaints Authority and Professional Standards. There were enough witnesses to confirm that no police officer was involved. After a few hours giving statements and hanging about, all those involved were released. Apart from reams of paper to be completed, life quickly returned to normal.

Steve and The Cap sat in the canteen mulling over events. They understood Ruby's thinking that Rory wouldn't survive prison, but to kill him seemed a bit extreme.

"But why kill herself, Steve? That's a bit weird."

"Who knows, Abul. Maybe she couldn't live without him. Maybe she felt guilty that she was responsible. I don't suppose we'll ever know. Come on, let's get out of here. I'll see you tomorrow."

Steve had phoned Alison to explain why he couldn't keep their date. She made him promise to call her as soon as he was leaving, which he did. Sitting alone in his office, he called Alison and they spent twenty minutes discussing their future and Steve's job. Alison felt there was too much violence but agreed that Steve loved his job.

Thursday morning in the office was quiet. The usual hustle and bustle, with Andy beavering away, was missing. Steve and The Cap were the only ones there; Andy was busy with the task force and Barry was back on Murder Squad duties. The Cap had a mountain of paper to get through in connection with both the Hackney murders and his statement from last night. Steve decided to let him get on with it and complete his own statement and get it into the system. That done, he sat back. He knew the task force would be in full swing. He thought about visiting the main conference room to see how things were going, but with a clear desk for now, he decided to excuse himself and signed off for two days' leave.

With the Hackney case coming up, he'd be busy preparing with the CPS soon enough.

Everything was under control. The Dr Graham murder had resolved itself and wouldn't lead to a trial. The Hackney murders were in hand with a court date set. John Peter Saunders was pleading not guilty, while Neil Ryder was pleading guilty by reason of diminished responsibility. The task force would report back but he had no part to play in it except remotely through Andy.

He headed for the car park with a clear conscience.

***

Steve and Alison spent the weekend at The Bull Hotel in Rye. They visited the care home where they'd first met, and Steve chatted to the people he'd last seen some nine months previously, including the ex-soldier Albert Spink, who'd been instrumental in helping solve an impossible previous case.

Steve had already bought a ring to give to Alison. Originally, he had thought they would enjoy a romantic weekend away, to give him the opportunity to propose, but he hadn't really planned for this to be in Rye. West Sussex wasn't the most romantic spot, but all in all it was probably the most appropriate place, so DCI Steve Burt and Dr Alison Mills became officially engaged that weekend. He didn't go down on one knee but spent the entire weekend on a different planet with the woman he intended to spend the rest of his life with. It was the best weekend he had ever had.

Steve was in the office bright and early to find Andy at his desk. The Cap was also there bemoaning all the paper he had to deal with. "The CPS can't go to the toilet without a form in triplicate. If this is being a detective inspector, I'm applying for a transfer to Traffic. They never seem to do paperwork." The Cap was frustrated by all the forms but managed a smile, telling his colleagues that he wasn't actually going to Traffic.

"Come in, Andy. Cap — before you transfer, let's hear from Andy about the task force."

Andy sat beside The Cap; he looked tired but excited. "I've never seen anything like it. I put all the parts on the big whiteboard. We already had a search warrant for The Fortress Club, and I assigned that to Vice. The superintendent had their men on that raid. I put Financial Crimes with them, and Miss Rough went in after the raid to grab all the accounts and contracts. I thought it best that they got there when people were about, so they went in at eleven on Thursday morning. I sent two fraud officers and a search team to get all the documents relating to the formula scam."

Steve interrupted. "How were James Rushdie and the guy Cutter?"

"According to the inspector from Vice, James Rushdie wasn't too pleased. He had to be restrained but guess what? He was carrying a Glock, so we've got him on firearms charges as well as drug dealing and pimping."

"Did the teams get everything?"

"Yes, as far as we know. Miss Rough was delighted. She said it was conclusive. I don't know what she found, but it confirmed the money laundering she had been talking about. The man Cutter arrived halfway through and tried to run, but they got him. All the girls who were there were herded up and they found a full list of everyone who worked there, so they'll all be charged."

"So The Fortress Club was a clean sweep?"

"Looks like it. A search team's going in again today to do a final run-through."

"Good work, Andy. What else?"

"The main drug raid was at Faversham — we got the Kent Constabulary to assist. The report that came back was amazing. They said it was on an industrial scale. They arrested everyone there, including an American who said he was a friend of Alistair Ramsay. He had the bottle to tell the officers he had protection and that they'd be in serious trouble if they arrested him. Needless to say, he's being held in the Chapel Hill nick."

"How much dope did they get?" This was from The Cap.

"They estimate that it's well over two hundred million dollars. It's the biggest bust ever in the UK."

"So was everything vacuumed up at Faversham?"

"No, it will take weeks, but we got all the staff and the managers, plus a load of documents giving dealer details. The superintendent from the Drugs Squad reckoned he'd enough follow-up to keep him going for years. Apparently, Faversham was a very sophisticated operation."

"Great stuff, Andy. What about the St John brothers?"

"We visited them early. I sent a search team and the superintendent from Serious Crimes sent a couple of DSs. They didn't get much but they were lifted on conspiracy to defraud and suspicion of murder after the fact. They screamed like pigs but one of the sergeants said the man Frankie just stood and laughed. They're calling for their lawyers. The super from Serious is going to review what they found and tie them to documents found at The Fortress Club before speaking to the DPP. He's confident they'll be charged with something."

"What about The Bell Tower Hotel?"

"I persuaded the commander to put a team in there from Thursday and not to wait until Friday. We got Kent to seal it off from around nine o'clock Thursday morning. It seems a few so-called 'delegates' turned up. They were collected by private limos from various private airfields during Thursday. We got the list from the club and the commander arranged for the schedule to be kept, except it was our guys driving. Immigration turned up early on Friday morning. There were fourteen in all, most of them from the Middle East or South America. They were all on false passports and, according to some, were there to bid for a secret formula. Some said they didn't understand. Immigration read them the collective riot act and cautioned all of them, and we took them back to their aircraft. According to one, we'd just saved them collectively over four hundred billion dollars."

"Wow! That's a lot for something that didn't work." The Cap was impressed by the amount of money.

"Anything else, Andy?"

"Not really. We kept getting reports and arrest details sent in all day. Everyone arrested was taken to a satellite station and interviewed. The statements came in fast and furious. I was up all night just loading them in, but I'd written a programme so that every time we did something it cross-referenced so that we knew we didn't miss anything. I think everyone was pleased but, oh boy, it was all, go."

"Sounds like a success, Andy. Take a few days off when you can. You've deserved them."

Andy stood up. "I'd better get back — I've still got a lot to do. How did the Thames murder finish up? I heard it's over."

Steve and The Cap looked at Andy in astonishment then laughed.

"Andy — you must be the only officer in the Yard that doesn't know. Both suspects are dead. Ruby shot her boyfriend and then herself." The DCI became more serious. "It was late on Wednesday night. The enquiry into how she kept the gun is still ongoing, but yes, the case is closed."

Andy smiled a knowing smile at his two colleagues. "In his statement, Julian St John said where she kept it. I can understand how she got it in — it's not very common to search in such warm places." Andy turned smiling — he'd evened the score.

Commander Southgate sent for Steve later in the morning, and over coffee in her office she brought him up to speed on events.

"DC Miller was brilliant. You'd think he'd never done anything else except direct cases. I think you'll have a job holding on to him. Oh, and by the way, I gave him the day off. He must have put in at least a thirty-six-hour shift."

"He's hard at it downstairs. I told him to have two days off when he can. I doubt he'll take them."

The commander finished her coffee. "You know, Steve, I've got three weeks left in the job. I've been a cop for more years than I can remember, but the buzz I got out of the task force job was the best I've ever had. I mean it, and it's thanks to you."

She continued: "The real prize was busting up this James Rushdie's drug operation. No one had any idea how big it was or how much stuff he was shifting. Apparently, the Faversham factory was enormous and geared to huge volumes. The people working there were nabbed by our Drugs Squad and the Kent force. Of course, rooting out a bunch of bent cops and customs officials, was another bonus. We had no idea that corruption within the force was so rife. Officers like Superintendent Dobson were held in high regard and were beyond reproach. It just shows that appearances can be deceiving.

The man Cutter is hiding behind a bank of lawyers, but he's a big catch. We had no idea he was involved in drugs and certainly not to these volumes. We've got enough on him to put him away for a very long time on drugs charges. It seems he's the main distributor for Rushdie and distributes the stuff through his oil distribution business." She drank her coffee and sat back contentedly.

"We don't have much on the St John brothers but the DPP's looking into various conspiracy charges, so we're confident they'll do time."

Steve also sat back. The commander had confirmed everything Andy had told him. He had a sudden thought. "I suppose Frankie will get the car now?"

They both laughed, enjoying Steve's sense of humour.

Both police officers sat in silence. DCI Steve Burt was happy that his work was done.

Over the next few weeks, everyone appeared busy either filling in forms or giving statements, but late one Thursday afternoon, Steve asked his colleagues and their partners to a special dinner the following night at his favourite Italian restaurant. He also invited Barry and Twiggy. Barry, who was now single, said he'd come provided that Steve wasn't setting him up with a blind date. Steve suddenly saw the possibility of seating Barry next to Twiggy and letting the rumour mill take care of the rest.

They all met as planned, and halfway through the meal DCI Steve Burt announced to his colleagues and friends that he and Alison were to be married. The evening became very jolly and noisy after his announcement. Congratulations were flowing, as was the wine.

Steve Burt looked around and then sat back, wondering how his life would change as a married man and wondering how long it would be before his next case.

THE END